PRAISE FOR

WANT NOT

"A complex, often hilarious, ultimately moving story about who we are and what we discard . . . A heartfelt affirmation of human value."

— *Washington Post*

"Jonathan Miles has produced a sprawling social novel of New York City . . . filled with many playful and keenly observed digressions . . . *Want Not* is fun. Read it and relish its pleasures now."

— *San Francisco Chronicle*

"With a light Midas touch, Miles turns all the glut and ache of late America into pure gold. If you're in that soul-hunt up the food chain and down the dial for something more satisfying than the hollow abundance of our contemporary lives, read this book. It is warm, complex, comic, honest, and never flinching. *Want Not* wastes not a word, while its pleasures are endless."

— Joshua Ferris, author of *The Unnamed*

"In this powerful, blisteringly funny novel, Jonathan Miles makes a startling discovery: We are what we throw away . . . Miles mines the depths of waste so artfully that by the end of this extraordinary novel, we're left with the suspicion that redemption may well be no more, and no less, than an existential salvage operation."

— Ben Fountain, author of *Billy Lynn's Long Halftime Walk*

"Rapturous prose [and] the blend of ideas and characters . . . result in a novel that's sharp and occasionally breathtaking."

— *Time Out New York*

"The underlying theme of *Want Not,* a book glutted with fascinating ideas, is human mortality. What is life for? How can we be happy? How can we be good? Is it possible to be both? And, arguably, the biggest question of all: If we're going to die, then what's the point of it all? Jonathan Miles doesn't have any more or better answers to these questions than the rest of us, but he's written a novel of uncommon grace and beauty in an attempt to find them out."

— *Pittsburgh Post-Gazette*

"The author weaves together three energetic, warm stories."

— *The New Yorker*

"Every generation or so an American novel appears that holds up a mirror to our lives and shows us exactly who we are right at this moment. *Want Not* is that book right now — a searing but compassionate look at modern Americans and their STUFF. A book about garbage and consumption and accumulation and disposal . . . but most of all about humanity. Simply put, the best book of the year."

— Elizabeth Gilbert, author of *The Signature of All Things*

"So luminous and so resonant . . . packed to the gills with heady themes and fierce writing."

— *Portland Oregonian*

"If there is a modern book that more artfully allegorizes the desperation and anxieties of the human condition through the lives of normal people, this reviewer hasn't come across it. Miles gives us the long view — the "big picture" — without having to go long, or big. With such simple, yet sprawling, beautiful and hilarious sentences, one can hardly imagine a world where art like this has disintegrated into ashes, radioactive trash heaps or stardust."

— *Washington Independent Review of Books*

"Thought-provoking . . . riveting storytelling."

— *Chicago Tribune*

"*Want Not,* Jonathan Miles's brilliant and original take on a culture—ours—that mindlessly seems to squander all that is dear, is as witty as it is mind-blowing and eye-opening. The combination of high-octane prose and Miles's compassion for his characters makes for a novel that stirs the collective conscience. A clear-eyed, exuberant entertainment."

—Helen Schulman, author of *This Beautiful Life*

"What is extremely apparent . . . is Jonathan Miles's extraordinary talent. Where so many writers are impressionists, Miles is more of a photo realist . . . Miles presents such fully developed characters, you come to know their essences."

—*Star Ledger*

"This is a novel with a strong point of view, but it's far from a polemic. Miles is as funny as he is observant, and he allows us to laugh at ourselves as he forces us to look at some of the more unattractive aspects of humanity. This is a hard novel to pitch in a few sentences, but it's an easy one to recommend. Simply put, it's one of the best of the year."

—*BookRiot*

"Before you gird your loins and stuff your birds for Thanksgiving, spend some highly rewarding hours with all the trash and waste in Jonathan Miles's new novel, *Want Not.*"

—*Bloomberg*

"With forthright wit and stunning intimacy, Miles doesn't hesitate to broach the uncomfortable consequences of unchecked abundance and desire. The result is a wild tangle of high-octane, entertaining prose, an astonishing leap for this accomplished novelist."

—*Booklist*

"For readers who relish extravagant language, scathing wit and philosophical heft, *Want Not* wastes nothing."

—*Kirkus Reviews*, starred review

WANT NOT

BOOKS BY JONATHAN MILES

Dear American Airlines
Want Not

WANT NOT

Jonathan Miles

Mariner Books
Houghton Mifflin Harcourt
BOSTON NEW YORK

First Mariner Books edition 2014

www.hmhco.com

Library of Congress Cataloging-in-Publication Data
Miles, Jonathan.
Want not / Jonathan Miles.
pages cm
ISBN 978-0-547-35220-6 (hardback)   ISBN 978-0-544-22808-5 (pbk.)
I. Title.
PS3613.I5322W36 2013
813'.6—dc23
2013027142

Book design by Cindy LaBreacht

Printed in the United States of America
DOC 10 9 8 7 6 5 4 3 2

Excerpt of "The Ridge Farm" from *Sumerian Vistas* by A. R. Ammons. Copyright © 1987
by A. R. Ammons. Used by permission of W. W. Norton & Company, Inc.

this one's for

LIZ

and for

DWIGHT & CREE

from their squatter
& forever pal

People forget, they cover, they kid themselves, they lie.
But their trash always tells the truth.

— William Rathje, archaeologist

        the odor of shit is like language,
an unmistakable assimilation of a
use, tone, flavor, accent hard to
fake: enemy shit smells like the enemy:
everything is more nearly incredible
than you thought at first.

— A. R. Ammons, "The Ridge Farm"

To what purpose is this waste?

— Matthew 26:8

PART ONE

THANKSGIVING, 2008

I

ALL BUT ONE of the black trash bags, heaped curbside on East 4th Street, were tufted with fresh snow, and looked, to Talmadge, like alpine peaks in the moonlight, or at least what he, a lifetime flatlander, thought alpine peaks might look like if bathed in moonglow and (upon further reflection) composed of slabs of low-density polyethylene. Admittedly, his mental faculties were still under the vigorous sway of the half gram of Sonoma County Sour Diesel he'd smoked a half hour earlier, but still: Mountains. Definitely. When he brushed the snow off the topmost bag and untied the knot at its summit, he felt like a god disassembling the Earth.

Micah would surely object to this analogy — the problem with dudes, he could hear her saying, is that y'all can't even open a freaking trash bag without wanting to be some kind of god subjugating the planet — before needling him for making any analogy at all. "You're, like, the only person in the world who overuses the word 'like' the way it's actually meant to be used," she'd once told him. Which was true: He was an inveterate analogizer who couldn't help viewing the world as a matrix of interconnected references in which everything was related to everything else through the associative, magnetizing impulses of his brain. Back in college he'd read that this trait was an indicator of genius or perhaps merely advanced intelligence, and while this had pleased him, he was also aware, darkly, that he'd inherited the trait directly from his Uncle Lenord, which wasn't a DNA strand he longed to advertise. Uncle Lenord, who repaired riding mowers and weedwhackers and various other small-engine whatnots out of his

carport in Wiggins, Mississippi, was a fount of cracker-barrel similes —
*hotter'n two foxes fucking in a forest fire; wound up tighter'n an eight-day
clock; drunk as a bicycle; spicier'n a goat's ass in a pepper patch* — but no one
had ever accused him of genius-level or even advanced thinking. Frankly
no one had ever accused him of any thinking whatsoever, with the possible
exception of the girlfriend of one of Talmadge's Ole Miss fraternity brothers. She'd interviewed Lenord for a Southern Studies 202 term paper about
the effects of clear-cut logging on rural communities, so presumably —
since the girlfriend scored a B-plus on the paper — Lenord had been forced
to think at least once. He debriefed Talmadge on the interview a few weeks
later, when Talmadge was home for Christmas break. "Girl had titties out
to here," Lenord confided. "Woulda jumped on that ass like a duck on a
Junebug."

With a gloved hand Talmadge sifted through the bag's contents: donuts, Portuguese rolls, kaiser rolls, bagels, cookies, cream horns, Swiss
rolls, challah, and muffins. The effluvia of the Key Food bakery department, most of it edible but none of it salable, discharged to the curb. He
transferred two of the Portuguese rolls and two pistachio muffins into the
burlap satchel he wore messenger-style on his shoulder, and then, remembering that Matty was coming to dinner, added another roll and muffin to
the bag. Then one more Portuguese roll, and on second thought another,
because he remembered that Matty ate like a pulpwood hauler.

The cream horns were fatally smooshed; otherwise he would've taken
three or four. Weed gave him a monumental sweet tooth. He considered
the cookies but they were nestled in a wad of paper towels drenched in
something blue — Windex, he guessed. The challah was hard as seasoned
firewood, and should have, he noted critically, been thrown out the day
before. Ditto the bagels, though he didn't care about them, since day-old
bagels were his easiest prey. Unger's over on Avenue B had the best ones
anyway, and Mr. Unger — testy, fat-jowled, an aproned old relic from the
bygone Lower East Side — put out two or three full bags of them nightly.
The only problem with those was Mr. Unger himself, who would sometimes charge out of the store to demand payment. Talmadge was always
quick to skedaddle but Micah relished the fight. "They're trash," she'd say.
"They're *my* trash," he'd reply. And so on and so forth until Mr. Unger
would fling up his arms and shout, "Freeloaders! Freeloaders!" The whole

exchange was avoidable since there was a two-hour window between the time that Mr. Unger locked the shop, at seven, and when the Department of Sanitation trucks rolled up at nine, during which time the bagels were free for the loading, but Micah operated on her own narrow terms—angry fat-jowled relics be damned.

After retying the bag and replacing it onto the heap, Talmadge went about frisking the other bags. He was after the pleasant dumpy squish that meant produce, which he found after several gropings. He wrestled the bag off the pile—it was unusually heavy, suggesting melons—and opened it on the sidewalk.

"Five dollars," he heard someone say. One of the canners at the bottle-redemption machines, about six yards down the sidewalk: a hunched, skittery black guy in a long charcoal overcoat, no taller than five-foot-five though possibly five-foot-ten if he would or could stand up straight, and while he looked about eighty—owing partly to his posture, but also his rheumy eyes which were capped with the kind of wildly unkempt and woolly gray eyebrows one saw in portraits of nineteenth-century lunatics—he was probably closer to sixty. With an empty plastic bag hanging from his hand, he was staring at the machine marked CANS as if squaring off against it in a brawl.

"Five fucking dollars," he said to it. He looked to his left, where a short, disfigured Chinese woman was waiting with a can-filled handcart and where another canner Talmadge called Scatman—grizzly-sized from the multiple overcoats he was wearing, and sporting his trademark vintage earphones—was feeding a huge cache of Evian bottles into the maw of the PLASTICS machine; then to his right, where Talmadge was watching him with an opened bag of mucky produce at his feet; and then finally upward to where a sign, perched above the bank of machines, read AUTOMATIC REDEMPTION CENTER. Talmadge had once suggested, jokingly, that he and Micah ought to transplant the sign to the Most Holy Redeemer Church around the corner on 3rd Street. She didn't think it was funny but then funny wasn't her thing.

Scatman wasn't scatting. Usually he serenaded his deposits, and accompanied his collecting, with mumbled scat-singing, or something resembling it: *skippity dip da doo, bop de-diddlee, bam bam bam*. Hence the nickname. Talmadge wasn't sure whether Scatman's vinyl-covered earphones—padded and brown and big as coconut halves—were related to the scatting, or if indeed they were even connected to anything, but he'd never seen Scatman without them, in warm weather or cold, so he supposed they served some function. As for the Chinese woman: Talmadge knew her, or was anyway familiar with her. She was a part-time canner who walked a fixed route in the early evenings, plucking cans out of the corner trash barrels with a plastic, purple-and-lime green pincing tool of the kind sold in toy stores. Their paths crossed often enough that she and Talmadge would sometimes acknowledge each other with a flick of eye contact or more rarely a nod. He called her Teeter, because the grievous shortness of one of her legs caused her to teeter down the street. But Hunch, and his five dollars—he was someone new.

"That's what I get?" he was saying to Teeter. "Five dollars?" She crinkled her face but said nothing. He looked back at the machine. "Well, mothafucka," he said, and chewed his lip for a moment. "Yo, man," he said to Scatman. "Five dollars. That right?"

"If that's what it say," said Scatman, without looking over, and in a voice Talmadge found mildly startling: Scatman spoke with the smooth basso timbre of an old-timey broadcaster. Smoother than that, even: a *parody* of an old-timey broadcaster. Talmadge had never heard Scatman utter words before, only the *bip*s and *bam*s and *ba-ding*s of his scatting, spluttered and muttered with all the grace and suavity of someone with an index finger lodged in an electrical socket. He'd reasonably expected to hear something more jagged.

"Motha-motha*fucka*," said Hunch, and then hit the machine with the side of his fist, rattling the fiberglass panel and blinking the lightbulb inside. This, now—this was more than mildly startling. Teeter flinched, then looked down toward the cans in her cart, pretending to notice something new about them. Scatman kept plugging away, staring straight ahead, his scat-free silence further starkening the moment. Talmadge was too busy watching their reactions, the gears of his brain gummed up by the sinsemilla, to monitor his own—something he realized too late. Before he could dip his hand into the produce, and with it the direction of his gaze, Hunch swung his own gaze toward Talmadge and shouted, "The fuck you looking at?"

Houston Crabtree was his name, and if he knew that Talmadge had christened him Hunch he might have tried corking Talmadge's mouth with a five-cent redeemable Coke can. Might have, that is, rather than would have, because a simple assault charge was an express ticket back upstate to the Mid-Orange lockup. And, most likely, to twelve weeks of Aggression Replacement Training: for Crabtree, the motherfucking cherry on top. Not that he'd ever let consequences stop him before. The first kid who'd called him a hunchback—this was back in Georgia, midcentury—found a baseball bat ringing his larynx. Kid was just seven years old but talked like Bobby Blue Bland after that. As a baby Crabtree had rickets, which'd crooked his spine, bent it like a fish hook, and the older he got, the worse his spine hurt, and the higher he needed to be just to roll out of bed. Some days, it was like walking around with an arrow sticking halfway out his back. Today, for instance. Today it *hurt*. Reaching in to those corner trash cans, stooping to root through those recycling bins, hauling that plastic bag over his shoulder like some dollar-store Santa Claus: today was like having a whole *quiver* of arrows jutting from his back. Today was a motherfucking Injun *massacre*. And all for five dollars. Five even: the precise amount, to the penny, of his urinalysis testing fee. Five dollars, and now this fatassed Don Cornelius saying "If that's what it say," like that's what it *didn't* say, and weeble-wobble Ching Chong behind him with a whole *truckload* of cans, maybe enough cans to clear his back parole fees *and* get a steak, a cheeseburger, whatever, anything besides that no-turkey turkey soup at the Renewed Horizons shelter. Five dollars, and now this glassy-eyed white kid staring at him as if there really *were* bloody arrows stubbling his back. "Yo," he said, angling a few steps closer to Talmadge. "I said, the fuck you looking at?"

Whether dread or meteorology was to blame, Talmadge didn't know, but he felt suddenly colder, as if a polar gust had just turned left on East 4th as it was nipping its way southward down Avenue A. The snow had been coming down in layers—a blast of chowdery snow followed by fifteen minutes of clear gelid air followed by another white blast—but now it was swirling, snow globe–style, and showing zero signs of another leisurely break. New York City hadn't seen this much pre-Thanksgiving snow in twenty years, he'd read earlier that day while checking Facebook at an internet café on St. Mark's Place. Busiest travel day of the year, and flights were running four hours late at LaGuardia blah blah click. The temperature must have been in the teens, he figured, with the wind so blowy that he had seen two people go by shielding their faces with folded newspapers. None of this bothered him, however—he had a boffo parka, cadged from a dormitory dumpster at Richard Varick College, and Matty was coming in on Greyhound. Plus, Talmadge loved it when the earth fought back, when it jostled and jerked like a horse shaking flies off its back. He'd muttered words to this effect after Hurricane Katrina leveled his parents' beachfront home in Gulfport, and only his stepmother leaping in front of him, screaming *no,* had stayed his father from committing second-degree murder or at minimum aggravated assault.

Crabtree was in front of him now, those wild eyebrows converged into an indignant, frowning *V.* But as he was sizing up Talmadge, his eyes bouncing from the trash bag between his feet to the FUCK HATE and HOLY GOOF buttons on his satchel to the black titanium barbell skewered through his right eyebrow to the tasseled, earflapped wool cap of vaguely Incan design atop his head, the anger in his eyes was getting nudged out by something like confusion. Talmadge was tall, yet so lanky and slim as to seem wispy—a "long tall drink of water," as his Uncle Lenord said, though Lenord had modified that to "long tall drink of bullshit" after Talmadge dropped out of college to, as Lenord put it, "let people draw shit all over his face." Slouchy and gawky, he seemed uncomfortable in his body, as if he were a victim of shoddy biological tailoring who'd been fitted with a frame one size too large. Or as if, at twenty-three, he still had some growing left to do, an impression bolstered by the palefaced splotches in his downy, flaxen beard and the boyish or possibly girlish softness of his big pacifist eyes. Even the tattoo on his left temple—a purplish star, which the tattoo artist in Hattiesburg told him signified celestial longing, a yearning for new (or possibly Renewed) horizons, new maps, new ways of being, a pure shine of light in the polluted darkness—reinforced the delicacy of his features, evoking, in its coloring and placement, something midway between mascara and an earring. Micah called him "angelheaded," which was only credible if you specified which angel—gentle Jophiel, perhaps, but not sword-swinging Michael. Yet the sentiment was fair: With his velvet-painted-Jesus visage, his spare, reedy chassis, and his timorous bearing, Talmadge Bertrand had the look of someone too sensitive for the scraggy existence of a mammal, with a face that wouldn't appear inappropriate above a golden harp. He could see Crabtree puzzling now at the sight of him, that freewheeling anger curving back on itself as the old man struggled to decipher the context of this angelheaded manchild rooting through the Key Food garbage. "The fuck you *doing?*" he finally said.

"Getting dinner," Talmadge said, which he sensed wasn't the ideal answer, given the situation, but it was the truthful answer, and really the only explainable one.

Quick and incredulous, Crabtree said, "You eating from the trash?"

"Yeah," Talmadge said. "Look at all they throw away. It's criminal, man, it's everywhere. Here, look here"—from the bag he pulled out a bunch of carrots, ferny green leaves attached, and bent a limp one to demonstrate—"there's nothing wrong with these, they're just soft. No difference if you cook them. And look"—now he fetched a fat tomato, blighted with a dark moldy blotch—"see, that just needs cutting out."

"Boy, what's wrong with you?" Crabtree said, the anger frothing back up. Five dollars, he thought, and now here he was messing around with a talking sewer rat. There wasn't no end to it.

"What's wrong with *them?*" said Talmadge. "There's hungry people in the world. There's people starving. And look at all this. They're *burying* all this food." At this point Micah's voice took over, as it always did, not just in the script but in Talmadge's inflections and intonations too, with even her zonked-hillbilly accent creeping in, as if he were wholly channeling her, or flipping the switch on some prerecorded message of hers: "It's a bankrupt system, man. Waste doesn't matter as long as it doesn't affect profits. They've built it into the system. Everything just gets rolled downhill. Check it out, man. Fifty percent of the edible food in this country never gets *eaten.* Half of it, seriously. Never makes it into a mouth. And no one cares, man. Because we've been *conditioned* not to care. We've been taught to dispose. And not just food, but—"

"What the hell, ratboy," Crabtree cut in. "Whoa, let me tell you something. You don't know your dick from your ass."

"Okay."

"Serious, man."

"Okay," Talmadge said again.

"Not if you think what you're doing can change *nothing.*"

With a meek shrug, Talmadge said, "I'm just changing me."

"Then don't be preaching at everybody."

"I wasn't preaching. You asked me—"

"Know what you are, man? Do you know?"

This was clearly a rhetorical question though Crabtree granted Talmadge a few unappreciated moments for response.

"You a *provocateur*," he said. "That's right. A *pro-voc-a-teur*. And that's bullshit, you know what I'm saying. Bullshit. That's *nothing*."

"Due respect, man, I'm just minding my—"

"Let me tell you something. Provocateur, man. That's what you are. I was with Bobby Seale in New Haven, you understand? The Black Panthers, man, you know what I'm talking about? New Haven. That was *war*, man. But this shit"—he waved an ungloved hand at the trash bags on the sidewalk, at the satchel 'round Talmadge's shoulder—"this shit is worthless, man. You ain't—you ain't even got a right."

"We all have a right," Talmadge mumbled.

"Shit," said Crabtree, then puffed his cheeks before unloading an aggrieved exhalation. Too cold for this shit, he thought. Too cold for anything. Weather like this, even a polar bear'd be crying for its mama, asking to crawl back in that warm mama-bear coochie to hide. The wind was spinning all those invisible arrows poking from his back, whirling them around in his flesh. He had pills back at the shelter but the pills didn't work. Reefer worked. Rock worked better. Junk worked best. But all his old nursing aids had been forcibly retired by The People of the State of New York v. Houston Crabtree. "Five dollars, man," he said blurrily, half to himself, a quarter to God, the rest to the dumbass kid. "I got fines to pay. No job. I don't pay the fines, I gotta go back to doing a bid."

The sudden shift in tone came as a relief to Talmadge, as though a knife had been lowered.

"I'm on a payment plan, you understand?" he went on. "Got behind six months. Parole officer say, shit, Houston, you can make that payment collecting cans. Cans! But I'm out here all day for five dollars. Shit is right. Ain't no way to make that payment. Make better money digging graves in Georgia and that's nothing, man, I did that."

Talmadge relaxed his face into a blank expression meant to show empathy. "You hungry?"

"Fuck you, man. I ain't eating that shit."

"Just asking."

"What you need to do — know what you need to do?" Crabtree's energy spiked again, and he wagged a long brown finger at Talmadge. "Incorporate. That's how you change shit, man. Not like this. This is just *provocatization*. You got to twist it from the inside. You gotta get up inside it to where you can cut the wires, you know what I'm saying? You need the initials, man. That's how you get inside. You got to be a corporation. Nothing happen in this country without the I-N-C-period, you understand?"

Talmadge didn't, but he nodded anyway.

"That's what I'm gonna do, one of these days," he went on. "Get myself incorporated. Nobody touches no corporation. Need a lawyer for that, though. Special-type lawyer."

"Sounds like a plan," said Talmadge.

"Lookit these boots, man," Crabtree said, kicking out a leg. The boots, made of thin green rubber, appeared to have been designed for a ten-year-old child in an equatorial nation. And when Talmadge looked closer he noticed two yellow dots at the toes of each boot: eyes. Dude was wearing children's frog boots. "I must've walked ten miles in these today. Sticking my hand into every goddamn trash can. Make me sick, man. Got cream cheese all up my arm. Ten miles for five fucking dollars. Ain't doing that again. My redeeming days is over. I'm done, baby. This motherfucker cooked."

"Jesus," Talmadge said, still marveling at the frog boots.

"That's right. You don't see no corporations walking 'round in boots like this."

"There's a nursing home or something on Henry Street. I can't remember the name, but I found some totally decent shoes there a few months back — in the trash. You just got to poke around."

"Fuck that," Crabtree said. "I had me some good boots, you know what I'm saying? Fucking *soldier* boots, man, I could've circus-walked that third rail in them, not felt nothing. Some motherfucker stole one of them at the Broadway Mission. That's why I don't stay there no more."

"Who steals one boot?"

"That's what I'm saying. Some one-legged motherfucker, that's who. Don't think I won't find him." To prove his intent, Crabtree squinted up and down East 4th Street. By now the snow was blowing sideways, strafing

Talmadge's pinkening cheeks, and sensing himself loosed from whatever threat he'd feared, he asked Crabtree if he'd mind him finishing up his "shopping."

"Suit yourself, ratboy," he said. This kid was hopeless, Crabtree concluded. Hopeless and stupid like the whole motherfucking world was hopeless and stupid. He remembered, back in the '90s, stopping at a crackhouse up the Hudson in Newburgh which the police had raided half a day earlier. Outside, on the stoop, broken yellow police tape flapped in the river breeze. Inside he found tweakers on all fours, a dozen or more of them, all of them scratching the floors like yardbirds, crawling from room to room, sniffing for any grit left behind in the commotion. He saw one skinny henpicker, barefooted, in a paisley housedress, licking the carpet. She'd comb it with her fingers, upturning the dust, then lick whatever grains she found. Kitty litter, mostly. Kitty litter was everywhere. For a moment he thought that was who the kid reminded him of, but then he panned out: That's what *everyone* reminded him of, himself included. Just a big mess of hopeless fools—or holy goofs, like the kid's button said— licking the carpet, hoping for that bitter buzz on the tonguetip, the promise of a fix. Money, pussy, cock, fame, the warm and righteous embracing arms of Jesus, a world scraped of all its scabs and scars: the fix didn't matter. Because most of the time it was kitty litter anyway. There was victory in knowing this, Crabtree knew, because once you figured out that nothing mattered, nothing mattered. Not even five dollars. Not even the cold. He rubbed his palms together, then seared his cheeks with their quick, passing heat. "You got a smoke?" he asked Talmadge.

"Not the tobacco kind," Talmadge said, immediately regretting it. *Idiot,* he scolded himself. It was always like this. He had this insuperable need to distinguish himself, at every flitting opportunity, from *normality:* from his father's sprawling, polished Ford dealership and Saints season tickets and rarely used inboard cruiser docked at the Gulfport Yacht Club, his relentless Rotarian striving; from his younger sister's BFD internship with Senator Thad Cochran, and her scotch-drinking, Phi Delt twit of a boyfriend; from Sherilyn, the forty-three-year-old, Clairol-blonde, hyper-Botoxed funeral-home heiress for whom Dick Bertrand had left Talmadge's mother midway through Talmadge's sophomore year at Ole Miss (as if Dick Bertrand had concluded his life wasn't clichéd enough); from the Joel Osteen/Rick Warren brand of styrofoam Christianity in which his mother had taken refuge after the divorce, which daily sustained her until five o'clock when she shifted to sauvignon blanc; and from the way everyone shunned Uncle Lenord as if he was some sort of anomalous black sheep, some unaccountably redneck outlier, when in truth he was just a mirror image of Talmadge's father, his baby-boy brother, minus the good fortune of two profitable marriages (Talmadge shunned Lenord, too, but for different reasons). Boneheaded comments like this — "not the tobacco kind," *Jesus* — were the frequent result.

"Baby!" Crabtree yelped, the arrows in his back going *boing* with excitement. Why not? Nothing mattered, he reminded himself. Except for Friday's urinalysis: that might matter. "Uh-uh," he said wistfully. "They got me nailed down so hard I can't piss anywhere *besides* a cup. Put my ass in the supermax."

Talmadge, who hadn't been kidding, said, "I was just kidding."

"Would do me right, though," said Crabtree. Unsteady now, thinking about it: "Take that chill off, you know what I'm saying?"

"Sorry."

"Can't spare a joint?"

"I was just kidding."

"That's cold, man. That's cold."

"Sorry," Talmadge said again.

Did matter, Crabtree decided, surrendering the point. That the prison thermostat never dipped below 70 degrees was an attractive detail Crabtree didn't presently want to consider. "Look like you got some decent greens there," he said, pointing at the grid of produce Talmadge was carefully laying out on the snow: spinach so wilted it appeared half cooked; three bananas, their skins tinged with umber; loads of bagged salad mixes, the plastic smeary in spots; a massive eggplant so soft that Talmadge's thumb punctured it; strawberries in their plastic compartments, the bottom ones fuzzed with ashy-looking mold; broken knobs of ginger root; a sizable mess of collard or mustard greens — despite his Southern rearing, Talmadge could never tell them apart — with crisp brown leaf edges, like singe marks; and six cantaloupes, so wet and spongy that they resembled fresh brains scattered on the snowy sidewalk.

Micah would have taken nearly all of it — she had a much higher tolerance for defects and rot, having been at this much longer. She also *liked* fruit and vegetables—helpful, since she was a strict vegan—whereas Talmadge, with some exceptions, mostly enjoyed the idea of them: the forkfuls of ideology he gulped down nightly, the bittersweet gratification of his adopted asceticism, the heroism of his caloric risk and sacrifice. When he swigged spinach like Popeye, it wasn't to inflate his own muscles—it was rather to bolster the earth's. Or to knock out the Bluto-sized idea that the earning and spending of currency was the sole means of survival for her hapless and swarming inhabitants. Or something like that—Micah could explain it all better. He could never confess to her, though, that sometimes, in bed, he'd close his eyes and fantasize about the roast beef po'boys at Lil' Ray's in Gulfport with an ardor that was almost sexual in nature; more than once, in fact, he'd sprouted an odd erection.

"Them grapes don't look so bad," Crabtree was saying, as Talmadge dug his hand farther into the bag. He'd been hoping for winter squash and/or sweet potatoes—it was Thanksgiving, after all—but he reckoned they'd been selling too swiftly to get chunked. Not to mention they had the enduring shelf lives of Twinkies. Whatever. Micah would make do; she always did. He just hoped Matty wouldn't be too turned off by her meat-less wonders—Matty had all the tact of a hydraulic log-splitter, something Talmadge credited, not altogether incorrectly, to Matty's New Jersey up-bringing. Back when he and Matty had lived together, in college, they'd more or less subsisted on the fried-chicken-on-a-stick at the University Avenue Chevron. The few potato logs on the side—those were strictly for ballast. Momentarily sidetracked by that reverie—him and Matty sprawled on their dorm beds at Deaton Hall, tripping on liquid LSD, then hiking to town through the brittle chromed aftermath of an ice storm to score some chicken-on-a-stick and lukewarm beer—Talmadge wasn't pay-ing close attention to what he was unloading from the bottom of the bag until he noticed Hunch's boots go skittering backward—the frogs recoil-ing, their yellow eyes appearing to widen in shock—and heard Crabtree let loose a thunderous howl.

"A rubber!" Crabtree was shouting. Jumping up and down, he mo-tioned for Scatman to come see. "Check this out, fool. They's a used rub-ber on the boy's lettuce!"

Which there was: a droopy, gelatinous sac of semen-stuffed latex cling-ing to the crown of a small pale head of butter lettuce.

"Hoo boy, don't that ruin supper," Crabtree said, clapping in delight. Because there it was, proof positive: the kitty litter on the carpet. The pot of shit at the end of every rainbow, the five-dollar cash-coupon at the back-cracking finish of a long day's redeeming. "Some stockboy getting it on in the back! Cleanup on aisle two, baby!" He waved to the fat-faced Mexican employee huddled in the flower stall outside the store entrance. "Yo, man, check this out! Y'all having a good time in there, ain't y'all?" He pumped his hips suggestively then, doubling over, clapped his hands again. "Get-ting fresh in the grocery store! Living it up, baby! That's what I'm talking bout. Love on the clock!"

Scatman, still plugging his Evian bottles into the redemption machine, ignored it all, but the Mexican slid through the plastic flaps of his flower stall to come see. He looked grimly bemused, as if surmising that Tal-madge had been seeking some particular treasure in the store's trash bags and this gooey item was it. Two teenaged girls in matching furry boots paused to see about the fuss; through her scarf, one of them muttered, "Gross," multi-syllabically, before the pair moved on. Cursing quietly, his face flushing, Talmadge corralled all of the produce back into the bag with the obvious exception of the butter lettuce which his fingers were in no mood to revisit. Violating Micah's code of etiquette, he left the plastic bag untied — as with virtuous backpackers, the scavenger's dictum was to leave no trace — as he pushed it, with his knees, back into the base of the pile. He wanted to say something to Crabtree — to tell him to pipe down, to stop laughing; that this was freakish, shit like this hardly ever happened; that the slop dished out at the burger chains along Third Avenue con-tained enough rat turds and body hair and pesticides and stray hormones and chemicals and various other effluvia to make a wadded-up condom seem as tasty as pizza cheese; that there was more at stake than just this, these two square inches of random spoilage, that we were gnawing the planet alive, all of us, that the entire mass-produce, mass-dispose system was like some terrible, endgame buffalo hunt, a horror-show of unpicked carcasses, and that *this* — this tube of driveled semen, flicked mindlessly onto food enough to feed a family — was Exhibit A, an ideal example of our blindness, of our pampered disregard and twisted self-indulgence, of the great unconsidered *flush* that defined civilization—but Talmadge realized it would be futile. Crabtree was in tears, flagging down passersby, performing an endzone-style two-step in his frog boots.

As Talmadge slid away toward Avenue A, the wind crunching against his face, he could hear Crabtree calling after him. "You see?" he was shouting. "I may be homeless, motherfucker, that's right, but I ain't making salad dressing outta some stockboy's jizz! You hear me, motherfucker? You hear me?"

2

HE NEVER HAD time to brake. By the time Elwin saw the deer, trotting across Route 202, it was three feet from his halogens, its final oblivious moments irradiated by the klieg lights of his Jeep Cherokee. *Ker-thunk:* Elwin's head and shoulders rocked forward as he hit the deer broadside, an improbably perfect T-bone that sent the deer sliding, on its side, far far down the road, in a straight line for a while, its splayed-out body whirling on the asphalt, and then finally, as the force of the collision dissipated, to the snowbanked highway shoulder like some tragically weak gutterball. Elwin didn't realize he was stopping until he was, in fact, stopped; some alternate self, his adrenalized Other, had pressed the brake pedal and turned the wheel, beaching the Jeep on the roadside. His chest was pressed tight against the steering wheel, his eyes fixed and unblinking, the sole evidence of his own continued existence the tiny smears of fog his breath was spraypainting onto the windshield. As his senses resumed, he heard a tinny clatter from the front of the Jeep, like that of a fan shredding plastic. He started to shut off the engine, then stopped himself—he worried it might not start again. Bleached by his headlights, the deer lay motionless, its alabaster belly facing him. Please, Elwin thought. Don't move. Be dead. Be dead.

In his thirty-eight years of driving, the last three of them in the deer-swarmed New Jersey suburbs, Elwin Cross Jr. had never hit a deer. He couldn't remember even swerving to miss one, though he saw them almost nightly on his commute back from Newark—grazing the road shoulder, or hightailing it across the Morristown golf course in such vast sovereign herds that the word Serengeti popped to mind. With a rifle, and later a compound bow, he'd killed a dozen or so in his lifetime, but that was years ago, back in his graduate school days when he was living in a commune—of a sort, anyway—in Pennsylvania's Skippack Valley, doing his slipshod Thoreau imitation, brushing his long hair out of his eyes while studying the *Foxfire* books as if they were Talmudic scrolls. About 150 pounds and 300 haircuts ago, he figured.

He got out of the idling Jeep to assess the damage. The front grille was munched and one of the headlights was dangling from its socket but the overall scene was better than he'd feared. He patted the hood as if congratulating a good dog. A plow truck zoomed past, trailing a slushy salted wake, then a sedan, but Route 202 was unusually quiet tonight. Or rather this morning, Elwin realized, not happily, after checking his watch. It was almost one.

He hadn't intended a late night—just a chummy, intradepartmental dinner with Fritz at a Portuguese restaurant in Newark's Ironbound, to discuss Fritz's Terascale Linguistics Initiative. But then Fritz had announced, over appetizers, that he and Annette were splitting, which had transformed dinner into a four-hour therapy session overlubricated with two bottles of midrange Douro red that Elwin was now fiercely regretting. He'd been drinking too much lately—sloppily, stupidly, the way his students drank; though, unlike them, mostly alone—and he'd been looking forward to an evening of sociable moderation. A glass of wine, a plate of potatoes and *bacalao* (of which he'd planned to eat just half, as his current diet book counseled; that plan had failed, too), some harmless shoptalk with Fritz whose notoriously boring company posed no danger to Elwin's ambition to be asleep by ten-thirty at the latest. But then the sudden declaration: "Annette left me." Followed by the questions: first from Fritz, "How do I deal with this?" then from the waiter, "Another bottle, gentlemen?"

This marked the second time in a month that he'd been forced to play marriage counselor: On Halloween, his assistant Rochelle had barged into his office, sobbing, because her estranged husband had switched his Facebook relationship status from "Married" to "Single," digitally squashing her hopes for a reunion. She'd been dressed like a witch that day, pointy hat, etc., and as she daubed her tears she piled tissue after tissue on his desk, diminishingly smudged with green pancake makeup. At one point, hoping to fish a tonic laugh out of her, Elwin said, "You're melting," but she'd just stared at him, with her lips puckered, sighing through her semi-green nose. The most helpful takeaway she gleaned from him was something like "things will work out," which, aside from being banal, was probably untrue. It was, however, the best he could offer: to Rochelle, and then tonight, to Fritz. All Elwin could figure was that he was now considered the departmental expert on marital collapse, owing to his and Maura's ongoing, downgoing separation. But this was absurd esteem—like saying the deer in the snowbank was now an expert on collisions.

Was he legally drunk? He doubted it. Poor Fritz, that fresh marital orphan, was the one who'd really be feeling the wine's kickback, just a few hours hence. But Elwin had no clue how much alcohol the current law permitted in one's bloodstream, so maybe. Until recently, he hadn't needed to consider his BAC in twenty-five years or so—and that was back when no one really thought to consider it anyway, back when uproarious drunk-driving anecdotes were a staple of the Johnny Carson show: the studio audience howling when Peter O'Toole told of snagging a covered bridge with a panel truck. He thought he was supposed to call the state police about this, to report the downed deer . . . but might the dispatcher instruct him to wait at the scene? Would he need to fill out an accident report? He imagined a flashlight in his eyes, the cop's leery squint, that dread highwire walk he'd seen doomed teens performing on the roadside. Damn Fritz anyway, he thought. Or rather Annette, not only for leaving Fritz but for telling him, on her way out, that she'd faked every orgasm of their seventeen-year marriage, up to and including the raucous, headboard-beating ones on their honeymoon that had made Fritz so giggly and proud that he'd eaten nothing but oysters for the rest of the trip. Elwin had squirmed madly when Fritz confided all this and even feigned a bout of heartburn after the oysters detail so that he could escape to a bodega across the street, for a stage-prop roll of Tums, hoping that in the meantime Fritz might reconsider the quality and quantity of guts that he was spilling across the table. It didn't occur to Elwin until he was outside, however, that he'd responded to the sad disclosure of Annette's fakery by immediately faking a physical condition of his own. He'd probably grabbed his chest and drawn and released a melodramatic breath in much the same way Annette had. Elwin's guilt over that bought Fritz another two hours of therapeutic drinking.

He rummaged through the Jeep, searching for something he felt certain he wouldn't find: ideally a knife, though anything sharp enough to slit the deer's throat—if appallingly necessary—would suffice. A plastic ice scraper, however, was the sharpest blade the Jeep contained, and it definitely wouldn't suffice. He grabbed the tire iron, more for his own mental aid than utility; if the deer was alive, he wouldn't possibly be able to bludgeon it to death with a tire iron. His goal was mercy, not a mob hit. Warily, he approached the deer. On his side of the road were woods, sloping upward. Houses lined the opposite side, where the deer was lying, but their windows were mostly dark; the shimmery aurora of a television glowed in one upstairs window, faint and bluesy, like a pilot light preventing the inhabitants' brains from freezing. When a car rolled past, spraying Elwin with a violent splash of light then a black wave of slush pellets, he envisioned the odd sight of himself—a fat, middle-aged, wine-rumpled man in a camel hair topcoat, armed with a tire iron, scampering across the highway at 1 A.M.; cop bait if ever there was such—but there was no way around it. If this was to be a hit-and-run, it would be a fatal one. He couldn't leave the deer to suffer, slowly twitching to death in the greasy moon-colored snow. Maybe other people could. He didn't think about it.

But the deer was dead. Or looked dead, anyway. Wanting to be sure, Elwin lowered himself to the ground and pressed his ear to the deer's chest, directly behind its foreleg. He listened, but there was nothing, not even the faintest quaver of a heartbeat—just the still, warm density of its body beneath him. He noticed a raw pink nipple, jutting from the white belly-fur. A doe, he realized, with an extra lump of sadness. Female deaths were always sorrier; with males, you could almost always cite a valid reason why they had it coming. The impact must have knocked the life right out of her, he figured, imagining, for the moment, that "life" to be something like the vaporous soul which, back in Catholic grade school, the nuns claimed you exhaled from your body at the precise moment of death, when it would go curling upward toward judgment like a campfire spark.

She was a pretty young thing, noted Elwin, who was now up on his knees and running a hand across her smooth dunnish fur. From this angle, it appeared she'd died a peaceful death: an obnoxiously anthropomorphic observation, he corrected himself, since in the wild there are no peaceful deaths—particularly deaths involving pavement. What a waste, he thought. What a stupid, stupid . . . waste. Stifling a nauseating rush of emotion, or maybe an emotional surge of nausea, he started to damn Fritz again, but then stifled that, too—Fritz had enough on his karmic plate. He warmed his palms on the doe's chest, falling snowflakes bunching between his fingers. The doe's eyes were open, aimed at the dead stubble of brush poking through the snow, just beyond the pavement edge. That's where the vultures would begin eating, he thought. Either the eyes or the anus—they always started at the vulnerable parts.

What happened next, Elwin would later blame on the wine—far too glibly, however. He'd once overheard, in the college library, an undergrad telling a friend that he'd moved back in with his girlfriend solely because he'd "got drunk." The friend protested: "After all she fucking did?" "Dude," he said, with a wag of his head, "I don't know. I was *drunk.*" The image of the kid staggering into an apartment with cardboard boxes of clothes and CDs, navigating stairwells in a cluelessly boozy stupor, had made Elwin chuckle aloud, mostly because it was so preposterous. The kid obviously lacked the mettle to confess, to his pal, that he was still in love with the girl in question, had forgiven her, couldn't quit her—despite whatever crimes she'd committed, up to though probably not including faking seventeen years' worth of orgasms. It was merely easier for him to pin it on a mind-bending beer buzz. So too with Elwin and the deer, though it wasn't quite so obvious at the moment.

During his Grizzly Adams years (that was Maura's phrase) he'd been fastidious about using every last bit of the deer he killed: the backstrap sinews for thread, the tendon sheath for glue stock, the hockskins for tool handles, the kidneys fried up in a pat of butter. He couldn't recall the precise source of his hardcore purist ethic—the chapter and verse, be it Leviticus or Leopold, that had instructed him to squander nothing of his kill, not even the musky, fudge-textured kidneys of an old stringmeat buck—but it likely derived from all the Native American texts he'd absorbed while writing his dissertation on Ned Manx, the last fluent speaker of a Pomoan dialect, native to California, known as Xotc. Not that Manx himself had anything to do with it. The old man—he was 102 when Elwin finished his dissertation, 104 when he died—loved Chicken McNuggets, *Dragnet* reruns, and a syrupy homemade wine he called Hoopa Juice, the empty pint-bottles of which he sometimes tossed out of the car window when El-win would drive him to visit his grandchildren in Cloverdale. Elwin had once, very gently, asked Manx how he reconciled the littering with the Pomo concept of *saltu,* the "spirit home" that infused the ancestral land-scape. *Saltu,* Manx replied, didn't apply to asphalt.

What happened next, then, wine-driven or not: Elwin grabbed two forelegs and started dragging the deer back toward the Jeep. He wasn't sure the meat was salvageable—he might find most if not all of it bloodshot from the impact of the Jeep; additionally, there was a decent chance that the paunch had busted, and that the resulting interior blast of urine and fe-ces was currently spoiling the meat—but abandoning it felt criminal, even if, according to the law, his current tack was actually the criminal option. He'd always heard that the meat of roadkilled deer, scavenged by the high-way department, went to homeless shelters, which was a pleasant idyll that nevertheless crumbled under scrutiny: Who was the mythological state butcher culling the fresh meat from the rotten? What team of state lawyers had hashed out the vicious liability issues of dumping wormy meat onto the plastic plates of homeless children? No, this was some analgesic fantasy someone had cooked up to soften the sight of fawns lying flyspecked and bloodymouthed on the Garden State Parkway. Elwin could guess what re-ally happened: the highway workers heaving the carcasses into the maggot-smeared bed of a hulking orange dump truck, the driver lipping a Marl-boro and cranking Supertramp on the radio while pulling back the truck's dump lever at some Meadowlands landfill, the deer slumping out of the bed in a tangle of rigor mortis–stiffened legs and split, sun-charred intes-tines. They buried them like everything else.

When headlights came sweeping around a curve to the south, Elwin immediately dropped the doe and glued his hands to his hips; he even nudged it with his toe, to heighten the impression of casual study. Just as quickly, when the car passed and no brakelights appeared, he re-seized the forelegs and scurried across the road. He was in dangerous territory now, and he knew it. If a cop happened by while he was heaving the deer into the back of the Jeep—Christ, just an imagined glimpse of the ramifica-tions caused his big belly to flip, sloshing all that Douro wine it contained. When he'd pulled the deer to the rear of the Jeep, he paused for a moment, panting, to listen for traffic. It took a few seconds for the panicked clatter in his head to subside, for the hysterical warnings and recriminations being shouted from his subcortex to die down, and then: silence, or what passes for silence in that swath of New Jersey: the low-grade choral hum of a million near and distant engine pistons, firing through the night, and as many industrial processes, the muted hiss and moan of sawblades and metal stamps and hydraulic presses and conveyor belts and coalfired turbines, plus the thrum of jets, whole flocks of them, towing invisible contrails toward Newark, and the insectile buzz of helicopters flying low and locust-like over fields of radio towers and above the scrollwork of turnpike exits, all of it fused into a single omnipresent drone, an aural smog that was almost imperceptible unless you stood alone and quivering on a deserted highwayside in the snow-hushed black hours of a November morning with a carcass hardening in the ice at your feet. Elwin's breath came in polar gasps.

But the road was clear. Now was his chance. He raised the Jeep's rear door and shoved aside the piles of papers stacked therein: Fritz's dutiful Terascale Initiative report, a sheaf of student papers on variable phonology, a three-page letter from Maura that even after a dozen rereadings he found indecipherable. Explaining to his students why he was returning their papers smirched with mud and blood was going to be difficult. Perhaps he could tell them, with a wink, that a dog had tried to eat their homework? But then that wouldn't address the blood. "So I killed it," he could say, then wait to be pilloried in the student evaluations. With one hand under the deer's neck and his other arm cradling its belly, Elwin hoisted it into the back of the Jeep, noticing, in mid-heave, two things: that the doe's flopping neck signaled it was broken, indicating a clean, instant kill; and that the fragile little *pop* he'd heard was from his own spine, which meant that in several dire moments, if he bent or turned too quickly in the wrong direction, he might find himself on his back in the snow, directly beneath the hot smoking tailpipe, immobile, and in epic howling pain, with a dead doe's fluffy white ass hanging halfway out of the Jeep. If there were worse ways to die in times of peace, he couldn't think of them.

Stepping back from the Jeep, he tested his spine by performing a slow, arrhythmic twist on the roadside. It was a risky use of time, this dance, but necessary. When he felt confident his spine wouldn't buckle on him, he scooped the doe's rear into the Jeep—gingerly, because he wasn't *that* confident—and slammed the hatch shut. Scrambling into the front seat, and yanking his seatbelt on, it occurred to him that this was the closest he might ever get to the sensation of driving a getaway car. It also occurred to him that he'd left the tire iron on the road, but that would have to be sacrificed; only a pinheaded bank robber would go storming back into the bank to retrieve his forgotten pistol. It didn't go unnoticed, furthermore, that he was suddenly, and weirdly, having more fun than he'd had in many many years.

"What the hell am I doing?" he asked himself aloud, and then, despite himself, he started giggling—so hard, and so irrepressibly, that he checked his face in the rearview mirror to see what a giggling Dr. Elwin Cross Jr., Imperial Grand Poobah (Rochelle's pet title) of the Trueblood Center for Applied Linguistics at Marasmus State College, looked like, in such an unusually florid state. Like a fool, he decided. Like a juiced-up, fatassed, Cumberland County redneck who'd just picked roadkill off the highway and would now be up—he hadn't considered this until now— until three or four or maybe five in the morning cleaning a deer that might or might not provide a single ounce of edible flesh, which he really wasn't sure he wanted anyway. "What the hell am I doing?" he repeated, but this time grimly, and without a subsequent giggle. At least tomorrow was the day before Thanksgiving, the start of the Marasmus holiday break, which meant he could sleep in, if needed. Except that he couldn't remember the last time he'd slept past seven. (Two hundred haircuts ago? One fifty?) But he *could* sleep in. And that's what mattered now, he thought: the *potential*. The potential of the deer's rammed flesh, the potential of untroubled rest, the potential of happiness, of brightness down the line, of "things"—what was that he'd told Rochelle, told Fritz?—"working out."

The dashboard clock read 1:37 when Elwin arrived home. "Home," however, struck him as an inaccurate term for the house Maura had ceded him; it'd been a home with her in it (at least he'd thought so), but she'd switched up the consonants on her way out the door, downgrading it to mere house. Either way: It was a three-story Colonial, circa 1890, majestic and maybe even ostentatious when it was built but having been divided and subdivided over the years, overhauled and underhauled, and modernized and plasticized, its honey-colored plank floors layered and relayered with linoleum sheathing, its pineboard exterior inhumed with aluminum cladding, its fireplaces bricked and a massive iron fire escape bolted to its flank, and with a ring of split-levels having grown around it in the early '70s, followed by McMansions in the '90s, the home-slash-house was now, Elwin had to admit, a weird eyesore. He'd made the offer on it himself, while Maura was still back in California, thinking they'd enjoy a renovation after all those years of living in prefab ranch houses—antiquing over in Bucks County, DIY Saturdays with a pot of chili simmering on the stove, the nerdy-fun detective work of historical restoration, et cetera. This had been a serious miscalculation. "Well, you've always liked rescuing things," was Maura's first impression of the place, her hostile tone more suited to a statement like *You've always liked my sister's ass.* She was so thoroughly cool to the house that she seemed ambivalent about unpacking the moving boxes, in retrospect a glaring signal. Had there been other signals? Hundreds or none, he couldn't be sure. He realized the preposterousness of saying he'd never seen the affair coming—does anyone?—yet the stark fact remained: He'd never seen the affair coming. And worse yet, the aftermath.

Shutting off the engine felt like an act of mercy. The noise had gotten worse, much worse, and the Jeep rolled into the driveway like one of those smoking, rattling, backfiring Model Ts you saw in Laurel and Hardy movies. He glanced at the upper windows of the house next door—home to Big Jerry, a retired lineman with Jersey Central Power & Light; his wife Myrna; and their twin boys, Christopher and Joey, who like their dad worked for Jersey Central—and was relieved to see them stay dark. Elwin wasn't certain, at the moment, that he could take Big Jerry, whose bombastic helpfulness caused him to preface nearly every utterance with "Whatchoo gotta do, see . . ." With a wince, he imagined Big Jerry stomping across the shared driveway, all too ready to dispense aid: *Whatchoo gotta do, see . . . is get rid of that fuckin deer.* By now, Elwin's wine buzz had worn off, having been flushed by the adrenaline torquing his veins for the last half hour—and that was ebbing, too. He shook his head after opening the Jeep's rear door and seeing the deer peacefully curled therein, like a napping child.

The immediate question was where to clean the deer. He settled on the fire escape at the rear of the house, the other option being to hang it from the big maple tree, streetside, which he nixed for obvious reasons. The only viewers he'd risk seeing the deer beneath the fire escape—and his lurid autopsy of it—were Big Jerry and family, an unpleasant but manageable potentiality. Their standard weekend apparel—camouflage overalls, ant-ler-emblazoned t-shirts—and the bowhunting targets in their backyard augured some measure of empathy.

Inside the house Elwin muttered hello to Bologna, a fifteen-year-old mutt that he'd found, as a half-starved, mange-ravaged, and seriously ugly puppy, on the side of the Ventura Highway licking a dead duplicate of itself—clearly, someone had dumped a litter there. Maura had never warmed to the dog, gladly bequeathing custody of him to Elwin when she'd moved out, which Elwin could have held against her but didn't—gassy, drooly, and dumb as a brick, Bologna was a challenge to love. The dog, deaf and more or less blind, raised his head, sniffed the air, then nes-tled his snout back into the dandery folds of his dog bed. "Hey boy," Elwin mumbled, headed downstairs.

From the basement he gathered a pair of rubber cleaning gloves, his old stag-handled skinning knife (stowed there with the rest of his Grizzly Adams paraphernalia: fishing waders, unwed flyrod sections, camouflage bib overalls, binoculars, a tin-plated manual meat grinder, magnesium fire-starter, a rifle cleaning kit, half-empty ammunition boxes, all of it per-fumed with the '70s, with the odor of mildewed ideals), three Hefty gar-bage sacks, a headlamp, two lengths of rope (one nylon, one sisal), a rusted hacksaw, and, after noisily dumping its contents into yet another Hefty garbage sack (he was improvising now), the twenty-five-gallon plastic bin he used for his recyclables. All this Elwin amassed on the snow, along with the deer, beneath the black gridwork of the fire escape.

Working steadily, he noosed the sisal rope around the doe's neck, tied it, yanked the knot to test it, then (standing tiptoed atop the overturned plastic bin) looped the rope's other end over one of the fire escape's iron rails. He pulled the slack through. With a heavy grunt, he tugged hard on the rope, drawing the doe's head off the ground so that it appeared an unfamiliar sound had just roused it from sleep. But that was as high as he could lift it. Hoisting the deer, he realized, was going to be more difficult than he'd planned; at 340 pounds (a weight deemed "morbidly obese" by his tactless primary care physician), Elwin wasn't remotely so fit as he'd been in his grad school years, back when he could've raised a buck like a yo-yo. Dropping the rope, he considered tying it onto the Jeep and hoisting it up that way, but this would entail parking on the back lawn, in eight inches of snow and probably atop the brick planters. He wiggled his arms like an on-deck batter, picked up the rope again, braced his boots against the snow, and pulled mightily. The doe's neck rose, then its limp forelegs, its torso, then finally its hind legs — slowly and smoothly, like a saint ascending — at which point Elwin, his overinsulated arm muscles seething, tied off the rope then collapsed onto the snow.

He lay there for a while, on his back, the soft-faceted snowflakes that the wind was sweeping off the roof grazing his eyelashes and powdering his lips. The deer he'd just lynched was dully twirling in the sideward glow of the 150-watt floodlight tilted over Big Jerry's back door. Light-years above him, partly screened by woolly black clouds, were two stars: Sirius and Rigel, guttering weakly. When Elwin was a boy, and begging for a telescope, his father had told him that the Indians took the stars with them when they were forced out of New Jersey, which explained the star-deprived blackness above Montclair as well as the overfreckled skies out west. Those few stars they'd left behind, like Sirius and Rigel, had been merely too big to carry; they were like abandoned monuments, a celestial Stonehenge lodged in the skies above Ho-Ho-Kus and Secaucus, the last physical vestiges of an erased civilization.

As the cold began penetrating Elwin's back, he wondered, idly, as he sometimes did, how he'd ended up here. Not the immediate here — face-up in the snow at 2 A.M. with a pendant carcass nearby — but the wider, more existential here: securely tenured and middlingly comfortable, yes, but piercingly alone, unloved and unheralded, a coroner of dead languages, dead marriages, and now (refocusing the mental lens) a dead and dangling deer. This was a question — How did I end up here? — that as a younger man he used to ask himself regularly, most often in a tickled and self-congratulatory mode: *How did I end up here* (limb-tangled in bed with this woman, so obviously out of his league; doing fieldwork in places he enjoyed hearing described as "far flung" — the Amazon, the Mongolian steppe, an Inuit village in Nunatsiavut; or accomplishing feats for which his Montclair upbringing had scarcely prepared him, like shooting a deer or tilling a half acre of meaty black soil in that Skippack Valley commune, or sewing up his own gashed arm, in a vocal haze of mosquitoes, after a machete mishap in a Bolivian Indian village)? The swivels of his life used to please him greatly. They were a rebuttal—not angry, but insistent—to the straight, level course of his father's life: from the Army to college to grad school to a teaching post to marriage to fatherhood to retirement to nursing home, each progression as engraved and invariable as the Stations of the Cross. Elwin had been different; he'd zigged, he'd zagged, resisting the tamped-down paths, the blatant grooves. For a while, anyway, until he found that same question, so luscious for so many years, beginning to curdle in his mind: *How did I end up here* (here, in yet another fertility clinic, Maura sighing and patting his fattening back; in yet another overstarched faculty committee meeting, and yet another classroom, ignoring his students ignoring him; back home in near-flung New Jersey, trapped in congealing Turnpike traffic; in a Morristown marriage counselor's office, watching the therapist's thatchy eyebrow ascend as Maura described sex with her new chef-lover as "frankly the most liberating experience" of her life)? Until recently, however, the question had never seemed final—the word *end* having always been exaggerated, a touch of young-buck melodrama.

But now . . . he was not yet at the age, like his father, when life shifts to past tense, when what *is* becomes what *was* and all the other verbs defining your existence go slumping into the preterite, crusted with apophonic alternations (*I sing* calcifying into *I sang*), and you can do nothing but marvel or wince at the irredeemable, irreversible arc of it—not yet. On this November night he was fifty-four years old. By no means, he told himself, was he beyond the future tense. But he could feel the past tense gaining on him, like the cold seeping into his back and dusting his face. He licked it off his lips and stood up. He had work to do.

He slid the plastic bin directly beneath the deer and lined it with one of the Hefty bags, then, after ditching his wristwatch and jacket and rolling up his shirtsleeves, replaced his leather gloves with the rubber cleaning gloves and fastened on the headlamp. With his knife, he made a tiny incision near the doe's pelvis, then squeezed his hand inside the cut; it was still warm in there, the gap exhaling a brief air-kiss of steam. Cupping the end of the blade with two fingers to prevent it from slashing the entrails, Elwin slowly cut upward, unzipping the doe's belly. When the organs flopped out, with a slurpy sound, he severed the connective tissue, scouring the area around the diaphragm with his hand and blade. The organs tumbled down—dark liver and multi-chambered stomach and grayish-purplish intestines—into the Hefty sack below.

He aimed his headlamp downward, to inspect the makeshift gutbucket, and was simultaneously relieved and dispirited to see that all the digestive organs had survived the collision intact: relieved, because that meant a burst of gastric juices or excrement hadn't spoiled the meat, and dispirited, because that meant he had to keep going.

He tied off the bung then pushed it through the rectum, and then, with the knife, cut off the rectum and a ring of the flesh surrounding it, letting the oblong chunk fall, with a gassy splat, into the Hefty sack. Not wanting to risk contaminating the meat, he slid the right glove off and used his bare hand to rip down the heart and lungs. Steam rose from the Hefty sack as from a pot of soup, a visual reminder, for Elwin, of just how cold he was— without his coat, and with his right forearm blood-wet and gore-gloppy. Only when he stepped back and focused did he realize his teeth were chattering.

He was just turning the corner of the house, headed inside, with his coat and gloves in his left hand and his mucoid, red-splotched right arm extended perpendicular to his body, when a pickup came roaring into the driveway, its headlights and foglights and aftermarket whatever-else lights bouncing over the potholes and freezing him in their comet-bright glare, before the truck came lurching to a stop.

"Shit," Elwin whispered. This was worse than being caught redhanded, he thought. He'd been caught red-*armed*.

The tinted window glided downward, releasing a potent blast of guitar distortion, sounding something like two chainsaws engaged in especially noisy sex, and revealing a glowing orange cigarette tip encircled by the ruddy, grinning face of Big Jerry's son Christopher. Or maybe Joey: It was hard to tell the twins apart. But no, it was Christopher. Joey, the more urbane of the two, drove a sportscar. "What up, Doc?" shouted Christopher, who had clearly—considering the hour, the beery warble of his voice and the canine droop of his eyes—just finished a typically monumental night of drinking in Morristown. Biting his lower lip, Christopher slung his head back and forth before turning off the music, then continued his headbanging for a few moments afterwards as if failing—maybe *actually* failing—to register the silence. The graceless, viscous way he came spilling out of the truck called to mind the organs plopping out of the doe's split belly.

Only when he tried to shake Elwin's hand, and was silently rebuffed, did Christopher notice all the blood. His eyelids leapt upward at the sight of it. Christopher had the kind of cold, windshield-washer-fluid-blue eyes that, on some men (Clark Gable as an antique example), women find devastating. Yet something was wrong with Christopher's set. They were *too* icy, too pale, and less roguish than sociopathic—zombie eyes. Christopher's other Gable-esque features—his cleft chin; his dimpled grin; his narrow whisper of a mustache—were similarly marred: the chin *too* cloven, and yeastily puffed, resembling a miniature set of buttocks adorning his lower lip; the dimples *too* deep, and too suggestive of the skull-lines beneath; and the mustache foppish and dated. He was staring at Elwin's out-held arm in mortal bafflement. "What'd you do, Doc?" he asked. "Deliver a baby?"

It was impossible to tell whether or not he meant this question sincerely. His father, Big Jerry, referred to Elwin as "Dr. Cross," but not out of respect—rather, because he enjoyed telling himself and others that a doctor lived next door, no matter what kind. He gleaned similar satisfaction from telling strangers what he'd paid for his house, in 1982, compared to its present value ($65,000 versus $320,000) and, whether they were interested or not, the amount of the monthly payment on the twenty-three-foot Bay Ranger he bought upon retiring, a not-insignificant figure—especially considering that, after nineteen months of payments, Big Jerry had used the boat only once. So for Christopher, whose curiosity, at twenty-two, was mainly limited to the varying shapes and sizes of New Jersey breasts and the still-unpredictable effects of legal beer consumption, Elwin was simply Doc—an ornamental doctor of some kind or other, be it linguistics or linguine, or maybe backyard obstetrics.

"No," said Elwin, after a long, pained pause. "Peek around the back."

"Fuck yeah," Christopher shouted, after doing so. "Nice one. I didn't know you hunted. Hey, we got a place on the Delaware we go. It's all managed and shit. Huge fucking bucks. Where'd you bang that one?"

"Two-oh-two," Elwin said.

"Two-oh-two?" The depth of his frown suggested advanced mental arithmetic. "What the fuck?"

"It jumped in front of me."

"Holy . . . fucking . . . toledo," Christopher exclaimed—slowly, but with increasing volume. He pitched forward in the snow to get a closer look at the deer. Elwin didn't follow. "You tee-boned this thing then brought it home?"

"I guess. Yeah."

"Where at?"

"Just past Harter Road. By Spring Brook."

"Was it dead?"

"Of course."

"Fuck the car up?"

"A little."

"A drive-by, wow," said Christopher, grinning. "That's fucking *punk,* Doc. Damn."

Elwin said, "Seemed like such a shame . . . you know, to waste it." His mouth was open to say more, but nothing emerged. He was overaccustomed to dealing with kids Christopher's age, having taught them for almost a quarter century, which was why his current unsteadiness felt so odd and inverted: He was feeling a total absence of authority. If Christopher were to turn on him now, and snap, "Shame on you, Doc" (for any number of valid or semivalid reasons: driving home from the restaurant half drunk, or even a quarter drunk; going seven miles an hour over the speed limit, thereby reducing his ability to brake and/or swerve for the deer; failing to report the collision; heaving the carcass into his Jeep despite his lack of hunting license and/or deer tag; butchering the deer in this macabre and presumably unzoned-for suburban setting; and so on), Elwin might bow his graying head and beg forgiveness from this twenty-two-year-old utility lineman who was currently struggling, pickled as he was by a dozen Bud Light longnecks and three Jägermeister shooters, to unite the flame of his Bic lighter with the swaying tip of the Marlboro Red between his lips. But Christopher did not say *For shame.* Instead, once his cigarette was lit, he grinned madly, and jutting his chin toward Elwin with what appeared to be newfound affection and admiration for his neighbor, said, "*Punk,* Doc. Totally punk."

"Anyway," Elwin said, "I've got to wash this arm off, and get some water."

"Right on. We gotta skin this bitch. I'll get my quad."

Meekly, Elwin protested, but Christopher was already scrambling toward his house, wobbling his way across the tiretracked driveway, past a row of beefy trash cans, and through the gate to where his Kawasaki quad was parked, beneath the sunporch. "Fucking crazy, Doc," he was shouting. "You the man!"

Inside the house, rinsing the bloody film from his arm under the warm stream of the kitchen faucet, Elwin cringed when he heard the guttural rumble of Christopher starting up the quad. Closing his eyes, with a wounded grimace, he imagined lights appearing in bedroom windows up and down the street, like flashbulbs at a press conference. This had somehow gotten entirely out of hand—if at any point it was *in* hand, Elwin reminded himself. Scooping the water in his cupped palms and lowering his face into its warmth, he wondered if this was the way lives crumbled: swiftly, within the flickering span of a night: one unfortunate, ill-considered decision leading to another, and then another, followed by another, until it was impossible to see where the logic had forked, where rationality had dissolved—until all traces of sense and sensibility were scrubbed clean, like the minor stars from the skies over New Jersey, and you were left with a mid-life professor attempting to explain, to a crowd of livid, orey-eyed neighbors wearing bathrobes and snowboots, and perhaps accompanied by a pair of cops, and maybe even by a graveyard-shift reporter mulling a Satanism angle, why Bambi's pink-nippled mother was dangling from his fire escape at 2-something A.M., her eviscerated organs steaming inside a recycling bin. ("You know," he could almost hear the neighbors whispering, "his wife *did* just leave him.") Elwin felt as if he was watching a video of his own demise. The decision, he felt, was whether to let it keep playing, ominous soundtrack-music and all, or fast-forward it. Bologna raised his head again, with a perturbed scowl, as Elwin rushed past him outside.

He found Christopher wiping the skinning knife in the snow, with the quad, looking as showroom clean as Big Jerry's Bay Ranger, parked beside the fire escape. "Nice knife," he said. Elwin looked around: no cops, no reporter waving a steno pad at him, no sleep-encrusted neighbors brandishing rolling pins. Not even a glow from Big Jerry and Myrna's bedroom window. Just the dark balm of New Jersey at night: the collective snore of

millions of exhausted commuters, awaiting their execution by alarm clock.
"You cool?" Christopher asked, pointing the knife at the doe.

"Be my guest," Elwin said, relieved—even thrilled—to stand back
and observe. He slipped his washed hands into his pockets, the way Pon-
tius Pilate might have done.

"My dad never lets me clean them," Christopher said. With his right
hand, he sliced the skin on the neck, just behind the ears, while pulling,
with the thumb and forefinger of his left hand, on the flap he was making.
He did an imitation of Big Jerry in full-choke cantankerousness: "'You'll
just fug it up.' Whatever."

"Where's your brother tonight?"

"That asshole," Christopher said. "He's nailing some broad up in Parsippany. He's whipped. We never see him." After he'd cut a collar-like ring
around the doe's neck, he made a vertical slice downward to where Elwin
had split the belly, adding a dramatic, Zorro-like flourish. "Beauty!" he
shouted, somewhat unclearly, then paused to light another cigarette. "You
see that new boat he bought? *Used* boat, I mean."

Elwin hadn't, but it wouldn't have been so easy to notice: Big Jerry's
backyard was a metallic garden overplanted with quads, jonboats, a Jet Ski,
a canoe, an antique Japanese motorcycle so frail and rusted it resembled a
cicada shell, and several engine blocks in varying states of dishabille.

"Your brother, you mean?"

"Yeah. Says it's a"—here his voice went lispy, queeny—"'perfect lake
boat.'" He took an intemperate drag from his cigarette. "Come *on*. It's
a twelve-foot jonboat. He's like, but it's fifty-six inches wide! Like that's
gonna matter in four-foot swells. The engine's worth more than the whole
fucking boat. And there's a big gash in the hull! Think he noticed it? Whatever. He's like, 'What gash?' What an asshole."

"Here," said Elwin, picking up the hacksaw. "We've got to get these
forelegs off."

"Oh yeah, right. I knew that."

While Elwin sawed, Christopher sliced, the smoke from his Marlboro
coiling above his head, the winddrift snow powdering the carcass like a
sugared pastry: two butchers working in tandem, the *scritch-scritch* of the
knife a call-and-response phrase to the intermittent rasps of the hacksaw.
After Elwin dropped the deer's right foreleg into the Hefty sack, he applied

the pink-gummed hacksaw blade to the left leg. Then he knelt in the snow, sawing apart the hind legs.

"Big night tonight?" he said, enjoying the silence but feeling obligated to break it.

"Naw. Same old shit, you know."

"You have to work tomorrow?"

"Oh yeah. Time and a half, bay-bee. Working Thanksgiving, too. That's overtime. They had us on call because of this storm but this was nothing. City got *bombed*, though. Long Island, too. Them crews'll be working all night."

"Careful now," Elwin said, after glancing upward. "You're pulling some meat off . . ."

"Okay, yeah. I got it. I see it, Doc." But in fact he was making a total hash of it, and Elwin was reminded that arming a drunk, no matter the task, was probably never a good idea. As he cut, Christopher swung his shoulders and hips about, in a woozy semi-dance, and sang, over and over again, the chorus to Mötley Crüe's "Doctor Feelgood," which Elwin suspected was in his honor. At one point Christopher's hip reeled dangerously close to Elwin's head.

Elwin said, "Easy now."

"So this broad tonight . . ."

"Yeah?"

"At McGuinn's, right? Donna. Fucking cuts me off after, like, three beers. I'm like, what the fuck? And she's like, after what happened last time, you're lucky to get anything."

"What happened last time?"

"That's the fucking thing, man. I don't know! It's my brother. I'm like, that was *Joey,* we're fucking *twins,* bitch. And she's all, it ain't my job to tell you guys apart. So I call Joey, right? I'm like, fucking bitch won't give me a beer because of whatever shit you pulled at McGuinn's. So he says, let me talk to her. So I give her the phone and she's, like, nodding and shit, then she hands me back my phone and she's like, I don't know who you called but that guy doesn't know you. He said you called a children's hospital. Fucking ICU."

Distantly, Elwin said, "Nice."

"Asshole! Then he turns his phone off. He's fucking garbage, man. And

you should see this broad he's doing, the one in Parsippany. She's like a total cow. It's like, grab a fold and fuck it. Not me, man."

"Yeah, well," Elwin said, cringing as he assessed the fuckability of his
own copious folds. He twisted the final leg off the deer and dumped it with
the other ones. "How's the meat looking?"

"Here, hand me that flashlight," Christopher said. "It's not bad, man.
Check it out. This side over here is kind of ripped up, but it's all right.
Make sausage out of that."

Elwin's eyes followed the flashlight beam. Christopher's appraisal, he
saw, was far too generous: The collision had rendered the doe's left shoulder ragged and jellied, reminiscent of cherry pie filling—completely unsalvageable. "It's already sausage," Elwin muttered. The flesh of the right
shoulder, however, appeared, if not prime, then choice: nicely striated and
evenly purple, just a shade lighter than the Douro wine that had indirectly
led to the doe's death, and layered with a webbing of diaphanous ivory fat.
"Better than I expected, actually," Elwin said.

"Nice bumper placement," Christopher said, and slapped Elwin on the
back. "Like bullet placement, right? Bumper placement. Hey, you got a
beer inside?"

"No, sorry," Elwin said, realizing he did but letting the lie stand anyway. "So let's get this skin off. You mind? The two of us can manage fine
without the quad . . ."

"Come on, with the quad it's like *that,*" snapping his fingers.

"I don't want to wake the whole street."

"Like *that,*" he said, re-snapping his fingers. "See that stainless-steel exhaust? That fucker's *quiet,* man. These new models, they gotta be. Some
law in California."

"Then let's be quick," Elwin said. "We need a rock or something . . ."

Christopher said, "A golfball."

"You got one?"

"I got *everything,*" he said, then took off running. The slam of the storm
door, as he rocketed into the house, was enough to shake the slumbering
icicles from the roof. He was back within a minute, holding a can of Bud
Light in one hand, and, in the other palm, flaunting a yellow golfball as if
it were a glinting nugget he'd just panned from a stream. Which wasn't so
far from the truth, as it turned out: "We used to fish these fuckers out of

the ponds at Spring Brook, when me and Joey was kids," he said. "Late at night, you know, 'cause they'd run you off if they found you. There's this pond, on the fourteenth hole—fucking *full* of balls. Just put some waders on, walk around with a landing net. Fucking bonanza, man. We got, like, five hundred balls one night *alone*. Sold them back for a quarter a ball— except for those Titleist balls, you know? Fucking dollar *per*."

"Not bad," Elwin said, plucking the golfball from Christopher's hand and inserting it into a fold he made with a skin-flap hanging from between the doe's shoulder blades. "Hand me that other rope," he said. After tying a slip knot, Elwin rung the nylon loop around the base of the skin covering the golfball, so that the ball was tucked inside the furry bulge, and tight-ened the knot. This would secure the deer's skin to the rope so that they could peel it from the carcass with a single motorized pull. "Your turn," he said to Christopher, tossing him the other end of the rope.

"We found this ball once," Christopher said, setting his beer on the rear fender so that he could tie the rope to the quad's hitch. "Had Saddam Hus-sein's face on it, right? The Iraq dude? And it said, 'Slam Saddam.' Fucking beautiful. I saved that one."

"Now let's do this *quietly*," Elwin said.

Christopher tapped his bootheels together, saluted, then mounted the quad. "Yippee-ki-yi-yay, motherfucker," he said, to nothing and no one in particular, before glugging down a long swig of beer and starting the engine. Elwin flinched at the noise—California's regulations were appar-ently generous with the decibel limits—as Christopher clunked the quad into gear and gunned it forward.

The ropes sprang tight, and the half-dressed carcass swung upward with an appallingly violent jolt. "Slower!" Elwin screamed. "Jesus! You're going to ruin—" Remembering Big Jerry, as quoted by his son, he cut himself off. No need to dunk the boy deeper.

Thick purple shards of flesh clung to the peeling skin; the yippee-ki-yi-yay force of Christopher's acceleration, Elwin saw, was shredding much of the meat. "Slower!" Elwin screamed again, this time more pleadingly. Christopher glanced back, his face contorted into a madman's conjunction of sneer and grin, but he either couldn't hear Elwin or was ignoring him— he revved the quad harder, and with his free hand, raised high and cradling his Bud Light, toasted the sparse night sky.

The beer can was what caught Elwin's eye first: sailing backwards through the air, it passed through the white glare of the porchlight for a single, spangly micro-moment, as the deer's skin slipped off the carcass, like a sock freed from a foot, and the quad, freed as well, went jerking forward. Christopher appeared to have zero control. Focused on his left hand and its ejection of his beer, he neglected the angle of his right wrist, fixed on the throttle. The quad bounced across the driveway, dragging the tangled, meat-specked pelt and throwing wet bands of snow behind it, before one of two things, or a combination thereof, stopped it: Christopher finding the brakes, or the row of trash cans he smacked impeding further motion. The cans exploded with a clatter, one tipping left, vomiting bulbous white bags onto the snow, and the other tipping backwards, shaking the entire length of vinyl fence. Elwin maintained a cringe as Christopher killed the engine and dismounted with the spooked but prideful expression of a rodeo bull rider.

"Lost my fucking beer," he announced.

Predictably, a light sparked in the upstairs window, and, after the miniblinds reeled upward into a slanting heap, Elwin watched Big Jerry's face, bisected by his fat woolly grub of a mustache, snarling and glowering behind the glass as he rattled the sash open and flung up the storm window. The raw force with which his head and naked shoulders popped out of the windowframe suggested a full-scale dive that only the width of his belly had thwarted, if not Myrna grabbing his ankles. In the mildest conversation, Big Jerry's voice was rich and grainy and preposterously loud, as if he were equipped with some sort of tracheal bullhorn. In California, one suspected, it would be illegal for him to speak. Now, stoked with the rage of his rude awakening, it thundered: "What the ever-loving fuck is going on down there? Christopher!"

"What?" the son barked back at the father.

"You piece of shit! It's three in the morning! Whatchoo doing?"

"Bite my ass!"

"*What?*"

"Bite my ass!"

"You get the fuck inside," Big Jerry yelled down, stabbing a thick bratwurst of a finger at him, "so I can put a gun to your stupid fucking head, and *shoot* it!"

The eerie calm with which Christopher planted his boots in the snow, in a wide and cocky stance, then slowly raised his middle finger to the window reminded Elwin of the famous image of that Tiananmen Square protester staring down a tank. Whether it was the first time he'd done something of that brazen, bird-fingered nature, or the thousandth, it felt epic all the same — at least to Elwin, who'd conducted his own youthful rebellions with excessively diplomatic tact, like a philosopher breaking with his mentor over some minor dialectic: thoughtfully, and with profuse apology. In response, the word *fuck,* in nearly all its grammatical derivations, rained down from the window like mortar fire. When Big Jerry had emptied his big mouthful, he clawed the air, cheeks puffed with rage, until small hands appeared on his shoulders and pulled him back inside. A few seconds later, Myrna replaced him in the window: frazzled and frizzy-haired, her drowsy eyelids beating weakly, but kind-countenanced as always — a cartoonist's rendition of the archetypal grandma face.

She said flatly, "Christopher, you gotta work tomorrow," adding, "and where's your hat?"

"Me and Doc just having some fun," he replied.

She brightened. "Dr. Cross?"

Reluctantly, Elwin moved out of the shadows, where he'd been cowering ever since Christopher had demanded an ass-bite.

"Oh *hello,* Dr. Cross." A church-supper smile. Or Rapunzel greeting suitors. "How are *you* tonight?"

This question didn't normally require contemplation, yet, for several intensely awkward, spotlit moments, Dr. Cross found himself wholly incapable of an answer. How was he tonight? Excellent question . . . other than being trapped in an absurdist nightmare which had begun, so far as he could track its course, when Maura had left him for the liberating sexual tactics of the Chef, and which was now culminating, here, in the blood-spattered, trash-strewn snow, in this dizzying, freakish alternate universe he'd tumbled into when the deer flashed into his headlight beams and his conscience subsequently unraveled him, and *especially* in these last few innocent moments that remained while Big Jerry's plump, shaking fingers dropped bullets into a gun barrel for the filicidal cataclysm to come, he was fine. Fine. Of course. This almost made him laugh. He was fine.

"Fine," he lied, with a cheery wave.

"Well, *good,*" she called back. Despite her smile, Elwin could see her waving a hand sideways, with hot insistence, to shoo Big Jerry, whose shadow was violently roaming the bedroom walls. "Will you send Christopher inside, please? He has to work tomorrow, you know."

"I'll let him know," said Elwin, standing five feet behind him.

"Thank you. Well, goodnight, Dr. Cross."

"Goodnight," he called back.

Her tone chilled. "Christopher, you need a hat," she said, before sliding down the window sashes. In fierce, spasmodic slants, the miniblinds came tumbling down behind them.

Immediately, Christopher asked, "You see my beer anywhere?" But his voice was quavery, fissured with hairline cracks. Shaking his head no, Elwin slipped his hands into his pockets. Despite his age, he felt small and childish beneath the window's rebuke, though not nearly so small and childish as Christopher now appeared, absently kicking at the snow while combing a hand through his gel-spiked hair—subconsciously, or so it seemed, feeling for a nonexistent hat. Christopher's meager, spindrift mustache, which had previously struck Elwin as foppish, struck him now as something sadder: a failed attempt to challenge Big Jerry's burly gray one, to defy his father's croaky, bullying manhood (and, perhaps, that of his twin brother, with his new used boat and fleshy girlfriend) by exerting his own nascent manliness, follicle by tender follicle. From that weedy mustache to his legacy job at Jersey Central, to the beer-drinking to the boat-collecting, it was imitation as insurrection, a simmered bid to defeat his father at his own game. Standing there, in his distressed low-slung jeans and rap-star parka, with a gold-plated chain rung around his neck and dandruff-like snow flecking the coifed black cactus topping his head, he bore the doughy stink of oppression, of undue kneadings and poundings. Elwin suppressed the desire to say something to him, something consoling and avuncular, partly because he knew it would be batted down hard—you didn't air shit like this, not in Jersey; better yet, you didn't *think* it—but also because he was oh for two on dispensing wisdom. *Things will work out* didn't cut it. Clearly, his powder was wet.

Finally, he said, "Thanks for all the help," with all its gently implied finality. "It's easy going from here."

"Yo," Christopher replied, whapping Elwin's chest with the back of his palm, and grinning unhappily, "that's what neighbors do, right?" He sucked back a belch, with obvious though appreciated discomfort. "That's what it's about, right?"

"Right," Elwin answered, adding softly, "You the man."

"Nah," Christopher said. He grasped for something else to say, some immodestly modest rebuttal, but none came; he was either too drunk, or too drained, or too flattered, or too mooky and young. "Nah," he repeated. Then his expression sagged, those ice-blue eyes drooping downward in private defeat. He ran his fingers through his hair again: still no hat. His shoulders slumping, and a sigh whirring through his nose, Christopher turned toward the house. "Fuck that old man," he muttered, and headed inside, lazily scanning the snow, as he went, for the four-leaf clover of his ejected beer. This time, when the door shut behind him, the icicles held fast; they'd been warned. Elwin listened, but there was no gunshot, not even the reverb of raised voices. When he looked up, the light in Big Jerry's bedroom was out. Back below the fire escape, he picked up the knife, and the flashlight, and resumed dismantling the deer.

By the time Elwin finished—having sliced and sawn the salvageable flesh of the doe into backstraps, tenderloins, shanks, a shoulder roast, and one dubious slab of ribs (both hams, having borne the brunt of the pavement, were wrecked), and having exhausted an entire roll of plastic wrap and half a roll of aluminum foil in swaddling the meat, the sheer glut of which forced him to evacuate much of his refrigerator's contents and even then spilled over into a cooler he dragged up from the basement, and having then collected and washed all the tools from outside, and bundled all the remaining deer parts (including the severed head, with its jutting pink tongue) into ever more black Hefty sacks, so that the multitude of trash bags piled against the house resembled the aftermath of some civic festival, and rubbed the snow with his boot to conceal or at least pinken all the bloody spatters and driplines, and (almost forgetting) untied the pelt from the quad hitch and stuffed it into yet another Hefty sack—the eastern sky was unblackening, the soft gray of dawn edging the horizon. He wanted to shower, but didn't have the energy; instead he undressed, emptying his BlackBerry and keys and change onto the nightstand, and collapsed into his bed, groaning in weak protest at the uninvited light creeping across the walls. From downstairs he heard the heavy click-clack of Bologna's claws on the floor, as the dog rose from his bed, then the *thwap* of the dog door flapping closed behind him. Poor old guy, Elwin thought. Must've finally picked up the scent of all that meat, like an astronomer viewing the glow of a distant star that's been dead five hundred years.

By force of ritual — or addiction, as Maura claimed: "Crackberry," and all that — he checked his BlackBerry before completely nesting in. Holding it high above his head, he noted the reddish-black gore under his thumbnail as he tapped the small screen. A message from his sister. He knew what that was about: his father, who'd also called — six times during dinner, it appeared. Also there were late-night emails from his students, which he ignored or skimmed ("I was wondering if the 500–750 words counted toward quotes used from the Lanza book, or [if] this limit [is] only in reference to our own thoughts and ideas expressed in the paper . . ."), various bits of Listserv pollution (DELETE, he pressed; DELETE; DELETE), and then one email, sent late that afternoon from Rochelle, in her semi-lovable, semi-competent way, which aroused a curious frown: "Somebody from the government called today," she'd written. "I wrote it all down but I can't find the message. SO SORRY!!! It was some governemtn [*sic*] agency. Department of Something :) It will turn up! You know it always does. Have fun with Dr. Horten tonight! ;) AND HAPPY THANKSGIVING!!!"

Somebody from the government, Elwin wondered, as he replaced the BlackBerry on the nightstand and, to depressingly little effect, flicked off the lamp. In his bleary, blood-encrusted state, which precluded logic or chronology or anything resembling cogent thought, he imagined only one possibility: the State of New Jersey, or maybe some obscure federal agency, wanted its deer back. They'd seen him, they knew. It was government property, and theirs to dispose of. He'd broken some sacred but little-known code, the New Jersey equivalent of *saltu,* enforced by the waste-management mobsters who got paid by the pound for every last scrap of metal, plastic, rubber, paper, wood, stone, fruit, vegetable, bone, and flesh they dumped into those mountainous, methanating piles. With his eyelids rolling shut he silently challenged them, all those myriad Big Jerrys he imagined storming his desolate house and raiding his fridge: Come take it, and me with it. Please. Why didn't you find me earlier? I'm *here.* And then, darkness: as black and airless as the Hefty sack in which the doe's severed head lay sideways, nestled on a pillow of her stiffening organs.

3

LIFESOLUTIONS 24-HOUR SELF-STORAGE was located on an otherwise farmy and intermittently wooded stretch of two-lane near the New York border: an agglomeration of steel buildings painted red, white, and blue and arranged in something like a hopscotch pattern. With its overexpanse of parking, its high, barbwire-crested fencing, and its excessively fulgent security lighting, it brought to mind a small-scale penitentiary. Sara Tetwick Masoli was there to retrieve a roasting pan, and maybe also (if she could possibly figure out which box it was in; she wasn't about to dig through them all) the china from her first marriage, but the process—plugging in her security code at the gate to induce its yawning, automated opening; plugging it in again on the keypad by the door; then traversing the long, fluorescent-lit hallway, her echoing heel-clicks as loud as ricocheting bullets, to the corrugated overhead door of Unit #592—made her mission feel weightier: an overdue conjugal visit, perhaps, or as witness to an execution. She unbolted the thick brass lock and, with a monstrous rattle, raised the door. "Oh my," she said.

She hadn't remembered the awesome *bulk* of it. Or the awesome disarray of it all, for that matter: No obvious starting point presented itself, no on-ramp into this miniature cityscape of stacked cardboard boxes and rectangular plastic bins and overstuffed square shopping sacks with various irregular bits (a pink bicycle handle here, a lampshade there) poking between the boxes. Everything had been pushed and piled toward the back of the ten-by-fifteen-foot unit, for which she'd been paying $59 per month for seven years, so that it sloped upward from where Sara, biting her bottom lip, and feeling like an irresolute mountaineer, presently stood. She considered bailing on the whole chore—that's why they made disposable roasting pans, right? And the china, like everything from her first marriage, was tainted anyway. "Honey," she said to herself, in the weirdly over-colloquial and vaguely black/Southern voice she often used when addressing herself in moments of indecision, as if equipping herself with her own personal Oprah, "you can bail on this." But no, she decided. I can't. It's just *stuff*. Get over it, honey. Start digging.

At forty-three, a widow and mother of a teenager (she wondered, now that she'd remarried, if she wasn't a "former widow"—but that seemed oxymoronic, like being a former amputee), Sara still retained a bright tang of youth. Something of the cheerleader she'd been, back in Ohio, still clung to her: in the nutty, summer-camp tint of her skin; in the elfin gleam of her smile, the nervous flutter of her laugh; and in the wheaty, sunlit color of her hair, which was the same shade of blonde you saw, chemically replicated, on women idling away their afternoons at the Neiman Marcus at the Short Hills Mall. Hers was natural, however. This was her inheritance from the Anglos and Saxons (quite literally: her father's people were English, her mother's German) who'd seeded her family tree, and was a point of feminine pride. Like the organic produce accorded its own VIP aisle at the ShopRite, her hair was value-added for what it lacked: ammonia, peroxide, p-Phenylenediamine. Her daughter Alexis used to say it smelled like apples, "or maybe celery. Something you eat peanut butter with."

Her figure, short and supple, was not quite so natural—a point of mild discomfort. Throughout her life she'd never minded her small breasts—dainty little knolls, no bigger than ice cream scoops, that disappeared completely under the gentle compression of a sports bra. Or at least she'd *thought* she'd never minded them. Her husband, Dave, suggested otherwise: that a bit of surgical augmentation ("nothing ridiculous," and his Valentine's Day gift to her) would provide an incommensurate boost to her self-esteem. Eight months later, she still wasn't used to them. They rode high and hard on her chest, pressing strangely against her clothing and threatening to spill out; and the way people stared, men and women both, she felt as if she was wearing a nametag ("Hi! My name is Candi"). She wasn't sure if she'd ever get used to them—or ever come to like them, as Dave had promised. But Dave liked them. She supposed that was good, but a part of her didn't like Dave liking them. It felt something like sexual roleplaying—not that she'd ever dabbled—but instead of having to wear some creepy nurse's or policewoman's outfit on the occasional weekend night, to maintain marital ignition, she had to wear it—or rather *them*—all the time. Even in the bathtub, where her silicone C-cups continued to surprise her, breaching the soapy surface like sea mammals rising for air. She missed the sight of her corrugated ribcage, looking elegant and slightly bohemian above the neckline of a dress. For years, since before her first marriage, Sara had gravitated toward women who, like herself, gravitated toward men in finance, but she'd never felt she was one of them. She'd lived in Prague, she'd had a decent if stunted acting career in her twenties (the unbalanced high points: her role as Anya in an off-Broadway revival of *The Cherry Orchard* and her appearance in a commercial for Coast soap, in which, ecstatically lathered in the shower, she cooed, "Oooooh, that scent!"), and now spent her summer weekends working a cooperative farm-share in Sussex County: She was different. Cold and gelatinous, her upgraded breasts argued otherwise, however. They introduced her before she could open her mouth, establishing (in her mind) the subjects of discussion: money or sex, both of which she found . . . uninteresting, or maybe just overworn. So they made the world go round: so what. Her silver Audi Q5 made *her* go round, and the only time she wanted to talk about it was when the car broke down.

"If I were a roasting pan," she said aloud, "where would I be?" In response, the piled boxes merely stared at her, unblinking, unyielding. She hadn't visited the storage unit in years—why would they recognize her? She moved the topmost boxes closest to her from right to left, noting as she did the brief descriptions of their contents written, in fat black Sharpie ink, on the sides and tops (ALEXIS, DOLLS; SARA, CLOTHES; ALEXIS, ART; LIVING RM, MISC.; and two cryptically marked ATTIC, ???). "Aha," she said, spying the word KITCHEN jotted on a box near the floor. The box was too small to contain a roasting pan, but she opened it anyway: an espresso maker; a citrus zester; a stainless-steel cocktail shaker onto which was etched MAR-KETBOLT ANNUAL MEETING, THE SCOTTSDALE PRINCESS, SCOTTSDALE, ARIZ., AUGUST 10–14, 2001; a pigtail-corded handheld blender; some individual tart pans; an analog meat thermometer; and a white apron, never worn (never even unfolded from the crisp square it came packaged in), emblazoned with the title WORLD'S BEST MOM. Nothing she needed.

She fingered the apron for a moment, its virginate starchiness, its embroidered sentiment. She didn't recall Alexis giving her this—oh, maybe vaguely—and almost snorted at the thought of Alexis giving it to her now: at the impossibility of it, that is. Alexis would probably just bookmark the title with asterisks, the way she noted sarcasm in her text messages: *WORLD'S BEST MOM*. WHATEVER. Alexis was at that age, seventeen, when mothers come into view as tyrants or imbeciles or both. Sara wasn't sure which category she fell into, nor did she much care; she'd been seventeen once, too, and knew these phases passed. Not that she wouldn't mind this one passing quicker. Just last night she and Alexis had had it out over college applications, over Alexis's mulish determination to attend Richard Varick College in the city, which was where her father had gone— along with every other Long Island meathead who wanted to break into Wall Street. Varick was okay, she supposed, but just barely—mid-tier, and wholly devoid of cachet. The great sin of parenting, Sara felt, was letting your children aim too low. Allow them to settle, and that's just what they'd do. Loose expectations were like junk food; kids just gorged themselves. She replaced the apron in the box and moved on.

What caught her eye, on the next box that she lifted, was the handwriting. It wasn't hers. BRIAN, it read, in unfamiliar blue cursive, and for a moment she failed to make sense of it. But then of course, she remembered. Her sister Liz had packaged up all of Brian's stuff for her. "I don't want to see it," Sara had told her, "I don't want to have it, I don't want it near me." But Alexis might, Liz had said, adding gently, "someday." It was Liz, in fact, who'd rented this unit for her, who'd done the initial piling which Sara, over the years, had occasionally supplemented with boxed-up obsoletisms (like the zester, displaced by her microplane, or the analog meat thermometer, displaced by a digital model, etc.) and various other non- or no-longer-essentials. With a small huff, Sara transferred the box leftward, in order to keep digging for the roasting pan, then paused. That was seven years ago . . . seven years and two months. And now she had Dave: the completion of her circle, the satisfying epilogue: the closure everyone had urged her to seek. She stared at the box, wondering how many like it were stacked here, and what they might contain, and bit her bottom lip again. Something irresistible, in an electromagnetic sense, drew her nearer to the box—some archaeological allure, like uncovering a time capsule while digging in the garden. But this was *her* time capsule—*her* archaeological record—*her* life, or at least some broken shards of it, dumped into all these cardboard squares. What harm could there be, at this post-closure point? Sighing, she sat down on the KITCHEN box, its top slightly crumpling beneath her weight, and after sliding some other boxes away with her feet, to clear some room, she opened the box marked BRIAN.

His face was the first thing she saw: impossibly square-jawed, with those hard Clint Eastwood eyes above that slanted overcocky grin, a dimpled half-Windsor knot at the base of that thick, not-quite-loutish neck. He was staring up at her, in grayscale, from a cut-out piece of newsprint more yellowed and crispy than she'd expected it to be: his obituary, if that's what you called it, from the "Portraits in Grief" series that the *New York Times* ran after September 11th. "Brian Tooney," the headline read. "A Winner in Life, and Love."

> Brian Tooney hated to lose. Whatever the game, be it Monopoly or one-on-one basketball or his latest passion, golf, he usually only lost once. "And that was always the first time he played," said his older brother, Robert. "After that, he'd hunker down somewhere to study and practice until he had everything down cold. Then he'd come back and stomp you."
>
> That competitive streak made Mr. Tooney, who was 34, a natural fit for Wall Street. He worked as a bond broker for MarketBolt, in the World Trade Center. "He loved the adrenaline, the charge of it," said his wife, Sara. On their second date, the couple bumped into a not-quite-yet-old flame of Mrs. Tooney at a midtown bar. Mr. Tooney, she later learned, tipped a waiter to "accidentally" spill a drink on the competing suitor, forcing him to beat a quick retreat from the bar.
>
> But Mr. Tooney had a soft side, too. His 11-year-old daughter, Alexis, brought it out in him most. "If she scraped her knee, and cried," his wife said, "he cried too." Almost every night, before bedtime, Mr. Tooney and his daughter danced together, usually to a Bruce Springsteen song. "'Thunder Road,'" Mrs. Tooney said, "was their favorite."
>
> The family had just moved, in June, to rural Sussex County,

N.J., because Mrs. Tooney dreamed of raising horses. "The commute was a killer," his brother Robert said. "But if Sara wanted to raise penguins, he would've commuted from the South Pole. That's the kind of guy he was."

For a long time Sara stared at the newspaper, her eyes darting from the text to the photograph and back, as if struggling to reconcile them. She heard the faint creak of her front teeth grinding. Finally, she said, "Fuck you, Brian."

And then it came back, as she'd feared (when setting that box aside) but not quite expected (when opening it). All of it: the initial splinter of that morning (Liz calling, saying, "turn on the TV"); the way Sara collapsed to the floor, rubbery and boneless, in perfect terrible tandem with the second tower's collapse; Alexis in pigtails screaming "someone tell me!" while Sara and Brian's mother clung to one another in the living room, Sara sobbing and Brian's mother hacking up broiled bits of her lungs, both of them incapable of speech; Brian's father's silent, sleepless vigil in front of CNN, a single omnipresent tear trickling down his old prizefighter's cheek; the four hundred MISSING posters they printed at Staples, and the clerk who glanced cautiously about for her manager before telling Sara there was no charge, go; the bobbing sea of yellow candles in Union Square; the smoke from the island's charred tip that went on and on, forever. All of which felt endurable and even lenient compared to what, for Sara, came afterwards.

Brian's brother Robert suggested the memorial. He offered to rent out A. J. Byrne's, the bar on 52nd Street where Brian had taken Sara on their second date and where Brian and Robert had had a standing date, for *Monday Night Football,* during the NFL season. Invite everyone, Bass Ale (Brian's regular) on the house, maybe a slide show if they could all bear it. "That's what Bri would've wanted," Robert said, and Sara had agreed. All Robert needed, he said, was an invitation list; he'd do the rest.

Brian's Outlook address book struck Sara as the natural source. The recipient lists on his constant stream of email forwards — New York Giants scuttlebutt, mostly, but also chain letters (typical Irish, he was superstitious to the point of paranoia) — must have included one hundred or more addresses. It was password-protected but that was easy: Alexis. As Sara scrolled through his inbox, averting her eyes from the text of the emails to avoid conjuring Brian's voice, she kept seeing one name—Jane L. Becker—over and over and over again. On September 8th, she noticed, there was a solid block of maybe twenty emails from Jane L. Becker. That Saturday, she remembered (because the days leading up to that Tuesday were engraved upon her memory in exquisite, even microscopic detail), she'd taken Alexis to her soccer game and then to West Milford for a matinee of *The Princess Diaries,* and Brian had stayed home to catch up on work. She wasn't so much suspicious—at that moment, Brian was the winged angel she spoke to in the dark, the vaporous essence suffusing the pillow that she fell asleep spooning every night, that sponged her 4 A.M. tears—as she was curious about the abundance, so, randomly, she double-clicked one of Jane L. Becker's Saturday afternoon emails.

I am completely worthless without your dick inside me, it read. *I feel like a crackhead. [A dick-head? ;)] God, I'm addicted. [A-dick-ted? Make me stop!] Seriously. I can't eat or sleep or work out or* ANYTHING. *All I'm good for is laying here thinking about you inside me. This is total torture. I'm suffering from withdrawal. What the hell have you* DONE *to me, Brian Tooney?*

To say she was stunned, as Sara later told her sister, trivializes the sensation—the overwhelming, airless, corporeal *suck* of it. The effect was like seeing the world turned inside out, and discovering that everything you thought you knew about existence was backwards and upside down. That trees caused pollution and smoking made you live longer and Santa Claus was real but also a well-known pederast: everything. Her stupor was so total that she didn't even register pain. Fortified by that numbness, though aware she was committing a spectacular mistake, Sara read, then printed out, every last one of Jane L. Becker's emails to Brian—from the earliest flirty messages (according to her email address, Jane L. Becker worked at Lehman Brothers; they'd met at a High Yield Bond Conference uptown) to the first, awkward postcoital note *(Are you okay? I'm really sorry if things got a little too, um, crazy last night. Call me?)* to the operatic, full-blown declarations that followed *(I had no idea what love was until I met you . . . I feel like Dorothy discovering Oz)* to the subsequent reams of hypersexed e-blather that caused Sara, weeping, and holding back her hair, to vomit into the wastebasket under the desk *(Sitting on your face last night was a whole lot better than sitting here in this CDOs meeting . . . whatever it is you do with your tongue, kiddo, you should patent it).* Precisely why she was printing them, she didn't know, but she felt a pressing need to marshal hard, physical evidence—multipurpose, eight-and-a-half-by-eleven, twenty-pound, ninety-four-brightness evidence, to be collected and examined and analyzed for some unimaginable but imperative prosecution. When Alexis woke up for school the next morning, she found her mother at the desk, never having slept, the overheating printer still whirring out page after page.

As for Brian's emails to Jane L. Becker, she read perhaps a quarter of them, and printed out none. She didn't quite recognize the voice of the Brian who'd authored them—his collected love letters to Sara, all of them predating their wedding, would fill five pages, six tops—and for a brief dizzying moment, slipping off the plane of reality as if stumbling off a curb, Sara wondered if this wasn't *her* Brian who'd written all this— that some intergalactic mixup had occurred, and this was *another* Brian Tooney's computer she was digging through. Because how could he have possibly written *this* to Jane L. Becker— *When we opened the drapes yesterday, and stood there looking out over Times Square, I wanted to break the window and scream down at everyone, Look at this woman! Look at this beautiful naked beautiful fucking woman! Like a king, right? Jesus, you make me feel like some crazy king*—just seventeen minutes (it was all there, timestamped in his Sent Messages box) before including Sara in a forwarded update, from the *Daily News,* about Tiki Barber's hamstring? And just forty-three minutes before he emailed Sara—individually, this time: *What did I need to pick up? Milk and what else? Total shitshow day.*

Two nights later, emboldened by a bottle of warm chardonnay she emptied after tucking Alexis into bed, she emailed Jane L. Becker. From Brian's email account: Imagining Jane L. Becker's expression, when his name appeared in her inbox, churned Sara's stomach with a toxic mixture of grief and glee. The TV in the study was tuned to CNN, on mute; that single portrait of the 9/11 hijacker Mohammed Atta kept appearing onscreen, in what seemed like an endless loop, the pundits seeking tea leaves in the glower of his expression. Yet somehow the sight of his face didn't rattle her. She didn't want to study it, or spit at it. Mohammed Atta had murdered her husband; Jane L. Becker, on the other hand, had murdered her. Sara emailed her a single question: *Why did you do this to me?*

At 11:49 P.M., three nights later, Jane L. Becker replied. *All I can say is that I'm sorry,* she wrote. *I am. He loved you.*

That final sentence wounded her worst of all, because it was a lie—even now, with Brian dead, with nothing whatsoever to be lost or gained, Jane L. Becker, this woman she knew only as a febrile swarm of words and emoticons, was lying to her. Because hadn't Brian written to her, over and over again, in terse but tortured emailese, that he *didn't* love his wife? (Sara was never Sara in his emails; only *my wife*), that he was no longer in love with her, had conceivably *never* loved her (not if you defined *love* as what he felt for Jane L. Becker)? After another bottle of chardonnay, this one properly chilled, Sara wrote Jane L. Becker one more email. It was a tremendously long note that she honed down to a single cold word: *Die.*

"Oh Brian," she whispered now, after seven years her tone more aggrieved than angry. She hadn't, as some widows do, rinsed his memory clean over the years. Instead, she'd extinguished it altogether—unable or unwilling to scrub the stains from it, to preserve the salvageable portions, she'd just . . . chucked it. When she and Alexis visited Brian's parents in Oradell, as they did two or three times a year, it was as if Sara was bringing Alexis to visit fond old neighbors, or relatives so distant it stressed the brain to map the familial ties—whenever Mr. Tooney brought up his lost son, or fetched the old photo albums for Alexis, Sara would flee to the kitchen to remove herself, bodily, from the connection. In Sara's carefully structured mind—where the fragments of her past were segregated into something like a caste system in which Brian was the sole untouchable and the rest curved parabolically upward from there—Mr. and Mrs. Tooney were not quite Alexis's grandparents; they were merely old people, vague obligations, suppliers of corned beef and hugs. It demanded some fierce mental acrobatics, this blotting of memory, but Sara had found it necessary. To do otherwise required confronting that inside-out world, or sifting through her twelve years with Brian to pan the truth from the lies without a single means of verifying which was which. He'd died, and then she'd killed him. It was the only way.

With an affected casualness, her body taut and angled, she rifled deeper into the box—but guardedly, with just two fingers of her left hand, as if fearful of an insect attack or some other, less palpable danger. She didn't like the pull she was feeling—this gravitational force threatening to vacuum away all the dividers she'd so diligently constructed in her mind—but she felt powerless to withstand it. Only after she'd devised a more clinical line of inquiry—what had Liz saved of his?—was she able to balance it, or rather submit to it, and continue in earnest, with both hands.

The organization of the box's contents was rhymeless, reasonless, reflecting Liz's haste and her unfamiliarity with what she'd been forced to stockpile: one of Brian's high school yearbooks (where were the rest?); loose photographs from disparate periods (Brian and Sara on the dancefloor at Megan and Robert's wedding, Brian voguing some comic disco pose, Sara's hands clasped, her face elongated with laughter; Brian and Robert as sunburnt teens, sitting in a canoe and making growly-faces at the camera; Brian at the zoo with Alexis on his shoulders, a mushy Popsicle tangled in his hair; Brian in his first office, grinning, his feet on his desk, an unlit cigar between his teeth); a folded, unread copy of the *Times* whose inclusion made no sense until she checked the date (April 18, 1993: Alexis's birth); two MetroCards and a Giants ticket stub; and, deeper in the box, a clear plastic tube filled with collar stays, a felt box containing all of his cufflinks, and a bottle of 212 by Carolina Herrera, his cologne. She swirled the bottle and stared at it. Why on earth had Liz saved this? Thoughtlessly, Sarah spritzed her inner wrist, then brought it to her nose. Regretting it instantly, she rubbed at her wrist to erase it. She knew why Liz had thought to preserve it, and the realization pricked her. Liz thought she might want him back. "Someday," as Liz had said, so softly.

Unfolding a manila folder, fished from near the bottom, Sara frowned. Here was the playbill from *Fosse,* the Broadway show they'd seen together, in 1998, when Brian's mother babysat Alexis and they'd spent the night at a hotel in the city; that evening had been a marital high point, and they'd even made love, again, the next morning, giggling like teens at their childless freedom. This time, with a faint roiling of her stomach, she didn't wonder about Liz—why had *Brian* saved it? And here was the invitation Brian had designed for Sara's thirtieth birthday, a surprise party—at the top were six headshots of Sara, carefully scissored out of photos: Sara as a child, as a teen, as a backpacker in Europe, and so on. (She'd found one of the decapitated photos beforehand, and, disturbed, confronted Brian. "Something we need to discuss?" she'd asked dryly.) Here, too, was the room service menu from the hotel in Barbados where they'd spent their honeymoon. And their wedding invitation. And a clipping, nineteen years old, from the *Post*'s lukewarm review of *The Cherry Orchard,* her name—the maiden

version—proudly underlined. Confused, and stung by the parallels between this manila folder and her memory of another one—the one she'd
filled, with that awful dossier of Jane L. Becker's emails—Sara dumped the
folder back into the box and sloppily resealed its cardboard flaps. *Enough,*
she said to herself, and cursed herself for having opened it in the first place.
Her pulse rate was incongruously high for a woman of her age and fitness,
seated. Scanning the boxes around her, she felt cornered by the blue writing
on their sides, the letters seeming to glow and throb with an almost menacing exigence: BRIAN, TROPHIES; BRIAN, CLOTHES; BRIAN, WORK STUFF.
Everything, she realized: Liz had saved everything. He was all here.

With a sudden, powerful chill, causing her to stand and step away from
the boxes, it occurred to Sara that this, rather than the Fresh Kills Landfill,
where the ashes and debris from the World Trade Center had been buried, and rather than the plot at Holy Cross Cemetery in Brooklyn, where
Brian's tombstone overlooked a narrow rectangle of unturned earth, was
Brian's true burial ground: that this ten-by-fifteen-foot unit, stacked high
with domestic debris, was his mausoleum. That she was standing in his
grave. She'd never felt anything at Fresh Kills, with her arm around Alexis's
shoulder at Mound 1/9, her eyes sweeping the site for any and all traces of
the dead, or the sacred, but finding only a garbage-strewn wasteland: tire-
treaded mudruts, sneakers, carpet scraps, listless, poisoned-looking gulls,
a white plastic bag snagged by a weed waving like a tattered flag in the
same gentle salt breeze carrying the odor of landfill gasses, leaking from
the rust-flaked pipes, toward their crinkling noses. Nor had she ever felt
his presence at Holy Cross, which, aside from the funeral, she'd visited just
once, with Alexis. Just the opposite, in fact: That was just a random marble
slab, its presence and location based only upon its proximity to the other
Tooneys buried beside it. There had been no corpse, and no ashes identified as Brian's—only his abrupt, traceless absence, and the smoke curling
upward from the end of the island like that from a smoldering cigarette tip,
and the stray brown hairs and lingering beery sweat-scent on the pillow of
his that she clung to, and had even kissed, not softly but passionately, in
those few pure days separating the 9/11 attacks from Jane L. Becker's attack. He'd been swept as cleanly from the earth as Sara had tried sweeping
him from her memory.

Except for this: these six or seven boxes of miscellaneous stuff—the golf trophies, the curled-edged photos, the cocktail shaker, the cufflinks—that refuted his absence, that proved, like fossilized footprints, that he'd been here, that he'd walked and golfed and drunk Bass Ale among us, that he'd transformed Sara Tetwick into Sara Tooney and imprinted his daughter with undeniable replicas of his own hard eyes and slanted grin which Sara struggled so hard to deny anyway. If ghosts existed—and Sara didn't believe they did—then this was where his dwelled. With a mental violence that surprised Sara, this realization—that Brian was *here*, in this climate-controlled tomb—clawed at her, pushing her back out into the hallway, and when the door opened, at the end of the hall, shattering the quiet and admitting a cold squall of outside air, she made a sharp, brief shriek, clutching a hand to her chest.

From down the hall, a short, round man in a bulky black overcoat stared at her. "Sorry," he said, waving. "We didn't mean to scare you."

Sara waved back, with a pageant-loser's synthetic smile. "Just startled."

This was a mistake, Sara scolded herself. This entire errand. She should have known better—but how? She'd just wanted her roasting pan. After rolling the unit's door back down and relocking the lock, she held the door to the outside open while the round man, followed by a morose, lanky teen, hauled in a white dresser of the disposable fiberboard variety sold at IKEA. "Thanks a lot," the man said, gasping for breath as he squeezed past her. "Put it down over here, Bobby." The teen didn't acknowledge her, as he passed, save for the furtive, appreciative glance he gave her breasts. For a moment, she stared at the dresser: at its chipped edges, and at the faint wrinkles and blisters in its veneer, puzzling over why they were interring it here. It was certainly no keepsake. When she glanced at the man, for some clue, he was bent over with his hands on his knees, as if defeated by the task. Something in that pose—his labored breathing, and the openmouthed, faraway stare he wore before his face drooped out of sight—made her wonder if the dresser had belonged to yet another dead pharaoh, and if they were bringing it here to be entombed like Brian's golf trophies. She noticed a sticker of a pink unicorn affixed to one of the top drawers, and, with a shudder of dark imagining, wondered if the man had lost a daughter. Something Alexis had mentioned—about one of her classmates flipping her car on Route 94 the weekend prior—came reeling back into her head. And when she looked again, the boy's torpid, bored expression appeared to her mournful instead, an adolescent/macho mask obscuring torrents of confused grief beneath, and the man appeared not just defeated but *crushed,* his limp neck suggesting an imminent, weepy collapse. Flooding with pity, she released the door, and moved two hesitant steps toward the man — to help him with his load, or perhaps, if indeed he crumpled, even embrace him. But when he lifted his head, revealing a wide grin spreading across his face, his cheeks as round and red as Gala apples, she immediately realized her error. "Hey, Bobby," he said to the boy, casting a curious sidelong glance at the busty, shrieksome woman hovering just inside the doorway. "Do your dad a favor, willya? Never get fat. I mean, Jesus, I gotta sit down."

Sara left LifeSolutions and drove forty-three miles to Paramus, to the Williams-Sonoma store at Garden State Plaza, where, for $229.95, she bought the same All-Clad roaster with the V-shaped rack that she'd packed up for the storage unit, two years before, to make room in the kitchen cabinet for the massive juicer that Dave had moved in with him. He was ardent about fresh juices then — proudly demonstrating the way the electric juicer gobbled down the carrots and celery and apples he stuffed into its plastic chute — and Sara, long accustomed to spending her holidays with either Liz and her family, on Long Island, or with Brian's parents in Oradell, hadn't used her roaster in years. Back in the antiseptic safety of her car, with suburban New Jersey passing by in familiar glints of big-box store signage and soot-smeared snow and the pointillist red speckles of brakelights, she felt feeble and childish for having fled her own storage unit, for imagining the boxes of Brian's stuff to be some kind of paranormal ark of the covenant, and, most of all, for buying the same damn roasting pan she'd gone to the unit to fetch. She comforted herself, just slightly, by noting that the new roaster had an anodized nonstick bottom, unlike the stainless-steel bottom of her other one, and that, as a bonus for spending more than $200, she'd received, for free, an All-Clad cast aluminum au gratin pan. Sara wasn't sure she'd ever use the au gratin pan, but its presence in the backseat, as she steered the car toward home, made her feel that, in some small but significant way, she'd come out ahead.

4

THE DISTASTE MICAH felt for Matty, from the instant she saw him, was, at first, entirely secondhand. He reminded her of someone, and though she tried and tried to identify that someone—even as she welcomed Matty into their apartment, embracing him in the living room and kissing his coarse, tobacco-scented tangle of beard before he offloaded his overscuffed, overstuffed backpack and dug from it a bottle of whiskey, as a housewarming gift—she couldn't pin it down. "Maybe someone from a movie?" Talmadge said later, but that was stupid and he knew it: Micah could count on her fingers all the movies she'd ever seen, and she'd never possessed a television, not even as a child. From the kitchen, as she cooked, she stared at Matty through the open doorway, straining to place the unpleasant evocation: at his slab of a beard, almost Hasidic in its wiry black lushness, and, covering his head's opposite pole, a broad Stetson hat whose wide brim shadowed his eyes and much of his narrow, pockmarked face. He was wearing a puffy, big-pocketed red ski parka over a faded black t-shirt onto which was screenprinted D.A.R.E. (TO KEEP KIDS OFF DRUGS), and nodding, as a beaming Talmadge explained the apartment to him, as blithely and steadily as one of those dashboard bobblehead dolls. In their six months of squatting here, Micah and Tal had never let another person into the building, and maybe, Micah thought, that's what Matty reminded her of: other people.

He'd come from Oakland on a packed transcontinental bus. "Three thousand, one hundred, twenty-two miles! Two days, twenty-one hours, and fifty-eight minutes!" he'd exclaimed to Talmadge outside the Port

Authority Bus Terminal, where Talmadge had found him happily smoking beside a bowlegged panhandler. ("Hey, thanks for the stogie," Matty told the guy as they left, prompting an admiring doubletake from Talmadge: Only Matty, he thought, could successfully panhandle a panhandler.) "Check this out, man," Matty said, as they began their trip southward, Talmadge walking and Matty rolling atop his longboard. "Some old lady *died* on the bus. Somewhere in Missouri, fucking *died*. She's like two rows in front of me, and this dude next to her, huge fucking black dude, I mean, check it, looked like Shaquille O'Neal, right? This dude stands up and he's grinning like he's embarrassed. Like he's just crapped his pants and it's so sad it's funny, right? He's looking all around, with that grin, until finally he's like, to everybody, 'I think this lady dead.' And everyone's just, like, staring at him. Like he's talking Navajo. Nothing. So I go check it out and, yeah, I guess she's dead, her eyes are open and shit. Dude is starting to freak a little, so I go tell the driver. He pulls the bus over and comes back and shuts her eyes and makes the sign of the cross on himself and asks if anyone on the bus knows her but no one does. By now dude is freaking *hard,* man, he is not sitting back down next to a dead lady, but it's a full bus. So I switch seats with him. Just till St. Louis. No big deal, right? But check this out, here, zip open the side compartment on my pack, no, the other side"—there Talmadge found a half-empty fifth of Heaven Hill whiskey, and, sensing the storyline, gasped, "You ripped this off a dead lady?"—"Dude! She had it in a paper sack over by the window. Like the cops were gonna save it. Look at you! Man, I thought a cracker like you would be all psyched. A dead lady's bourbon. That's, like—what was that shit we had to read in Tutweiler's class? Faulkner, right. That's like spooky Faulkner shit. That's right up your alley.

"And, hey," he went on, with a slewed grin, as they waited for the light to change on 39th Street, "that's your big thing now, right? Recycling?"

"Something like that," said Talmadge. "You'll see."

Thirty-plus blocks later, on what looked to Matty like a shabby and unremarkable East Village side street, Talmadge stopped in front of a narrow brick building, painted red, and coolly surveyed the streetscape. Bright yellow leaves from caged sycamore trees carpeted the sidewalk and dappled the curbside snow mounds; the few pedestrians moved past with that New Yorky oblivion in their eyes, unheeding, uninterested. "Nice," Matty said,

noting an encircled *A*—the anarchy symbol—spraypainted on the padlocked door. Behind the iron bars shielding the first-floor windows was
plywood that appeared to predate him and Talmadge. "We gotta be cool,"
Talmadge warned, glancing an additional time, to his right and to his left,
before crouching down on the sidewalk to unlock the steel cellar doors
with a key attached to the carabiner he wore hooked to a belt loop. "Okay,
go fast," he urged Matty, once he'd pulled up one of the doors, and the two
of them, fast and furtive like burglars, slunk beneath the sidewalk. Talmadge scanned the street one last time before pulling down the doors and
sealing him and Matty in a cold, turpentine-scented darkness.

Talmadge also carried a penlight on the carabiner, and when he flicked
it on, so that he could relock the cellar doors from the inside and light their
path through the basement, he heard Matty whisper to himself, "Whoa,
what the fuck." A half inch of oily water covered the floor; psychedelic
rainbow swirls glimmered in the flashlight's thin beam. Lining the walls
were chain-link cages, which had once housed tenants' overflow goods—
now empty, they imbued the space, at least for Talmadge, with the feel of
a medieval torture chamber or some other horror-strewn dungeon. Even
after six months, Talmadge still couldn't navigate the basement without
hearing, inside his head, the screams of victims being skinned or sawn or
slowly impaled, and owing to that, as well as his fear of rats, he moved
swiftly and skittishly past the cages to a set of concrete stairs at the far end,
ripples of water from his boots sloshing against the walls. Blinking, with
his hands splayed in front of him, and cursing the wetness seeping into his
sneakers, Matty struggled to keep up.

"It's almost impossible to find a squat in Manhattan," Talmadge was
saying, as they climbed another steep set of darkened stairs, the flashlight
beam bouncing across the walls and presenting a split-second montage
of architectural decay: loose and leaning nail-studded boards; crumbled
plaster; random sections of iron pipe and ducting; a sheaf of unused plywood sheets; a chandelier dangling from the flaked ceiling like the desiccated corpse of a mountaineer strangled by a fall. "We lucked into this
one. We met some Christian anarchist dudes in Austin who'd just moved
out, and we were like, why not? Micah was getting tired of Austin anyway.
Supposedly the guy who owns the building is some superrich hippie who
doesn't know or doesn't care how many buildings he owns. They called it

the Tampon Tower because the guy's family invented tampons or something like that. It's been abandoned, like, forever—watch your head. See that? You can tell there was a fire here once. The latest date on the shit we've found is 1987. Whatever, man. It's home."

"Right on," Matty said shakily.

At the top of the third staircase, Talmadge said, "Come on inside," smiling and swinging his open hand back like a realtor at a condominium open house. Decrepit yet weirdly clean, with diffuse gray light coming from the unboarded windows in the rooms to their left, the main room was dominated by a massive oil painting, housed in one of those baroque bronze frames you see in museums, on the wall opposite the doorway. In the painting was a roly-poly nude woman, lounging on her side, surrounded by wooden bowls piled high with fruits and vegetables; Matty's eyes were drawn, predictably, to her pale flat nipples, but also to the strange detail, in the top left corner, of an infant on horseback watching the woman through an open doorway. The painting looked vaguely valuable, in a minor-work-of-the-High-Renaissance way, but, as Talmadge explained to Matty, they'd fished it out of a construction dumpster on Bedford Street. "We call her Maybelle, the goddess of produce," said Talmadge, pursing his lips as he stared at the painting alongside Matty. Thoughtfully, he added, "She *looks* like a Maybelle." In the center of the room were a folding table and two metal chairs; a rickety side table and an upholstered, army-green recliner, its seat fabric worn down to whitish fuzz, were the only other furniture in the room. Against the streetside wall, on the floor beneath one of the boarded windows, was a kerosene wick heater, which accounted for the room's pleasant balminess. On the wall to Matty's right someone had painted: *Foxes have holes and birds have nests but the Son of Man has no place to lay his head. Matthew 8:20.* Noting Matty's bewildered frown, Talmadge explained, "The Christian anarchists. Kinda some weird dudes."

Matty's frown, however, was not aimed at the graffiti; he hadn't even read it. Rather, he was struggling to syncretize the Talmadge Bertrand with whom he'd spent two years at Ole Miss—freewheeling, ultra-funded, Chi Omega– and Widespread Panic–chasing, Land Cruiser–driving, hard-partying, weed-loving Talmadge Bertrand—with this Version 2.0 Talmadge: the apocalypto downtown squat, the purple star on his temple, the way he'd recoiled from the looted whiskey and had canvassed trash bins on the long walk from the Port Authority like a deer grazing its way down a forest trail. The voice was the same, light and mild as before, and the face more gaunt and fuzzy (like Matty could talk, with that elongated afro below his bottom lip) yet still familiar, but Talmadge seemed hypnotized and . . . and, well, not *stoned*, because Tal had almost always been stoned, but another kind of stoned, a deeper, aura-altering kind, like one of those chanting, hollow-eyed cult members you sometimes saw on TV, praising King Dwight or the Prophet Bob as ATF agents led them from their raided compound or out of some sick jungle fortress. Though on second thought: That was overkill, man, Tal wasn't like *that*. But *still*, Matty thought, as he noted the absence of lamps and the excess of candles in the room—an entire wax skyline on that side table alone—and realized, with an almost physical jolt, that Talmadge was living, in deepest gaudy Manhattan, without electricity: What the fuck?

The answer appeared from the hallway to his left, looping her naked arms around his neck and planting a noticeably wet though somehow chilly kiss on his cheek: This was Micah, and this, Matty thought, explained everything. Not that she was quote-unquote beautiful; her face, with its overgrown eyebrows and robust nose and jaw, was at certain angles mannish, and there was a faint thickness to her—the cushy way her goosepimpled upper arms settled on his shoulders—that would make Matty, a connoisseur of internet porn, click to another model, were she beckoning to him from his computer screen. Her hair was in dreadlocks, dark and glossy at the roots but woolly and hay-colored at the ends, and she was wearing an aquamarine tank top, with a pink bra beneath it, and an ivory floor-length skirt that swished about her legs. Her left arm and shoulder were overlaid with tattoos—a sleeve of flowers growing out of her wrist—that complemented the downy brown tufts of hair spilling from her armpits, and a silver stud glinted from the side of her nose. If she wasn't Matty's type—in his time out west, he'd developed a thing for Asian girls—he could understand the allure anyway: She was like the cakey, crumbly, worm-turned soil that farmers scooped and lifted to their noses in the early spring and sniffed like truffles. Discovering soil like that made people stop and settle, froze wagon trains in their tracks. She was beautiful the way Kansas, which

Matty had watched pass outside the bus window as an infinite sheet of gold, was beautiful. She could make you want to put down roots—could make you want to grow.

"Here," Matty said, digging the fifth of Heaven Hill whiskey from his pack. "A little Thanksgiving present." A quick wink at Talmadge. "Some of it evaporated on the ride."

"Thank you," she said, cradling the bottle. "That's sweet."

Talmadge said, "Micah's straight edge."

"Oh shit," said Matty, grabbing the bottle from her and slamming it into Talmadge's chest. "I know *he* still parties."

"Yeah," she said lightly. Matty missed the subtle signal of tension—a dimple that formed just below her left eye, when her jaw tightened—as he shook one of Talmadge's shoulders. "I haven't seen this dog in, like, what, three years? Four?" he said. "I used to live with him so I can relate to the nightmare you're living."

"You two went to college together, right?"

"Matty was on a soccer scholarship," said Talmadge.

"Briefly," Matty said.

"But—your accent," Micah said. "You're not—Mississippi?"

"Jersey, baby. Mahwah. Yankee all the way. Ole Miss offered me the best deal. I was gonna be like General Sherman and burn the whole state down. But I ended up burning too much other shit with this dude."

"You gonna see your parents?" Talmadge asked him.

"Nah. We sorta cut things off after all that shit went down in Portland. They don't know I'm here."

"Portland's cool," Micah said.

"Yeah, well, mostly I saw Salem. I did some time at the, erm, prison there." The jumbled way he revealed that—the cheeky "erm" rubbing against the stoical "I did some time"—suggested that Matty hadn't yet figured out how to talk about the nine-month prison term he'd just finished. "Possession with Intent, total bullshit. But Portland was—hey," he said to Talmadge, "the hell you laughing at?"

"Sorry, dude. It's just weird hearing you say, 'I did some time.'"

Stiffening, Matty replied, "Yeah, well, it's weird seeing you digging lunch out of a trash can, asshole."

"Fucking Santa Claus," Talmadge said, tugging Matty's beard.

"Oscar the motherfucking Grouch," Matty replied, tousling Talmadge's hair.

"I'm getting back to my cooking," said Micah. "Y'all be good."

Other people, she thought, as she sniffed a watery hunk of tofu (two days expired) and set it aside on a warped wooden cutting board latticed with old knifemarks. Yeah. Maybe that's all it was. In the fifteen months they'd been together, she'd never met any of Talmadge's friends or family. It was as if he'd sprung from nowhere and/or nobody—this half-formed man-fetus she'd found, nude save for a pair of boyish white Hanes briefs, clawing the dirt at Burning Man, trying to bury a glo-stick in the alkali flats. She'd just broken up, the day prior, with Lola, her girlfriend of three years, and had been wandering the Playa in a dismal funk. She'd been looking for a ride somewhere—anywhere, she didn't care—but no one was leaving until after the Burn. Thus she was trapped: unable to return, even temporarily, to Lola (their breakup had concluded with the phrase "Have a good life"), yet powerless to escape the Black Rock City limits. Drifting through the camps, amid all that strident glee, she felt like a lost child at the circus. Burning Man was Lola's thing: For four years she'd run an info tent preaching the gospel of Freeganism, a mishmash philosophy (its name derived from the compound of "free" and "vegan") to which Lola had converted Micah in the early bloom of their relationship. Lola loved all of it: the rowdy tent-revivalist vibe, the earnest salesmanship, dispensing brochures and instructional tips ("with reclaimed produce, look for a nine at the beginning of the price look-up code—nine means organic, four means Monsanto"), plus the whole mindfreak carnival tableau: the psychobilly and surfbilly blasting from the camps beside them, the art cars and drum bands, the psychonauts and pole dancers and ravers and pervs and Deadheads and Goa trancers and the topless old earthmothers with their flapjack breasts and the slackjawed pyros at the Burn, their dilated orange eyes chasing the spark-swirls heavenward. Micah, on the other hand, hated it. True, the first time had been cool, like the ideal lover simultaneously exotic and comforting; by the third time, however, she'd come to despise it, likening it to the Las Vegas strip sans money. Everyone was after something, she'd decided, nevermind all the communal/tribal atmospherics. Everyone had an angle, an itch they'd come to have scratched. She felt like MOOP, the Burning Man acronym for "matter out of place," meaning the litter strewn across the desert after the camps were dismantled: foreign items found where they don't belong. There on the Playa, back in San Francisco with Lola, neck-deep in the whole catfighty activism scene (LGBT rights, antiwar, antiglobalization, ecofeminism, freecycling—Lola was freelance, she did them all), everything, life, all of it: She was matter out of place, she was Micah out of place. She was MOOP.

So too was Talmadge, swimming on the ground, caked in white gypsum dust—alone and, from what Micah could gather, as she scanned the makeshift camps around him, abandoned. Some frat-boy types, suckling twenty-four-ounce cans of beer, were watching him from outside their RV, laughing. "Don't touch the fish!" one shouted to her. "Fish gotta swim!" another called. She knelt down beside him. Rivulets of powdered drool ran down his chin and a long rope of mucus swung from his nose. She couldn't tell if he was trying to bury the green glo-stick or was paddling after it, like a bass tailing a minnow, through the kaleidoscopic eddies of his mind, but it didn't matter either way: He was obviously tripping, and tripping badly. "Can someone help me?" she called to the frat boys. One called back: "She caught the fish!" Others: "Reel him in!" "He's getting away!" "Don't eat the fish!" Finally one of them walked over and said, deadpan, "Is this your fish?" "Just help me get him up," she said, and together, with awkward grunting difficulty, they lifted Talmadge to his feet, in the process scraping his underwear down around his thighs. "I see fish dick!" one of the frat boys exclaimed.

The crowds parted and hushed, crucifixion-style, as they hauled Talmadge limply through the dust. Hopelessly slack, his legs trailed behind him, his toes leaving curvy snake trails in the dust. Every now and again he would splutter something unintelligible but anxious-sounding, then revert to a blank drooly stare. "Where are we headed?" asked the frat boy, who'd introduced himself as Cooper, and for a long while Micah didn't answer. She didn't know. Or rather, she knew but didn't want to admit it: They were taking him to Lola's tricked-out camper van. "Over this way," she told him. "Who is he?"

"The fish? I don't know. Said he was a Beta from Mississippi."

"What's a Beta?"

"Beta Theta Pi. It's a fraternity. He just kind of stopped by and sat down. Said he'd done a massive bump of Special K and needed to chill.

Then he started getting all freaky and took his clothes off. When it got too weird we just rolled him the fuck away. Dude is *out* there. He's in the K-Hole, man."

Lola sighed, not unhappily, when Micah appeared begging for help. Micah never needed help—that had long been one of Lola's issues. "You wouldn't grab my hand if you were drowning," Lola had once told her, but now here she was: not drowning herself, but lugging another drowning victim toward her—close enough. She helped Micah and Cooper unload Talmadge onto one of the two narrow mattresses in the camper van and, because she worked part time as an EMT, checked Talmadge's pulse and pupils. "Ketamine, you said?" she asked Cooper, who waved his hands in front of his chest, to absolve himself of responsibility, before easing himself backwards into the passing herds, shouting "Bye, fish!" once he was safely absorbed in the crowd. To Micah, she said, "They call it the K-Hole. A high-enough dose sends you there. They say it's like a pit you fall into, separated from your body. Big-time hallucinations, total lack of exterior awareness. That explains the ataxia. We treated a girl at some club in the Castro who was like this. Supportive care, mostly. They tend to pass out after an hour or two." Without asking too many questions, though her expression suggested distrustful bewilderment, she told Micah to close the curtains, to stay close beside him, to avoid questioning him so as not to induce anxiety, to keep the "environment" gentle and dim. "Like a womb," she said. "What he needs right now is the security of a womb."

Outside the van, in the dust-glittered sunlight, Lola paused before shutting the rear doors. "I was hoping you'd come back," she said. When Micah didn't respond, she shook her head sadly, staring, then shut the doors, enclosing Micah and Talmadge in that familiar dingy must, with Lola's Freegan 'zines stacked against the sides, her and Micah's clothes crammed in cardboard liquor boxes, the light seeping through the red-bandana curtains suffusing the van's interior with the plummy dimness of a photographer's darkroom.

"There now," Micah whispered, as he murmured to the ceiling. She stroked his crusty hair with her left hand while her other hand, palm pressed flat against his bony hairless chest, monitored the slow cadences of his heart. Though his eyes were open, he didn't seem to register her presence; blinking, and softly jerking, they weren't quite corpse eyes, but seemed just as distant, tuned to some outer-galactic channel she couldn't see or hear. "There now," she whispered again, this time with her lips at his ear, close enough to feel the heat of her breath reflected back upon her, and to inhale the smell of his skin: ripe and slightly sweet, like the inside of a squash. Her hand slipped off the cliff of his ribcage to the corrugated plains of his belly and lingered there—maternally, the way a mother strokes her sleeping child, but sensually as well—faintly, chastely, and if not quite subconsciously then something close—in the way her hand orbited his navel and then glided over to his arm, her fingertips gently mashing the long stringy muscles they discovered corded there. For a long time, she watched him, as if enthralled by some sculpture from antiquity: his stony litheness, the chisel-marked grace of his long arms and torso, the floury sheen of dust that imbued his skin with a matte luster of fired clay.

Noting the dust swirls left by her hands, she fetched the bucket of water she and Lola had been using to sponge-bathe themselves. Talmadge's eyelids flickered as she squeezed the sponge over his chest, the cool water dribbling down his ribs and pooling at his navel. As clinically as she could, she slipped off his underwear and dropped it to the floor. Humming lightly, she guided the sponge up and down his body, the fresh nude skin it revealed appearing like smears of color on white canvas, as if she wasn't so much washing a man as creating one, daubing him to life with the tawny, chewed-looking sponge. The burbling sound it made, when she wrung out the sponge over the bucket, was like a mountain stream she remembered from childhood, where the stream—an unnamed trickle, on the blue-green edge of the Smoky Mountains—went spilling over some moss-glazed stones two feet down into a limpid pool in which Micah would cool her feet, the cold blissfully stinging her curled toes. The evocation was pleasurable and for a long while she reveled in it. Meanwhile the sponge traveled everywhere: ruddying his cheeks, glistening his hair, smoothing the oily curls in his armpits, polishing the grille of his attenuated, countable ribs. She paused, at his penis, but sensing no reaction when she ran the sponge between his thighs to their humid intersection beneath the chicken-skinned orbs of his testicles, she continued.

She hadn't been with a man in four, five years, she realized; enough years, in fact, that most of the men had been more properly called boys. (Lola never understood the way Micah's affections could toggle back and forth between genders; she'd claimed Micah was self-delusional, owing to the backwoods way she was raised, or else just plain greedy. That was another of her issues.) Those encounters, however, had almost always been swift and mechanical, their narratives circumscribed by custom if not biology; unlike with women, there was rarely time to linger, to explore, to pass an hour doodling random fingertip patterns on another's skin, or mapping the riverine trails of postcoital sweat. Always there was that lurching, insistent erection. With selfish male lovers, it ended there, at the guttural, sleep-inducing finish. With the selfless ones, however, the lingering and exploring was always directed at her, on her; they couldn't bear reciprocation. She'd never noticed, for instance, the embossed line of flesh that ran down the underside of the penis and divided the testes, so straight it seemed surgically crafted. Or the accordion pleats of the slumbering penis, or the nimbus of frizzy hair on the testicles that, neither silky nor coarse, reminded her of the soft, pliable, ultrafine thorns on the canes of a certain wild berry she used to graze upon during her childhood summers. Cupping his fever-warm testicles in her right hand, she drizzled his groin with water from the sponge in her other hand, then swabbed his lolling penis, shifting it tenderly from side to side as one adjusts a sleeping infant. When she felt a delicate pulsing, at its base, accompanied by a quick, brittle-sounding inhalation from up above, she stopped, wagging her head as if to revive herself from a dream. Stroking his hair again, she whispered, "It's okay, lie still."

After shedding all but her panties, she nestled herself beside him on the narrow mattress, pulling a maroon flannel sheet over them both. Passing in and out of sleep, she shushed him, whenever he'd start to murmur again, pressing a finger to his lips. Micah had no idea who he was, or what he would say or do when the technicolor fog cleared from his brain, when he climbed back out of the hole they claimed he was in, but she trusted the narcotic peace she was feeling with her body coiling his — the contact high from his flesh pressing against hers. Something more than a samaritan impulse had drawn her to him, she felt certain — like her father, who she guessed was at that very moment reading scripture aloud to himself in the grainy darkness of his cabin, Micah believed in invisibilities. She didn't share her father's faith but had faith just the same.

Only Lola, commandeering the other bed an indeterminate number of hours later, broke the spell. "Jesus," she muttered, looming above them. "When I said he needed a womb, I didn't mean it literally."

But Micah didn't care—was surprised, in fact, at just how little she cared—pretending to be asleep while Lola grunted and sighed herself to sleep a yard or so away, and then truly sleeping, beautifully hard, despite the music and screams and howls from outside, until just before dawn. Talmadge was spooning her when she awakened, his face buried between her neck and shoulder; she could feel his jaw unfolding into what felt like a smile when she moved. Silently, and with animal ease, she took his hand in hers. Four days later, they were in Austin together, and eight months after that, New York City.

Which was where she found herself now, on Thanksgiving, chopping tofu into squishy little squares then limp carrots into rounds, while eavesdropping on Talmadge explaining the intricacies of squatting to Matty. "Water is key," he was saying. "Just like in nature. You've got to have a water source. The Christian anarchist dudes took care of hacking that. Can't even tell you how stoked we were to turn the faucet on and see all that nasty rusty water coming out. That was like, everything." Micah smiled, remembering Talmadge's head-cocked befuddlement when she shrieked—*shrieked,* jumping pogo-stick style in the kitchen, then nearly tackling him with an ecstatic embrace—when water came spurting from the tap in diarrheal squirts. "What else is it supposed to do?" he'd asked, nearly as giddy as Micah but uncertain why. (Their Austin squat had been communal, shared by six other people, with all the infrastructure hurdles having been cleared years before.)

She remembered, too, as she fired a match to light a homemade penny stove, his infinite, boyish fascination with the stoves—this whole life, she sometimes felt, was an epic ceaseless adventure for him. A British backpacker in India had taught her how to make the stove: With a knife or scissors, you sliced up three Heineken cans ("has to be Heineken," he'd instructed; something about the can shape) to make a base, burner, fuel cup, and simmer ring. The burner, about three-fourths of an inch tall and made from a can bottom, got its edges crimped and its sides and bottom punched with holes, including a quarter-inch hole in its convex center. Once assembled, you placed a penny over the quarter-inch hole, which somehow (this was what Talmadge could never figure out) sealed the burner and stabilized the heat; after sliding the stove under a tripodal pot support (for one stove, Micah used irrigation stakes; for another, bent bicycle spokes), you filled the fuel cup with alcohol and lit it. (HEET, a cheap, methanol-based gas-line antifreeze, was their preferred fuel; according to Talmadge's calculations, they averaged eighteen meals per twelve-ounce bottle, which went for two dollars at an auto-parts store at Cooper Square: eleven cents per meal.) Micah had two of their four penny stoves going now: On one, simmering gently, was a pot filled with lentils, wild rice, garlic, onions, basil, and cashews, and onto the other she placed a pot containing the carrot rounds, olive oil, and vegetable stock.

From a shelf above her she pulled down a cast-iron Dutch oven; after checking it for roaches, she blew the dust off the bottom and set it on the counter. Nearby was a beige disk of dough she'd made from whole-wheat flour, salt, soy milk, and olive oil. The olive oil wasn't right but it was the only oil they had right now. This was for the pumpkin pie Talmadge had requested. "We gotta have *something* traditional," he'd said. She dropped the dough into the Dutch oven and patted the center down to form a basin at the bottom. Arching her body sideways to read the recipe Talmadge had found on the internet and reproduced in his barely legible shorthand, she combined, in a mixing bowl, the chopped tofu with the contents of a dented can of organic pumpkin purée that Talmadge had scored, last week, from the Whole Foods dumpster. He'd rushed into the apartment that night like a man clutching a winning lottery ticket. But this was foreign to her: She'd never made anything like a pie before, and the vagaries of scrounging food from the trash rendered recipes more or less useless. You got what you got, and you did the best you could with it. Having never measured anything before, unclear in fact as to the difference between a teaspoon and tablespoon, she guessed at the amounts of ginger and cloves and cinnamon and allspice and sugar that she dashed into the mixture. After mashing everything together into a thick orange gloppiness, she dumped the mixture into the crust, fitted the heavy lid, and set the Dutch oven on a third stove. She lit it, and rejoined the boys in the main room.

"Pie's on," she said.

"Sweet," Talmadge moaned.

"You're making a pie?" Matty said. "Damn. This is better than Grandma's."

Talmadge said, "I was just kinda explaining the Tampon Tower."

"Yeah," said Micah, crinkling her nose. "Not my favorite nickname . . ."

"One thing I should kinda probably warn you about," said Talmadge to Matty. "There's bed bugs pretty bad. They snuck in on a mattress we found." He yanked down his shirt collar to reveal a small galaxy of red bites. "They don't seem to affect Micah so maybe you'll luck out."

Matty's horror was blatant. "Maybe," he said, "I can get some . . . kind of spray?"

"That's cool, whatever," Talmadge said.

Matty raised the whiskey bottle to his lips; his spooked expression suggested the desire for fortitude rather than flavor. Some of his mother's insect phobia—she'd once thrown out everything in the kitchen cupboards, even the canned goods, after discovering a single dead weevil in a box of Cream of Wheat—had wormed its way into his own subcortex, and he couldn't stand bugs. In his ideal world, the world's citizenry would band together to conduct a mass slaughter of any creature in possession of more than four legs and/or unfeathered wings. He understood this was ecologically vile but longed for it anyway. As he'd often said, to his parents and his defense lawyer and the very few girls (three) with whom he'd hooked up for longer than a month, he was only human.

Talmadge watched a brown bubble form inside the bottle, then skitter upward through the liquid as Matty raised the bottle, as if it were fleeing Matty's lips. Big gulp, he noted.

"Matty ripped that off a dead lady," he announced suddenly.

Matty blew a mist of bourbon. "Dude!" he said, then wiped his mouth with his sleeve.

"Micah's cool."

"What dead lady?" said Micah.

"Damn, man. That was my *gift*."

"It's funny," said Talmadge, though he wasn't sure it was.

Rolling his eyes, and punctuating his speech with theatrical sighs, Matty explained, "Some old lady died on my bus. Somewhere in Bumfuck, Missouri. No one wanted to sit next to her so I was kind enough to volunteer."

"Then he klepto'd her bourbon," said Talmadge.

"I was doing her a favor! Like . . . like if you'd died in our dorm room, okay? It woulda been only polite to pry the bong from your hands."

"Oh, I get it," said Talmadge, grinning. "It was just good manners."

"Hell yeah. What if, like, the driver radioed ahead and the old lady's *daughter* was there to get her off the bus?"

"Was she?"

"Naw, I'm saying *what if.* How's that gonna look? Her dead mom on the bus hugging on a sack of whiskey. No girl needs to see that."

"She was *hugging* it? You, like, pried it out of her hands?"

"No, figure of speech. It was next to her, up against the window."

"So you were just, what, tidying up the scene?"

"Right! See, man, I let her die with dignity—with *pride.* It's all good. No one got hurt and everyone's happy. Well, I mean, not *happy* . . ."

"Her daughter's not happy," said Talmadge.

"But she coulda been *more* not happy, that's what I'm saying."

"Unless she likes whiskey."

"Why you jacking with me?"

"I don't see an issue," said Micah.

"*Thank* you," said Matty.

"Unless, you know, the whiskey was poisoned," she said, "and that's what killed her." Repartee like this was rare for Micah, and Talmadge's heart surged: God he loved her. The girl could *hang.* Even with Matty Boone, who for a few troubled moments appeared to be seriously considering the possibility of poisoned bourbon.

"Dude," Talmadge whispered to him. "You're so dead."

"Who would poison an old lady?" Matty said.

Talmadge replied, "Her daughter."

Busting into a loud, fat laugh, Matty exclaimed, "I made the daughter up!" He held the bottle out to Talmadge. "Here, man," he said. "Drink up. Blood brothers against the wind. We go down together . . ."

"Here's to you, Maybelle," Talmadge said, swinging the bottle toward the painting, and Micah winced as it went vertical. Whiskey had been her father's preferred medicine, in his case moonshine, and she dreaded the bosky smell of it on Talmadge's skin tonight. She didn't mind the weed, to which Talmadge had mostly limited himself since his self-described "come-to-Jesus" moment at Burning Man. The rest of it, though . . . she worried.

"Ah, death . . ." said Matty, reclaiming the bottle from Talmadge; the word hung there, awkwardly, as if Matty was quoting something he couldn't remember the rest of. Shrugging, he fetched a box of cigarettes from the side table and drew one out of the package. Micah's eyes were drawn downward to where he'd ground two previous cigarettes into the floorboards. A sliver moon of ash already skirted his chair.

"Here," she said, sliding a ceramic plate from beneath one of the fat candles, for him to use as an ashtray. The plate, which was trimmed with gold paint and petaled like a flower, had come from the trash of a nursing home on Henry Street, and there'd been something poignant about it, she remembered, as with the teddy bears she often came upon, or the wedding dress she'd once unearthed. With some discarded objects you could almost feel the history embedded in their cell structure, the heat of their absorbed sentiment, as if you might be able to hold them to your ear to hear their stories told, the way a seashell confides its memories of the sea.

"Whoa, check this out," Matty said, skimming the plate's inscription. Acidly, he read it aloud: "'God bless our home . . . Bless this home, dear Lord above, with Happiness, and with thy Love.'"

Embarrassed, Talmadge said, "You find what you find out there. If it ain't broke, what the hell . . ."

"I like it," said Micah.

"You find what you find, right," Matty said, setting aside the plate while knocking a gray spiral of ash to the floor. To them both, he said, "On the real, though, I'm still trying to, like, uh, digest all this. What's the point again? I mean, like, eating from the trash . . ."

As if physically dodging the question, Talmadge leaned quickly back in his chair so that Micah could field it.

"It's about . . . well, a lot of things," she began. Exhaling deeply, she smoothed the wrinkles of her dress on her thighs. Something about the smoothing evoked the nineteenth century: a pioneer woman fixing to explain salvation to a savage. "I mean, the trash, yeah. Okay. Foraging is about refusing, on a totally personal level, to join in the overconsumption that's just, just sucking the life from the planet. It's about shunning commodity culture, or disposable culture, whatever, it's different words for the same thing. The amount of waste this society generates, it's enough to feed and clothe and sustain entire other countries. And I'm just talking, like, reclaimable waste now. *Multiple* countries. So it's not only possible but doable to survive off that waste stream. I mean, check out the pumpkin pie cooking in the kitchen . . . Exhibit A."

"Right, okay," said Matty. "That's, like, Freeganism, right? I met some Freegan chick in Portland—"

"Freeganism is a marketing term," Talmadge sniffed.

"Yeah, we don't go in for all the *ism*s," said Micah. "Once you're an *ism,* you're political, and that's a dead end. The labels are just another domestication device. Look at environmentalism. Everyone's favorite pet *ism.* The golden retriever of *ism*s, right?" She smiled at Talmadge, from whom she'd cribbed that line. "I guarantee you that someone, right now, maybe even on this block, is replacing an incandescent lightbulb with one of those compact fluorescent ones and feeling all nicey and righteous because they're *helping* the planet. And at the same time, right now, someone else is buying a hybrid car because they want to save the planet. And think about that word, man, *buying.* You just have to sit back for a second and think about the whole psychology there. Those people are doing their part, in their minds. They're paying their money, they're doing their part. They can go to bed tonight knowing they're, like, on the side of the angels. That they're the good guys—"

"Wait," Matty said. "Go back. Those are bad things?"

"They're *meaningless* things," Micah replied. "They're placebos, get it? They're meaningless tools that the system has devised to make people *think* they're doing something, and to get them to buy something at the same time. It's like, okay, this architect who got this big environmental hero prize, from the president or something, for putting this so-called 'living roof' on a freaking truck factory in Michigan. Planted native grasses and shit up there, called it songbird habitat. I mean, Jesus, just roll that around in your head for a while. Our environmental heroes are the assholes designing *truck* factories. I mean, my fingers can't do those stupid air quotes fast enough."

"Yeah, but what are you *saying?*" Matty challenged. "Like, everyone's supposed to be eating from a dumpster?" Talmadge leaned forward, stiffening in his chair and averting his eyes from Micah's. This was the side of Matty he'd dreaded: the disruptive, pigheaded Yankee side, dismissive of anything unfamiliar. Like that of a chained dog barking at every stranger, his initial reaction was always to catapult threats or insults. (On their first visit to town together, as Ole Miss freshmen, Matty had looked up at the Confederate war memorial overlooking the Oxford town square and announced, "That's way too fucking big for a second-place trophy.") Talmadge noted the level of whiskey in the bottle; from what he remembered, liquor didn't soften Matty's edges. He was regretting, now, spilling the beans about Matty jacking that bottle from the dead lady. He'd thought Micah, who shoplifted fairly regularly, might find it amusing, and maybe even respectable, since she deemed waste a greater crime than theft. He'd been puzzled by his own queasiness and had wanted Micah's verdict. But attitudes colored actions: If Matty acted like a dick, he thought, then that story just dickened him further. I shouldn't have said anything, Talmadge decided, staring at his boots.

Unflapped, Micah responded, "Don't get hung up on the foraging. That's what everyone does. Everybody gets all freaked out about the diving, the whole Freegan thing. What I'm saying is that you can't fight the system, or even change it, if you're part of the system, if you're beholden to it. Because the only weapons the system puts into your hands are different lightbulbs and cars. Chemicals in the same bottle but with a green label and flowers on it. The same old shit with a different label. They'll comfort you by saying the way out is through *nonsystemic* change. That's the whole Al Gore thing, right? That we can all *modify* the system to quote-unquote save the planet while maintaining the status quo. But it's bullshit, man. It's *beyond* bullshit. The status quo isn't sustainable. Nonsystemic change doesn't help when it's the system that's the problem."

Her tone was gaining forcefulness, the inherited embers of her father's fire and brimstone reddening inside her. Cold, techno-dry words like *nonsystemic* came off her tongue with improbable heat and passion.

"So to answer your question about why we live this way?" she said, raising her hand to encompass the apartment, the cooking smells drifting from the kitchen, the pink sores on Talmadge's shoulders, the dainty salvaged plate that Matty wasn't using for an ashtray. "To stay out of the system," she said. "To say no."

Talmadge had never heard Micah put it that way, and resisted the down-home urge to spring from his chair shouting amen. But Matty scrunched up his face and, lifting the bottle to his lips, said, "See? That's where shit like this always gets a big *fail* from me. It's like all the brothers in prison talking about the *Man*. Who's the Man? They didn't know. The guards, the cops, me, whoever. The Man. So all this shit about 'the system' is like . . . I mean, whatever. What the fuck is 'the system'?"

Caustically, Matty laughed, looking to Talmadge for support; but Talmadge had resumed studying his bootlaces, his amen dunked in the muck of his discomfort.

"Civilization," Micah said.

"Say what?"

"Civilization."

"Uh . . . go on."

"The entire structure of society. The way it's driven by growth. The whole concept of *progress* which is as arrogant and stupid as Manifest Destiny."

"Manif . . . ?" Matty's lifted hands conveyed the question mark.

"You know, the idea that white people were ordained by God to settle the West and murder the indigenous peoples. Totally indefensible today, in the exact same way that civilization will be indefensible a hundred years from now. Civilization is like, like some drug that we can't get enough of, can't resist, that we're helpless without. But producing that drug requires the systematic destruction of the planet. Every ounce of civilization requires, like, a hundred pounds of soil and air and water, and then generates, like, fifty pounds of waste. The math doesn't work, right? It's simple. At the end of the equation there's nothing but waste."

Dropping his cigarette, then screwing it into the floor with his bootheel, Matty said, "Then why not live in the woods? I mean, Jesus, if civilization is the problem, what are you doing living . . . downtown?"

"Because there's no woods *left*," Micah said flatly.

"Come on. I know the shit's bad, global warming and all, but—"

"Listen, it's *gone*," she said. "It's all claimed. It's all surveyed. There is no wilderness left."

"Okay, but what I'm saying is, listen, I just come off a three-thousand-mile bus ride, right? And I was staring at a whole lot of empty . . ."

"And all of it's on someone's schedule for drilling or developing or irrigating or whatever. They're just the last few remaining puzzle pieces that haven't been fitted yet—"

"Parks?" Matty squeaked, and Talmadge could see he was now just fighting to fight.

"The so-called wilderness areas that the government sets aside," Micah said coolly, "are like elephants in a circus. You know, with their legs shackled in irons, performing tricks for the crowds. They're no more natural than that. They're managed, they're groomed, they're scenery, set dressing. Look, my daddy tried that, living off the grid. Bless his fool heart, he's still trying. But he'd be the first to tell you, there is no off the grid. Not anymore. The grid reaches everywhere. Tell some Eskimo woman in, like, the most remote regions of the Arctic that she's living off the grid, and you know what she could say? She could ask you why her breastmilk is contaminated with crisis levels of PCBs. Okay? Go out into the middle of the Pacific Ocean. The very middle, as far from any land as you can get. And you know what's there? A floating garbage patch that's nearly the size of Africa. One hundred million tons of debris. So tell me where the grid ends. Show me the city limits sign of civilization."

"You're kinda freaking me out," Matty said. He was surrendering, Talmadge saw. Micah was beating him down. Or was she cornering him?

At this Micah grinned, and, seeing the curl of that smile, Talmadge exhaled for what seemed the first time in minutes. "Good," she said softly. "If the world isn't freaking you out, you're not paying attention. And what's everybody doing about it? Changing their lightbulbs."

"While the, uh, polar bears are dying," Matty snorted agreeably.

"Yeah, right, but it's not about polar bears." Matty was taking her side, Talmadge noted, but she wasn't letting him off that easily. "I mean, no offense to polar bears, but if people think it's just about polar bears then they won't even change the stupid lightbulbs. That's what the system *needs* you to think. Look, you know how genocide works, right? The leaders convince people that certain other people are different. That they're the *other*, right? Like the indigenous peoples, all over the world. They're so different, primitive, barbaric, evil, whatever, that we can kill them. *Should* kill them. That's how they get wars to work. But the whole polar bear thing is like, like the flip side of that. I mean, the polar bears are just one example, but it's like . . . they're the *other*. But what I mean about the flip side is that instead of being the enemy, they're the victims. But they're still the other, get it? And it's the same deal. The more we separate ourselves from them, the more we say it's about them, the less we understand that there is no other. And the less we understand that everything we're doing to them, we're also doing to us."

"Right," Matty said.

But Micah was like a spring that, while released, had more uncoiling to do, more energy to expend. "That drug, civilization? It requires more than destroying the planet. It requires that we destroy *ourselves,* too, with, like, murder and rape and war and genocide and by burying ourselves alive in waste. But that's just the surface wounds, understand? There are deeper wounds. Have you ever seen a chicken farm?"

Matty shook his head.

"They keep the chickens hunched over all the time so that their breasts overdevelop," Micah said. "They snip off their beaks because if they don't the chickens will rip each other apart from the stress. They use artificial lighting to disrupt the daily cycle so that the chickens eat as much as possible, all the time. They pipe in, like, elevator music to keep the chickens from rioting. They pump them with massive amounts of antibiotics because without them, in those artificial, like, circumstances, the chickens will die. But a lot of them die anyway from this thing called ascites. That's when the heart and lungs can't keep up with the rapid growth rate. The chickens *grow* themselves to death, right? Too much too fast."

Matty, who had happily scarfed down a KFC three-piece dinner in Grand Junction, Colorado, while the bus was refueling, stared at her, unfazed. He wasn't getting the chicken talk.

"Poor chickens, right?" she said.

He nodded, thinking *tasty* chickens, too.

"There's good people who want to change all that, make it more humane," she said.

"Cool," Matty said.

"But they're not seeing the bigger picture. Almost everything that's happening to those chickens is happening to us. The natural world can't sustain us anymore, so we've resorted to all these artificial means to keep the system working, to keep it from collapsing. I mean, it all lines up, when you think about it, even the freaking breastmeat fixation. The only difference is that the chickens get eaten at the end. We get pumped with toxins and stuffed into a steel box. But that's it, get it? You see what I'm saying, man? The chickens aren't the other. They're us. We're all locked in this system together. We're not in wire cages but they call it the grid anyway. We're even losing our ability to think, our, like, *primal* ability, but it doesn't matter because they're pumping us with synthetic drugs designed to make us content to, to not even *try.* Antidepressants, ADD medications, whatever. Just take a pill and change the lightbulbs, right? That's the prescription. That'll make everything all right. Just keep smiling and buying."

Micah was almost startled, when she looked up, by the rapt, unblinking stares she was fielding from Talmadge and Matty, as if she hadn't known these thoughts of hers were being channeled through her vocal cords. She hadn't even registered Matty's responses.

Foggily, she said, "What was the question again?" This was a standard laughline for verbose after-dinner speakers who'd lost their trail of thought, but there was no mirth in it—Micah's expression was funereal, earnest. Waiting, Matty and Talmadge said nothing.

"Oh yeah," she said, nodding, reentering the world from what her father called "the sermon current"—the powerful tide that seems to lift and carry a preacher away from his congregation and into some sacred subliminal wormhole. "Why we do this, right? That's why. That's why. I don't want to smile and buy. We need to weep, and scream, and . . . fucking *resist,* man. The whole thing is rigged," she said, and looking to Talmadge, she added, "And we're not playing."

For a long absorptive while they were silent. "Shit," Matty finally said, as he lit another cigarette, the clicks from his failing lighter sounding like the hammerings of a spent pistol. "You guys are fucking serious. That's cool." Looking around the room, he added, "I could get into this." Only then, as Talmadge and Micah followed his gaze, noting the orange fire-nub of the cigarette glowing like the first star emerging in the dusk sky, did they all realize how dark the room had become.

Talmadge snatched the lighter and aimed it—with a grip trembling from love and something like missionary zeal, a religious euphoria—at a candle. He struggled to suppress the smile his mouth was forming, which struck him as inappropriate, boyish, selfish; unable to stifle it, however, he covered his mouth with a hand, as if thoughtfully rubbing his beard. "I could get into this," Matty had said. Here was his past, aligning with his future. Here was a wholeness: a mission, a woman, perhaps now a comrade. Though their companionship had been brief, Matty was Talmadge's only durable friend; everyone else he'd abandoned, as their lives had calcified (in Talmadge's view) and his had swelled and flowered. He chided himself for having worried about Matty and Micah: about the whiskey, Matty's cynicism. Here they were, only a couple of hours into their reunion, and Micah—sweet holy Micah—had already converted him, or at least neutralized any of the expected wariness, the harsh volley of what-the-fucks. Something about the power of three: They'd been alone for so long, he and Micah. In that time they'd learned things, *understood* things, broken code after code. There was satisfaction, Talmadge realized, in passing it on, in widening the circle. It felt good to come down from the mountain, to be human again. In the yellow candlelight everything felt ancient and true, and the world outside, as for the earliest Christians huddled in their desert caves, debased yet redeemable.

Talmadge yearned to say as much—to *declare* something, to translate these feelings into language, language that would rouse them to action, to crash gates, storm trenches—but there were no words in his mind; only a warm radiant blur of emotion. Yet the silence was overripe, he felt; the moment needed seizing.

But Matty beat him to it. "How's that pie coming?" he said, causing Micah to leap up, "Oh *shit*," and flee into the kitchen. Talmadge watched Matty take a long, hard swig of whiskey, sucking on the bottle harshly and sloppily, the way old movie villains kissed resistant damsels—and then, unless Talmadge was mistaken, wink at him. But no, Talmadge decided, that mustn't have been a wink. Just smoke in Matty's eyes, or a trick of the shimmering candlelight. "She's some'n, huh?" he said to Matty, who replied with a thumbs-up and a crooked, inscrutable grin.

5

THE MEMORY OF the deer was still imprinted upon Elwin's spine as he slid a two-drawer steel file cabinet out of the rear hatch of his loaner car, which he'd parked beside a snowbank on Henry Street in lower Manhattan. Objecting to this new burden, his spine telegraphed a complaint that went buzzing from his dorsal horn to his thalamus before being expelled as a loud, emphatic grunt made briefly visible by the cold air. Elwin paused, with the cabinet half discharged, and scanned the sidewalk for—for— for what he didn't know. Help, advice, maybe an unattended forklift. Or maybe some drowsy vagrant with a WILL WORK FOR FOOD sign pitched upon his lap, because Elwin had the goods for a fair deal: Haul this cabinet across the street to the Roth Residence, that big old cranky-looking building right there, take it to room 109, the door's marked CROSS, and there's a plate of seared venison medallions in it for you. Medium rare, and glazed with a cranberry–port wine sauce. Peas and onions, too, and buttered carrots just like my mother used to make, back when she was—

But there were no drowsy vagrants. Only some kids, underdressed for the weather, making choppy snowballs and pitching them, violently, at a chain-link fence. From his brain's amygdala, this time, came another message, this one more diffuse, darkening his mind the way an octopus's ink clouds the sea: There's no one out there. You're alone as ever, bucko. This message—a familiar one—he expelled as a dim sigh. The file cabinet hit the street with a sharp clank.

The loaner car was a painfully small, egg-shaped domestic model for which he'd traded his Jeep at a body shop on Route 24 — permanently, as it turned out. "I see my new ad brought you in," said the owner, referring (he had to explain this to Elwin) to a dead buck splayed on the roadside, just beneath the body shop sign. "Found that one here this morning. I should hang him up with a banner saying DEER COLLISION EXPERTS." His name was Sal, according to the blue patch on his shirt. Elwin had found him eating a footlong meatball sub at nine-thirty in the morning, a mildly impressive feat; faint whorls of tomato sauce spotted all the paperwork. Classical music was emanating from a conspicuously high-tech stereo system in the corner — and not just any classical music, Elwin noted: not the philharmonic Quaaludes you heard on public radio stations, but something jarringly avant-garde, Luciano Berio or somesuch. When Elwin complimented the soundtrack, however, Sal glanced back at the stereo as if he'd never noticed it before, shrugged, and dusted the hoagie-roll crumbs off the paperwork before sliding it toward Elwin.

"Been a crazy fucking month," he'd said. "Hunnerd and fifty deer collisions already. Fucking suicide bombers, how they're acting." The worst-case scenario, he said, was two weeks in the loaner car; "unfuckingbelievable" was how Sal characterized his backlog. Rightfully concerned about the seating capacity of the little loaner — several years earlier he'd been ejected from a roller coaster because the safety bar couldn't fit over his belly, causing his young niece to perish from terminal embarrassment — Elwin asked if there might be a larger vehicle . . . something with more "trunk space," he said. Bearing width issues of his own, Sal saw right through the ruse; looking Elwin up and down, he said, "Tight squeeze but you'll be okay."

But then Sal had called him three hours later. "Your insurance company put the ixnay on the repair," he told Elwin. "They wanna total it out."

"Total it out?" Elwin squawked. "It's just some front-end damage!"

"On a '98 model, buddy," said Sal, a funereal cello sonata playing loudly in the background. "Your guys, see, they go by the fifty-one percent rule. If the repair cost tops fifty-one percent of the Blue Book value, she's a goner. Totaled. Finito. Kaput-ski."

"How can it be totaled? I drove it to you."

"Talk to your agent. I'm just repeating the news, okay?"

"I love that Jeep," Elwin said.

"Love is cheap," Sal advised. "Come back at me after the holiday, okay? I'm up to my fucking earballs."

The file cabinet, salvaged from the Trueblood Center's basement, was a gift to his father, though as with all gifts self-interest played a supporting role: Elwin couldn't bear his father's room any longer, piled as it was with the elder Cross's research for the book he was trying to finish, or what Elwin's sister Jane, rolling her eyes and squiggling her hooked fingers to make air quotes, called his "research." Four-foot-tall stacks in the corners; precarious-looking piles on the windowsill, on the nightstand, the dresser; and a disheveled tower of manila file folders that had recently bloomed on the room's single chair, forcing Elwin, on his last visit, to commandeer another chair from the room across the hall. Before all this—the swift mental skid and subsequent diagnosis of Alzheimer's disease that had landed Elwin Cross Sr. in this nursing home—Elwin's father had been painstakingly neat, a model of chilly organization. His three children had been born two years apart, and their heights, as adults, were precisely two inches apart; even his DNA was well-ordered. "He'd alphabetize the ties in his closet if he could only figure out how," Elwin's mother used to say. But now he'd grown slipshod, with everything out of place—his files, his glasses, his memories, his semantic processing, his brain's crudded neurons. He was like a carpenter whose constant misplacing of his hammer limited him to pounding no more than a dozen nails a day, the bulk of his energies directed toward searching. Owing to this, Jane thought it cruel to encourage his writing. "How is he capable of finishing a book when he can't remember Mom died?" she'd told Elwin. "It's not fair to egg him on. And, Jesus, that room. He can't look anywhere without it staring him in the face. It's just wrong. It's like sticking him in a maze that doesn't have an exit. I mean, it even looks like a maze in there."

So Elwin had engineered a compromise. As the middle child, that had always been his role: the Henry Clay of the Crosses. The file cabinet he was now lugging across Henry Street would ease some of the clutter—open the maze, at the very least—and buy his father some time, though it wouldn't assuage Jane's fears (or cold suspicion) that their father would be eaten by silverfish long before the Alzheimer's could claim him. When he'd returned home from California, three years before, Elwin had thought the reason was to protect his father from the disease—a security detail that he partially blamed for the demise of his marriage. (Maura had been content, if never giddy, in the L.A. suburbs. The dutiful move to New Jersey, and the acid it generated within her, had thrown the marriage's fragile pH level off kilter.) More and more, however, he felt as if he was protecting his father from Jane's various acids.

Even as a teenager, tilting against his father for all the standard reasons, he'd never quite comprehended his sister's hot animosity toward their father, admittedly a tyrant though of the classic benevolent order. That she could sustain the animosity now—no matter how she tried to frame it as "realism" versus Elwin's presumed idealism—was an even darker mystery. "Is it possible that Jane is just, deep down, an asshole?" their younger brother, David, had emailed Elwin from a remote village in China, where he taught basic English while struggling to gestate a novel that, after twenty-plus years, was verging on the mythical. But then David, who was curiously alone in christening himself the family's "black sheep," came equipped with his own set of complications; distance, in this case, did not equal objectivity. He'd seemed to covertly relish the fact that Jane's third husband, a Tribeca anesthesiologist, had more or less wiped out their father's retirement savings by handing them over to Lawrence Muntner, whose arrest and conviction for operating a gargantuan Ponzi scheme had dominated newscasts a year and a half earlier. Maybe it assuaged some guilt David was feeling for contributing nothing to their father's care; Elwin didn't know. Elwin was sanguine about David's absence in the financial schema, however. His little brother's bohemian act—which at this late stage was no longer an act—exempted him, in Elwin's mind, and to a lesser though still surprising degree in Jane's. Though, "when that book of his gets made into a movie," she'd said, "we're socking him with a big fat bill. Interest included."

Noting Elwin's struggles to reconcile his load with the building's double set of entrance doors—the exterior of which bore the phrase "A LIFE FULFILLMENT COMMUNITY"—a familiar male nurse helped him carry the cabinet to his father's room. "Special delivery," the nurse announced, visibly startling Elwin Cross Sr., who was propped up in his bed examining an envelope. The elder Cross frowned at the file cabinet. "What's that for?" he said.

The nurse, glossy-faced and blubbery, with a neck the size of a wheelbarrow tire, replied, "All your stuff, man."

"What stuff?"

"That stuff."

"That's not stuff."

"Whatever. All 'em papers."

Elwin's father hadn't seemed to notice his son, leaning against the file cabinet and breathing way more heavily than his cardiologist would deem appropriate. Up went Elwin's hand, for a meek wave that his father also didn't register; at this he felt a negative tingle. His father's doctor had warned Elwin that it might happen one day: You'll walk into his room, and he'll ask who you are. He won't recognize you. "You need to be prepared for that," the doctor had said, neglecting to explain how. But surely . . . not *yet,* Elwin thought, staring solidly at his father as if to transmit some kind of telepathic introduction: *Hey Pop. It's me. Don't you dump me too.*

"Put it over there, Boolah," the elder Cross told the nurse, and in the same flat executive tone said to his son: "How was traffic?"

The negative tingle vanished, deactivated by relief. "Fine," he said, far too brightly, and for that matter inaccurately: At the mouth of the Holland Tunnel he'd been trapped inside that blue egg for forty-five minutes, the steering wheel wedged hard against his belly no matter how he adjusted the seat. Scanning the radio, he'd discovered a weird surfeit of Billy Joel songs, causing him to conclude that Billy Joel must have just died—a fair hypothesis for why all of radioworld seemed to be paying him sudden and synchronous tribute. This saddened him, not because he liked Billy Joel—he didn't—but because Maura did, and though their marriage was apparently over, he was still somehow conjoined with her, so that, imprisoned inside the Holland Tunnel, he felt the stab of her grief vicariously, as if some emotional satellite linkage had yet to be disabled. But none of the DJs mentioned any death, and neither did the cycling newscasts on the AM dial, so after a while Elwin realized he'd conned himself into mourning Billy Joel for Maura while both of them—albeit separately—were probably off somewhere giggling, as alive and vital as ever, while his poor belly flesh was slowly enveloping the base of the steering wheel in the manner of a white blood cell engulfing a pathogen. Another forty-five minutes in that tunnel, he felt sure, and full phagocytosis would occur, with the steering wheel becoming an indelible fixture in his gut.

"Boolah, meet my son." A brusque wave. "Dr. Cross the Junior."

Boolah, who'd been introduced to Elwin a hundred and thirty times before, said hidy.

"He's an expert on dead languages."

Boolah nodded like he always did. Like most of the world's peoples, he had no response to that, even with practice.

"Boolah," Elwin's father said to his son, "is an expert on the New York Giants."

Now it was Boolah's turn to brighten, if just for a moment. "Played two seasons at Defensive Back, '88 and '89," he said, which actually was news to Elwin. Elwin was about to ask him more about that—Elwin wasn't a football fan but he was drawn to tragedy, and a former NFL star changing bedpans showed potential for that—when he saw Boolah's expression darken. "Blew out my knee, y'know, so that was that. Not something I talk about. Ain't that right, Dr. Cross?"

"They say he's famous," said Elwin's father.

"Hush with that already," said Boolah.

"But then I must be famous, too—look." He spread open his hands to reveal the heap of plastic-windowed envelopes splayed atop his bedsheet. "It's the only way to explain the amount of mail I receive. Junk—all of it junk."

"I'll help you clear some of that," Elwin said. "But later. I brought you dinner. I just need to fetch it from the car."

Boolah protested: "We got turkey today, man. It's Thanksgiving."

"We eat at five," said his father.

"Turkey at five," said Boolah. "With all the trimmings."

"I'll be back in a sec," said Elwin.

"He don't eat turkey?" said Boolah to Elwin's father.

"It can't be five already," came the response.

Elwin's father's room was on the first floor, four doors down from the lobby where a dozen patients were gathered, in varying models of wheelchairs, around a bulky, low-def television. Not one of them, Elwin noted, was watching the football game on the TV; instead they sat slumped in their chairs, arms hanging as loosely and slack as their lower jaws, as if in the late stages of carbon monoxide poisoning. One woman was wearing an XXL sweatshirt emblazoned with a gleeful turkey and the word GOBBLE! A taut plastic sack of urine, dark as lager, peeked out from beneath a man's gym shorts. Some were asleep, or if not quite asleep in a state much like it: eyes closed, heads comfortlessly lolling, consciousness cranked down to a low sludgy stasis. Others appeared to be scrutinizing the walls, which were painted the pale sulfurous yellow of a banana's flesh. Their eyes rolled toward Elwin as he passed, but blurrily—as if an instinctual response to perceived movement, like the reaction mechanism of sea urchins. He was merely a sudden dark break in the wall color, for some of them—a flickering anomaly, an unmoored memory sinking too swiftly to rescue. He felt their failure as he went by, and felt guilty, as if just by his passing he'd bullied them into futile exercise—reminding them that he was no one they knew, because they no longer knew anyone.

Elwin couldn't help himself, he hated this gauntlet: It was like wading through death. Or near-death: death's waiting room. The women were almost bald, their crusted lipstick askew and their hands pre-curled for the rosary that a mortician would equip some of them with, and the men tremulous and incontinent, their faces saggy and mole-splotched. But then it wasn't their decrepit physicality, their exteriors, that repulsed him—not primarily anyway. Elwin was hardly without his own sags and splotches; in fact, an honest appraisal in the mirror (something he'd avoided for years) would reveal him as *mostly* sags and splotches. Rather, what repulsed him—no, frightened him; suffused him with dread and pity—was the blankness of their interiors: the stale pudding he saw in their eyes, the larval lethargy that was either the cause or the result, the chicken or the egg, of their confinement here. Only scarcely did Elwin ever hear them speak, and, even then, it was usually in confounded response to a nurse's shouted inquiry. When visitors came—which to Elwin, who saw his father twice a week, seemed scandalously rare—the scene often evoked bad community theatre: synthetic grins, bellowed lines, squishy sentimentality, and unimpressed children made fidgety by their yearnings for a digital screen. No wonder his father barricaded himself in his room, Elwin thought, almost proud of the old man's cantankerous vanity (unlike Jane, naturally, who claimed their father was "antisocial" and "retreating inside himself").

He was not unaware that this admiration might be filial vanity on his part. On his first visit here, recoiling from this same dread gauntlet, he'd immediately phoned Jane to protest. "It's a human junkyard," he told her. "We can't stick Dad in here. Have you seen these people? There must be scads of better places over in New Jersey. Places with . . . activities or something, maybe a Ping-Pong table, I don't know, a coffee lounge. A library larger than what could be contained on a steel pushcart." "A Ping-Pong table? For God's sake, El. That's the only nursing home left south of 86th Street," said Jane, who was complicating matters by singlehandedly funding the portion of the nursing-home bill that the remainder of their father's pension didn't cover—as an unspoken penance, perhaps, for her husband's squandering of most of the elder Cross's retirement. Or, in a less generous interpretation, as a means of exerting control. "I'm not going to drive to fucking Jersey once a week so that he can have access to a goddamn Ping-Pong table," she said. "He's never even played Ping-Pong."

"I meant that . . . symbolically," Elwin said. "I retract the Ping-Pong table. But can't we ever be civil about this? Why do you have to talk like that?"

"You're the linguist," she replied. "You tell me."

Outside, on Henry Street, he discovered that the snowball-wielding children had turned against his loaner car. The little blue egg was dotted with the cold crusted whorls of a snowball ambush. He didn't blame them; he'd grown to hate the car, too, and not just for the hilarious practical joke it had played on him by suggesting the untimely death of Billy Joel and thereby conning him into an odious bout of pity for poor Maura. How could his insurance company deem his Jeep "totaled"? Elwin knew what "totaled" meant: mangled, upside down, charred, gutted by the Jaws of Life. Not deer-dinged and operable, like the Jeep. Didn't anyone use Bondo anymore? So his Jeep had a broken nose; that wasn't grounds for dialing the mortician. Elwin was fond of his insurance agent (she was the only person who sent him a birthday card every year), but this was an outrage. If he wanted to save the Jeep—which was still running strong, after 110,000-plus miles—he'd have to fund the bodywork himself. To the Consolidated Mid-Atlantic Insurers Co. of Morris County, New Jersey, it was scrap metal, its death sentence determined by some sort of actuarial calculus that didn't allow for a bit of old-school, pinch-and-tuck repair work, or for that matter take into account the Springsteenian affection a man can develop for a car after a dozen years of driving it, even on the Turnpike. By that metric, his dog Bologna should have been put down four years ago, when a Pacific Gas & Electric truck had backed over Bologna's leg and Elwin had paid $4,000 to have a titanium rod installed between Bologna's already arthritic joints. By that metric, maybe Elwin's father was totaled, too — the cost of his care outweighing his value, as his memory further blackened.

Elwin fetched the two plastic-wrapped plates from the passenger seat and walked back to the Roth Residence. Boolah opened the glass doors for him again, directing him to the nursing station, where he heated the plates in a microwave while the desk nurse argued with someone — presumably a lover of some kind — on the phone. "What'd you think flowers was gonna do?" she hissed. "Who you think paid for those flowers anyway?"

Trying not to eavesdrop, or to appear to be eavesdropping, Elwin studied an array of motivational sayings pinned to a corkboard between studio portraits of kittens: *RN means Real Nice. Nurses are IV Leaguers. Patients Require Patience.* When the microwave beeped its finale, he waved thank you to the nurse, who didn't respond, then cruised past the clutch of wheelchair patients, this time without looking, or at least appearing to be looking.

"I didn't say they warnt nice, fool," he heard the nurse say behind him.

"They've got turkey here, you know," his father said, when Elwin set one of the plates on the tray. "Boolah said so." He flicked the rim of the plate with a fingertip. "What'd you bring me, anyway?"

Unlike Elwin, with his forty-eight-inch waist and stovepipe-thick ankles, Cross Sr. was thin to the point of scarecrow. As a child, Elwin had never graduated from drawing stick-figure portraits of his father, even as breadth and curves had blossomed in his portraits of his mother — the accuracy of the stick figures had always sufficed. Add a bowtie and you were verging on photorealism. He'd filled out, just slightly, since moving into the Roth Residence, but his appearance was still dominated by bones: from those of his long narrow fingers to the craggy heights of his cheekbones. He was unshaven today, a paltry scruff of white brightening the sharkskin color of his jaw—a lapse that he blamed on the nurses. But if the nurses hadn't groomed him, that meant he'd combed his own hair, with a wavy if considered part on the side, which Elwin (always on the lookout) deemed a good sign; his dad hadn't given up. He was still trying. His eyes were still exuberantly blue, his hearing still crisp, his movements still coiled and twitchy like those of a schoolchild monitoring the classroom clock. He still looked—physically, anyway; to Elwin, anyway—like an inappropriate candidate for forced bed rest.

"It's venison," said Elwin.

His father harrumphed. "I thought you quit all that years ago. The Davy Crockett act."

More to the floor than to his father, Elwin said, "My new neighbors are big-time hunters." A curl of steam—rich and faintly sweet-smelling, like the odor of a scabbing wound—rose from his own plate.

"Well," said the elder Cross, obviously uncharmed by his Thanksgiving supper. "They do have turkey here."

"This is more authentic," Elwin countered. "It's what they ate at the original Thanksgiving."

"Oh goody," said his father, fumbling at last for a fork. "A history lesson."

"Please don't start, Dad," Elwin said, girding himself for the standard-issue laments: the word *history* triggering Historical Studies, as in the New School's Department of Historical Studies, which Jane, in overselling the Roth Residence and Manhattan to her father, had said would welcome him as an adjunct instructor. ("*Might* welcome him," is what Jane later told Elwin she'd said. "As in, the Nobel committee *might* award you the prize in linguistics. Come on. I had to tell him *something.*") His father felt he'd been hornswoggled, whether by his children or the New School or both; he'd even planned the course he wanted to teach ("Genocide: Historical and Cultural Frames") and had drafted a loose syllabus, which he was still revising.

Except, this time, the laments didn't come. Perhaps the mental cue wasn't strong enough, or perhaps that particular grudge—which had lodged in his otherwise fenestrated memory the way a shard of roasted meat gets lodged in one's teeth—had finally shaken loose. Instead of kvetching, Elwin Sr. was chewing, with his head cocked to the left and one

eye partly closed: his thoughtful expression, Elwin noted with pleasant surprise—the way he used to look when a clever graduate student asked his
opinion on, say, the effectiveness of cavalry charges at the Battle of Has-
tings.

"You know," he said, two pink specks of meat tumbling symmetrically
from both edges of his mouth, "we shot a deer one winter. One of the best
meals of my life."

Elwin froze, his own forkful of meat a mere inch from his lips. "*You*
did?"

"No, not me. A kid from Kentucky. Jenkins, or something like that."

"When you were . . ." A pause. "When?"

"Christmas Day, 1945," his father said. He sawed another bite from
the venison, dipping his head down, almost ravenously, to meet the fork.
"Kid shot it with his M1 and cleaned it and cooked it himself. Some kind
of stew, I think. Two corporals went and raided the basement of a beer garden, too. Filled up a Jeep with beer. Camp heroes, those guys. How was the
traffic?"

"Fine," Elwin lied again.

"Still blowing out there?"

"Not as much. Where was this?"

"What?"

"The deer."

"The deer? Austria. On the Enns River, near Steyr. The Russians on
one side and our boys on the other. We were always trading rations. You
could get just about anything for a can of Spam. They loved that Spam."

As casually as he could, because his father had always refused to discuss
his wartime service, Elwin said, "You've never mentioned that before . . ."

"The deer?"

"No. The war."

"Well, it was a long time ago." At this Elwin's father glanced off to the
side and skewed his mouth in the way he'd always done when telling a lie.
His incapacity to lie smoothly was the stuff of family legend: surprise parties blown, secrets fumbled. Elwin registered this, but just briefly, because
it made no sense. The war *was* a long time ago. In any case, his father was
quick to swerve the conversation: "So what's new?" he said. "How's my
sweetie?"

"Maura?"

Slyly, "You got another one?"

"We're separated, Dad. You knew that."

"Oh Christ. I guess that's right. Why?"

"We've been over this."

"Yeah, yeah. You know I forget things sometimes. It's the medicines." Ribot's law, Elwin reminded himself: The dissolution of memory is inversely related to the recency of the event. Christmas memories from 1945 remained tightly glued. The recent totaling of his son's marriage, on the other hand, wouldn't stick.

"She moved out," Elwin said flatly. To explain, as he felt obligated to do, he went with an old standby, the geographic gloss: "I don't think Jersey agrees with her."

"Jersey doesn't agree with anyone," said his father. "That's its charm. Why the hell would she leave? You're a big shot now. The director."

"It's complicated, Dad. Eat your supper."

"Complicated, how? She didn't run off on you, did she? With someone else?"

"As a matter of fact . . . yes. This isn't news. You've known all this."

"With who?"

"A chef."

"A chef? Why? You're a great cook."

"I don't think it was strictly a dining option. Can we not have this conversation?"

"Well, I think she's a fool. You're a good catch. A big shot. She'll be back."

"Let's not talk about it," said Elwin, testing a bite of the venison. Reheating it in the microwave had cooked it past medium-rare; it was gray in the center, and tough. The portion he'd cooked for himself the night prior—his first homecooked meal, he realized, in more than a month— had been pleasantly and not quite expectedly tender, though the circumstances of the deer's death had cast an uncomfortable pall over the meal. Whether from the lack of fair chase, or the broader symbolism of its killing (the eternal *whoops* that defined man's relationship to nature), he couldn't bring himself to enjoy it, and rushed through the meal while distracting himself reading the portions of the *Times* he'd skipped that morning. Enjoying it felt immoral, not unlike the way he'd once felt eating a spider monkey—tasty, but repellently infant-like—during his fieldwork with a tribe in the Amazon basin. The deer was what commercial fishermen called bycatch—the accidental and unwanted victims hauled up in their nets. Seahorses, dolphins, that sort of thing. And yet the clear virtuousness of eating bycatch, rather than abandoning it, didn't seem to offset, for Elwin, the melancholy of its blundered presence on his plate. This struck him as irrational—the less moral tack would have surely been to cede the deer to the buzzards and landfill-fillers—but then the dams and dikes of rationality were usually powerless to withstand emotion. On a somewhat related track, he wondered if his father's dentures would be able to withstand the meat's sticky toughness.

Maybe not: Elwin Cross Sr. had stopped chewing, though a wad of food was visible inside his cheek. But his dentures weren't to blame. He was gazing past his son's shoulder, toward the hallway, confusion muddying his eyes.

"What is it?"

"We should call your mother," he said. Urgently, as if he'd forgotten her birthday, their anniversary. "Here, pass me the phone."

"We can't."

"Sure we can. They let me call long-distance here. Is she long-distance? Pass me the phone."

"Try to remember, Dad."

"Remember what? Jesus, you kids. Always with the memory games."

"Why can't we call Mom?" Emotionlessly, professorially: the Socratic Method as Alzheimer's therapy.

"They let me call long-distance. Look over there—at the goddamn phone bill. I can call anywhere I want. I can call Timbuktu."

"No," said Elwin. "Just try to remember."

"Remember what?"

"Why we can't call Mom."

The elder Cross took a breath, sucking in his lips so that they disappeared entirely into his mouth: the way children imitate the toothless elderly. He sighed through his nose as his lips reemerged, his face suddenly colorless, his eyelids blinking and reblinking like those of someone emerging from a nap. "Because she's gone," he said finally. "She died."

"That's right."

"Okay. It's just . . . I knew that. I did." He resumed chewing the gray mushball of venison stored in his cheek, then said glumly, "This is good. What is it?"

"It's venison. I told you."

"Right. You told me."

"It's okay."

"The goddamn medicines, is the thing." With a knife he glumly rolled the peas around on his plate. "They say it could be a potassium deficiency, too."

"I know. It's okay."

They ate in silence after that, avoiding one another's eyes. His father was embarrassed, and though he knew it was wrong, Elwin was embarrassed for him. Their forks squeaked against the plates. From across the hall came the sound of moaning, bovine and forlorn-sounding, or maybe just excremental. Nurses glided past the open doorway, their crepe soles whispering *sffft sffft* to the floor tiles. A telephone rang in a distant room, an old-fashioned analog ring: the past calling to say hello.

"So tell me," his father finally said, then paused, his strain visible. A pained but familiar ellipsis filled the room. "Tell me — tell me what's bold and new in the field of linguistics."

"Well," began Elwin, grateful for this new swerve. After decades of longing for a deep or even semi-deep conversation with his father — about the war, about his childhood, about his father's infrequent but cataclysmic night terrors that had so traumatized Elwin and his siblings as children (their father curled into a ball in the upstairs hallway, weeping madly, their mother cradling him while ordering the children to close their bedroom doors and go back to bed) — Elwin now mostly desired small talk. Work (meaning his, not his father's), the weather, bodily matters. Every other subject bore them straightaway into a fog of hurt and humiliation.

"I did have an interesting call yesterday," Elwin said.

"Oh yeah?"

"From an outfit called Attero Laboratories. Connected to the Department of Energy." This was the call Rochelle had fumbled, the one that had loomed strangely and ominously over Elwin as he'd lain in his bed, exhausted and bleary-headed, after dismantling the deer. The caller had left a voicemail the next day, and the fierce urgency with which Elwin had dialed him back seemed, in retrospect, dodgy and ridiculous—further cause for concern about his own mental state. His physician had prescribed antidepressants, after his and Maura's split, but Elwin had resisted taking them because of the potential for weight gain as a side effect; now he was reconsidering. Numb and fatter: There was the best suit he could drape upon his future.

"Energy?" said his father.

"It's still a bit unclear. Apparently Congress has commissioned the department to come up with a warning system for a nuclear waste depository out west. In New Mexico."

"Congress? What did they call you for?"

"That's what I asked. An 'Expert Judgment Panel,' is what he said. A few weeks of meetings, here and there."

A slight *pshaw.* "Since when are you an expert on nuclear waste?"

"It's an interdisciplinary panel. Physicists, geologists, nuclear scientists, philosophers. A folklorist. Even an artist."

"And a linguist."

"And a linguist, right." From deep within him Elwin felt a tiny, reflexive, decades-old prick of defensiveness about his chosen field. His father had never quite approved, dismissing much of linguistics as "theoretical posturing." Chomsky, Lakoff, et al. Elwin had long ago resigned himself to the idea that his area of specialization—applied linguistics, the application of linguistics to real-world problems—was a direct response to his father's distaste, a bid for his respect. "There's a language death component," he said. "Whatever system they implement has to be effective for ten thousand years. The full radioactive lifespan. So the question—presumably the reason I got the call—is how to communicate when no language has proven itself durable for—well, for really a fraction of that time."

"Hell of a riddle," his father said, licking whipped yams from his spoon.

"It is, isn't it? Of course I said yes. I mean, ten thousand years. It's mind-boggling. Old English, that's just a thousand years old, and barely comprehensible. Middle English is five hundred, and that's hard to read, too. Swadesh's formula says that any language will undergo a total lexical transformation in ten thousand years, though I think that's way over-stated—more like five thousand. So the question is how you communicate over deep time."

"Communicate what?"

Elwin's shoulders slumped. "Dad, I just told you—"

"No, I mean, what's the message?"

"Oh. That. Well, it's . . . something along the lines of, 'Keep Out,' I suppose."

"Here be dragons."

"Something like that. Apparently there was another panel already, a Futures panel, that came up with all sorts of these wild scenarios for us to address. Human extinction. Extraterrestrial interference. Radical stuff. But it all has to be factored."

"Human extinction," his father said, not quite as a question.

"Every possible scenario," said Elwin. "It's all rather science-fictiony, isn't it? Might even be fun, I don't know." He pondered this for a moment, as it emerged unedited from his mouth: Fun? Maybe, in the way a crossword puzzle or riddle book could be fun: as a mental distraction, a reprieve from the colorless lassitude of marital collapse. Some people—Elwin envied them—had children to get them through. Must be hard to wallow, he thought, while searching for lost mittens, packing lunches, darting from soccer games to ballet practice, fielding questions about why the sky's blue or why they always build gas stations across the street from other gas stations. All he had, on the other hand, was Bologna, and his father, and rooms full of students who he'd long ago realized didn't care what he was saying. And a 1998 Jeep Cherokee, nursing a busted nose in a lot at a Route 24 bodyshop, that would soon be wondering why this minor injury—no fault of its own—had caused Elwin to abandon it. "I could stand a little fun in my life right now," he said, as much to himself as to his father.

"Huh." At this the elder Cross snorted, and drew his fork around his plate. His mouth was curled into something like a smirk.

"What?" Elwin said.

"It's just funny, when you think about it," he said, cocking his head and closing one of his eyes. "All the terrible effort of human civilization, the great big arc of it. And in ten thousand years the only intelligible trace of

it might be your 'keep out' sign in the desert, stuck in a big heap of trash."
He lifted his eyebrows and wagged his head. "Sucks the wind out of your
sails, doesn't it?"

"I hadn't thought of it like that," said Elwin.

"Well, it's rather chilling, when you do," said his father. "Nice of you to
cheer me up like that, son. Adds a whole new perspective to the day." Joy-
lessly chuckling, he said, "Merry Christmas to you, too."

"It's Thanksgiving, Dad."

"Same difference. Where's Boolah?"

"What do you need?"

"I'm done, that's all."

"With what?"

"My dinner. That was good. Compliments to the chef."

Chef: Elwin winced. Compliments to the chef indeed: for poaching
Maura from him, for ending civilization as he knew it. Among the myriad
injuries from Maura's betrayal was that she'd spoiled, for Elwin, the stal-
wart pleasures of eating in restaurants. The mere sight of a toque, or even a
sauce-painted plate, was enough to put him off his feed. That was one reason he'd become a bleak regular at Burger King and sometimes Taco Bell:
no chefs in those joints. Just workaday cooks, trying to earn enough for a
down payment on a new tattoo and wholly uninterested in fucking Elwin's
wife.

He gathered up his father's plate with his own, then dumped the uneaten portions into the trash can by the bed, drizzling the plastic liner with
gloppy, plasma-like streams of the cranberry-port sauce. In the bathroom
he rinsed the plates in the sink, searching for something with which to
scrub them. After a paper towel proved ineffectual, dissolving into mush,
he used his naked hand, rubbing at the yam remnants to dislodge them
into the faucet stream. The insignia on the back of the plates, which were
of the oversized, wide-rimmed, plain-white variety used in fashionable restaurants, rewound Elwin's memory back to the plates' origins: Maura buying a dozen place settings at a Napa boutique and crowing about the good
price that'd struck Elwin as grossly excessive though he'd kept that to himself. She'd left them when she'd moved out, all twelve settings, despite his
suggestion she take them. "What am I going to do with twelve plates?" he'd
asked, yielding from her a disinterested shrug. Perhaps they were no longer

fashionable, or maybe her chef had a thing for square plates—whatever the reason, she didn't want them anymore. He remembered staring at the plates with tender sympathy, then, as if they too were victims here—innocent spectators, caught in the crossfire. The bycatch of a marriage. Only after realizing that twelve plates meant he could conceivably go almost two weeks without running the dishwasher did he come to appreciate the relinquishment.

Washing his hands, he noticed the red, quart-sized sharps container, for needle disposal, affixed to the wall beside the mirror. On it was a label emblazoned with the familiar international biohazard symbol: a plain trefoil, or triple Venn diagram, with its three overlapping circles superimposed upon a fourth circle at the center. He studied it for a while, the water gushing uselessly over his hands. It looked vaguely heraldic, and also, with its evocations of the Holy Trinity, not-so-vaguely Christian—like something you might have spied on a shield during the Crusades. But what did it *say?* he wondered. He tried fishing meaning from it, failed, then tried willfully misreading it, to see if he could glean an erroneous message from it. At this he failed, too. It was a blank symbol, he decided, that wouldn't look out of place stitched onto an athletic shoe, or stenciled onto the back of a fashionable porcelain dinner plate. A leftover corporate logo, slapped onto medical waste. Meaningless. Only when he heard his father call did he realize the water was still running.

"What is it, Dad?" he said. "Want me to help get you started with the file cabinet?"

"The file cabinet? No. That's a nice one, though, isn't it? Boolah got it for me. No, pass me that stack of files over there on the chair. No, underneath there. The green folders. I think it's the green ones. Just hand them all to me."

"What about the mail?" Elwin said.

"What mail?"

"Right there, beside you . . ."

"Eh, it's junk. It's not worth the effort. Anyway your mother handles all that."

"Dad," Elwin said. The dilemma was always whether to correct him or let the delusion slide, and was mostly decided by Elwin's energy level. Sometimes the effort felt constructive; other times, a waste. You could jog him back to reality, but not for long—the duration of the visit, at best. "We just went over this, remember?"

"We went over it, right."

"About Mom."

Vacantly, he said, "All about her, sure."

"Look, I'm happy to help you—"

"No help needed. I've got to get some work done. And you've got your sweetie waiting for you at home."

This time Elwin didn't object; he just lowered his head, wishing his father was right (though resisting the wish, or trying to, the way he tried and failed to resist cleaning his plate) and wondering, not for the first time, if there was a kind of dark bliss built into dementia: an immunity from death and abandonment, a way of fixing a point in time so that nothing can change, nothing can be rewritten, no one can leave. Hail hail, the gang's all here—for good.

"I can stay," Elwin said, masking the truer sentiment: *I want to stay.* Which itself masked an even truer one: *I have nowhere else to go.*

"I've got lots of work to do," his father said. "You probably do, too. What's new in the world of linguistics these days, anyway?"

"Just the same-old," sighed Elwin. Game over, he thought. Finito. Kaput-ski. "That's fine, Dad. No worries. It was good to see you." Then, softly: "Do you have your glasses?"

"Right here. Or, right over there. Somewhere. Oh, right here." He smiled at Elwin, then reached out his hand—awkwardly, like a businessman closing a meeting. Confused, Elwin responded in kind, then watched as his father took Elwin's meaty hand in his own spindle-fingered one and patted it, gently, three times. Elwin was momentarily struck by the sight, by the Sistine Chapel–ish disparity between his hand and his father's: the age, the shapes and sizes, the vital pink heft of his versus the frailty of his father's dwindling grip. It was like interspecies contact, or deep-time communication: a connection defined by distance.

"Jane says she might visit tomorrow," Elwin said.

"That's nice of her."

"I'll try to swing back by on Sunday."

"You're a good kid," his father said, then fumbled his glasses onto his head, licked a finger, and opened the topmost file folder on his bed.

Dismissed, Elwin stood there for a while, watching his father read, noting the way his father's lips trembled slightly, like those of a child restraining himself from mouthing all the words, and the way his eyes zigzagged along the page. For a moment he pondered the irony: that in fifty-four years he had never needed his father as much as he did now, yet his father was gone, or, if not quite gone, then cemented in the past, and unable to receive signals from the present. But then he decided it wasn't an irony, it was merely the broken gears of time, or the way life can feed you when you're full (youth) and starve you when you're hungry (midlife). Elwin fetched his coat and plates and drifted toward the doorway. He looked back once, as he left the room, but his father didn't look up. In several minutes, he knew, his father would forget he'd ever been there.

"Happy Thanksgiving," the desk nurse told him on the way out, but she didn't look up either. The world is casting me aside, it's burying me, Elwin thought, descending the steps outside. As he walked he glanced backwards once, to make sure he was at least depositing footprints in the snow, that not every trace of him was being extinguished—that he too hadn't been totaled, at least not yet—not yet. The radio was naturally playing Billy Joel's "Scenes from an Italian Restaurant" when Elwin started the car. Cursing, he flipped it off, but not before the melody had latched onto his brain, the "oh oh, oh oh, ohs" of the chorus hounding him all the way across the river to New Jersey.

6

AN HOUR AFTER eating Thanksgiving dinner, Dave Masoli was staring into the toilet with wide-eyed awe and admiration. He couldn't recall ever making anything so beautiful as this in his life. Not even the Cashomatic Pay-Day eLoans deal, in which he and his partner had scored a $1.3 million debt portfolio for $12,750 in a bankruptcy auction and started clearing a profit on it within *two* hours. But no, that was business, while this—this might be art. Suspended in the toilet was what could only be called the *perfect* turd, the turd a man might aspire to produce his entire life but despite daily attempts never achieve: an unbroken coil of three (Dave counted) equidistant loops so smooth and unblemished that it looked machine-made, like the compression springs on a shock absorber. Even the ends were flawless, not pinched or severed but rounded and polished-looking, as if milled on a lathe. And the color! A deep and unstreaked chocolaty brown: not Hershey's bar brown, but that other one, the more bitter candy bar he'd always traded to his brother on Halloween—Special Dark, that was it.

Dave was stunned. How could he, the humble son of a Turnpike toll collector, a man with no discernible artistic talents save finding money where others thought none existed, have possibly squeezed something so precious and perfect out of his ass? Standing over the toilet, he wondered if this was what childbirth might feel like: the sensation of being on the sweet end of a miracle, the bodily pride, the instinctive urge to nurture and protect. But then . . . how could he preserve this glory? Flushing struck him as criminal. Leaving it, dishonorable—and anyway, no one else in the house (certainly not now, with the house overrun with Sara's relations) was sensitive enough to appreciate a thing of beauty like this. Whoever came next would just say *ewwww*, look away as the toilet scarfed it down, then creep back downstairs whispering about the unflushed potty like it was some lowgrade family scandal, eager to finger the dirty culprit, the poo vandal.

Then a solution occurred to him: From his pants pocket, down at his ankles, he fished out his cellphone camera and aimed it at the toilet. Three digital clicks later, he verified the turd's glory with the camera—it looked as majestic, in five-megapixel resolution on a 2.5-inch LCD screen, as it did in the bowl—before flushing it all away, wincing then sighing as it collapsed and splintered in the cruel vortex of water. Walking back downstairs, to where his in-laws were gathered around the big-screen, he felt a sense of accomplishment that he hadn't felt in weeks, a proud, delighted buoyancy that was evident to everyone, even his dense mother-in-law, who remarked, as he settled back into his chair in the living room, that he looked like the cat who'd eaten the canary.

"Canaries? I thought we ate turkey!" exclaimed her husband, persisting in the geezer-slash-bumpkin routine he enacted whenever he and Sara's mother came east from Ohio, which they pronounced "Oh-*HI*-ah." Dave knew he was supposed to laugh at this, if only to be polite; just two years (re)married, he remained within the statute-of-limitations period in which he was obligated to care, or pretend to care, about what came dribbling from his in-laws' mouths. This time, however, he let everyone else do the laughing for him: Sara's older sister Liz, who'd recently cut her blonde hair short and shaggy like a schoolboy's, confirming—aesthetically, anyway—Dave's longstanding suspicion of ulterior lesbianism; Liz's husband Jeremy, a skinny nailbiter who worked for a nonprofit something-or-other (nonprofits also striking Dave as vaguely lesbo); their twelve-year-old son Aidan, who Sara claimed was autistic but who Dave suspected was just weird; and Bev, his mother-in-law, who chuckled loudest of all, punctuating it by grabbing her husband's knee and giving it a good hard lovey-dovey wiggle. "Ohhh, Raymond," she said.

"Well, they do things differently back east," said Raymond. "Didya eat a canary, Dave?"

The temptation, properly resisted, was to flip out the phone and display the snapshot he'd just taken: *Yes, Raymond. As a matter of fact I did.*

Then, courtesy of my astounding, amazing, even miraculous bowels, I turned it into . . . this. Truth was, however, Dave actually *liked* his father-in-law, who struck him as the most hypoallergenic human being he'd ever met: Mortimer Snerd reincarnated as a (retired) suburban schools administrator. Sure, you'd never want to share a battle trench with him, and you'd definitely want him on the *other* side of a business deal . . . but sharing a couch with him on the holidays, once or twice a year: eh, not so bad. Dave's former father-in-law, on the other hand — there was a ball-buster, a Brooklyn vice cop who knew every angle, was always glaring narrow-eyed at Dave as if just about to place his face from an old Wanted poster. Always pissed off and sourheaded, as if begrudging the fact that he'd been born a few hundred years too late to earn dowries on his trampy daughters, the trampiest of whom Dave had squandered six years of his life on. So Raymond Tetwick was an upgrade — corny jokes and all. Dave let the canary inquiry slide.

"What'd I miss," he asked Raymond instead, nodding his chin at the television while reclaiming the glass of beer he'd left on the side table.

"On the game?" said Raymond. "To be honest, now, my mind wandered . . ." As if Dave couldn't make out the digits on his own eighty-two-inch LCD screen, Raymond leaned forward, squinting, and reported, "Looks like the Cowboys are up by, looks like fourteen."

"Felix Jones just ran it in for forty-six," muttered Aidan, who was sprawled on the carpet, his head propped against his father's shins.

"That's *right*, Aidy," said Jeremy, a long shock of gray-brown hair flapping forward as he patted his son on the shoulder with a degree of pride more suited to Felix Jones's father, high-fiving Jones on the sidelines. "That's great. You knew his name and everything."

Dave rolled his eyes. No wonder the kid was a freak. And why, he wondered, did liberals all sound the freakin same? One part Mister Rogers, one part Jeff Spicoli, condescending and vacuous at the same time. Like the way homos all sounded the same, Dave thought, exhuming an old barroom disquisition: why sticking dicks in your mouth resulted in a lifelong lisp. Did cocksucking tear some hidden, hymen-like membrane in the male mouth, thereby altering the air-to-saliva ratio (as in the gas-to-air mixture in a fuel injector) so that the words came out all wet and slushy-swishy? Were scientists studying this? Probably not, Dave guessed. Too *incorrect* to address. Global warming, on the other hand: That was an open-and-shut case, as clear and tidy as a prime-time whodunit. But this — this was just, *ooooh,* a wiggly *mystery.* Dave made a mental note to bring that up with Jeremy sometime, as a verbal noogie, when he was feeling less charitable (and accomplished) than at present. He enjoyed watching Jeremy stammer; it made the holidays bearable.

Dave's eye-roll hadn't gone unnoticed. Aidan smirked at him, commiseratively, as if in agreement about his goo-gooey father, thereby confirming Dave's suspicion that whatever was wrong with the kid — up to and including the various food allergies that had forced Sara to more or less cook two separate Thanksgiving dinners, one of which went more or less uneaten — wasn't clinical.

The Raiders fumbled on the Dallas twenty-four. Though he'd claimed to be rooting for Dallas, Raymond went, "Ohhhh," and shook his head, as if heartbroken by the brute injustice of it all; Dave got the feeling that in Raymond's vision of the perfect world — call it Raymondville — all games ended with a hunky-dory tie, and the only legal sexual position (here Dave's mind was wandering) was the even-steven sixty-nine, although, as he assessed Raymond and Bev from that unsavory mental angle, Dave highly doubted that they'd ever graduated from the mild injustice of missionary position. Because he'd neglected to call his bookie in time, Dave didn't care about the game's outcome. He suspected no one else in the room cared, either — certainly not Jeremy, who seemed frustrated that his offers to help Sara with the dishes kept being rebuffed, and who was presently molesting a thumbnail in a way that didn't suggest he was anxious about the Raiders' chances. Maybe Aidan, but then, with that kid, who the hell knew? "I'm saying this sucker is over," Dave announced.

"You never know, Dave," said Raymond, which is what passed, in Raymondville, for a heated rebuttal.

"*I* do," Dave said, with an incontrovertible snort, then slid his almost-empty beer glass off the side table, swirled its skimpy contents to signal his purpose, and stood up. The self-satisfied groan he released, upon rising, was loud and carnal enough to cause his sister-in-law Liz to glance up in jumpy alarm. Her semistricken expression, which she quickly hid by turning toward the television screen, brought a pleased simper to Dave's face, as if he'd whispered *boo* and she'd promptly drenched her panties. He knew she despised him, probably had from the start. He didn't know why—he considered himself a solid guy, a more-than-decent provider with a business that was ka-chinging in this weakening economy, who took primo care of Sara and her daughter, bought 'em whatever they wanted, rubbed Sara's feet when they were achy from jogging, drove to the Rite Aid at midnight when the girls ran out of tampons; *solid,* right?—but figured it might have something to do with him being Republican and her being a liberal feminazi-slash-closeted-lesbo who talked, openly, about her two youthful abortions—*two!*—the way Sara talked about her old TV commercial jobs: disparagingly, but with what Dave sensed was secret pride. As if she'd *endured* something, come through fire or someshit, and was stronger and wiser for having done so, unlike (thought Dave) the two babies she'd flushed without even as much fanfare or feeling as he'd accorded his recent super-turd, two babies denied the chance to be strong and wise or at least, like Aidan, autistic and allergic. Fair enough: She didn't like his kind, and he didn't like hers, but at least he could be civil about it. Civilly, he asked, "Anyone need a refill while I'm up?"

A bland chorus of *nope*s answered him. Jeremy felt compelled, naturally, to apologize for his *nope,* citing the long drive back to Port Washington, to "the Island," which Dave ignored, saying "Suit yourself" to no one in particular.

"Where's Alexis?" Raymond asked.

"Still in the *bath*room," muttered Aidan, his tone strangely vituperative, as if he'd been waiting forty minutes for the potty to clear.

"Be kind," Jeremy hissed at him, and this time, instead of patting Aidan's back, gave the boy's neck a two-fingered massage. The tactile line between approval and disapproval, Dave noted, was awfully slight. "Alexis," Jeremy informed him, "has Irritable Bowel Syndrome."

"What's that?" Aidan said.

"Means Lexi's no good at pooping," Dave explained.

Aidan said, "That's funny."

"It's actually very serious," Jeremy corrected.

"It's a little funny," said Dave, striking off toward the kitchen. Along the way he noticed a tiny curl of mud on the carpet—must've fallen out from between someone's boot treads—and scooped it up, then dunked it into the foamy dregs of his beer glass. He was trying to remain unbothered by all the disarray that houseguests engender: the multitude of drippy boots in the mudroom, the coats heaped upon one another in wayward piles, the sink overrun with coffee mugs and egg-encrusted plates, the trail of abandoned newspaper sections charting his father-in-law's creaky passage from room to room. Dave was big on a clean house, a clean car, believing you could tell much if not everything about people by the state of their furnace filter, the organization of their freezer, and the level of rinse aid in their dishwasher. He considered these things—the house, the Cadillac Escalade in the garage, the furnace filter, the subzero freezer, all of it—testaments to his success, showcases for what he'd achieved, at the age of forty-six, via a mixture of sixteen-hour workdays, savvy timing, the investment capital spending spree of the mid-'90s, a rare and precious grasp of human frailty, and (even he would admit) deliciously loose federal regulations.

Dave was in the collections business, though the term he preferred— insisted upon, actually—was "debt acquisition," which had a much more gilded, Wall Street-y ring to it than "collection agency," or, worse (though more accurate), salvage or junk debt collection. The word *collection* had a dirty taint—trashpickers, ragpickers, stamp and baseball-card nerds, that sort of thing—which was why, publicly anyway, he banned its use at ARC (Acquisitions and Asset Recovery Corp.), the company he had founded in 1996, except in the required legalese ("This is an attempt to collect a debt and any information obtained . . .").

Privately, however, the ban was intended to position Dave farther up-field from his father, who *was* a collector, and nothing but—a toll collector on the New Jersey Turnpike who'd blown his twenty-eight-year career by offering a boozy-looking carful of coed-looking girls (Catholic high schoolers, as it turned out) a free pass through Lane 8 of the Bayonne tolls if one of them (the daughter of a state senator from Neptune, as it turned out) would flash him some fresh white tit. Ordinary night-shift hijinks on the Turnpike, but this marked Sal Masoli's tenth such complaint, plus the senator wouldn't stop huffing and puffing, so the Turnpike Authority eased Dave's father out with an early-retirement package and a listless farewell party conspicuously unattended by management. Now he spent his nine-to-five hours dialing and redialing sports call-in shows to complain about the various "bums" spoiling athletics in the tri-state area. Once or twice, in the car, Dave had heard his father on the radio. It was a miserable experience, like happening upon a photo of your mom on the internet with a schlong up her tush. "Sparta Sal," the hosts called him, and usually tried to hurry him off the air. "Breathe, Sal, just breathe," they sometimes advised. After pulling the plug on one of his rants, a host pondered aloud: "What's the opposite of a fan? Is there a word for that? Anti-fan, maybe?" His cohost added, "I think Sparta Sal actually *hates* sports," to which the first host said, "I think Sparta Sal might hate *life*. Bennie in the Bronx, what's shakin . . ."

Dave's memories of observing his father at work were suffused with shame and disgust, not from his behavior—the old man enjoyed showing off for his son by flinging pennies back at startled drivers, skimming a dollar here and there for the boy to stuff into his jeans pocket, shouting *Fuck you very much* to drivers of Mercedes or BMWs as they passed beneath the gate arm—but from the job itself: the cramped little booth with its fogged-up windows and its grease-whorled cashbox and its squeaky vinyl-clad chair from which yellow stuffing leaked like the split guts of a woodchuck on the Palisades Parkway, the air around the booths layered with bands of leaden smog that choked tears from Dave's eyes, the way drivers ignored his father (many of them used their tollbooth intermission as an opportunity to pick their noses) as though he were a vending machine or some other nonhuman coin-sucker, the sad ceaseless sameness of the transactional exchange: *dollar-thirty,* like strophe and antistrophe, *dollar-thirty, dollar-thirty.* This, to Dave, was *collection,* and he wanted no part of it; like his father, it felt below him.

Acquisition, however: That was different. He loved the word—"I've got an acquisitive mind," he was fond of saying—nearly as much as he loved the word *asset,* which scored double bonus points for containing the word *ass* and thereby evoking his number-one favorite female attribute. ARC, which Dave had spun out of a one-man bounced-check collections company he'd founded as a Rutgers undergrad, specialized in stale debt portfolios. Not the "firsts," the industry term for delinquent accounts that hadn't yet been charged off, and which sold for twelve cents on the dollar; these were too pricey for Dave, plus the big boys, the publicly traded outfits, kept an exclusive grip on those. And not even the "seconds," the charged-off accounts that had stymied prior collection efforts. Dave's forte was in acquiring packaged portfolios of dead debts—years-old, out-of-statute consumer credit accounts, which he could usually score, *en masse,* for less than a penny on the dollar—then, using a proprietary algorithm he'd developed for sifting out probable payers on those accounts, extracting payment on those debts.

The profit percentages were outlandish, as unfathomable as unicorns: math at its giddiest. The Cashomatic PayDay eLoans deal, for instance: $12,750 for $1.3 million in abandoned accounts. His "acquisition teams"—forty-seven employees working out of a giant phone bank in a Sparta office park, using scripts (written by Dave himself) that were notorious industry-wide for the way they strained the legal boundaries established by the Fair Debt Collection Practices Act—had already wrested more than $285,000, mostly in arbitrary settlements with the debtors, from those so-called dead accounts. Dave adored doing the numbers, dancing his hairy fingers across a calculator's keys: a 2,235 gross profit percentage, and still growing. Water squeezed from a stone. Financial Lazaruses, called forth from their tombs. There's profit everywhere, he was fond of saying, so long as you know where to look.

At least once a week—more frequently if he was feeling down—Dave would roam the phone banks, dispensing backslaps and thumbs-up signs to the good employees (the "acquisitors," in ARC-speak) while scouting for the weak ones. The weak were easy to identify: Their mouths were closed. They were the ones nodding—patiently or impatiently, it didn't matter—while Mrs. X from Milwaukee or Mr. Y from central Ohio (Raymondville, possibly) tried to explain why the debt was no longer valid or why he couldn't pay now or why the account belonged to an ex-husband who'd absconded to Orlando with that chippie from the Meineke muffler shop, etc. This was where Dave liked to swoop in, commandeering the employee's computer mouse to click the TERMINATE CALL icon, then removing the headset from the employee's head and fitting it onto his own head, coolly adjusting it like an astronaut prepping for liftoff. Leaning across the desk, he'd click INITIATE NEXT CALL. "Take notes," he'd command.

Because Dave could work miracles, on the phone. Fiber-optic cables were like a frizzy extension of his will; by the power of his voice, he could move people's hands toward their checkbooks, dictate the numbers they scrawled, could extract from them their bank and routing numbers as easily as a cane-pole fisherman drawing bream out of a farm pond. Not through charm (though his arsenal included a salesmanish version of that) and not through its antithesis, coercion (though browbeating was an old specialty of his), but through a counterbalanced combination of the two that called to mind an expert dog trainer, with the *sit* and *stay* commands swapped for *shut up* and *pay.* The key, he'd discovered, was never to listen to the debtors, because listening only complicated what was in essence as simple and choiceless an exchange as passing through the Bayonne tolls. You had to let them talk, of course — they hung up if you didn't — but you couldn't *listen* to them talk, because then some empathetic instinct might kick in, causing their problems — the ex-husband gone south with his chippie, the disability preventing them from working, that sort of thing — to infect *your* problem, that being how to most efficiently convince them to pay money on a debt they had every liberty to ignore. Because, if you kept your focus and your distance, you could get them to do almost *anything.* Not all of them, of course — but *enough* of them.

This was a lesson Dave had learned young, as a college student, when he'd taken a part-time job with a 1-900 psychic hotline. A killer student job: flexible hours, fair pay, crazyass stories for the amusement of his Kappa Sig brothers. All he'd had to do was answer a dedicated phone line between the hours of, say, 4 P.M. and midnight, and bend the callers' questions and dilemmas into a set of provided scripts. One night an old woman called. She'd lost her brooch. The "Lost Objects" script — he had scripts for everything: love, death, illness, sports predictions — instructed him to tell her the object was in a "place of meaning," and to walk her through the history of the loss without ever asking, as a parent advises a child with a misplaced toy, the last place she'd seen it. But Dave was bored. "Did you look under the bed?" he asked her. When she said yes, he told her to look again. "Now?" she said. Now, he answered. He waited six minutes — with the meter running at $3.99 per, though, since he didn't work on commission, this was insignificant — until she returned to the telephone, panting, to say nossir. "Check behind the refrigerator," he told her next. It was so friggin *beautiful,* listening to her grunt as she heaved the fridge forward, that Dave had to bite his sleeve to muffle his amazed laughter. For the next seven weeks Dave experimented with increasingly absurd variations on this theme, persuading people to throw away their toasters, mail him nude Polaroids (that worked with two chicks, both of them ferociously ugly, but he'd kept the photos anyway), rename their pets, bet their savings on racehorses with eleven-letter names, and, in one instance, urinate into the scotch bottle of an abusive and potentially unfaithful husband (to which he also listened, until he heard the presumed husband enter, midstream, and heard the caller say "ohmygod" before the line went dead). It was like long-distance puppetry, and Dave excelled at it.

"Mrs. Garcia," he would say, as the employee avoided Dave's bossman stare by eyeing the keyboard in pseudo-concentration, "I understand your predicament. I *empathize.* But I gotta predicament, too." (A pause, as he prepared to deepen his voice, serrate his tone.) "Mine is that I've got an apparent case of fraud in front of me. You borrowed seven hundred dollars from Cashomatic PayDay, and the account history I'm looking at"—a lie, since Dave had no access to histories—"suggests you never intended to repay that money. That smells like fraud. That fits the definition. But—no, no, you need to listen, this is important—Cashomatic is willing to settle this without formal legal action. Without any kind of seizure. Without anyone showing up, unannounced, at your home or place of work. I'm authorized to waive the interest and penalties on this debt, and cut the principal by"—this fraction was always dictated by the debtor's resistance level—"half. But you need to decide *now,* do you understand? Because there's a deadline on this account, and it's scheduled to move to our legal department tomorrow morning. And I can assure you things get ugly, not to mention *extremely* expensive, from there."

The end result: Marcella Garcia of Holbrook, Arizona (a cashier at Jack in the Box whose stated predicament involved rebuilding her life after a bout of methamphetamine addiction while caring for a brain-damaged three-year-old), pays $412.50 ($62.50 added to the settlement as a "processing fee") on a $700 payday loan on which she defaulted twelve years earlier, a loan Cashomatic charged off ten years earlier (before going bankrupt in the wake of a books-cooking scandal) and which was expunged from her credit history five years earlier—a debt, therefore, that wasn't presently affecting her, adversely or otherwise. The end result: $412.50 for a debt that ARC paid 6.6 cents to acquire, and which Dave spent seventeen minutes collecting, or as he put it, "recovering." The end result: the American Dream, at least from Dave's end of the phone line, by which the son of a

Turnpike toll collector acquires and assetizes, acquires and assetizes, marries a hot widowed actress who knows the correct way to pronounce "Bulgari," then sets her up in a 4,400-square-foot house with a three-car garage and a swimming pool and the builder's top-of-the-line "Brazilian hardwood" option. "There," he would tell the employee, clicking TERMINATE CALL with a fat prideful flourish. "Keep *your* mouth moving, not theirs. You play them right, and they'll do anything. Get 'em to pee in a scotch bottle if you want. *Anything.*"

In the kitchen he encountered Sara from the backside, his favorite view. He'd met her this way — on a standing-room-only New Jersey transit train out of Penn Station, him seated, her standing, that cotton-clad rump just inches from his twitchy rabbity nose; relinquishing her his seat had sparked small talk, then the exchange of cell numbers, then dinner in Sparta, then by and by this: her standing in the kitchen they'd designed together, loading the Thanksgiving dessert dishes into a custom-panel Viking Intelli-Wash dishwasher — and three years of full-frontal togetherness plus one surgical enhancement had done little to broaden the specificity of his attraction. He set down his beer glass and placed his hands on her hips, paying tribute to that attraction by giving her rear a few herky-jerky but affectionate crotch-thrusts. He calculated the odds of her unbuttoning her slacks right then and there as being about seven million to one, give or take a million, but then what were the odds of him having sculpted a triple-coil turd? Biology was his amigo today.

Or maybe not. Startled and jostled, Sara muttered "Jesus, Dave" as three dessert spoons went fumbling from her hand down to the floor.

"What?" He was still pumping a bit.

"Seriously, Dave," she said, bending to retrieve the spoons. From her forehead she wiped away a few strands of blonde hair disheveled by his dry-humped endearment. "Enough."

Dave shrugged, rebuffed, then investigated the refrigerator. "Any more of that pie left?" he asked.

"Tell me you're not still hungry."

"I didn't say I was hungry," he said. "I asked if we still had some of that pie. There's a difference."

"I saved some for Alexis."

"She won't eat it. No dairy, remember? Bad for the you-know-what."

"Well, let her decide that. Everything okay out there? I'm almost done . . ."

"It's all good," Dave said, shifting glass containers around in the fridge, unpiling and repiling them. "Your sister's scowling, Jeremy's doing his knitting. Hey, where's all the beer? Christ, I bought a whole case."

"Jeremy put it outside."

Dave straightened. "Outside?"

"In the snow," she said. "Smaller carbon footprint, or something like that."

Dave's jaw dropped loose. "But more of *my* footprints, jeezum." He shut the refrigerator with a sour grunt. "So, really . . . I gotta put my fucking boots on to get a beer?"

"Sorry," she said, raising her hands to denote helplessness. "You know how he is."

"Fruitycake, that's what."

"Be nice," she said.

"I'm always nice." There went that grin of his, the same one he'd flashed her that evening on the train when she'd agreed to give up her cell number. For mysterious reasons people called this a "shit-eating grin."

"Am I nice, or am I nice?" he went on. "I'm nice."

"You're nice," she agreed.

"I'm *so* nice, see, I'm gonna go dig around in the snow for my own friggin beer." This he said with the benevolent gusto of someone heading out to donate a kidney, just for the altruistic hell of it. Dave knew Sara shared enough of Liz and Jeremy's liberal tendencies for him not to belabor the carbon footprint issue. Better to play along, he thought. He waited to be buttered with praise.

"Want to be even nicer?" she said, in a decidedly unbuttered tone.

"I think I'm red-lining already."

"Take the trash out for me?"

Dave sighed through his flat nose. Snubbed, scolded, and then saddled with a chore. This was not lifting his buzz. Practiced in the art of "recovery," however—in extracting from people what they don't want to give—Dave made one final attempt at Sara's affections, giving her right buttock a firm, piggy, I'm-not-done-with-you cupping. "That's nice, too," he said quietly, in what he thought was seductive understatement.

But Sara said nothing—just hit the switch for the sink disposal, which gurgled and slurped and filled the room with a harsh machine racket that seemed intended to drive him out. Not even a coquettish wink, or the promise of "later" that she used to whisper in his ear. He stood there, looking victimized. Frankly he thought he deserved a little something-something for having put up with Liz and Jeremy all day, for biting his cranberry-sauced tongue when Jeremy had launched into a rant about "factory farming" at the dinner table, thereby insulting the turkey Sara had so expertly, Food Network–edly roasted. But no: *nada*. He feared his holiday might have peaked on the potty.

Bundling himself like a polar explorer, he cursed the forced switch from Weejuns to snowboots and all the political deviance it represented. Outside, he was distracted from the search for his organically chilling beer by the spectacle of his kingdom, all 2.11 acres of it covered in a moon-colored blanket of snow so plump and waveless that it resembled marshmallow cream. After dumping thirty inches on northern New Jersey, the snowstorm had finally ebbed, and the landscape—quiet to begin with—seemed gripped by a weird, muffled stillness: a snow coma. Dave dragged the trash bags down the path that Raymond had shoveled for him ("good for the old ticker," he'd said, pink-faced and jolly). He heaved them into the roller bin beside the garage, then paused to take stock of the bestilled landscape from this slightly different angle.

Pedro, the only Mexican plowman Dave had ever encountered, was out on Russell Lane, scritch-scratching the pavement as he cleared the driveways to three houses, almost identical to Dave and Sara's, and twelve empty lots. For a moment Dave felt sorry for Pedro, pulling a holiday shift, then wondered if Mexicans even celebrated Thanksgiving. He didn't recall any beaner pilgrims. He also didn't know why the developer forced Pedro to clear the driveways to the empty lots—who was going to scope out homesites during a blizzard?—but then Dave's low opinion of the developer precluded any reasonable theories. The sufficient answer was: Because he's a prick, that's why. Dave would have gleefully organized a lynching party among the neighbors if there had been any neighbors to organize.

Greg Russell—that was the developer, the greasy grand poobah of Russell Estates, LLC—had promised an "ultra-exclusive" neighborhood of fifteen luxury homes. Two years later, however, Russell Estates consisted of the house Dave and Sara had built, a smaller one built by a Pakistani orthodontist, and the model home; the rest of the development was bare graded dirt poked with weak little FOR SALE signs. From what Dave had gathered, Russell had never had the proper funding to begin with; just the land, a bulldozer, and a boneheaded mixture of hope and greed. The rumor was that he'd scammed the 112 acres—gorgeous rolling hills, about 60 acres of them covered in second-growth hardwoods, plus a wide ribbon of wetlands bisecting its middle—from an old spinster he'd befriended. This was way back when, when she and her brother had operated a chicken farm on the property, but the brother died, the old lady morphed into a chickenless shut-in, and then came Russell to the screen door, offering to mow her lawn if she'd let him deer-hunt on the back sixty. No one knew how, but Russell had somehow weaseled her into deeding him the land, which he'd promptly started logging three days after her death. Cleared the whole damn parcel, laid a horseshoe-shaped road on it, then constructed a rococo, foam-concrete entranceway—RUSSELL ESTATES: A LUXURY COMMUNITY—with columns, caps, pediments, three thousand dollars' worth of pansies, and a foam-concrete sculpture of a bucking stallion onto which a local yahoo had painted red tears (probably, Dave and Russell agreed, one of the eco-ninnies who'd opposed the subdivision permit). Dave should've figured Russell for a fraud—he prided himself on his radar that way—but Sara had gotten all misty-headed about the views (they *were* pretty magnificent, if you were into that sort of thing) and about the "community stables" and equestrian trails Russell had promised for the long term. She'd swooned. Whispered hot breathy things in Dave's ear, things that'd gelatinized his good sense.

There were no stables, of course. Hardly any houses, for that matter. Just Pedro, the Snow Spic, clearing this oxbow to nowhere, while King Dave of Masoli stood watching from on high. He'd sell the goddamn house if the real estate market hadn't tanked; right now they'd be gobsmack lucky to break even. And, Christ, all the issues; Russell's houses were built to last a season, tops. An offset crack in the foundation. Drippy white stains between the pool's deck and bond beam. Popped nails and buckling in all the windows. The veneer already peeling from the kitchen cabinets, which weren't supposed to be veneered to begin with. Insufficient flashing around the chimney, resulting in a water-logged attic. "What'd you expect?" his golfing buddy Pete had said to him. "The houses they build these days, they ain't designed to outlast the warranty period. Back in the old days, they built 'em to pass down to their kids, y'know? Who the hell you know now who's living in the old family homeplace?" Into Dave's mind had entered a vision of himself occupying his parents' shabby little bungalow in Rahway, causing him to shudder so violently that he shanked the ball with his seven iron.

Surveying the not-neighborhood now, he decided it didn't look quite so abortive and barren beneath all the snow—though maybe only in the way a corpse doesn't look so bad after someone drapes a sheet over it. Regardless, it was better than the view inside—Jeremy no doubt explaining why the Cowboys cheerleaders' uniforms were sexist and exploitative, rather than magically delicious—so Dave fetched a cigar from his shirt pocket. He lit the cigar, a high-end Nicaraguan torpedo. As always, life improved. Unlike the proverbial cat to which he'd been recently likened, Dave had never eaten a canary, but he guessed they might taste something like this.

Except soon the cigar began to stink. He pulled it from his mouth and stared at it. Number eight on *Cigar Aficionado*'s top twenty-five cigars of the year, with a Sumatra seed wrapper around Costa Rican leaf, ten bucks a pop, supposedly heavy on pepper and leather flavors with an espresso-bean finish. And it smelled like a friggin skunk fart. But then, no, scratch that: Bringing the cigar to his nose, Dave sniffed its smoke plume, twice, then a third time, finally acquitting it from blame. So what the hell *was* that smell? He flipped the lid on the trash bin beside him and took an investigative whiff. All he got there was a mixture of gravy odor and whatever the chemical was that they impregnated the trash bags with to make them smell like a mountain meadow or feminine deodorizing products. Just about then, however, with his nose probing the trash bin like a wine expert's assessing an old Bordeaux, Dave recognized the smell—unmistakable, once he'd pegged it. He grinned, and not only because he was instantly transported back to 1984 when Bon Jovi opened for the Scorpions at Madison Square Garden and Matt Rocca showed up with some trip-weed his hippie brother had brought back from Kathmandu. Sauntering farther down the path, his cigar jutting from his smile, he turned the corner to the dark little alcove where the central air conditioning unit sat hidden inside a semicircle of dwarf boxwoods.

"Busted," he announced.

Alexis shrieked in terror, her arms gyrating so wildly that she ejected the contents of both hands—her cellphone shooting one way, the joint she'd been smoking the other. But she wasn't alone. Some kid was standing beside her, a slim shadow raising his hands slowly to show they were empty.

Pricked by the indignity of her surprise, once she'd identified her stepfather behind the orange nub of his cigar, she pouted at him and snarled, "What are you *doing*, perv?"

"I know what *I'm* doing," he replied, his mad hatter's grin fading as he sized up the terrified-looking kid frozen beside her. "What're *you* doing?"

"It's medical, okay?" she said, bending to retrieve the joint and cellphone from atop the snow. With her coat sleeve she wiped the snow from the phone's screen. "It helps with my condition."

"It helps you shit?"

"Whatever," she said.

"Who's this?"

"Who's what?"

"Who's *what?* Him."

"That's Miguel." To Miguel she said, sighing, "My stepdad."

The kid nodded, dropping his hands, while Dave leaned in for a closer look. The kid was Latino, he noted, and—no way around it—a handsome little devil, with a narrow smoldery face and soccer-star frame. Skittish-looking, but Dave guessed that was to be expected in the present weed-perfumed circumstances. Dave snorted. "Who's Miguel?" he said to them both.

"He goes to Sussex," answered Alexis, Miguel affirming this with another nod. "Let's not make an issue out of this, okay? With you-know-who?"

Dave pursed his lips. *Goes to Sussex:* This was a cryptic answer, even for the reliably cryptic Alexis. And what precisely was the issue she didn't want Sara digesting, he wondered. The pot—or the presence of Enrique Iglesias here, hiding in the shrubs?

She and Dave had what might be called an "understanding," despite his geopolitical alliance with Sara. Or if not an understanding, then a kind of caustic accommodation—a mutual tolerance manifesting itself in the kind of thorny banter that cocktail waitresses engage in with their dumpy regulars: lewd jokes, hard-edged teasing, recurrent bouts of eye-rolling. He called her Lexi, which Sara abhorred ("that's a stripper name," she protested), and, privately, she called him "perv," owing to her exploration one night—accidental, but exceedingly thorough—of his unsavory internet browser history. That discovery—in which she'd reveled, acidly, for the power it gave her—had shifted the relationship, infusing it with something oozy and potentially toxic but also, to Dave's thinking, kind of . . . stirring. It was as if they'd lowered their human masks—the do-right businessman, the Honor Roll teen—to reveal something meaner and more reptilian behind them: the lecher, the blackmailer. The benign teasing she'd formerly directed Dave's way—dubbing him her "step-guido," taunting him for the undone top buttons of his shirts, his Rocawear sweaters, the tinted windows on his Escalade, the way his dancefloor moves were limited to punching the air in slipshod time with a song—had turned darker, aimed deeper. She'd redrawn her cartoon of him, depicting him as a goatish old sadsack, as discontented with his life with Sara—albeit far differently—as she herself was. "Having a little *me* time?" she'd say, as she passed by his home office. "I'll just close the door for you," punctuating it with a cold wink. Or in the aftermath of a spat between him and Sara: "Guess you'll be working late tonight, huh?" This had chafed Dave, at first, until he'd formulated a defense, which was more like a plea of *nolo contendere:* Copping to the perv charge, he'd taken to constantly quizzing her about her own sexual hijinks, real or imagined, with just enough quasi-parental disapproval in his tone to maintain a staged sense of decorum. As in, "I hope you kept it to just a blowjob tonight," when she'd roll in late on a Friday night. Or, in the present instance, as he watched her peck away at her cellphone while poor Enrique/Miguel stood there wetting himself: "What're you—getting a little action out here in the bushes?"

"You wish," she said.

"I just stopped by to say hi," the kid piped in, adding, with a thumb cocked in the direction of the plow truck uphill, "while my dad's working."

Huh. Dave processed this while chewing his cigar. So this Miguel was

Pedro's son. He did a little kneejerk calculus, putting one and one and then maybe one more together to solve the alcove equation: Miguel must be her dealer. Sure, okay—that made sense. Jumping out of the plow truck to drop off a—what'd they used to call it? A dime bag, yeah—while Papa Pedro scraped the Lane to Nowhere for whatever Frito-Lay products Russell probably paid him with. Then naturally sneaking in a little product test with Lexi. This was sweet. This was dirt. Dave grinned. "So, what," he said to her, "you got a prescription for that?"

Alexis snapped shut her phone and said, "It helps, okay?"

"Bet it does." He grinned at Miguel, who did not grin back but instead licked his lips and glanced sideways in a manner suggesting he was still mired in the disagreeable process of wetting his pants.

"Seriously," she said. "Look online. It's, like, the best treatment ever for IBS." As if to demonstrate her point, she pursed her lips around the joint, blazing the ember at its end. The long hiss of her inhale came to a sharp stop, however, as she coughed the smoke back up. The resulting cloud was thick and dense enough to obscure her face altogether. Waving away the cloud, she barked a few more coughs, her chagrined efforts to suppress them almost poignant. She tried passing it to Miguel but he waved his arms no: not the groovy-cool *I've-had-enough* wave no, Dave noticed, but a more adamant, appalled refusal, an *I-don't-even-know-what-that-illegal-shit-is* wave no, all of which widened the smile behind Dave's cigar. "Amateur," he sniffed.

"Like—you'd know," she spluttered.

"Hand it over."

Miguel peeked around the corner, presumably hoping for a rescue by his dad.

"Fuck off," she said.

"You need some instruction," he said. "Give it here."

She did so, but reluctantly, as if fearing his instruction might involve throwing it down into the snow, coupled with a lecture about the evils of dope, etc. When he replaced his cigar with the joint, crabbing up his face as he took a long macho drag from it, her mouth flopped open. "This is so fucked up," she said to Miguel. "I'm getting high with my stepdad."

"Yeah," came Miguel's reply.

"Yeah . . ." Dave echoed him, but then it was his turn to cough. "Gaw," he cried, his cheeks wiggling, shoulders shaking, as he hacked the smoke back up. The coughs, searing and unstoppable, bent his body and yanked tears from his eyes. Doubled over, he offered the joint back to Lexi, certain he was about to see pinkish lung flecks dappling the snow. Just how would he explain *that* at the emergency room? Snatching it back, she sniffed, "Amateur."

"Jesus," he wheezed. "What the fuck *is* that? That's *harsh*. Holy . . ."

"It's medical grade."

"Christ," he said, still wheezing. He put a hand to his chest while leveling a cold glare at Miguel, who had somehow, he couldn't help feeling, just shown him up. "I'm cured a' *something*."

Alexis took another drag from it, more gently this time. No coughs followed—just a smooth, vampish exhale (were those *smoke rings?*) that felt, to Dave, like cocky one-upmanship. Now everyone was showing him up. Pouting, he wondered if he'd suddenly morphed into a Raymond—the impotent old coot, publicly tolerated but privately mocked. You wouldn't want him having your back in a fight against some guys from Hopatcong High, but sharing a joint with him outside by the trash cans . . . eh, not so bad. This was an intolerable thought. "Not that *I* need any curing," he said, brushing his chest as if the purpose of his hand there had been to dust snow off his coat, rather than to salve the fierce pain he'd been feeling. "Not in the shitting department, anyway. Here, gimme another toke of that."

He hadn't smoked pot in—what, twenty years? And in that weedless meantime he'd turned against it—bitterly so, after then-candidate Bill Clinton made his oily crack about smoking but not inhaling it. He'd forgotten, until now, how much damn fun it had been, sneaking out back of the house as a teenager, giddy and terrified as he fired up a bowl, then floating back inside to giggle right beside the old man at whatever was on the tube. He'd had a girlfriend back then, Alcee Vercellino, who wouldn't fool around *unless* she was high; though after that, man, it was no holds barred. She'd unstrap her bra before he'd even dug a hand in there. They'd drive to the Newton Reservoir in his mother's big brown Delta 88, find the blackest, most secluded place to park, jam some Styx or Molly Hatchet into the cassette player, pass a poorly rolled joint back and forth in the backseat, and then just go *at* it, like rabbits, stoned rabbits. (Dave still saw Alcee, every now and then, at the ShopRite, and once at the Home Depot over in Newton. She'd gotten fat as a house, which gave him the liberty to pretend he didn't recognize her.) Shifting from his reminiscence, which left a warm, briny residue in his mind, he looked down at Lexi and wondered what the setup was for kids like her: whether or not the Newton Reservoir was still fuck central, and how these poor kids managed to get it on comfortably without the plush generous expanse of an Oldsmobile's backseat. Shit, at seventeen, she had to be getting it on—but where, and with who? He sized up Miguel again, tilting him sideways in his imagination so that he was on top of Lexi, then tilting him the other way (whee!) so that he was under Lexi . . . naw, he decided. Lexi was too snotty to be plowing the blowman's kid. Wait a sec—too snotty to be blowing the plowman's kid, he'd meant. What was this shit?

"Thanks for the overshare," she said coolly, immune to his insult. She was used to him making fun of her Irritable Bowel Syndrome, which he sometimes called Irritable Butt Syndrome. "Glad to hear *something's* working for you."

"Seriously," he said, his voice pinched and wheezy from trying to hold the pot smoke captive in his lungs. "I'm the world's greatest shitter."

Miguel put a hand to his mouth, stifling a laugh.

"I didn't know there were, like, competitions," Alexis said.

"Here." He fetched his cellphone from his belt holster. "Check the proof."

"What, you keep a record?" Apprehension paled her face.

"I got proof, just hold on," he said, squinting at the phone, thumbing its buttons.

"You're so fucking *weird.*"

"Check this," he said, holding out the phone.

Jumping back from the sight of it, she bounced into a dwarf boxwood before Miguel caught her. "Fuck!" she bawled. "Did you just show me a picture of your *shit?*"

He turned the phone inward, smiling, to re-admire the photo. "That's what you're aiming for on the can, baby. That right there."

Flatly, she said, "Ohmygod, I am so going to hurl."

"I'm just sayin, that's a keeper." He was still admiring it as she passed the joint—now just a half-inch nub—back to him. He offered a view to

Miguel, who did that same crossed-arm wave with which he'd refused the joint, but when Dave said, "C'mon," with a fat exhale of smoke, Miguel leaned in gingerly and took a wincing peep at the photo. "That's an achievement, right there, huh?" Dave said, turning the screen back to give it another look of his own. He frowned at it, rotating the phone. "It's kinda corkscrewed, isn't it?"

"I cannot fucking believe you took a photo of your own . . . *shit*. That is so, so wrong. You're, like, the ultra-perv." Like an unexpected gas bubble, however, a burst of laughter escaped her, which caused Dave to laugh, too: those raucous, infectious, irrepressible marijuana giggles. "Oh my fucking *God*," she squealed, that sideways smile now open and wide. Miguel just shook his head, by all appearances hoping his father might lasso him at the soonest possible moment.

"And I don't even need no performance-enhancing drugs," Dave said, taking a final, fingertip-scorching drag from the dying joint, then flicking it down to the snow.

"You are so, *so* sick," Alexis said, as a clear compliment. Another spasm of laughter convulsed her.

"What, 'cause I poop?"

"No, perv. Because you take *pictures* of it."

"Just this one. That's a framer."

"Uh, *no*."

"Uh no, *what?* Like you can do better?"

"Dude, I can't even *do*, remember? IBS?"

"Wah wah." Dave made a sad-clown face. "Excuses."

"You're really a dick, you know that?"

They froze, suddenly stricken. "Dave?" a voice was calling from around back.

"Oh shit, it's Uncle Jeremy," Lexi hissed.

"Fuck me," Dave snapped, panicking. Jeremy finding him getting high with Alexis: That was nothing short of the apocalypse. Liz would sound the sirens at full volume. The entire world would crack open, sending Dave to his death in a hot bath of lava. "Okay, call me," he heard Alexis saying to Miguel, and from the corner of his eye he saw Miguel plant a quick smooch on Lexi's cheek before he went scampering toward the front of the house. Dave wasn't worrying about Miguel just then. He stomped his boot in the snow, roughly close to where he'd tossed the remains of the joint. Then he stomped again, beside there, and once more, beside there. He looked like he was trying to kill the rare New Jersey snow snake.

"I'm gone," Lexi said, scooting out between the dwarf boxwoods and fleeing toward the front of the house, the same scamper-route Miguel had taken. Dave started to follow, then reconsidered, then reconsidered his re-considering, his feet going one way then the other.

"Dayyy-eeeve?" Jeremy shouted again, either louder or moving closer. Jeremy's shouts, Dave couldn't help noticing, sounded like yodels.

"Right here," Dave called back, sucking on his cigar to build up the biggest, masking-est Costa Rican leaf cloud possible, then gulping cold air and re-sucking it like a hungry infant at the dry end of a bottle. Very very slowly, he walked back down the path, trailing a steam engine's billow of smoke. At the corner of the house he collided with Jeremy.

"The beer's right by the door," Jeremy said, all measly-faced and con-trite.

"Been looking everywhere," Dave mumbled, still puffing wildly on the cigar. His mouth felt like he'd been chewing on a sweater. In addition, he couldn't feel anything from the waist down, as if his thighs had broken loose and would at any moment abandon his torso to continue down the path. This, he knew, would be regrettable on several levels.

"Sorry, man," Jeremy said. "Thought I'd save you a few kilowatts, stash-ing it out here."

"I can spare the fucking kilowatts," Dave grumbled.

Back in the family room, Jeremy and Dave found everyone (save Lexi) still gathered in front of the big-screen, Sara now nestled between her mother and father, the Cowboys having maintained their lead into the fourth quarter, Aidan still watching from the floor with that far-out, far-off expression of his, which might possibly be evidence of another marijuana habit in the extended family. Maybe pot brownies were a remedy for glu-ten allergies. For the first time, Dave noticed how big the kid's feet were — they were huuuuuge, like floppy clown feet, maybe larger than Dave's own feet, which he felt the immediate need to check, to confirm they hadn't scooted out ahead of him.

Dave was lurking at the edge of the room, examining Aidan's sneakers vis-à-vis his own Weejuns, when Raymond exclaimed, "Dave!'" Startled,

Dave glanced up. Raymond was six inches off the seat, risen with glee as if they were reuniting after a multi-year separation. "Thought a bear might've got ya," he said. Dave watched Bev's eyes crinkle in amusement. So did Raymond, who crinkled his own eyes back at her. Crinkle crinkle crinkle. "Did a bear get ya, Dave?" he said.

"Bear . . ." This was as much as Dave could say, and even this he didn't say skillfully. More like "Burrrrrr . . ."

All eyes, none of them crinkled any longer, turned toward Dave. "You all right, honey?" Sara asked. At this a jolt of panic went rattling through him, and he pulled his gaze away from Raymond to meet Sara's stare directly. She looked baffled. And possibly angry. He noted an irked eyebrow, riding just a bit higher than its opposite-eye partner, the way the fur on an annoyed cat's spine rises. Could she smell it on him? Holy fucking macaroni. Could everybody? And where were his goddamn legs? "Yeah," he said, more chirpily than he'd intended—more chirpily, in fact, than he'd ever spoken the word *yeah* in his life. Like a chipmunk had hijacked his vocal cords. Then, by dint of explanation, he added, "It's cold out there."

"That's my fault," Jeremy said, returning to his position behind Aidan. He seemed genuinely penitent, which Dave liked to see.

"Well, take a load off then," said Raymond. "You sure were right about those Cowboys. It's just . . . a massacre, I tell ya."

Sitting—God, sitting down felt like the greatest thing that had ever happened to Dave. It was as if he'd spent the entirety of his forty-six years upright until some samaritan had confided to him, "You know, bending your legs, and putting your ass on something—it's really quite pleasant, give it a whirl." He emitted one of those meaty-sounding groans that tended to alarm Liz. Beyond the physical relief, however, sitting also brought some clarity to his mind. To wit: "Medical-grade" marijuana, whatever that was, was a vastly different species of grass than the shit he'd been smoking in 1980, back when Alcee Vercellino weighed 110 pounds and would put out, oh so spectacularly, for a doobie hit. He was in over his head, he realized, and needed to be *very* careful; he didn't remember ever feeling this way, back when he'd sit giggling at *Barney Miller* punchlines beside his father—he'd never felt this woozy and trippy, this freakin *legless.* Also: Aidan's feet weren't really *that* enormous, upon closer inspection. Must've been the angle, he thought. Huh. Furthermore: The color quality on his eighty-two-inch LCD screen was miraculous, and incontrovertible proof that God not only existed, no matter what Liz and Jeremy might say, but that He loved us all. It was as if God, wearing a divine Best Buy jersey, had personally installed a rainbow in Dave's family room. As well: There was a beer in his hand, but he couldn't explain how it had gotten there. And woweee was it cold.

The Raiders threw a TD with four minutes left on the clock. "Ope, ope, ope, *ope,*" Raymond chanted, though the Raiders' chances—Dave swung his hundred-pound head at the big-screen to confirm this—were nil. Along the way he noticed a one-inch zipper gap at the top of Sara's slacks, a little almond-shaped cleft opening just below a minor roll of bel-lyfat that he'd never detected before. This wasn't much to behold—it was Thanksgiving, they were all puffed and bloated—until his gaze shifted two feet to her left, where Bev was displaying a similar gap in her own zip-per, topped by a much fuller, much more major tube of bellyfat. His gaze went darting back and forth, from paunch to paunch, until he'd incised a mental line between them, at which point a whole series of lines appeared in his mind's eye, a visual grid superimposed upon the two of them: one from Sara's lush lips to her mother's parched, lipstick-clotted lips, from Sara's longish golden hair (the hair that had been lathered, so sexily, in that old Coast soap commercial, the one in which a younger Sara had cooed, "Oh, that scent!") to the fluffed white poodle curled atop her mother's scalp, from Sara's long, slightly Olive Oyl–ish neck to Bev's also long but wattled scrag, between their identical sockfeet . . . he'd never quite noticed, until now, with all that THC floating through his brain, what an exact replica of her mother Sara was. Could he stand that, twenty years hence— fucking Bev? He looked at Raymond, who was thrilling at the last point-less minute of the game, saying "Oh boyo" when the Raiders threw for a first down. Shuddering, he envisioned himself in Raymond's cheap little blue house in Ohio, wearing Raymond's clothes (navy cardigan with over-sized buttons over a plaid flannel shirt with easy-on snaps in the back, twill putter pants with an elastic waistband and fake fly), begging Bev for some gray nookie. *That's* what he'd worked for? Surely Raymond must've spent a thousand and one nights walking outside, to plead with the moon: *More. More. I want more.* But here Raymond was. Here Dave was. The game ended. "They sure gave it their goshdarn best, didn't they?" said Raymond to no one.

Dave's cellphone beeped. Grunting, he unsheathed it from its holster and flipped it open. What appeared on the screen brought forth from him an explosive, room-shaking laugh, as if he'd belched up a Roman candle. He stifled it as best he could, though not before everyone's attention — quizzical, from some quarters; contemptuous, from others — had been drawn to him.

"What is it?" Sara asked.

On the screen was a photo message. In the photo was a single, small, demure-looking turd, like a fat little *perfecto* cigar, lying at the base of a toilet — Dave recognized it as the toilet in the downstairs half bath. In the photo's foreground was a raised middle finger, its fingernail adorned with chipped purple polish.

"Pete," he lied, with a fingertip sponging a tear from his eye. "It's Pete. You know how Pete is." He snapped the cellphone closed. "Not for family consumption." He frowned at Aidan. "Man stuff."

Vacantly, Sara nodded, while Liz shook her head and gave Jeremy a peeved black look signaling *Time to go.* Dave tried to suppress further giggling by drinking his beer, but the actions clashed, causing the beer to boil and go spurting down his chin and neck.

"Something's wrong with Uncle Dave," said Aidan.

"Be polite," said Jeremy, kneading the boy's shoulder in very very clear agreement.

7

THE EAST RIVER, on its short, telescoping passage from Long Island Sound to Upper New York Bay, picks up speed as it forks at Roosevelt Island, then slows back down until it narrows near Delancey Street and the Williamsburg Bridge, where it begins hastening again as it goes churning 'round the bend at Wallabout Bay and past the yellow-pine caissons sunk beneath the Brooklyn Bridge. At this point it is flowing at a slightly faster pace than the average human walker—more equivalent, that is, to the ever-hustling pedestrians of Manhattan. On its western bank, from 125th Street down to the South Street Viaduct, the river's course is hugged by the FDR Drive, parts of which were built upon rubble imported from Bristol, England, after the German Luftwaffe bombed Bristol to gray smithereens. Prior to that, the river lapped Front Street, one block to the west, which has retained its name despite no longer fronting anything; before that, it bordered Water Street, two blocks farther westward, and no longer, of course, on any water; and before that, the East River met Manhattan at Pearl Street, which was named for the glittering oyster shells that once adorned its shores. This fattening of lower Manhattan, 350 years in the making, was accomplished via landfill, the streets and buildings overlaid upon the shattered remnants of bombed foreign ports, upon infinite piles of brown earth hauled from where hills were leveled and cellars and subway tunnels dug, upon shipwreck debris, broken stoneware, ash, offal, horse carcasses, dung, apple cores, glass shards, grease, and other assorted garbage, piled onto the banks via shovels, pails, horse-drawn carts, bulldozers, and dump trucks.

A few blocks north of Delancey Street, four stories above solid Manhattan schist, Talmadge Bertrand tucked the last of the Thanksgiving leftovers into the snow on the roof, to keep them chilled until tomorrow, and glanced eastward toward the river, across those landfilled blocks whose history Micah had taught him. His cheeks were reddened, but from warmth rather than cold, and an interior warmth at that: from contentment, and possibly even joy, though at this late hour he was too stoned and booze-headed to parse the distinctions. In some odd and uplifting way, he'd felt like a bona fide adult for the first time in his life tonight. They'd *entertained,* he and Micah, like some old married couple . . . but some *cool* old married couple, he amended himself, some cool old married couple still fond of loud music and loosey-goosey late nights, like the Hendersons back home though (on second thought) without the suicidal son and the daughter in rehab and all the rumors about swinger parties that his mother had kept in circulation for at least fifteen years. Micah had set the table with hand-sewn cloth napkins, arrayed it with candles, and decorated it with orange and yellow sycamore leaves she'd gathered from Tompkins Square Park. She'd even fetched him and Matty a little decanter type of thing, to make their whiskey look proper. (A fifth of Heaven Hill on the table, she'd said, was too country even for her.) And man, the freakin dinner she'd cooked: a tofu roll that she'd stuffed with a mixture of onions, celery, bread, and walnuts, plus some herbs and other stuff; cranberry sauce (from dented cans, but she'd doctored it up somehow); curried carrots, like she must've tasted when she was in India, or so Talmadge figured; and some sort of vegetable mashup whose ingredients he couldn't quite inventory but that he'd been unable to stop eating. Plus that re*donk*ulously good pie.

He kept glancing across the candlelight at her, as she listened to Matty going off on one of his unhinged, semi-hilarious rants, and every time she'd smile or laugh Talmadge felt this blast of . . . it was like heat, but low-grade heat, not like the heat you felt during sex, which was burning heat, big fat log heat blazing you from the inside out, but more like the softer, moister radiator heat you felt afterwards, when it was over, and you were just lying there, recouping your breath and wanting so badly to say something but never knowing what. After all these months spent in each other's exclusive company, tonight he'd been able to glimpse himself and Micah through another person's eyes—Matty's, which were kinda screwy eyes, but whatever. And what he'd seen through that lens, he'd liked. Something true, something ancient, something *sustainable*.

He stood there for a while, by the thick steel-clad door, looking toward the river, his heart hot and melty. It didn't look like a river, from his vantage—just a ribbon of blackness interrupting the dense urban light grid, an absence rather than a presence. His eyes were drawn to the long glinting bridges spanning it, with the stalled traffic on the Williamsburg Bridge resembling a festive string of white lights hung for the season. Then he peered upward, to where a narrow sliver of moon hung tilted in the sky, so minimized by the quivering radiance below it—by the million-windowed incandescence of Manhattan, its infiniteness of glowing filaments, the excess lumens hurled skyward into a blue-yellow penumbra—that the moon appeared quaint and obsolete up there, like a rowboat docked beside a cruise ship. He recalled his father's glee after purchasing an electric bugzapper for the family fishing camp, up on Black Creek near Uncle Lenord's. Dick Bertrand had hauled Talmadge, aged seven or thereabouts, onto his big pleated lap and said, "Watch this": moths and gnats and fireflies and beetles and dragonflies orbiting the blue cylinder until, *bzzzzp,* they'd hit it and explode, two thousand volts of electricity spraying bug parts into a micro-dappled circle on the concrete porch. "Dumb little buggies," Dick Bertrand told Talmadge, patting the knob of his kneecap. "They think it's the moon. Ain't that somethin?"

Back downstairs, in the shuddery bronze light of the apartment, he checked on Matty before making his way to the bedroom. "You good, dude?"

From the floor, where he was laid out beneath a wool blanket, Matty signaled thumbs-up. "The Son of Man," he said, cocking his thumb toward the biblical passage graffitied onto the wall, "has a place to lay his head."

"Matty 8:20," Talmadge said, circling the room to blow out the candles.

"You got it, man." Slyly, with one side of his mouth curved upward, Matty added, "I might get frisky with Maybelle tonight."

Pausing to ogle Maybelle's pale, impastoed haunches, Talmadge said, "Be careful. She's a handful." Instantly, however, he felt an odd twinge of guilt. Despite her fecund nakedness and come-hither pose, he'd never considered Maybelle *in that way* until just now: as a pinup, a wet dreamscape. He felt as if he'd just mentally undressed the Virgin Mary, and was grateful to blow out the final candle so as not to risk the sight of Maybelle looking stricken and blasphemed. Poor pure Maybelle. He'd just handed her over to Matty like a druglord's party favor.

"Awesome," said Matty, wiggling down deeper beneath the blanket. "That was a cool night, man," he said. "I think we killed the dead lady's whiskey. Thanks for the chow."

"That was something, huh?"

"Fucking amazing. You got a cool chick."

"Yeah," Talmadge said. He sensed this compliment deserved more and better words, but he didn't possess them. "Yeah," he repeated. "I do." Then he announced he was baggin' it, and went feeling his way down the hallway to where Micah had been asleep for hours.

In their bedroom was a futon they'd cadged from an NYU dumpster. On both sides of the futon were plastic milk-crate nightstands, Talmadge's red and Micah's blue. At the foot of the futon were other plastic crates, filled with their clothes: Micah's clothes were folded into neat little mallstore stacks, while Talmadge's were squished and stuffed into the crates, sleeves and pantslegs overflowing the tops. A pair of backpacks were positioned against the near wall, and against the far wall was a choir pew salvaged from the renovation of St. Margaret Mary's on Second Avenue that they'd re-employed as a bookshelf. This sat beneath an ancient sheet of plywood boarding the room's window, onto which had been sprayed, probably decades ago, an indecipherable graffiti tag that might or might not have spelled out *jewel, jews, jaws,* or *jawas* (as in the hooded pygmy scavengers from *Star Wars:* Talmadge's preferred interpretation). Propped against a corner, too, was Micah's banjo, an heirloom from her mother, who'd gone missing just before Micah's twelfth birthday.

Though familiar, this was all barely visible to Talmadge as he tiptoed into the room, with only the nearest edges of the room's topography discernible in the dim orange glow of the kerosene heater. Aware that he was swaying from the whiskey, he navigated his way slowly, so as not to disturb and disappoint Micah by kicking something over and/or lurching toward the bed, lout-style. He undressed as quietly as he could, wincing at the heavy cowboy clink of his buckle as his belt unspooled onto the floor.

From outside, a siren yelped: one of those short, sharp squeals that New York City cops issue to nudge idling vehicles out of their path, or to put potential do-badders on notice. Underlying that was the base hum of the city, chordal and constant, like the grind of some massive hidden gears, the subterranean hamster wheel that powered the city. Talmadge was still unaccustomed to the sound of it. Like the crickets back home in Mississippi, rubbing static into the aural nightscape, the urban hum redefined silence. It went mostly unnoticed, beneath the higher-decibel soundscapes (the sirens, the sanitation truck brake-squeals, the carhorns, the seismic subway rumbles, the fragmented pedestrian babble, the irregular gin hoots of the smokers congregating outside an unmarked cocktailery four doors down), until bedtime, when Talmadge often found himself lying in the darkness trying to identify its source: air traffic, maybe, or the vibrations of the FDR Drive to the east, or a hundred thousand vacuum cleaners being operated all at once. White noise, people called it, but this seemed inaccurate to Talmadge. Snowfall: that was white noise. This noise was the color of a truck axle. He slid beneath the sheets with a movie burglar's stealth.

He was startled, then, when Micah rolled over, sharp and alert. "Hey, baby," she whispered, with what sounded like noontime wakefulness.

"You still awake?" he said. "Shit, sorry." How long had she been up — and had she been listening to him and Matty as they'd sat drinking and toking in the living room? He rewound the audio of his memory, scanning the mental tape for regrettable snippets he might need to address. He prayed she hadn't heard him and Matty caterwauling about the night a monstrously drunk Chi-O pledge named Chivers Holley had peed Talmadge's bed during sex, forcing Talmadge to request a replacement mattress from the dorm's RA. Three nights later, when he returned to the dorm room with Chivers after a more sober date, he found a plastic painter's tarp draped over his bed. After Chivers had stormed off in debased fury Matty came bursting into the room, gasping with nasty laughter. This was not the kind of reminiscing you did around Micah ("That poor girl," she would say, forcing you to think *That poor girl* and feel not amused but rather ashamed of your crass eighteen-year-old self). Nor, for that matter, did you crack jokes about getting it on with sweet chaste Maybelle. "I was just kinda chillin' with Matty," he said, adding as a preemptive defense, "Just kinda like, talking dumb college stuff."

"Naw, it's cool," she said, propping her head on a hand. "Y'all have a good time?"

"Yeah, yeah, you know. Good to reconnect. There's not many old friends, you know, I'd wanna hang with . . ."

"Yeah," she whispered.

"But, I think he's a little freaked."

"Bout what?"

"You know, the squat, the diving, the whole anti-civ rap . . ." This was true — even after Micah's lecture, Matty still kept surveying the apartment and mouthing *What the fuck?* — but Talmadge meant to illustrate another point: that the here-and-now Talmadge Bertrand was a distinct and even antithetical creature from the Talmadge Bertrand who'd laughed gutbustedly as Chivers Holley went sniffling down the dorm hallway. That he'd experienced a Great Awakening after emerging fetal and sinless from that ketamine hole in the blood-red light of that camper van, waking to a face so tender and wild he felt sure he'd died and this was Heaven, with her as his guide or his holy reward, dribbling water onto his lips with a teaspoon, whispering *hush*. That he'd renounced all his old citizenships, rewired his thinking, had thrown himself — heart, soul, mind, the "whole ench-o-lada" as Uncle Lenord would say — in with Micah: was *hers,* on almost every level. "Baby," he said, smiling a smile invisible to Micah in the darkness, "you didn't know me back when."

She said, "I know you now," and drew a fingertip across his chest, rousing the few stray pale boy-hairs.

"Well, yeah." He shrugged. "I'm just sayin."

"Are you good with you?"

Talmadge frowned. "Am I good with me — what?"

"Are you happy?"

"Am I *happy?*" he replied, the question's preposterousness causing his head to lift fractionally from the pillow. "Shee-it. Happy as a dog with two tails."

At this she laughed, lightly but appreciatively, poking his chest with her fingertip. "That's a new one, man."

"Uncle Lenord," Talmadge said. "I got hundreds."

Micah scooched closer to him, laying an arm across his chest and her cheek against his clavicle. She let out a long and conclusive-sounding sigh, as if she'd been waiting up all night to gauge his happiness quotient, and, now that she'd done so, could finally rest. This wasn't typical Micah, however. She tended to lead without glancing back; you either kept up or lost her. Talmadge knotted his forehead, wondering if he needed to ponder *her* happiness, and thinking how bizarre that would be at the end of a night like tonight, when his swollen sense of contentment had been all but popping his shirt buttons.

Out of nowhere she asked, "Are you hard down there?"

"Am I *hard?*" he spluttered, his head rising off the pillow again. "Harder than a—"

A fingertip mashed his lips. "Don't say it, man," she laughed.

"Uncle Lenord's pillow talk."

She let out a pleasantly appalled groan and rolled onto her side so that her back was toward him. "I want you to do something for me," she said.

He spooned himself beside her, his penis lurching upward as the blood came roaring into it, its head tapping her buttocks with a sudden though invited insistence. "Put it in," she whispered, and with his right hand he tried sloppily directing it, the head prodding the firm dry crevasse of her ass cheeks until pushing it downward he felt it sliding across the humid bristles of her pubes. He retreated, and then gave a delicate thrust to cleave it inside her. Missing his mark, he let out a yearnful moan and reached a hand around to clasp her right breast, the pliable lusciousness of it beneath his hand provoking an almost violent rocking of his hip. She yelped lightly as he jammed himself into some incorrectly sensitive spot, her hips recoiling. "Here," she said, reaching down and taking him into her hand to aim him herself. His chest went tight with trapped breath as he squeezed into her, the head probing the foldsome entrance gently, even meekly, before she pressed herself into him and he felt the whole shaft engulfed by her tender slickness and his breath came pouring out in loud airy heaps.

As he thrust himself upward, burying his face in the corrugated lushness of her dreadlocks, he seized her nipple between his fingers. Then he felt her remove his hand from her breast and transfer it to her belly. "Just like this," she whispered. "Don't move it."

His eyes came fluttering open. "What?"

"Just don't move it. I wanna feel it just like this, as I fall asleep."

Obligingly, he froze himself as best he could, though bewildered and not a little stung by the command. He felt himself pulsing inside her in sharp rhythmic bursts. To distract himself he focused on her belly beneath his hand, rubbing a wide and ethereal circle around her belly button until his fingertip chanced upon a tendril of pubic hair and the heady sensation of it buckled his hips, his dick blundering deeper. She clutched his hand, impounding it beneath hers against her belly, and whispered sleepily, "Still. Just still."

"This is weird, baby," he protested. "I don't know if I can."

"Please," she said, and he redoubled his effort, resisting the fervent tugging from his groin, his dick's stallion determination to pull the weight of his body ever deeper into hers. He clenched his teeth in struggle. "Like that, baby," she murmured, slow and drowsy, her voice barely audible above the city's hummy layered drone. "Be still. I just want the fullness of it. Just the fullness."

PART TWO

I

"STUPID STINK BUG," Alexis finally said to it. The bug was head-butting the walls of her room but might as well have been head-butting Alexis herself, the way it was—she'd just texted this to Miguel—"buggin the shit" out of her. She'd complained to Dave a million times about the bugs, about the way they came seeping into her room by the dozens, where they'd gang on the windowsills until by flicking on a light she'd incite them to riot and with growly buzzing they'd go divebombing her room, divebombing *her*. One of them got caught in her hair once, right behind her ear, which seriously might have been the worst experience of her life—top three, anyway. She didn't know why *her* room had to be their gateway, when her mom's room and Dave's office were right down the hall, nor did she get how nature—which, as she understood it, was supposed to be really frag-ile—could be so superabundant, so invincible, and so . . . annoying. You couldn't squish stink bugs, because when you did they spewed out that poison gas of theirs that smelled like rotting cilantro, and because Alexis despised even fresh cilantro, this was not not *so not* an option. Vacuuming them didn't work either: That just made the vacuum itself stink, thereby broadcasting the odor to the whole house every time someone used it. After Alexis's 379th complaint, her mom bought her some eco-variety of bug spray at the ShopRite, which was made out of mint oil and for some reason had a photo of a golden-Lab puppy on the label, but it didn't really do much more than annoy the stink bugs back. Doused in the stuff, they'd drop to the floor onto their backs and kick their legs for a while, like ba-bies in a crib, the cilantro and mint smells mingling into some nightmare

Thai salad odor. Dave swapped out the "bullshit green stuff" (his words) for a can of Raid, which he'd deemed "the good old bad stuff," whatever that meant, but it smelled the way bug spray probably should smell: toxic death, Satan's morning breath, the end of the world. Exhaling a measure of her aggravation through her nose, she flopped sideways on the bed to reach for the can beside her nightstand. Scooping it into her hand, she texted Miguel an update with her other hand: "Raid. Die stinkbug die."

"^5," he responded, as she rose from her bed: a high-five for her killing mission.

The stink bug seemed to sense her purpose. They were weird like that. From the window side of her room the stink bug went buzzing over to the door side, as though making a break for the hallway. Fat chance: Alexis's door was closed, because Alexis's door was always closed. The bug bounced off the poster taped to the door, on which her name was broken down into an acronym: AWESOME, LOVING, ELEGANT, X-CITING, INTELLIGENT, SUR-PRISING. She stood in the room's center, waiting for the bug to land some-where—though from her observation they didn't really land so much as crash. This one got lucky, colliding with a stack of her laundered clothes. It steadied itself on the folded corner of a blouse—a mint-green checked one that her friend Gus, depending on his mood and/or meds, called her "cowgirl shirt" or her "Taylor Swift shirt" or her "truck-stop hooker shirt." Alexis didn't like cowgirls or country music and definitely not truck stops but she did like the shirt—way too much to drench it with Raid. With her fingertip poised just above the button she pantomimed spraying the bug, in order to scare it off her shirt, but gingerly, because she also didn't want her shirt fouled with insectile cilantro stink. *Ping:* "Iz it dead yet?" Miguel texted. While she paused to answer—she always tried to be witty with him, but unable to devise a way she just tapped "No"—the stink bug made a calculated leap to her dresser, perching itself atop a framed photo-graph of her dad and engaging in what looked like push-ups and felt like taunting.

Four photographs of her dad were on the dresser top, reclining in-side Target frames. This one was the largest. In the photo he was holding Alexis, mere days old, with an unlit cigar clenched brashly between his teeth: a victor's pose, with her as his trophy. Of all the photos in the world she loved this one the most. Her mom had unearthed it for a seventh-grade school project about genetics, and, as with the other photos on her dresser, Alexis had framed it herself. Lauren Shprinzel, who'd been her best friend back then (before Lauren's older brother got killed in Iraq and Lauren went half-crazy and full-emo and asked everyone to start calling her by her brother's name), told Alexis her dad looked like Bruce Willis. This was a serious stretch, to Alexis's eye, yet ever since then she'd found herself drawn to Bruce Willis movies—nestling into one when she'd happen upon it while channel-surfing, or ordering one up on pay-per-view when she was feeling lonesome or depressed. The resemblance was negligible at best, but there he was anyway: her dad, saving the earth from a hurtling asteroid, going back in time to stop a killer virus, taking a samurai sword to a rapist in a pawnshop basement. There was odd comfort in seeing him— or some vague approximation of him, some dad-like avatar—kicking ass in the cinematic afterlife. On that same genetics project, she'd put down "hero" for her father's occupation. Her mom objected to that: "He was a bond trader, honey," she'd said. "Put down bond trader instead." (Alexis refused.)

She studied the bug for a while, which would've been more like her had she been high, which she wasn't. It looked like a gray-brown shield with legs—like a video game version of a bug, she thought. No-frills insect evil. Dave said stink bugs had come from Japan (or somewhere like that, she didn't remember), and they weren't around when he was a kid. This one crawled along the top edge of the frame, pausing directly over her dad's head. She thought maybe she could blast it from there by spraying it point-blank at an upward angle, but she didn't want to risk it. So far as she knew, that was the only copy of the photo in existence—back when she was born, people still used those old film cameras, like the one her Grandma Tooney still brought out every time Alexis visited. ("Oh, you're just the spittin' image of him," her grandma would always say, with such a surge of emotion that it seemed she'd never noticed this before.) Still, Alexis drew the nozzle close to the stink bug, to fully gauge the risk. The bug shifted slightly away from her, and then, with obliviousness or nonchalance or probably with neither because it was just a stink bug, it jumped frog-like and sideways off the frame. Pure predatory instinct jammed Alexis's finger-tip down onto the button, unloosing a fierce and sustained mist of poison that spattered the bug in mid-flight—along with everything behind it.

That it went tumbling floorward barely registered to Alexis. She gasped. Positioned behind the photos, in a sequin gown, was the Barbie doll her dad had given her just before he died. The Barbie had taken the Raid blast head-on; the stuff was dripping down her face and shoulders in milky-gray streams, like in the videos Dave was so fond of watching on his computer. "Fuck," Alexis said aloud. She was almost a decade removed from playing with Barbies, but this one—this one had meaning, this one was way more than a plastic doll. That's why she'd posed it there, at the corner of her dresser—to remind her of that last birthday with her dad when he'd de-livered that long rectangular giftwrapped box to the table and joked about there being a hamster inside (because a hamster was what she'd asked for). And now she'd just . . . gassed it. With Dave's stupid Raid. Because of the plague of stink bugs in this stupid house that no one had asked her opin-ion about buying, in this room she'd been assigned without any consider-ation as to whether she wanted it . . . "Fuck," she groaned, and grabbing the poisoned Barbie by its teeny waist she fled into the hallway.

And ran smack into her mom, who leveled a baffled frown at her, one eyebrow scooting up her forehead. Icily, she said, "Barbies?"

Alexis blurted, "Stupid stink bugs!" brushing by her mother toward the bathroom. "They're all over my room! Can't we call a freakin exterminator or something?"

Her frown only deepening, Sara followed Alexis into the bathroom where Alexis was stripping off the sequined gown to rinse the Barbie in the sink.

"Did one of them spray Barbie?" Sara asked, with more bemusement than concern. You could hear it in her voice: a faint trace of *huggie-wuggie* baby talk.

"No, I did. With Raid." Alerted by her mother's tone to how little-girlish and ridiculous she must look, bathing a Barbie in the sink, Alexis sighed and explained, "Dad gave this one to me."

In the mirror, as she took an exfoliating bar to the doll, Alexis saw a different, darker frown appear on her mother's face. She brought her gaze back down to Barbie whose fixed smile and wide eyes, despite the suds, formed an expression completely opposite to her mom's, if a little ghoulish as well.

"No he didn't," her mother said. "I did."

"Whatever," Alexis said, barely audible over the faucet's hiss. "Dad did. Right before he died. I remember him giving it to me."

The way Sara rolled her eyes suggested exasperation, but sadness too. That here-we-go-again routine she sometimes did. "Alexis," she said, "I bought that one for you. I remember the dress on it. And the ring. I got it at the Toys-R-Us at Rockaway Square Mall. I bought you that, and those awful rhinestone jeans you wanted from the Limited Too. Do you remember those?"

Alexis reassessed the drippy Barbie in her hands. She noted the ring: a big fat chunk of silvery plastic on the doll's hand. Its yellowy hair, whatever it was made of, had clumped from the water. Wringing out the hair, she said, "I think you're wrong."

"Does it matter?"

It did, of course, but she couldn't quite say how—not to herself, and definitely not to her mom. "Not really," she mumbled.

But it did—*did*. She'd never understood the imbalance: how her dead dad could mean so friggin much to her, yet mean nothing to her mom. Why the only mementoes of his existence were in *her* room. Why her mom couldn't even acknowledge him as the hero he was. The first time her mom went on a date after 9/11—maybe it was a year later, but to Alexis it'd felt like September 12th—Alexis had thrown a huge tantrum, crying so hard and inconsolably that Aunt Liz, her babysitter for the night, had to call her mom back home. The second date went the same way, though instead of calling Sara back Aunt Liz had sat Alexis down for some "girl talk," during which they'd struck a deal for Alexis to act cool in exchange for staying up as late as she wanted. She hadn't said this to Aunt Liz, because with her you just listened, but the question throbbed: How could she think of *replacing* him? She'd hated all the replacement candidates her mom had paraded by her over the years: a miserable line of middle-aged losers who spent three minutes pretending to be interested in Alexis before ignoring her altogether. Then came Dave, the culmination of loserdom, who'd somehow won the pageant. "Guess what?" she remembered her mom announcing. "Dave and I are getting married": with the same level of excitement or import she might've used in announcing the purchase of a new car. What she hadn't said then was, "Guess what? We're moving, too." Into some tacky plastic faux-mansion in a zombie subdivision. Nevermind about the house you grew up in, dear, the one where your dad taught you to walk, where he danced with you to the Bruce Springsteen "screen door" song—we're chucking all that for some . . . dude. Dave.

"Well, poor Barbie," her mom said, but by now Alexis had already snuffed out her sentiment, and didn't respond. She thought about trashing the Barbie right then and there—the wastebasket was right beside the sink—but doing so struck her as too aggressively spiteful, almost certain cause for an undesirable bout of sit-down talk. Talking about anything with her mom yielded one of two results: her mom brushing off whatever the issue was, often with some variety of condescending unhelpfulness *(it's a phase; getting over it would be the best thing; once you're grown up you'll laugh about this)* delivered with a smile less sincere than Barbie's; or her mom overreacting and dragging her to a counselor, like back in eighth grade when Gus posted video of one of his salvia trips on YouTube—salvia was a legal herb and the high passed quickly, it wasn't a big deal—and Susan Vitarelli's mom instigated a school-wide freakout. That was her mom's philosophy, as far as Alexis could tell: ignore the issue altogether, or else hire someone else to deal with it. She gave the Barbie's hair-clump one more halfhearted wringing and returned to her room, abandoning her mom to the bathroom door frame, to which she was presently clinging as though girding herself for an earthquake.

She lobbed the nude Barbie onto her bed and sank down beside it. Then she texted Miguel: "Bug dead." When a minute passed, without any reply, she brought the phone back up and looked at what she'd sent him, cringing. *Bug dead:* the lamest text message ever sent. Averting her eyes from her own lameness, she gazed at the Barbie, whose soggy hair was leaving a little seep of wetness on her comforter. She waited another minute or so, until the silence was too much for her, and carrying the Barbie by its hair she took it to her closet and chunked it into the corner. She knew it was a plastic doll but the constancy of its smile unnerved her anyway; something about it felt betraying. She spun around at the sound of her phone pinging, but when she fumbled it into her hand she saw it was only Katie Horner, wanting to know if their history assignment was due tomorrow or Friday. "Tmrw," she typed back. Why hadn't Miguel responded—besides the fact that she'd sent him an appallingly lame text? She leaned back onto the pillows on her bed, half submerging herself in their vapid plushness. Why wasn't he in love with her?

That's when she noticed, in the furthest reaches of her peripheral vision, the stink bug, staggering out from behind the corner of the dresser. Flopping itself forward on Raid-slackened legs, it was slowly—painfully slowly—heading her way. "Jesus," she whispered. She tried to ignore it, sinking deeper into her pillows and foundering in the awfulness of her loveless solitude, but she couldn't help monitoring, with equal measures scorn and admiration, its creaky, gasping progress across the beige carpet. *Bug NOT dead* went through her mind: the imaginary text message to this boy whom she wanted so badly and stupidly to be in love with her. She closed her eyes, but even in that blindness she could see the stink bug coming, could somehow feel its advancement on her skin. Finally she propped herself up onto her elbows, and, with a sigh, slid off the bed. The stink bug halted, seeming to groggily sense her shadow as she stood looming above it. A shoe-sole would finish the job, but she was barefooted, and anyway . . .

Alexis ripped a page from the school notepad on her nightstand, and slipping it under the stink bug, which tumbled into the semicircular tube she'd made, she carried it to her window and dumped it, gently, onto the sill.

2

FOR THE LONG cramped flight to San Francisco to attend his first meeting of the Waste Isolation Project Markers panel, back in January, Dr. Elwin Cross Jr. stuffed his carry-on bag with a half pound of homemade venison jerky; a tin of Altoids to counteract any close-quarters social effects of the jerky; his laptop and BlackBerry and their tangled black contrails of charger cords; seven amber vials containing his Metformin (for metabolic syndrome), Lipitor (cholesterol reduction), Avapro (hypertension), Colcrys (gout), Meloxicam (bursitis), Elidel (eczema), and Clonazepam (anxiety), plus a squat little bottle of baby aspirin and a pack of lozenges said to prevent snoring; a thick packet of background information, dressed in staid government-issue binders, that he'd been sent for meeting prep; and four books: *The Half Way to Healthy! How to Shed Pounds and Feel Great with One Simple Fraction,* by Simon Levine, MD; *Alzheimer's Essentials: A Practical Guide for Caregivers;* a fiercely underlined copy of *Surviving Infidelity: A Man's Guide* pressed upon Elwin by Fritz during one of their increasingly squirmy conversations (how he missed the old boring Fritz! Heartbreak had liberated Fritz in the worst way, unleashing years of pent-up testosterone. "The keisters around here!" he'd say after a walk through campus. "You just want to . . . bite them!"); and an oil-splotched edition of the *Haynes Jeep Cherokee Repair Manual 1984–2001,* which Elwin considered the most pleasant if least comprehensible of the four books.

The Haynes manual, in fact, was what Elwin fetched first, after wedging himself into a window seat and reciting a plaintive little prayer that the center seat would go unoccupied. His thighs needed that overflow space.

He usually booked two seats, if a Business Class seat wasn't available, but this time around he'd been too embarrassed to ask the government travel coordinator for two. The current political mood, he'd calculated, probably ruled out this sort of taxpayer-funded largesse; merely imagining the coordinator's apologies was humiliation enough.

The congressional temperament was playing an unexpectedly large role in the Waste Isolation Project. Bill Owens, the project administrator from Attero Laboratories who'd recruited Elwin for the panel just before Thanksgiving, had confessed a measure of anxiety about whether Attero's contract with the Department of Energy would be renewed; from what Elwin could surmise, the company'd lost its primary benefactor when the Senate Energy Committee's chairman lost his Senate seat, in a much-ballyhooed upset, to a right-wing candidate who wanted to abolish the Department of Energy because the word "energy" was nowhere to be found in the Constitution. "So we're fast-tracking this," Owens said, with much apology for the bimonthly meetings this would entail. Only later did the irony of fast-tracking a ten-thousand-year mission occur to Elwin.

He flipped open the Haynes manual randomly, to the chapter on brakes. Along with a pair of Banks TorqueTube headers, K&N filter, Flowmaster Cat-Back exhaust package, Alpine stereo system plus Rockford Fosgate subwoofers, and whatever else added up to $1,387.62, the Haynes manual had come into his possession via Christopher, who'd made a seductive case for a "massive upgrade" of the Jeep after guiding Elwin through a satisfying round of bodywork repairs. Overwhelmed by the purchase options ("On the headers, you want ceramic-coated or stainless steel?"), Elwin had surrendered his credit card and dispatched Christopher to the AutoZone with tongue-in-cheek instructions to "go crazy." The subwoofers alone were proof that Christopher had taken him literally. Though stung by the gone-crazy receipt (visibly enough for Christopher to posit a quavery, item-by-item defense, which merciful Elwin, sensing another failure being inked onto Christopher's record, stopped midstream), Elwin was nonetheless enjoying the after-hours camaraderie in the garage: the banter, the loud cruddy rock 'n' roll, the soul-tickling way a can of cheap beer tastes when plucked fresh from a cooler. Twice Christopher had dragged Elwin with him to McGuinn's tavern, where Elwin had felt like a folk hero after besting the all-time high score on the video trivia game ("That's my *neighbor,* motherfuckers!" Christopher shouted) and where a bartender dressed in a striking if unseasonable miniskirt had three times called him "big cutie," which he dismissed on a rational level and yet, on another, fudgier level, savored like a perfect potato chip.

There was something soothing about the Haynes manual, Elwin had discovered: the way its schematics and enumerated instructions offered wrenchable solutions to just about every predicament, the way it broke down the mysteries of combustion and locomotion and made every-thing—even the grand opera of engine replacement—seem so elemen-tary and doable, so one-two-three *possible.* He'd even taken to reading it in bed, as a sleep aid; it seemed to ease those terrible minutes between turning off the light and falling asleep when one is so profoundly naked before the truth of one's circumstances. Why weren't such manuals written for life, he wondered. *(Haynes Linguist Repair Manual, 1958–.)* For marital tension, he imagined: "Remove the tensioner mounting bolt (see illustration). Use a drivebelt tool to turn the tensioner clockwise for belt removal. Replace the belt." For ennui: "Add 12 oz. octane booster to the fuel tank." That sort of thing. He assessed the trio of other repair guides in his carry-on—how to repair marriage, obesity, the dissolution of his father's mind, all of them loaded with obtuse directions to "try to let go," or to "re-envision yourself," or to mollify the stress of an afflicted parent by "taking time to focus on *you*"—and found them all flaccid and useless in comparison. Where, he wanted to know, were the *real* instructions he needed: what socket to use, what fluids to check, what nozzle to clean, which fuses controlled what and how to replace them? Oh, to be a machine: diagnosable, restorable, upgradeable, *functional.*

"Dr. Cross?"

Elwin looked up. A tall narrow man, roughly his own age with a rect-angular gray band of a mustache and shaky blue eyes, was leaning toward him with his hand extended. "Rick Carrollton, from Columbia," he said. "They said they'd put us together on the flight out. I'm there in the, uh, middle."

"Of course," Elwin said. (Carrollton? Columbia? He drew a blank. The middle! Yet another prayer spurned.)

"So pleased to meet you," said Carrollton, as Elwin, in 13A, was unsuc-cessfully attempting to reduce his spillover presence in 13B by tilting his buttocks toward the window. "I'm a big admirer of your work with linear optimality theory."

Emptily, Elwin said, "Oh, why thank you," at the same time chiding himself for neglecting the information packets which would have supplied him the material for a polite retort. As a younger, more ambitious (and skinnier, more married) man, he'd have digested the whole packet weeks beforehand, thereby equipping himself with bouquets of flattery to distribute to his colleagues. But that's what flights were for, he'd decided this time—cramming. The open Haynes manual on the seatback tray, he realized, suggested a slackness even deeper than he wished to admit.

"And I see you're a mechanic as well," Carrollton said, with a chin-nod toward the manual.

"Amateur."

"Boy oh boy, I don't think I've cracked the hood of a car in twenty, thirty years. Used to love it as a kid though. My old man had a '68 Pontiac Tempest, you remember those?"

Elwin didn't, but nodded anyway. It was already clear he wouldn't be reading anything on this flight.

"We'd fiddle with that darn thing every weekend," Carrollton went on, a honeyed tone of nostalgia seeping into his voice. "Safe to say that car was the love of my life back then. I'd drive it to school and pop the hood at lunchtime like everyone else, you know, stand there waiting to be complimented. Or wait for some girl to be impressed, but, jeez, I don't remember that ever actually happening, right?" A chuckle and a head wag, aimed at his former self. "You got kids?"

"No," Elwin said.

"I've got a boy in high school, he's a senior now. I don't think he could change the oil on his car at gunpoint." At this he sighed and went silent, suggesting to Elwin that there might be other, more troubling incompetencies worth noting about his son. Then he snorted and said, "Heck, I don't know that I could change my *own* oil anymore." As if to buttress his point, Carrollton splayed out the fingers of both hands, obliging Elwin to appraise them along with their owner. They were unsmirched, soft-looking, Westchester County hands, like you'd see in an advertisement for a high-end wristwatch. "Don't get much honest labor, these hands," he said.

"Good for flicking a mouse around, that's about it." Another chuckle and a head wag, aimed this time at his current self. "Ahhhhh," he said, lowering his hands to rub his knees as if a bout of poly-cotton scuffing might restore their old integrity.

In the long pause that followed—one of those unnerving in-flight lulls during which one is tempted to crack open a book or magazine but fears the rude signal it might send—Elwin found himself studying his own hands, remembering in passing the way his father's hand had seemed so fragile and avian in comparison. His were soft-looking, too, but in a different, more upholstered way than Carrollton's. Squishy, doughy-looking hands, with gnawed fingernails and cartoonish dimples. Good for grabbing a cheeseburger, that's about it. He noted his gold wedding band, which had been resized so many times through the ever-swelling years that by now it was scarcely thicker than tinfoil. He hadn't had the heart to abandon it yet, though by this time stubbornness was as much to blame as sentiment. He wasn't sure if Maura had noticed it when she'd stopped by just before Christmas, but he hoped so. Maybe he'd wear it forever, like some sadsack from a George Jones ballad, and exact his posthumous revenge when Maura would spy it gleaming upon his refrigerated finger at his funeral and break into how-could-I-have-hurt-him-so sobs. Or, more likely, he'd finally wriggle it off his finger when Maura cut it out with all the "autonomy" crap and decided whether she was divorcing Elwin for the chef or coming back home. But then what would happen to it if she finally *did* pull the trigger? The question suddenly chilled him: What did people *do* with their wedding bands after a divorce? Tuck them away in rarely opened drawers, pawn them, sell them on eBay, have them melted down into tiny, bitter ingots? What *happened* to all those rings? And—what had Maura done with hers?

Her pre-Christmas visit had been a pity stop, he knew that. She'd claimed she'd left some shoes in the closet, but since the closet offered up no shoes but his own, he suspected it was a ruse. Elwin had been on his way down to the garage to meet Christopher when the front door shivered with timid little knocks. He was dressed in his (amateur) mechanic's uniform: oily Marasmus State t-shirt, jeans, a knit skullcap. He looked like a hobo, whereas Maura looked as if she'd made a detour on her way to the city for dinner; she was dressed for foie gras. He fixed her a cup of tea, and then, after deciding that the beer he was craving would only intensify the hobo impression, fixed a wan cup for himself. Their conversation was civil but stilted, like that of opposing generals forced to make small talk while their aides type up drafts of a surrender agreement. Aside from real estate, mostly they'd talked about his father: an easy neutral ground.

"You'll like this," he said. "Dad says last week that he's thinking about divorcing my mom. He's upset that she never calls."

"Oh God," she said, directing a tragic-looking smile into her teacup. Then she looked up frowning. "Why'd you say I'd like that?"

"I don't know," Elwin said, cutting his eyes sideways. Because what he'd meant, semi-consciously anyway, was: *You'd* no doubt like the idea of divorcing a corpse. Abandoning a helpless being, blaming someone else for your own unhappiness.

He said, "It's a figure of speech."

"Okay," she said.

"Anyway, I told him I had plenty of advice to give him on *that* subject." Wincing, he realized too late that he'd overemphasized the word *"that"*— had in fact almost growled it. He'd set the exposure setting all wrong; what was meant to be light, or half-light anyway, had instead come out terribly dark.

He wasn't alone in noticing. "You see, there you go, El," Maura said with a sigh. "You don't need the little jabs. Is that really what you want—a divorce? I know this has been—painful. Okay? I know."

Did she know? Here was a woman, the former-and-perhaps-yet-again Maura Crandall, who'd awakened him at 3:30 A.M. on a Tuesday to announce she'd been having an affair with one of her publicity clients, a chef with the appallingly daytime-soapy name of Fernando, and that after much "terrible" consideration—not to mention sixteen years of marriage—she was moving in with the chef. She wasn't "leaving" Elwin, per se. She didn't want a divorce, didn't want to "lose" Elwin; no, what she wanted, more than anything else, was "autonomy." Nothing is more lonely, she said, than living with the wrong person, but before Elwin could sink his chin all the way into his chest she said she didn't think he *was* the wrong person—just "half the right person." He was simply, she said, "not enough." Just like that: short flat staccato sentences, rehearsed so many times that she'd worn the inflections off of them. And then she'd left, before Elwin had even grunted himself into a fully seated position on the bed. He'd always prized her directness, but—this was too much. Subsequent counseling sessions daubed in some context—a lukewarm array of resentments ranging from their childlessness (the fault of his clinically sluggish sperm) to his weight, from their nonexistent sex life to (startlingly) his habit of peeing while sitting down "like a girl," and to all the cool calm academic success he'd enjoyed while she'd pinballed through careers as a political pollster, grants administrator, bookstore manager, interior design consultant, and finally restaurant publicist—and yet, context or no context, Elwin felt sure he'd never recover from the brutality of that announcement, that 3:30 A.M. pickaxe to his chest.

He'd stared at Maura across the kitchen table. There she was, the woman he'd married seventeen years before, the woman to whom he'd dedicated the lion's share of his decidedly non-leonine life: that same wheaty hair, same rectangular face and severe mouth, same droopy shoulders, and that same inscrutably flat expression so many people had misconstrued over the years as disapproving or uninterested or bored or dense but that Elwin knew stemmed from her insecurity, a diffidence so crippling that even her facial muscles were bound by it. Or was it her? In the later years of their marriage Elwin had noticed, not with dismay but with begrudging acceptance, his wife seeming to *fade,* both physically and mentally. Every birthday seemed to sap her of more and more color and more and more energy, until, at about the time they'd moved from L.A. to New Jersey, she seemed to have altogether lost her capacity for excitement, developed an immunity to exhilaration, taken on the demeanor of a washed-out watercolor. A natural condition of aging, he'd presumed, or maybe a vitamin deficiency. Yet in the past year something odd and disturbing had happened: her colors (eyes, skin, hair, even her clothes) had grown exotically vivid, her speech more electric, her gestures as dramatic as a silent-movie siren's. She'd been colorized, remastered with Dolby surround sound, converted to 3D: had morphed into a Pixar version of her former Elwin-ized self. Even the way she was sipping her tea at his table—there was bona fide *gusto* there, as if this was her first-ever taste of Earl Grey and within minutes she'd be describing it with zealous detail in an exclamation-filled diary. Was this the result, Elwin wondered, of addition or subtraction? Meaning: adding Fernando . . . or subtracting Elwin?

"So what do you want?" he finally asked her, when they'd waded through the small talk.

She sighed, and ran a fingertip across the table in a circle. "That's the problem, El. I think I want everything."

A long silence, before Elwin asked, "And where does that leave me?"

She shook her head, and for the first time since that 3:30 A.M. soliloquy he saw a trace of moisture in her eyes. "I don't know," she said. She reached for his hand, but he drew back. "That's the worst part," she said. "Not knowing what you want. Or wanting what you can't have. I don't—I don't *know.*"

"So, wacky stuff, huh?" Carrollton was saying.

Elwin startled, realizing he'd just drawn his hand back the way he'd done with Maura. He looked at Carrollton as if Carrollton himself had just tried to hold it. "I'm sorry?"

"The Markers panel," Carrollton said. "Gotta confess, I figured it was one of my postdocs pranking me when I got the call. But then that spiel . . ." he said, throwing up his hands to denote . . . well, Elwin wasn't sure what. "Not every day an engineer gets thrown in with Byron Torrance, you know?"

The engineer. Now it made sense, his deprecation of his hands: At some point, Elwin reckoned, he'd given up the blissfully hypnotic tinkering that had led him into engineering, swapped his calipers for class rosters. It'd been the same way for Elwin. At some point he'd gone from actually preserving languages to preserving his various centers for the preservation of languages, to the maintenance of his little sinecures. Of the world's 6,500 languages, only 600 would survive another generation, and what was Dr. Elwin Cross Jr. doing about it? Eating dinner with potential donors to the Trueblood Center. Sitting still as a pimple through committee meetings. Checking his email. Resisting constant memo pressure from the Dean to "harness social media" to advance the "Trueblood mission." (Now there was a concept, Elwin thought: using Twitter to stanch the red tide of language death. An idea on a par with arming a militia to combat gun violence.) Informing his father, over and over again, that he was a widower. Studying a diet book whose premise was that portion size, rather than a plague of sapped willpower or sedentariness or high fructose corn syrup or Happy Meals or anything else, was to blame for the fattening of America, and that one could achieve a healthy diet by eating only half of everything and dumping the rest in the trash. At what point, he wondered, had he been forced to devote all his energy, constitutional or not, to mere *existence?*

As to Byron Torrance, the subject of what appeared to be starstruck elation from Carrollton, he was a semifamous genome biologist fond of making scientifically imprudent forecasts about the future of humanity. Armed with a Panglossian view and a whizcrack publicist, he regularly plopped himself onto studio couches to spin comforting predictions for basic-cable late-night talk-show hosts. Chief among his theories was that humans were extinction-proof, owing to their ability to manipulate flora and fauna, and that genetic engineering would temper the evolutionary perils of what he deemed an unavoidable (but not calamitous) human monoculture. More prudent scientists, whose books didn't sell one one-thousandth as many copies as Torrance's and whose media exposure was limited to alumni-magazine profiles, had already parlayed his name into a verb: to "Torrance" something was to proceed apace on the blithe assumption that everything will work out somehow. George W. Bush, for instance, had "Torranced" the war in Iraq. The mortgage industry, for instance, had "Torranced" the subprime loan market. Dr. Elwin Cross Jr., for instance, had possibly "Torranced" his marriage.

"My first thought, of course," said Carrollton, "is why the heck are we *burying* this stuff anyway? Well, maybe not *my* first thought . . . my daughter's, actually. She said to me, 'Why can't we just shoot it all into the sun?' Nineteen-year-olds, you know. They're all such self-appointed *geniuses.*"

Elwin glanced at the shape of Carrollton's mouth to confirm the sneer he'd caught in his tone. Carrollton's children appeared to be a source of acid displeasure, an engineering project gone wrong. "Interesting idea," said Elwin.

"Yeah, I did some reading on it. It's an old idea, actually. Main problem is orbital velocity. Turns out it's awfully hard to get anything to the sun. The better bet, apparently, would be to eject it from the solar system. Just give the stuff a one-way bus ticket, like Giuliani did with the homeless back in the nineties. But then you run into a statistical trap. As in, the one percent failure rate of rockets. Can't risk a payload of radioactive waste blowing up over Yellowstone. Or Paris. Not to mention the costs involved. Astronomical, pun intended."

Elwin wasn't quite ready for this discussion but began anyway, "Well, burial has proven —"

Carrollton cut him off. "Frankly, I like my son's idea the best. Since radioactive decay emits about two kilowatts of heat, my son (I loved this) says we should bury it underneath the interstates in thick steel containers. No more icy roads. Wouldn't even need to salt 'em anymore."

It wasn't clear whether Carrollton was making fun of his son's proposal or endorsing it. When Elwin had explained to Christopher his whole warning-future-civilizations-about-buried-nuclear-waste mission, Christopher had cited the radioactive spider bite that'd transformed Peter Parker into Spiderman as a way of questioning the gravity of the whole enterprise. As if to say: Relax, Doc. Maybe there's an upside to be considered, like super powers. Christopher was clearly a Torrancian. "You've got interesting kids," Elwin offered.

"Yeah," said Carrollton, not in the least bit scrutably. "Anyway, that issue's settled. What's your angle here? I'm just the materials guy, as I understand it. You tell me what kind of marker you're building, I tell you what to build it out of. Though, personally I've a theory that . . . well, let's just say it wouldn't be *popular*."

"Go on," Elwin said, ignoring Carrollton's question about his own angle since Carrollton appeared to be ignoring it too.

"What? Oh, sure. So we've got a quarter-million barrels of radioactive waste buried in salt flats, two thousand feet below New Mexico. With a ten-thousand-year hazard period. And we're supposed to devise a marker or marker system to keep people away from this stuff. But what do we know about the deep future? Not squat, right? Will the United States last ten thousand more years? Inconceivable. Will civilization as we understand it last that long? Highly doubtful. But will *humanity* last ten thousand more years? Barring the unthinkable, something like a mega-meteor strike, it seems probable. Genetically modified, maybe, or cybernetically enhanced—whatever. *Homo sapiens.* So there's your one constant. Human nature."

"I'm following," said Elwin. (This whole spiel, he could tell, had been rehearsed as many times as Maura's 3 A.M. declaration, not to mention his father's recurrent questions. The bartender at McGuinn's had probably called others "big cutie," too, though he preferred to think otherwise.)

"I got to thinking about this with regard to the pyramids," Carrollton went on. "That's one of my areas of research. Four or five years ago we did a microstructural analysis of the Khufu pyramid, figured out there was a geopolymer involved, like cast concrete, and not just cut limestone like everyone'd thought?" The interrogative way he said this suggested the expectation that Elwin might break in at any moment to say, "Of course! Holy shit, that was *you?*" Elwin didn't. "Got some media notice on that one because it pushed the date of concrete development back by about twenty-five hundred years. Anyway . . ."

"Human nature," Elwin nudged.

"Right. Well, I went to the pyramids. Thought-wise, I mean. I was thinking about them in terms of engineering, of course. Specifically, what lessons they might offer about protecting the message core of our marker system, whatever it's going to be. From the elements, vandalism, intrusion, et cetera. But then something . . . something dawned on me. Khufu, right? The Great Pyramid? Khufu was looted by the time of the New Kingdom, let's say 1500 B.C., but probably long before then. So it remained undisturbed for less than a thousand years. King Tut's tomb, on the other hand, was safe for about thirty-two hundred years. A much better run, if you're thinking about it in terms of intrusion prevention. So I asked myself what the difference was."

"What was it?"

"Well. Khufu was *grand.* Khufu was a *monument,* writ large. The greatest wonder of the ancient world. Tut's tomb, however, was either built over, or flooded over, or used as a dumping ground—it disappeared. It was hidden. No one thought to loot it because it *wasn't there.* Are you following?"

"Vaguely," Elwin admitted.

"Yeah, well, that's where human nature comes in." Here Carrollton leaned in, lowering his voice. Out of politeness, Elwin leaned in too. "Let's say it's the year 5510. Civilization has collapsed, then reemerged.

Viral catastrophe, resource depletion, whatever the cause. But humanity has inched its way back, okay? You're exploring the New Mexico salt flats though the name New Mexico means as much to you as, I don't know, the Tumulus culture does today. What are you looking for? Doesn't matter. But you come upon this massive, super-forbidding, intensely *permanent* monolith in the middle of all this nowhere. There's writing all over it, courtesy of this crackerjack linguist four thousand years earlier (that's you), but you can't make sense of it. So what do you do?"

"Curse the linguist, who clearly wasn't so crackerjack."

"Bwah! Maybe," Carrollton said, which Elwin didn't quite appreciate. "No, look, for starters, here's what you *don't* do: You don't get the heck outta there. Uh-uh. You set up camp and you dig and you pick and pry and poke to try to figure out what's so damn *important* here. Because clearly, like the pyramids, this site *meant* something to someone. This site had *value*. And because you're human, you want to know why."

"Fair enough," said Elwin.

"Well, there's my argument." Here Carrollton paused. Elwin blinked. "You see? We're talking about building a modern-day Khufu when we might be better off building Tut's tomb. Building something that isn't *there*. Put another way, maybe the best marker for all this waste material would be no marker at all. Throw some standard-issue government concrete on it for the short term, let erosion do the rest. Be gone in a century."

"Out of sight, out of mind," Elwin murmured.

"Exactly."

Elwin weighed this for a while as the plane rose, watching through the window as Newark dropped farther and farther beneath him. The multi-colored shipping containers, stacked at Port Elizabeth, looked like a giant circuit board, a teeming matrix of *stuff* parked beside the long charcoal smudge that was Newark Bay. Then the intestinal snarl of roadways south of the Ironbound, as the plane banked westward, and the quilted neighborhoods out toward Scotch Plains and Watchung—then clouds, gray and linty-looking, devouring the view. Elwin turned back to Carrollton.

"Several issues with that," he said, more brusquely than he'd intended but then something about Carrollton was itching him. "First off, Tut's tomb *was* opened. Whether it was safe for, what'd you say, a thousand years or three thousand years—that's a fractional difference."

Carrollton blew the air from his cheeks. Obviously he'd been hoping to find an ally, seeking to line up support for his do-nothing proposal. "It might be worth noting," he said, "that it was opened by archaeologists, rather than looters."

"To some people those would be synonyms," Elwin said. "Motives aside, the result was fundamentally the same. The tomb was opened, explored, emptied."

"You have to keep in mind, it's a theoretical construct—"

"But secondly," Elwin countered, "there's a moral component."

Carrollton frowned.

"The warning, the marker system itself, would seem a moral obligation. Something like the warning label on a pack of cigarettes."

"Ah huh," Carrollton said. "But is there anyone who'd argue, realistically, that those warnings are in any way effective?"

"Maybe not. They weren't to me, thirty years ago. But there's a strong argument to be made that they're morally incumbent."

"Morally incumbent," Carrollton repeated, as if he'd never heard the words conjoined. "Well. I'm not sure the analogy works, but it's a valid point." He pursed his lips, lifted his eyebrows, sank a little into his seat. "Like I said, you know, I expected resistance."

With a smidge of pity, Elwin said, "I wouldn't say resistance . . . ," though he did think Carrollton's idea was only half an inch from crazy. Then again, he thought the whole undertaking was only half an inch from crazy, too: budgeting $120 million for a monument to waste in the New Mexico salt flats. "You know, it's funny," he said. "I've been talking about this with my father a good bit . . ."

"Your father?"

Elwin bristled at the condescending smile Carrollton was giving him, as if he was expecting Elwin to relay some ha-ha idea *à la* his son's proposal to insulate highways with radioactive waste, or his daughter's to blast the stuff into the sun. To credential his dad, Elwin said, "He taught history at Montclair State for almost forty years," then immediately undermined it by adding, "He's got Alzheimer's now, but . . ."

"Sorry to hear that."

"It's . . . funny."

"Funny?" Carrollton must've thought he meant the Alzheimer's.

"No, what he says about it. He says the whole project is the most depressing thing he's ever heard."

"The Markers project? Depressing, how?"

"Just the idea that . . . this is the deepest time capsule we've ever conceived. Aside from the *Voyager* mission, this is the longest-range communication attempt we've ever undertaken, as a society. And what's in the time capsule? Spent fuel rods, warhead shavings, Pyrex tubes, rags, junk. Just a big radioactive pile of . . . shit."

Carrollton was grinning. Elwin felt certain he'd greeted his children's ideas with the same supercilious grin. "But that's all *any* civilization leaves behind," he said. "Think about it. Not a single library survived antiquity. It's just tombs and trash heaps. Historically speaking, we are what we bury. Biologically, too. There's a hundred thousand terabytes of data in a single gram of human feces. Talk about shit."

Elwin turned to the window and watched the silver wing slice the atmosphere, squinting from the sunlight that was bleaching the cloud layer beneath them and somehow feeling, through the soles of his shoes, all two hundred thousand pounds of turbine thrust that were hurling him westward and detaching him from the earth. Carrollton was vacantly thumbing the SkyMall catalog while monitoring the flight attendant's progress up the aisle with the beverage cart. Elwin revisited the Haynes manual, but, finding none of the usual comfort in it, pulled the Waste Isolation Project information packet from his bag and for half an hour or more, while drinking half a glass of ginger ale and munching half a bag of peanuts, trained a hard stare upon its pages.

Suddenly, he asked Carrollton, "Whatever happened to the car?"

Absorbed in the in-flight movie, Carrollton had to yank out an earbud. "Say again?"

"Whatever happened to the car?"

"The car?"

"The Pontiac," Elwin said. "The Tempest."

"Oh, *gosh,*" Carrollton said. "I haven't thought about that car in twenty, thirty years." He rubbed at his mustache and shut one eye in half concentration. Then he looked at Elwin, with something like amusement and distant melancholy, and said, "I have no earthly idea."

3

AT THE GLASSED front of a three-story Finnish clothing store on 34th Street, a slim young man with narrow crescent sideburns wearing a charcoal linen blazer and a subtle black headset stood monitoring the entrance. From bag to bag his eyes went zigzagging, as shoppers funneled in and out of the store, but he did not open the door for the shoppers, nor greet them, nor even acknowledge them; he merely watched, with his hands behind his back, rocking back and forth on his heels, mute and expressionless, as the outflow of white bags went swinging past his kneecaps.

Out back, on 35th Street, another man sat monitoring the store's rear entrance. This man was older, and though he was Latino like the man out front, his skin was browner and pocked, his face rounder and more puff-cheeked, his torpid eyes reddened by infection and the incessant rubbing the infection aroused, with no sideburns to mention. Dressed in a plaid flannel shirt, sleeves rolled up high and neck buttoned low, along with knee-stained navy workpants, he was sitting with his back against a concrete wall and with a fingertip drawing figure eights on the pavement between his legs. Nearby, a crouching three-year-old girl was angling a red crayon over a Dora the Explorer coloring book. At regular intervals the man would look up, glancing first at the girl and then at the bright-orange loading-dock door and then at the big steel dumpster, where two women were sifting through bags of clothing. One of the women was his wife, who'd come north from Guatemala with him four years before. The other woman was Micah.

Together the women untied a black plastic bag and went rooting through its soft contents. After a while Micah held up a loose-fitting floral blouse with a grosgrain bow at the neckline and said, "Hey, *mira.*"

The woman looked up. She was broad-faced, with a flat Mayan nose and thick chapped lips, the buttons of her purple blouse straining at her middle.

"Para tí," Micah said.

The woman asked, *"¿Qué tamaño?"*

Micah checked the size. *"Diez y ocho,"* she said, and the woman cocked her head, reaching across the bag to caress the shiny fabric between her thumb and forefinger.

"Raso?" she said, and Micah nodded. It was satin. Frowning, the woman asked, *"¿Dónde se corta?"*

"Here," Micah said, and rotating the blouse she showed where the cut was: a twelve-inch gap down the back that a store employee—possibly the young man out front—had sliced with an X-Acto knife before disposing of the blouse and sending it out to the dumpster. Everything in the bags had been similarly cut—some beyond repair, some salvageable. They did this to prevent scavengers from returning the clothes for cash, or so went the story Micah'd gotten several weeks earlier when she'd buttonholed the store manager. Why couldn't they stain the clothes instead, she'd asked, so they'd still be functional? Or donate them? The response was something along the lines of: "Corporate policy." Swiftly followed by: "I'm sorry, I've got customers."

Shrugging, the woman took the blouse from Micah and smiled. *"Gracias,"* she said, then shouting to her husband—"Hector! Hector! ¿Te gusta?"—she held up the blouse for him to judge. Her husband raised his head, squinting, and then shielding his eyes from the low orange sun he gave her an uninterested thumbs-up. She sighed, and then he croaked, *"¿Para mí?"* and when the little girl giggled the woman giggled too, and with a glance toward Micah rolled her eyes, endearingly embarrassed. *"Para mí,"* she whispered, wagging her head, and with a newfound lightness she set the blouse aside and continued rifling through the bag. Micah paused and stood up, staring at the man then the child then the woman with a sudden tenderness, as if her mental lens had just been smeared with a film of sentiment. She couldn't help feeling as though she'd just glimpsed something lovely and intimate, however small: something that disinterred a memory from her own childhood she couldn't quite pin, perhaps less a memory of a scene or event than the memory of an emotion, a remembrance of unlikely happiness. "Micah," she said to the woman, extending her hand, and after a moment of confusion the woman took Micah's hand and said, "Marcella." They exchanged smiles, then went back to work, tugging clothes from the bags, analyzing cuts, sifting and sifting.

Micah's haul was slight but not insignificant: a t-shirt for Talmadge, sliced down the side but easily mendable; a batik-patterned sweatshirt for herself, equally mendable; and a crocheted dress that was probably irredeemable but worth a try anyway. There remained one more bag to open, but when Micah tore it open she found baby clothes spilling out. She dug deeper into the bag, hoping for more, but her hands found only more of the same: tiny fist-wads of fabric. She thought of the girl, now scribbling heatedly in her Dora the Explorer coloring book, lying on her stomach on the pavement and kicking her legs, and probed the bag for larger sizes. Spying a blink of pink fabric from near the bag's bottom, she pulled it up.

It was an infant's onesie, she saw—useless. Yet something about it gave her pause and when she spread it out atop the bag she realized what: The onesie had been sliced straight down the middle, from neck to gusset. Micah glowered at it, feeling a harsh stab of anger in her chest, an upsurge of bile bubbling in the rear of her throat, as she imagined the employee cutting it—what could he have been thinking (because it was surely a he), performing a gratuitous vivisection on this almost-infant, this cotton baby shell, poking the blade into its belly and then ripping it downward—at best he'd been thinking it was mere fabric, a $12.95 commodity, a casualty of corporate policy, but still—how could he have reconciled it in his mind, that blithe and unwarranted destruction, how had he divorced the act of slicing open a onesie from the thought and image of the baby it might have clothed? Micah flattened it onto the bag, kneading the sheared flaps together as if to close the wound, but then shaking her head and breathing hard through her nose she held it up to show Marcella and said, "Jesus, *mira esto . . .*"

Marcella looked up from a pair of men's jeans, a warm gentle expression overtaking her face. She put down the jeans and clasped her hands together. "*¿Está embarazada?*" she asked.

"No," Micah stammered, then repeated it, *no I'm not pregnant,* the hot red flush of anger on her cheeks replaced by blushing the same color as the onesie. Once more she said no, while Marcella blinked at her in bewilderment. Micah started to explain, gathering the Spanish phrases in her head, but then stopped—unsure of her anger, unsure of herself, unsure why she was holding the onesie so tight and tremblingly. Marcella shrugged and resumed her scavenging while Micah brought the onesie to her chest. It wasn't that the store had sliced *any* baby down the middle (symbolically or otherwise), she realized. No. What had enraged her was that the store had sliced *her* baby down the middle, the baby that (she further realized, the thought so dizzying that the dumpster felt waterborne) until that very moment had been a mere embryonic pulse in her imagination, an unformed craving that like the memory the Guatemalan family had evoked was vague and featureless, a buried emotion, a half-heard signal. Yet here it was, clear now, unburied, laid out before her as a pink swath of fabric floating atop a black sea of polypropylene.

She wanted a baby. There: that was it, she'd said it, and the ridiculousness of it—the reversal—almost caused her to laugh aloud. For years she'd sneered at "breeders," lambasting them for their egomaniacal, acquisitive desire to slather more of themselves upon the earth, overpopulation be damned. More privately, she'd long ago vowed to never have children because of the compromises they forced in one's principles—more precisely, because of the compromises she herself had forced her father to make, because of the snake she'd turned out to be, however inadvertently, in her father's doomed Eden.

The story of that Eden, as she'd absorbed it over the years, went something like this: John Rye had been a clean-shaven industrial engineer in Knoxville, Tennessee—a Vietnam vet, bass fisherman, small-scale collector of vintage Indian motorcycles, lackadaisical member of the First Pentecostal Church, and (people whispered) something of an odd genius—before God had commanded him to flee to the hills with his pregnant wife. This message had not been conveyed by a burning bush but instead by a burning Ford Fairlane station wagon John Rye had come upon late one night in 1981. He'd been out low-riding in his truck, a pint of peppermint schnapps tucked between his thighs, when, rounding a wooded bend, he'd come upon the Fairlane—upside down, with its top halfway crushed, lying crosswise in the road. Already the car was in flames; by the time John

Rye was out of his truck, sprinting forward, the blue-yellow flames had swallowed the car whole. Flailing arms or legs appeared as silhouetted squiggles in the front and rear windows. He tried moving in, scampering low toward the car the way he'd scurried toward Huey helicopters at Bien Hoa, but the heat was like a shimmering, impervious wall, bouncing him backwards. He looked behind him, and then to the left, the right, but there was nothing and no one there: a galvanized guardrail coruscated by the fire's reflection, and beyond it a blackness of pines. The flames had screams inside them, two kinds—the low, moany, guttural pain-screams you heard after mortar attacks, and the higher-pitched squeals you heard from wounded rabbits and children. He doubted there were rabbits in the car. Helpless, John Rye dropped to his knees in weepy prayer.

That's when God spoke to him. Not in words, as he'd later tell his daughter. No, God speaks in images. (This was why John Rye came to see film and television as especially poisonous: They approximate the voice of God.) The visions came in spastic flashes; the sensation, he said, was like trying to read a newspaper thrown into the wind, as the pages went flapping by. He saw a lush green mountainside, a narrow pewter stream. A woman's pale ankles in the stream, surrounded by an armada of floating yellow oak leaves. A smooth gray boulder, tall as three men, wider than a semi. An Appalachian bristle fern, unfurling from a rock crevice. These were not images from some internal album, flitting through his mind; that is, they weren't memories. Kneeling on the roasting asphalt, he never once closed his eyelids, yet the visions were distinct from what his wet eyes were seeing—not superimposed atop his view of the burning car and its charring occupants, and not peripheral either. Separate: as if he was trading visual frequencies with someone else, the way radio signals sometimes overlap, or eavesdropping on another consciousness. As an engineer, he was rational enough to recognize the impossibility of this. Clearly, the only reasonable diagnosis was spiritual: the slideshow voice of God.

In time other vehicles arrived. Their drivers saw John Rye in their headlights, bent before the blazing wreck with his arms spread wide. After a while a contingent of firemen hurtled past him pulling a heavy cloth hose, and a state trooper's big gentle hand came to rest upon his shoulder. This stanched the visions, but by then John Rye had seen enough.

He disappeared for seventeen days, during which time his wife Janie (six months pregnant with Micah) filed a Missing Persons report with the state police and his coworkers held a seven-minute, company-wide prayer vigil. There was no trail for the police to follow until a single transaction in Vonore, Tennessee, some fifty miles south of Knoxville, emptied the Ryes' cautiously tended savings account. John Rye returned the following day. It had taken him all that time to find the landscape he'd glimpsed in those visions, driving the dirt backroads at the edge of the Smoky Mountains National Park, hiking along streams into the thick sunless woods, sinking his boots into rhododendron must, sleeping on the forest floor and sustaining himself, as he'd done in Vietnam, with a diet of peanut butter and grape juice.

The boulder, the bristle fern, the pewter mountain stream: All this he'd located in a thick holler of second-growth hardwoods tucked between the Great Smoky and Unicoi Mountains, near the southwestern edge of the national park. He tracked down the land's owners — descendants of a defunct family logging company — and offered three times the going rate per acre. From that cash deal — brokered on a Saturday evening at the home of a bewildered Vonore attorney in overalls who kept asking if John Rye understood that, because of its border with the park and the TVA's Adahihi Dam holdings, the land was more or less inaccessible, except by foot, and therefore "kinda worthless" — he emerged with seventy-seven acres. With the deed in hand he returned to Janie at 4 A.M., shaking her from sleep. "John?" she said, noting a new and unrecognizable quality to his eyes, as stark and strange as if they'd changed color.

The couple was packed and gone before sunrise. "Are you sure it was really God? God himself?" she asked him on the drive south, drinking what might've been the last Coca-Cola of her life through a straw. The tone of his *yes* was enough for her.

For seven weeks, while John Rye built a windowless cabin out of poplar and locust logs, they lived in a tent. The closest spot to park his truck was a forty-minute walk from the boulder-and-stream homesite, so John Rye had to haul everything overland: He drove pigs through the woods, humped sacks of flour and sugar on his back, dragged a crateful of chickens up the sloping deerpaths on a skid. In the meantime Janie prepared a garden, in a clearing John Rye had sawed, and combed through her Bible seeking precedent for this vision God and a Ford Fairlane had dictated to her husband. Janie was not without her own secular smarts—she'd completed twenty-two hours toward a Master's degree in Environmental Science from the University of Tennessee–Chattanooga and worked briefly at the Oak Ridge National Laboratory—but this did not override her faith in both God and her husband's peculiar genius. At night she drank dandelion-root tea and languidly rubbed her swollen belly while John Rye, gaunt and exhausted, slept from dusk until dawn, too tired to even witness nightfall. He had to take Janie's word about the abundance of fireflies. Three months later, Micah was born in a summer thunderstorm. Moments after she emerged from her shrieking, dust-caked mother, her father carried her outside and washed her in the rain, braying, stomping his boots in the deep shiny mud puddles.

She'd described her childhood as magical, to Talmadge—as a nineteenth-century idyll, *Little House on the Prairie* relocated to 1980s Appalachia. She taught herself to catch brook trout by standing stone-still in the stream, with a dress on, luring in the trout with the shady lee her dress made, and then, with a quick whap of her hand, batting them to the bank. She roamed the woods with Tusker, a stray Plott hound they'd adopted (a boar hunter's dog, they figured) after it refused to scram. Every year, after his annual trip to town to pay taxes and load up on supplies, her father delivered stacks of books into the house, culled from library discards, which Micah and her mother would bust into like children assaulting presents beneath a Christmas tree. She helped plant corn in the spring, harvest greens and pick hornworms off the tomatoes in the summer, butcher hogs and goats in the fall, gather kindling in the winter. Her greatest childhood fear, she'd told Talmadge, was a tyrannical rooster her father nicknamed Ho Chi Minh, or Ho for short; the rooster was always jumping her in the yard, drawing blood more than once. But she had no scalding nightmares to recall, no moments of dread. She described hardships (failed crops, coyotes mauling livestock, a lightning-struck oak that came down on the chimney) but little tragedy—only a miscarriage by her mother, when Micah was five, that prompted a three-month rift in her parents' marriage during which Janie turned against John Rye, God, and personal hygiene, in that order, though eventually she recovered her devotion to all (in the reverse order).

But that was before they were discovered—before everything changed.

This happened in the autumn of Micah's tenth year. A young agent with the Tennessee Wildlife Resources Agency happened upon the family homestead while searching for black bear poachers. Appalled by what he'd witnessed—Micah, barefoot and grimy, being homeschooled in a hand-hewn log cabin lacking plumbing and electricity; John Rye, butchering a pig and sporting what the agent reported as a "ZZ Top–style beard" that was speckled with blood; and Janie Rye, making soap by stirring a pot of grease and lye and hickory ashes with a spicewood stick—the agent called the state's Children's Services Department. Two sheriff's deputies flanked a social worker (stumbling uphill in a pair of red peep-toe flats) to the Ryes' cabin, where Micah was seized, at unnecessary gunpoint, and driven to the hospital in Maryville. She'd only been in a vehicle once before, when one year earlier she'd accompanied her father on his annual supply run to Vonore. When the social worker dialed the car radio in to a Huey Lewis song, Micah began to cry, because the unfamiliar noise hurt her ears; the social worker, however, interpreted this crying as tears of grateful relief, tightening her grip on the steering wheel and accelerating the car as a tear of pity rolled down her own cheek, the righteousness of her career choice confirmed. At the hospital Micah was given a battery of tests and a fusillade of shots by a chainsmoking doctor whom she overheard muttering, to a nurse, "Where do they ever find these backwoods imbeciles?"

A three-month stay in foster care followed. Her foster parents called her Tarzan and took personal offense at her distaste for Hamburger Helper. They dressed her in hand-me-down, Chicago Bulls–branded clothing from their teenage son Zack, who played Atari video games for hours at a time, sometimes eating his Hamburger Helper with one hand while maneuvering the joystick with the other. Though she could read at a high schooler's level, and had several stanzas of William Blake committed to memory, she was placed in the first grade, where, because she physically towered over the other students and because she was woefully unequipped to converse with them, she was isolated and predictably scorned. When a third-grader named Brad Bonds smeared dogshit on the back of her shirt, at recess, she did what she thought was reasonable and removed the shirt; this provoked a military-level response from the recess monitor, who draped her naked torso with his sportcoat and kept his eyes trained on the ceiling as he marched her to the principal's office. The following day, she beat Brad

Bonds to the pavement with a red plastic baseball bat, causing blood to leak from his ear. This, however, only aggravated the harassment. In gym class the boys took turns spitting loogies into Micah's hair.

In the meantime her father pressed a legal battle to have Micah returned to him and Janie. This required making humble amends with Janie's parents, semi-prosperous retirees who were reasonably incensed that John Rye had "kidnapped" and "brainwashed" their daughter, then hidden a grandchild from them. They refused to hear anything about his sacred calling (which he exaggerated, inventing detailed instructions from God to mitigate what might be seen as the vagueness of his actual calling), suggesting that his invocation of the Christian Almighty was a disguise for something uglier, like Hare Krishna–ism or Catholicism. Could he even *imagine* the shame, they asked him, when people asked about Janie and they could provide no answer? "After a while," her father confided, "we just took to saying *Alaska*." They were suspicious about Janie's absence, waving away John Rye's explanation that she'd needed to stay back to tend to the animals and crops; her father even asked, the ice in his scotch-and-soda trembling seismically, "Why should we believe she's even still alive?" When they asked to see a picture of Micah and John Rye had none, Janie's mother fled the room in tears, viewing the lack of photographic evidence as bedrock proof of his egotism and parental unlove. In exchange for their aid, they made demands on John Rye—annual visitations, public schooling for Micah, and for the Lord's sake some indoor plumbing—to which he submitted with an escalating series of winces.

The bureaucratic hurdles he faced were staggering. He and Janie had breached laws regarding proper medical treatment, education, adequate shelter, even emotional neglect (for isolating Micah from other children). As a favor to Janie's parents, a family friend and Knoxville lawyer named Fred Taylor helped John Rye navigate his way through the court system. "You understand, however, that getting your daughter back to you doesn't mean y'all will be able to go back living that way, right?" Taylor asked John Rye one afternoon, in his law office on South Gay Street. By this time John Rye had shaved his beard and cut his long hair and outfitted himself in new clothes from the Gap. Bands of louvered sunlight striped the wall. John Rye held his head in his hands. "Do you?" Taylor said. Red-eyed, tight-jawed, John Rye nodded. "Whatever it takes," he whispered.

Three months is what it took: three months of hearings, depositions, court-ordered meetings, several different upbraidings by several different judges, and three subpoenaed appearances by Janie (whose increasingly weakened mien caused her mother to once break down sobbing and attack John Rye's chest with her fists). On a wickedly cold morning in February, Micah was handed back over to her father outside the Knox County Chancery Court building, along with a sheaf of notarized paperwork. On the ride back home John Rye stopped to buy her a Coca-Cola and some candy — during her suburban quarantine, she'd developed a mad crush on Reese's Pieces — and picked up a two-liter Coke for Janie, as well. They didn't say much on the drive. Micah laid her head against her father's shoulder, grazing on her Reese's one piece at a time, as the town gave way to farms then to steep-sided woods. "It's all over now, sweetness," John Rye said, lightly patting her knee as he steered the truck off the pavement and down a grass path that winter had turned pewter.

The absence of chimney smoke was the first distressing sign John Rye noted, as he and Micah crested the ridge. Then: an eerie silence, as if coming upon a ghost town or blast site. No loping, barking, slobbersome greeting from Tusker, no chickens pecking the yard. He quickened his pace, Micah saying, "Daddy, Daddy, wait," as she struggled to keep up, tripping on a loose stone, tumbling earthward. He veered off toward the livestock pens, sprinting now, shouting *Janie Janie* as he hurdled the fence. When Micah caught up with him, clambering onto the fence, he was twirling near the pigpen the way a wild horse panics at its first corralling. At his feet were the remains of their pigs, four of them, picked over by vultures, what was left of their skin gray and crispy and curled upright. "What's happened?" Micah said, as her father jumped past her, hurtling toward the cabin. There he found Tusker, alive but only barely, unwilling or unable to rise, his skin sucked tight to his ribs. The dog thumped his tail at John Rye, throwing up dust clouds. In the goat pasture he found only gnawed and shattered bones. Micah fell onto Tusker, kissing his ears and rubbing the washboard contours of his sides, while her father shouted for her mother, shouted until his voice went gravelly and then was gone, shouted until night had fallen and Micah had collapsed into an inadvertent blank sleep on the dirt floor beside Tusker.

They never found Janie Rye.

Nor did the mystery ever clear. Had they not seen Janie, at her three court appearances (when she'd walked down the mountain to meet John Rye's truck at the road), certain hypotheses might have applied: that she'd broken her neck in a fall from the mulberry ridge, eaten the wrong species of mushroom while foraging in the deep woods, etc. But the hogs had died, John Rye concluded, before her disappearance; whatever had happened to her, it wasn't a freak accident. Some sort of breakdown had preceded it. He kept playing and replaying back his memories of their three drives to Knoxville — what she'd said and hadn't said, the long grim silences he'd construed as being byproducts of their invaded, smashed-up lives, the way she'd vacantly dismissed his apologies for making her singlehandedly shoulder the upkeep of their homestead, the cloudy stare she'd given him when he'd driven away the last time. He'd watched her, that time, in the rearview mirror, a lone spindly figure on the roadside, pale and immobile, becoming smaller and smaller in the mirror before vanishing — not before he'd tapped his brakes, unsettled by her stillness — as he'd crested the hill. He wondered now if she'd ever hiked back uphill, or if she'd stood there, absorbing the roadside silence, gauging the choice between the tangled leaf-strewn path leading home and that clear striped asphalt road leading . . . where? Had it all been too much for her — the reunion with her parents, the raw scorn of the social worker and judge, the forced inventory of her last dozen years — the psychic pricetag, with compounded interest included, of her obedience to a secondhand filmstrip from God?

Deputies roamed the woods behind splotchy bloodhounds, interrogated John Rye for hours. They asked about the possibility of another man ("Look around," John Rye snorted), asked if he'd held Janie against her will, if he'd ever smacked her around ("A man's got a right sometimes," one of the deputies goaded him), asked over and over again about the miscarriage and what they'd done with the tiny red fetus. They inspected his guns, unbolting them, shrugging. One deputy picked up Janie's banjo, dumbly plucked a string.

John Rye hissed, "Don't you touch that."

"Easy, cowboy," the deputy replied.

"I said put it down."

Flaunting the banjo electric guitar–style, the deputy took three steps toward John Rye and, grinning, said, "You gwine go all Rambo on me?"

John Rye said nothing.

"Are ye?" the deputy said.

John Rye felt his molars grating together.

The deputy leaned in close enough for John Rye to smell the midmorning's Slim Jim on his breath. "We gwine find her," Micah heard him whisper. "We know what you done."

But they didn't: find her, or come close to establishing her fate.

"So what'd they ever decide?" Talmadge had asked Micah. This was early on, when they were riding back from Burning Man to San Francisco in the back of Lola's camper van. At this point Talmadge was still unsure of the dynamic — unsure who this girl was who'd rescued him, clothed him, fed him, and was presently captivating him with her mad sad sylvan history; unsure also who the other girl was, the butchy surly one driving up front; and furthermore unsure what his role might be in this inscrutable threesome, if any. Fate had handed him something new and alluringly weird; best to roll with it.

"Missing person," she'd explained. "No note, no signs of suicide, no signs of anything. Like she'd ascended to Heaven, man — body and soul and everything."

This dissatisfied Talmadge, who despite his Catholic upbringing had little patience for open mysteries. "What do *you* think?"

The question seemed to knock her off balance, as if, improbably, she'd never quite formulated her own hypothesis. "At first," she said, haltingly, "I thought — I mean, I guessed I hoped — she'd just gotten lost. Like I'd gotten lost a lot, you know? Somewhere out by the gum swamp, where it's easy to get all turned around and shit. That's what I'd tell my daddy at night — that Mama'd gotten lost, that she'd come back, and he used to put his hand on my cheek and say, 'Then God's gonna lead her back home.' But after a while I guess I knew that wasn't true. After that I used to — I dunno, I guess I wanted to believe she'd died some peaceful death, got snakebit in some beautiful holler or something, died with a smile thinking bout us even though, I mean, who dies with a smile? I was just a kid, man."

"What about now?"

"Now?" She sighed. The imbalance Talmadge had noted earlier began to make sense: She didn't much like her hypothesis. "Now I think she must've just . . . *gone*, you know? Hitched a ride somewhere, I don't know where. Just started all over again. Changed her name, changed everything. Maybe she had more inside of her than anyone knew." Another sigh, a wag of her head. "More conflict, I mean. More . . . look, Daddy couldna been easy, he wasn't easy as a daddy, so . . . she just—left."

For a long while Talmadge was silent, hushed by his proximity to genuine human tragedy—something he'd never personally experienced, unless you counted Dick Bertrand ditching Talmadge's mother after twenty-three years of marriage and all the resultant domestic mayhem that had engendered, all of which, while genuinely painful to him, Talmadge understood as middle-class farce: tragedy wearing a pair of pleated khaki trousers and sipping a gin and tonic on the lawn. Still, he bristled at the openness of the case. People didn't just *vanish*. Not with Facebook and everything. "What about your dad?" he pressed her. "What's he think?"

"That," she said, pausing to inhale, "is where things got ugly."

At first, she explained, John Rye blamed himself. For leaving Janie alone all those weeks, overloaded with chores and crunched by fear and loneliness; how terribly it must've ached, he realized, to be feeding those snuffling pigs every morning, casting scratch grain to the chickens, all the while friendless and ignorant of the whereabouts of her child and husband, and then, worse, holing herself up in that cabin come nightfall, staring at Micah's empty bed or maybe curling herself atop it as if to make sure the straw mattress didn't exhale its telltale dent. He'd seen Janie wrecked by the loss of one child; to lose Micah, even temporarily . . . she couldn't have withstood it, he now realized. It must've been too much. This line of thinking led to wider self-recrimination, as he expanded the circumference of his guilt: for neglecting Janie's role as the not-seer of divine orders, as the disciple to his prophet, for having demanded double faith from her— faith in his sacred flaming vision, but also faith in *him,* as the messenger, the reporter, the interpreter of that vision, in him as holy vessel. Had he deserved such faith? And had he—had he really—(these doubts came to him in the predawn darkness, as he'd watch Micah asleep with Tusker, watch their ribs rise in syncopated rhythm)—had he really actually *seen* what he'd thought he'd seen? What if he'd misread the message? What if it hadn't been God?

He'd known a gun-team leader back in Vietnam. Corny college kid from Indiana, everyone called him Early. Early went out on patrol with

his squad one day, but some dipshit grunts up on a hill, noting movement in the bush, opened up on them with mortars without knowing
what-all/who-all they were shooting at. Friendly fire: They took the whole
squad out. Owing to V.C. snipers, John Rye's squad couldn't get down
into the valley until the next day, when they found Early, lying face-up in
a ditch, mangled but smiling. "Jesus?" he'd asked, all beatific-like, as if the
Son of Man Himself—decked in fatigues with a Lucky Strike tucked behind his ear—had come to fetch him at the head of a heavenly infantry
squad. "Not yet, asshole," one of the corpsmen joked, but Early said again,
with tender recognition, "Jesus," looking straight into the gas mask of the
corpsman, who flipped Early over before John Rye could warn him not
to . . . then, boom. Early'd been booby-trapped. The explosion shattered
the corpsman's gas mask, blinding him instantly. For several long minutes,
despite his whole side having been blown out, Early kept calling to Jesus
like a happy kid playing Marco Polo in a pool, until finally another corpsman, trying to pluck the glass out of the blinded corpsman's shredded eye
sockets, shouted, "Will someone please tell this motherfucker that Jesus is
busy and will call him back later?" Remembering this now, John Rye drew
an ugly crooked line in his head between himself and Early: Jesus hadn't
been there in that free-fire zone. And maybe Jesus hadn't been there beside
that fiery Ford Fairlane on Thorngrove Pike. Maybe it had all been a trick
of the mind, optical adrenaline, some sort of merciful psychic response to
the trauma he'd witnessed: the brain overlaying random postcard images
of serenely verdant earth to screen the sight of all that trapped burning humanity. An eleven-year trick of the mind that had sent him fleeing into the
woods and had cost him the only woman he'd ever truly loved.

At this juncture, John Rye could have repented or relented—same difference. Surrendered to his doubts, come down from the ridge, started
fresh back in Knoxville. He didn't. Instead he dug in, burning those weedy
doubts out of his mind—it'd been God all right, he decided, and who was
to say Jesus hadn't been there that day in La Drang Valley, invisible but to
Early's doomed eyes?—and finally acquitting himself, after that long mental trial, for Janie's disappearance. The latter he accomplished by widening
the circle of blame further—diffusing it, letting it bleed over his property
lines to the outer world. Janie, he told himself, had been happy *until*. Janie
had been fine *until*. *Until* the State of Tennessee had invaded, *until* Micah

had been swiped from them, until John Rye had had to go off on his terrible chase to bring her back home where she belonged. *They'd* done it,
not him. *They'd* run Janie off. Or maybe, he got to thinking, they'd done
worse—paranoia trailed his grief, and late at night, as he pieced and re-
pieced the evidence together, other, darker theories blossomed. He thought
of that bucktoothed deputy, fingering Janie's banjo, that Slim Jim on his
breath smelling like moldered lust. And, too, he thought of the deputies
who'd come to take Micah, with their service pistols drawn, and the way
they'd eyed Janie as she'd clung to her daughter . . . he'd seen that kind of
look before, on GIs sweeping through rice-paddy villages on Search & Destroy missions, surveying the skin-curves of the daughters and the mama-
sans, knowing their M16s gave them the privilege to take anything they
wanted, sometimes taking all they wanted back behind a hooch while the
rest of the squad waited smoking cigarettes, one of them shouting after a
while, "Jesus, Randall, get a move on already! You don't gotta make her
come too."

Homemade corn whiskey fertilized these theories. The whiskey he got
from a neighbor, Motee Lusk, who'd come calling during the search to offer the use of his coondogs and been impressed by John Rye's primitive
setup. Motee, who was seventy and lived on disability, had an ideological
beef against government in any form, and after a while was spending long
afternoons at the cabin appending exclamation marks to every one of John
Rye's theories while contributing ever-darker scenarios of his own. "They
mighta got rid of her just to chase you out," he offered. "Been coal-com-
pany men crawling up and down this here valley. Me and you sittin square
on what they want."

During these slanted, boozy hours Micah was all but forgotten. "You
gwine cook that girl supper?" Motee would sometimes say at twilight, jogging John Rye back into the present. "Fry her up some bacon, how bout."

By this time John Rye had said to hell with the re-custody agreement
and all its stipulations, had burned the paperwork in the fireplace—this
came as a relief to Micah, who had zero desire to ever return to a school—
and told his daughter he'd shoot that goddamn social worker if she dared
show herself on their ridge. Motee loaned him a battered AK-47 which the
two men would occasionally take turns firing down the ridge—drunkenly,
and without much aim. Micah made the discovery of her first menstrual

period during one of these firing bouts and for several terrified minutes feared she'd been struck by a ricocheting bullet.

In time Motee's nephew and grandsons started hanging around, ostensibly to hunt but mostly to pass a quart jar of white dog down the porch. "You respect this here man," Motee told them. "He been privy to the voice of God." Respecting Micah, however, wasn't listed in the rules. John Rye either didn't see or ignored the doggy looks the boys directed at Micah, too preoccupied by his status as the leader of what they'd come to call the Unicoi Holy Freedom League, the boys mumbling "I hear that" to every anti-government rant and scriptural snippet John Rye could muster, their eyes fixed upon Micah, nevertheless, as she'd dump slop for the pigs or stand chopping at the earth with a hoe. It wasn't long before she'd outgrown her mother's old bras, and the boys took openmouthed notice of the loose swing of her breasts and the way her nipples embossed her dressfront.

Micah was not without her own curiosities, and one day, at fourteen, she led the youngest, gentlest, and gawkiest of the Lusk boys, Johnny, down to a deep hole in the stream where she often went swimming. Sharing a sixteen-by-twenty-four-foot cabin with her father, she'd noted the way a man's nether regions could expand and contract; getting out of bed in the morning, to head to the outhouse, her father's bedclothes were often strangely tentpoled at the middle. After daring Johnny Lusk to skinny dip, she asked him what made a man's thingamajig get big.

After he'd shown her she floated nude on her back in the cold spring water, watching the backlit oak leaves flitting and swaying greenly above her, feeling strangely nonplussed.

"Is that what sex is?" she asked Johnny, who'd retreated to the shore to put his clothes back on, itchy to leave.

"That's right," he told her, chewing on a blade of grass, not looking at her.

"I can't say I like it all that much."

"I ain't sure you're supposed to," he said.

If John Rye possessed any inkling about what his daughter was doing with the Lusk boys (after Johnny came Nate and T.J., though never Wade despite his insistent pleas) down at the swimming hole (and by the side of Wisner Creek, in the bed and the cab of T.J.'s pickup, and in the trailer

Nate shared with his mama and three sisters), he never let on. Harlotry, he would've called it, in full Old Testament rage. By this time, however, Micah sensed she'd become less a person than a symbol to him: a spectral memory, like Janie, that he used for stoking his own resentment and that of his disciples. A martyr to his jumbled cause. Railing against the government, the authorities, all the enemies of liberty, he would often cite the abduction of his wife *and* daughter, as if Micah wasn't standing there behind him with a plate of hot fried chicken for him to eat, rolling her eyes. No doubt puberty was also a factor. He *had* lost his little girl—as irrevocably, in some sense, as he'd lost Janie. This new woman-child who'd taken her place bewildered and frequently unsettled him, and though a distant gleam of tenderness still lit their relationship—without irritation Micah cooked for him, swept and cleaned the cabin, fetched him rags wrung with cold springwater when it felt as if the morning light had cracked his head open like an egg—he found it ever harder to talk with her except about the livestock, weather, or snake-sightings. Wordless hours crept by after nightfall, during which they seemed like different species of birds forced to share a nest. Consequently Micah spent more and more evenings at the Lusks' trailers, zooming back and forth on Motee's four-wheeler, while John Rye read scripture aloud in the empty cabin by the glow of a lamp powered by a generator Motee had generously donated to make refrigerated beer available to the members of the Unicoi Holy Freedom League.

T.J.'s trailer was where Micah met Leah. Leah was nineteen, from Marin County, California, trippy and lithe and so resolutely blonde that you had to look discourteously close to confirm the presence of eyebrows. Her venture capitalist father had made millions backing internet browser technology in its protean days; Leah disdained the family wealth—a barcode tattoo on her neck was a rebuke to the "commodification" of humanity—though not earnestly enough to forswear her trust fund. For several weeks she'd been hiking the Appalachian Trail solo, aiming to thru-hike all the way to Maine before winter. At a gas station near the trailhead she'd met T.J. and Wade, who, after elbowing each other about the wedgie-like cling of her denim short shorts, invited her back to the trailer to help them drain their brand-new case of Bud Light. Leah didn't drink, but, having vowed to embrace every possible life experience along the trail, took them up on the offer anyway. Wade rode in the truck bed on the drive back, his amazed and paled face so close to the rear window that T.J. kept slamming the brakes to squash him into the glass.

Micah was sixteen that spring, and unbearably restless. Only her mother's wretched legacy was restraining her from hiking down to the highway and hitching a ride out into "the World," as her father scorned everything beyond their property lines. Back during the war, "the World" was what they'd called civilization: that infantryman's dreamscape of hot meals, soft bedding, dry clothes, English-speaking girls, mortar-free nights. For John Rye, however, it had become code for something different: a society in thrall to the idols of materialism, stripped of its old core values, its honor, its ancient natural balance. The World, he thought, was what God had ordered him to flee, and what had later stolen Janie from him (whether by force or seduction, it didn't matter). When Micah, as a young girl, had asked him about the airplanes she saw coursing high above the mountains, John Rye had answered, "It's people trying to escape the World."

"What happens?" she said.

"Nothing," came his reply. "They run outta fuel and have to come back down."

Yet here was Leah, fresh from the World and embracing rather than fleeing its horrors. The way she talked reminded Micah of a shaken can of Coca-Cola (her second-favorite World attraction, behind Reese's Pieces): frothy, bubbling, impossibly sweet. She displayed none of the sour lassitude of the Lusk women, who spent the bulk of their days and nights smoking generic menthols on the trailer steps, looking withered and put out, as if waiting on a locksmith on account of their bozo husbands' drunk and absentminded ways. Leah had soft scarless hands with unchewed fingernails, and she smelled like the inside of a pumpkin blossom, half floral and half vegetal, an alluring mixture of winsomeness and nourishment. She'd been to Africa ("must be shitloads of niggers over *there*," Wade cut in, to which even T.J. objected, slapping Wade upside the head and saying *Shut the fuck up*) and to Europe and to the Galápagos Islands, where, she said (rapidly, effusively), she'd talked her way aboard an Ecuadorian Navy boat to patrol for shark poachers. When she grabbed Micah's hands, in a flurry of excitement about some sea lions with which she'd hobnobbed on the island of Floreana, Micah gasped with what felt like the strongest surge of pleasure she'd ever experienced. Almost immediately she recognized the sensation as love. This identification was not difficult to make; she'd never seen a sea lion before but felt sure she'd recognize one if it came waddling up to the cabin. When Leah offered to cut Micah's hair—which hadn't been cut since her mother's disappearance, its tattered split ends hanging slackly past her waist—the Lusk boys finally gave up on her, conclusively slapping their knees then stomping outside to sulk. "At least she didn't drink none of our beer," Wade said to T.J., in limp condolence.

The next morning, John Rye awoke to the sight of Leah asleep on his floor, swaddled in a synthetic orange sleeping bag. Tusker was lying beside her, as if he'd dragged her inside the way he'd done with squirrels and rabbits as a leaner, faster dog. Micah was already up, piling squarely folded dresses into an Army Surplus rucksack.

"I'd do for some water, if you don't mind," John Rye said from his bed. The previous night's combination of Leviticus and moonshine had left singemarks on his brain. Even his tongue felt charred. When Micah delivered it, he asked her, "Who's that?"

"My new friend Leah," she said, shifting back a few steps to make the subsequent announcement more formal and, she hoped, less contestable: "I'm gonna hike to Maine with her."

John Rye took a long desperate swig of the water. "All right," he said quietly, then repeated it. He pulled himself up and over to the edge of the bed and ran a comb of three fingers through his beard. "What's in Maine?"

"The end of the trail."

"I see."

He raised his feet and stretched his toes, examining them with a scowl.

"And the whole world, Daddy," she went on. "I'm sixteen. I can't be living like this forever."

Still inspecting his toes, he said calmly, "Like this, how?"

How? For a few moments she stammered—not wanting to hurt him, not wanting to desert him the way her mother had (maybe) deserted him, not wanting to accelerate the desolate downward spiral that her mother's disappearance had set in motion—then argued around the edges: "With nobody but the Lusks to talk to! With nothing but the Bible to read. With nothing in my life but . . . seventy-seven acres, Daddy. You should *listen* to where Leah's been. France, Africa, the Gapa . . . Gapagalo Islands . . ."

He just stared at her.

"They're in South America," she said.

"I know where they are."

"Then how come I didn't?"

He paused, cocking his head. "We got plenty other books besides the Bible . . ."

She snapped back, "You ain't brought a new book home since Mama disappeared," which brought a flinch to his face. As if by ricochet, an identical flinch quirked Micah's face: She wasn't cushioning her blows enough. "There's something like six billion people in the world, Daddy. And I don't know but, like, ten of 'em."

"The Lusks, they're good boys," he protested. "You seen how they help us out."

She could've batted down this point in a millisecond, by noting the varied degrees of help they'd given her in semen form. Instead she said, "I can't understand what's wrong with the World 'less I see it for myself, can I?"

The question—cleverly indisputable, Micah thought—hit him like a droplet of water on a hot skillet. "You been out there!" he exclaimed, with enough vocal force to make her shoulders jump. "What happened, back at that school? You recall that? And what about them people they stuck you with?"

"I ain't saying I'm moving to Knoxville!"

To which he shouted back, "And I ain't saying you can't . . . go."

The confused frown on her face belied the tandem surges of relief and joy she was feeling. She moved three steps toward her father, close enough to touch him. "Then what?"

For a long while John Rye re-examined his toes and said nothing.

"Oh, Daddy," she finally said, tossing her arms around him and kissing his neck, which tasted of the turpentine he dashed himself with, cologne-style, to ward off tick bites. In later years, when she'd tell the story of her childhood, she'd resent the *pity* that inevitably followed it, and the disdain her listeners would often heap upon her father for "imprisoning" (Lola's term) her and her mother in the mountains for all those years ("a classic caveman maneuver, cloaked in religion": Lola). How could he have *done* that to you, they'd ask, interpreting Micah's tenderness as some filial subset of Stockholm Syndrome, sometimes trying to fish suppressed rage out of her to induce a therapeutic reckoning. Yet there was no rage within her, or even mild disgruntlement. Any pity, she thought, should have been steered his way: for trying and failing to shield her. He'd tried to remake Eden, and she'd been the snake, or if not the snake the apple—the thing that'd opened a portal to the lesser world, that'd brought evil down upon them. "Then what?" she said.

"It's just a bad world," he said quietly.

They were both startled by Leah, drowsily countering from the floor, "It's a *beautiful* world."

Turning to Leah, Micah released her father, who cut his eyes toward Leah as well.

"Was," John Rye said to her. "Once." Nodding toward Micah, he said, "She'll see."

That was the last time she'd seen her father, though, care of the Lusks, they corresponded two or three times a year. Last she'd heard, the doctors had forced Motee to quit drinking, on account of his liver, and John Rye was attempting the same. He'd finally plumbed out the cabin, too, after devising a way to harness wind power into an old truck battery for running a well pump. Every one of his letters ended with the same ambiguous question: "Where in the world are you?"

Following their five-month walk to Maine she and Leah had flown to San Francisco—the flight so terrified Micah that Leah force-fed her some contraband hashish somewhere over Ontario, which did the wild opposite of calm her down; this was nearly cause for emergency medical care, and, coupled with her father's moonshine dependency, quashed all further curiosity about chemical enhancements—where for six months they lived with Leah's ex-sister-in-law in a cottage on Telegraph Hill. The ex-sister-in-law, Julie, also called Micah "Tarzan," and smirked at Micah's childishly rapt fascination with saltwater, sushi, mangoes, tampons, bookstores, transvestites, Rollerblades, the zoo, silk sheets, panhandlers, espresso, the cruise ships docked alongside the Embarcadero, and the high-end, keypad-controlled, Japanese toilet in Julie's bathroom that glowed in the dark, cleaned and massaged one's rear with a pressurized jet spray then dried it with blasts of hot air, and played any of six soundtracks including traditional Japanese harp music which Micah found magnificently and exotically soothing.

A flock of feral red parrots nested in a date palm in their backyard.

Micah found that if she stood still long enough, with bits of apple on her outstretched palm, a few of the parrots would eat from her hand and even perch on her forearm. At first this was cause for ticklish fun—and for Julie to quip to Leah, as she peeked through the blinds, "I see your wild child is finally making friends"—but after a while, as the thrill and wonderment wore off and Micah found she could pet and even (she thought) communicate with the birds, she came to see the parrots as a prime rebuttal to her father's indictment of the World. They were proof, she decided, that wildness *could* coexist with civilization, that a balance could be struck, that the World hadn't been degraded beyond rescue. With a parrot roosting on her wrist, pecking apple from her palm, she would place her other hand over one eye and take a mental snapshot of the bird backed by a red spray of pyracantha and the wild blue haze of the Pacific in the distance; then she would transfer the hand to her other eye, to take in the opposing view: the houses piled atop one another on Telegraph Hill, the Bay Bridge, the Transamerica Pyramid, all the clamor and concrete abutting the water. And then the hand would flip back—to the parrot, the Pacific—and back again—to the skyscrapers, the iron fire escapes, the quilted city blocks— and Micah, radically in love and overwhelmed by the vast rich multitudinousness of this new World, would whisper to herself: *You were wrong, Daddy, just look how you were wrong.*

Then came Dilly. Dilly lived next door; he was in his mid-fifties, wore a constant uniform of Hawaiian-print shirts and tassel loafers, and was equipped with a colostomy bag concealed beneath a decorative beaded pouch. Dilly didn't like the parrots. They squawked. They dropped little greenish turds on his patio and its wrought-iron table. And, he claimed, they were an invasive species, like kudzu or mitten crabs, that was stealing precious food and resources from the beleaguered native birds. Parrot-feeders like Micah, he complained to Julie, were only aggravating the situation. Dilly was fulsomely emotional about it all, saying that while he didn't wish to start a "conflict" with Julie ("as a neighbor I have nothing but love for you," he said, afterwards spelling out *love* for bonus effect), the squawking was inciting migraines and, he said (patting the colostomy bag), he was "terribly worried" about the potential hazards of all those germ-laden "poos." Julie apologized, hugged him, and promised an immediate stop to the feeding.

Micah was incensed. All through dinner that night she pleaded her case—at one point Julie groaned, "Is there *anything* else we can talk about?" to which Micah replied no and silent Leah slid farther into her chair—and then long, long into the night, until Julie finally told Leah, "If Tarzan says one more fucking word about those parrots, I want her gone. As in, *tomorrow*."

"What does he mean, the squawking bothers him?" Micah kept on. "That's like saying the ocean being blue bothers you. Or the leaves falling off the trees."

"For fuck's sake, welcome to reality!" Julie howled back. "Welcome to civilization, okay? It's not a zoo. It's *my* house! It's *my* neighbor! Get over it! Find another fucking . . . hobby." Then she threw up her arms, in Leah's direction, and went clomping off to her room in thick exasperation. In the morning she told Leah it was time for them to go. Micah's presence was warping her *chakra* something bad.

So they traveled to India for three months, Leah and Micah, though not before dumping two hundred pounds of birdseed in and around Dilly's patio. Obtaining a passport for Micah proved a serious hurdle, requiring the aid of her father's Knoxville attorney, Leah's father's attorney, and two forged documents. Micah's passport photo, taken at Walgreens, was the first formal portrait of her life. For hours and hours she stared at it, rubbing it with her thumb as if to disprove its flat one-dimensionality, as if to make tactile contact with this piece of herself trapped beneath laminate. The blue passport itself was her solemn badge, signifying newfound allegiance to the World, and though it mesmerized her, with its official notice from the Secretary of State and inscrutable numeric coding, it also felt treasonous: a vinyl-bound repudiation of all that John Rye had tried to shield her from. On the long flight to Mumbai, dulled by regular doses of Xanax that Leah administered ("It's nothing nothing *nothing* like the hash," Leah promised), Micah wondered about the girl in the photo: Was she friend or foe? And of whom?

They roamed from hostel to hostel, watched their underwhites turn malevolently green in the cold waters of the Ganges at Haridwar, observed a ritual cremation pyre at the Manikarnika Ghat in Varanasi, made slow giggly love in a pink poppy field outside Bundi with their lips dyed crimson from chewing *paan,* dispensed thousands upon thousands of rupees to children on the beach at Chennai, and reveled in their conversions to vegetarianism (Micah) and Jnana yoga (Leah). Mostly, however, India made Micah cry. This wasn't an unusual reaction to the country, where American women had been known to come sniffling up to hotel registration counters after staring out the window openmouthed on the five-mile taxi ride from the Mumbai airport. But Micah's response was different from that. It wasn't the makeshift blue shanties and lean-tos, or the women thrashing clothes on rocks, the men squatting to defecate in the shade of Peepal trees, or the naked, cinnamon-colored children cooling themselves in puddles—all this was too familiar, even nostalgically comforting, to faze her. What wrenched her, instead, was the unnatural *landscape* of the poverty: the scale, the density, all the degraded details. The coolant-green, battery-acid-yellow swirls in the puddle those children were cooling in. The mustardy burning-trash haze that strangled the breeze those women were sucking into their lungs as they paused between thrashings. And the hunger: the everywhere night-and-day hunger that seemed to her so impossible— how could so many be so hungry and contaminated, yet the earth still be spinning, the newspapers publishing, the factories factory-ing, the lovers loving, the preachers preaching? How could God justify this lopsidedness, with endless Hamburger Helper granted to one side of the world and what looked like *nothing* to the other?—and yet so insurmountable, so unrelievable at the same time? It can't be like this but it is; it must change but it can't. A thought scratched at her: Was this the World her father had warned her about? Was this sensation of enraged helplessness, rather than God's voice, what had sent him into the woods?

One afternoon, beside a biscuit stall near the Anjuna market, she watched a pair of toddlers scraping stray lentils—so few she could probably have counted them—out of a discarded plastic bowl with their fingers. A backpacker's leftovers, plucked from the street: She'd seen the disposal, and the rapid scavenging too. With tender formality, the pair took turns scooping equal-sized gobbets from the bowl, the boy licking his fingers clean while his sister dug in, and vice versa, then vice versa again. The sight was not extraordinary, by any means, but something about it—the mature resignation on the toddlers' faces, perhaps, or the poignancy of their diplomacy—struck Micah as unbearably, crashingly tragic. For a long while, jostled by crowds of backpackers and trinket-hawkers and scam artists poking metal rods into tourists' ears to sell them bogus ear cleanings, Micah waited to see if a mother might appear, her chest as tight as when she'd waited all those weeks and months for her own mother to reappear. To this story, at least, she needed an ending. Then Leah came to fetch her.

"Been looking everywhere, Jesus," Leah said, her voice tinged with a burr of annoyance. "You have got to see these bangles down this way. They're so freakin *you*." She tugged at Micah's arm, and then, sensing resistance, asked, "What's wrong?"

"Everything," Micah wanted to say, but didn't. Instead she bit her lip and kept staring, forcing Leah to survey the scene for clues. Leah frowned, shifting her weight to one leg with the audible harrumph of someone hamstrung by a riddle. She saw a splotchy humpbacked cow ambling through the litter. A mustachioed man pedaling a rickshaw down the street, a giant black vat of something tethered to a trailer. A woman sitting crosslegged and shut-eyed behind a basket of bananas. A torrent of motorbikes, a rainbow of sari-draped women. And then there, at the side of the biscuit stall, the two toddlers: expressionless, the boy in a crouch, rocking on his heels, and the girl picking listlessly at a knee-scab, their exhausted bowl of lentils overturned beside them.

"Them?" she asked, and Micah nodded. When Micah said nothing more, Leah sighed with enough theatrical emphasis to be heard over the street clamor, and said, "Yeah. It's awful."

For a few respectful beats, she waited, then tugged at Micah again. Again Micah resisted.

"Okay," said Leah, drawing a pink thousand-rupee note from her beaded change purse. "Let's do this."

Micah watched as Leah made a swift, efficient beeline for the children. She had the air of someone conducting an unpleasant business transaction, similar to the way she'd approached a hosteler in Mumbai after contracting 240 volts through her finger via a ceiling fan switch: her gaze level, her posture impeccable, her movement crisp and considered.

The boy peered up at her indifferently. Then, spying the rupee note, he raised an open palm which Leah covered with the money. She said something to the children that Micah couldn't hear, and the boy nodded weakly and passed the money to his sister, who examined it with the same enervated half-interest she'd given the scab on her knee. Leah turned back toward Micah, almost but not quite smiling, and Micah watched—with a sudden sadness more focused and intense than the sadness preceding it, though far less scrutable—as the crowds parted for Leah, fell back to let her stride untouched through the visible shimmers of heat.

By the time Leah was beside Micah again, yanking her toward the bangle stall with blithe tenacity, Micah was no longer in love with her. Micah would agonize about this, and reconstruct the scene over and over again in her head in an effort to determine just what had broken the spell and if perhaps it was just a sag rather than a snap, but it wasn't, and she was never quite able to pinpoint the cause: It was as if the indifference on the boy's face, as he'd squinted up at Leah, had been transferred to Micah via some telepathic, love-smothering infection. She was suddenly, even violently immune to Leah as she encircled Micah's wrists with various bangles, deliriously colored yet uniformly drab, her inability to select one impelling Leah to buy half a dozen of them for her, the languorous, charmed way Leah sidled up to the shopkeeper contrasting so starkly with the way she'd approached the smeary-faced children crouching beside the biscuit stall. It wasn't as simple as a case of insufficient pity, of Leah's casual regard for the toddlers revealing some hidden chilliness within her, or the way she'd used her father's money as a kind of salve, like the rosebud salve Micah's mother used to rub onto Micah's scrapes and insect bites, in order to rescue not the children but the moment, *her* moment; Micah had dismissed those theories by nightfall. No, something larger had come between her and Leah, she thought, something that had little to do with Leah and possibly just as little to do with *her* and Leah, or her and anyone. In those moments, as she'd watched the children scooping salvaged lentils into their mouths, love—the act of it, the narcosis of it, the exclusivity of it—struck her as an indefensible luxury on a par with the computerized toilet in Julie's apartment or the cruise ships towering above the Embarcadero. The memory of her and Leah tattooing each other's bodies with *paan*-dyed lip-prints amidst a coral sea of poppies—which had seemed, in its silky recollecting, an inexhaustible fount of pleasure—had come back to her corroded and drained of color, etched by guilt. In its wake, with fierce vividness, came another memory: "It's a beautiful world," Leah sleepily announcing from the wide-grained floor of the cabin (a line she'd repeated, over and over again, in that swaying field of poppies), and John Rye wagging his head and saying, "She'll see." Had she seen? But seen what?

This came near the end of the trip, which, coupled with a bout of giardiasis that reduced Leah to a dismal, shuddering groan-state, relieved Micah of the immediate need for painful declarations. She had only the vaguest bookish notions of what happened at the end of love, and of how you treated its remains. Still, Leah knew. The teasing and playfulness commenced a slow fade-out, leaving only somber affection. Every touch lingered, as if each was the last. The clearer farewell came when Leah fell ill and they reversed roles: Where Leah had been the older, wiser guide to the exterior World, the midwife for Micah's entry into civilization, Micah became the guide to Leah's interior landscape, nursing her through the cramps and cradling her head while she vomited, applying cool damp rags to Leah's forehead just as she'd done for her father. She spent her eighteenth birthday in a luxury hotel suite in Mangalore (Leah abandoned the freewheeling hostel-and-streetfood mode of travel the very instant she got sick, handing Micah a heretofore-unseen Amex card), reading an Ivan Illich book she'd scrounged from a hostel while monitoring Leah's sleep from a silk-cushioned rattan chair.

For the rail trip back to Mumbai and its international airport Leah dosed herself so heavily with Xanax that she spent most of the journey immobile; every few hours she would stagger to the bathroom, her crusty, slitted eyes of limited use to her as she'd feel her way down the aisle, then sink back into her seat like a water buffalo submerging itself in mud, dunking herself into a brown subconsciousness.

Theirs was a first-class car with air conditioning. Across from them, in a sheenful pinstriped suit, sat a middle-aged Indian man holding a cordovan briefcase atop his lap, as if fearful to place even an inch of distance between the briefcase and himself. Because this reminded Micah of Dilly with his beaded colostomy bag, and because the man's suit reminded her of all the lawyers who'd milled indifferently about the courtroom during her custody hearings, she took an instant dislike to the man — this despite the warm, beatific, slightly amused expression he aimed at her throughout the long ride, and his endearingly clumsy attempts at conversation. "I see that your friend is ill," he said, several hours out of Mangalore. "Yes," replied

Micah. "That is extremely unfortunate and I am sorry to hear it," he said, before another hour passed between them.

That's when Micah noticed the plates. The first one, barely: a white disk flitting in and out of her peripheral vision, from outside the window, quick as a diving bird. But then another, and a minute later another. She glanced at the man to see if he'd noticed them too, but he was staring straight ahead as he'd mostly done since Mangalore, engaged in some businessman's version of meditation. Noting her glance, however, he smiled and nodded and parted his lips to speak. Sharply, Micah returned her gaze to the window where, again, she watched a polystyrene plate sail by. Bewildered, she stood up and, leaning over Leah, peered out the window at the tracks. How had she not noticed this before? Thousands of smeary plastic plates were strewn alongside the tracks, where bonesleeve dogs were licking them along the dirt here and there—a fringe of multicolored saucers lining the tracks for as far as she could see. As she watched, more and more plates came coursing by; passengers were apparently flinging them out the windows of the car or cars in front of theirs. Her grimace, as she fell back into her seat, was acute enough to provide the businessman an opening.

"This troubles you?" he asked, jutting his chin toward the window.

So he *had* noticed. But because his tonal emphasis was on the word *troubles,* Micah construed the question as a challenge, as if he was goading her to pass judgment on his country and his countrymen's habit of chucking their trash out the window. Still, it *did* trouble her, so she met the man's eyes and said, "Yes."

"Me too!" he blurted, then laughed as uproariously and incredulously as if he'd just discovered they were cousins. "It is *terrible!*"

"Well," Micah demurred, not sure if it was terrible or just ugly.

"But there is an explanation," he said, raising and shaking an index finger. "To proceed you will tell me your name."

"Micah."

"Mica!" This seemed to him another happy discovery; the way his eyes glowed, Micah half expected him to say it was his name too. "An extremely important mineral," he said, his voice shifting suddenly into professorial mode. "Did you know that the Kodarma district in Jharkhand has the greatest deposits of mica in the world?"

"I didn't."

"It is *true*."

"Okay."

"I am pleased to know you."

"Yeah," she said. "Cool."

He craned forward so that his arms were bunched between his torso and briefcase, as if he had a major confidence to reveal. "Now I will explain this unfortunate scene," he said. "In the past, not so long ago, when you bought food for your journey, it came to you wrapped in banana leaves. This was how it was done. You would eat your meal, and throw the banana leaf out the window. Like this!" Stiffening himself upright, he whipped his arm toward the window and laughed a bubbly little laugh; he was clearly cherishing some recollection from childhood. "I remember this! And the cattle would line the tracks to eat the leaves. That is the prior situation."

Micah said, "What happened?"

"Plastic!" he exclaimed. "Do you know its history? A man named Alexander Parkes exhibited it at the Great London Exposition in 1862. It was to be, in his view, a replacement for ivory." At this the man lifted his eyebrows, and awaited a reaction from Micah. When none came, he frowned. "Which comes from elephants."

"Right," she said. "I know that."

"You know this! Then you will be most interested to know that Great Britain, during its control of India, consumed enough ivory to require the deaths of four thousand elephants a year."

"That's awful," Micah said.

"I am in agreement with you!"

"But . . ."

"Yes." He waved a finger. *"But!"*

Micah waited.

Lowering his finger, the man sighed. "This is our condition. We do not solve problems. We replace them with other problems. You are too young to comprehend this but in time you will reach these conclusions. One could contend that Alexander Parkes saved the elephant from a swift and inevitable extinction. This is in fact my contention, and not only because my business happens to be plastics and their molding. But in order to preserve elephants we must also have—this."

As if by conjuring, another polystyrene plate went whirling past the window.

"But what was wrong with the banana leaves?" Micah asked.

"A most incisive question!" Perhaps too incisive, because the man fell into a brow-knitted silence for a while, his smile drooping. "But to ask that," he finally said, "is to ask why this train we are on is preferable to a cart. Or why this berth we are in is preferable to the sleeper class car ahead of us. It is to question progress. To question motion."

Micah frowned.

"Also," he went on, "the plastic costs less money for the vendors, and is not vulnerable to rot."

Micah turned her attention outside: a sheet of pure cloudless blue above a scrubby green flatness.

From behind her shoulder the man said, "You must select what you see when you look out the window. You may see plastic, up and down the tracks. This is understandable, and you are right to be troubled. But do you know what I see?"

She turned to him. "What?"

"I," said the man, "see elephants."

For the remainder of the ride Micah stared out the window in search of elephants, metaphorical or otherwise. Despite the man's lawyerly suit, she liked him, and wanted him to be right—wanted the elephants to fill her with the same faith and solace that the red parrots of San Francisco had. But all she saw was plastic, mile after mile of it, floating in bronze-colored ditches and snagged in camphire shrubs. When she glanced at the businessman, she saw he was also scanning the trackside, and she wondered if he too was watching for elephants, whether for his own benefit or hers. But there were no elephants, and after a time their absence began to feel oppressive, as though the two of them were waiting for someone to arrive whose dire tardiness was now casting doubt on the arrival itself.

As the train slowed into Mumbai, however, Micah finally saw one, and springing up from her seat so that her torso draped Leah she pressed her nose to the glass for a deeper look.

The elephant was standing at the head of a traffic line at a railway crossing, waiting for the train to pass, a snarl of Padmini cabs and auto rickshaws behind it. Tethered to its back, atop layers of blankets, was a plywood platform with steel railings on which sat a barefooted teenaged boy. Almost at once Micah felt the fizz of the sight go flat. As the train rolled by she drew her gaze first to the elephant's eyes, which were dry and saggy, brimming (it seemed to her) with a kind of sorrow that persists long past the indulgence of tears, and then, panning upward, she looked at the boy's face. Sullenly, perhaps impatiently, he was watching the long train go by, and for a fugitive moment their eyes locked, his and Micah's, with what felt like a violent and unexpected snaring, as in a lock clanging shut. She lost her breath. His were hard, narrow, predatory eyes, like those of T.J. Lusk glancing up at her from behind the covers of a girlie magazine after a pint of white dog, eyes that refused to register her as a fellow human traveler, that were chilled by something she didn't understand and wasn't sure she wanted to understand: an ice-core of anger or resentment or nihilism or maybe just sour hopelessness. The boy's head turned, as he tracked the passage of her face behind the smudged glass, and when at last he disappeared from the windowframe Micah rolled back into her seat — suddenly and confusedly aware of a wetness in her own eyes, of fetal teardrops at their base. She looked to the businessman, to see if he'd noticed, and if so wanting him to explain why the sight of this precious elephant felt more hopeless and dismaying than that of the plastic-strewn tracksides. But he hadn't. He was back to staring straight ahead, an oblivious almost-smile on his lips, his hands splayed atop his briefcase. When she swung her gaze back outside the window she saw only plastic again, whole ditchfuls of it.

His had been a false choice, she realized: the plastic or the elephants. The elephant she'd seen had not been spared or saved or otherwise preserved. Instead it had been coerced into service as a cog in the plasticized system, had been mechanized as the boy atop it had been. This was what civilization, the World, forced upon us: false choices. It stung her pride to acknowledge it, but it was true: Her father had been right after all.

But then maybe she'd been operating under her own version of a false choice too, she wondered now, ten years after kissing Leah goodbye forever at a Heathrow boarding gate and setting off on her own, knee-deep in that polychromatic abundance of slashed clothing in the dumpster off 35th Street, kneading the onesie with her thumb. Between rejecting the World and surrendering to it. Between abstaining and succumbing. Why couldn't there be some sort of middle path — or if not a middle path, because that reeked of acquiescence, then a three-quarters path, or a fifteen-sixteenths path? She didn't quite know what she meant—her brain was firing willy-nilly, thoughts and emotions streaming and colliding in her head—but through all the mayhem in her mind she was seeing another way forward, a freshly dug and profound new truth. To start over from scratch—this meant creation. She peered down at the onesie. It wasn't mere coincidence, she realized, that God had deigned to speak to John Rye during Janie's second trimester of pregnancy. Because her father hadn't meant to merely *escape* the World; not for himself anyway. His goal, she saw now, had been to make a new and better world for *her*, his child—with his hands, the only way he knew how. So perhaps she hadn't been the snake in Eden after all, not the cause of all the doom that'd befallen it. She'd been the cause of the dream of Eden itself.

Into her pack went the pink onesie, and with a flurry of effusion that startled and nearly knocked over Marcella she hugged the woman, who shot a grimacing glance to her husband as she patted Micah's back. He just shrugged, and as Micah climbed out of the dumpster he returned her farewell waves with a gringo-bemused grin—just as the security monitor emerged from the orange loading-dock door for a cigarette and, seeing them there, came charging at them shouting, brandishing the cigarette like a weapon. Backing into the alley, Micah waved at the security monitor, too, but he ignored her, haranguing the husband in Nuyorcian-inflected Spanish while the man leapt up to help his wife out of the dumpster and while their little girl went on coloring in her book, wonderfully (Micah thought) oblivious to it all, ensconced in a better world of her own waxed making. From 35th Street Micah turned south onto Broadway, charging through the sidewalk crowds like an ice cutter parting bergs, headed straight for Talmadge.

4

DUMPING HIMSELF INTO the sofa Dave emitted a sound like a juicy air-brake blast from a tractor-trailer: *"Pppppbbbbbbbfffffffffffttttttttt."* His collapse was so forceful, in fact, that it caused a wave in the foam-core cushions that went all the way down-sofa to where Alexis was sitting with her legs folded beneath her, thereby dislodging the finger she was using to type a text message. "Shit," she said, sending an inflammable scowl Dave's way. "You just made autocorrect change dammit to donuts."

Dave didn't respond. Instead he rubbed his eyes and craned his neck and then sat there with his mouth open in what appeared to be an approximation of death or at least a coma. He was fresh from dinner with Tim, his senior VP and general manager, and Tim's wife Susan, whom Sara couldn't stand for reasons she'd tried unsuccessfully explaining to Dave on the drives to and then from the restaurant. Something about how Susan was unable to talk about anything besides politics and her kids — always the insufferable (Sara's word) kids, with the twenty-minute play-by-play rehashings of their latest hockey games (lately augmented with cellphone video footage) or Brit Hume–level analyses of their student council maneuverings. Dave didn't find Susan all that bad but then again he didn't really listen to her. Regardless, to his thinking, kids and politics (of a kind, that being his) scored higher on the topic list than shopping, Sara's main conversational subject. (Sara had tried to engage Susan on that one back when they'd met, but had backed off for good after Susan raved about a sale at Kohl's.) The dinner had been fine, otherwise — or maybe *not* fine, now that he considered it. Tolerable. But exhausting. He felt as though he'd been smiling for a group photo for the last three hours, waiting for the fucking *cheeeeese* that'd allow him to be human again. Like he'd suffered the equivalent of a power-steering fluid leak—by which he meant, his own power to steer other people. When had *that* started?

Righting the tilt of his head, he scowled back at Lexi. "Whaddaya, sexting?"

Tap, tap. She didn't look up. "You wish, perv."

"Kinky donut messages."

"'They're home, dammit.' *That's* what I'd meant to type, okay? Before you, like, burped yourself down."

"Who's they?"

"Guess."

"Oh, right. Us. Me." He frowned. She was wearing those low-slung sweatpants of hers that tended to creep down her hips to expose just an inch-long coin-slot of butt-crack, which he tried not to look at except when he didn't try, which was maybe half the time. Sometimes he resented that humid-looking inch, while at other times he resented being equipped with downwardable eyes. At still other times, however, the sight of that shadowed little crevice provided him the only jolt to his existence all day, the only hint of life's magnificence. He thought it all very complicated, which was why he tended not to think about it. "Must be texting your dealer, then."

"Yeah, right. My *dealer.*"

"Tell him I said hi."

"Right," she said. "Perv says hi. Send."

It was 10:32 P.M. Said so on the fancy Italian clock on the wall. He rubbed his knees while examining his loafers which also happened to be Italian. Well, Italians made good shit. Like his dad used to say: "The Chinese mighta invented noodles, but we Italians invented *spaghetti.*" He scanned the living room, pleased to see it tidy save for the disarray of papers on Lexi's end of the coffee table, then drew his gaze back to himself: also tidy, but definitely not pleased. What was he *supposed* to be doing at 10:32 P.M. anyway, with a belly full of ricotta-and-chive gnocchi, diver scallops, truffle rémoulade, roasted cipollini onions, and key lime semifreddo, and with his brain overrun with echoing dinner chat? Besides the obvious, that is. (Sara had already Heismanned him on that front.) *Digesting:* right. That was it. Digesting dinner, digesting the day, digesting his life. He brushed a hand across his middle and with a kind of philosophical softness asked, "You ever get that feeling like you're full but you're not full?"

"Yeah, it's called Chinese food."

"We didn't eat Chinese."

"Can't help you then."

"Like you *should* be full, you know, but you're not? Full, I mean."

Her phone dinged, and in trained response her chin sank and her thumb went scrambling across the keypad. Like a fingertip on a soap bubble, the ding also caused whatever vague inquiry had been swelling inside Dave's head to vanish: pop. Needing auxiliary stimulation, he glared at the television screen. Some tiny lipsticked girl-child in a tiara was getting hug-squashed by her mom in slow motion while spooky horror-movie music thrummed. Clearly this wasn't going to end well—not stimulatingly, for damn sure. "The hell you watching, anyway?"

"Dumb reality show," said Alexis. "Take the remote."

He thumbed it. *SportsCenter.* That'd work.

"Where's Miguel?" he said.

"What?"

"Your dealer."

"He was never my *dealer*. God. Where'd Mom go anyway?"

"To bed."

"Can't you follow her?"

Dave grunted. The short answer, of course, was no. He tried thinking of the long answer but it was also just no, or maybe *noooooo.* An analytical knot appeared on his forehead. "Whaddaya mean, 'was'?"

"Was what?"

"You said, '*was* never my dealer.'"

"What's with the shakedown?"

"Oh, I got it. *Was.*" He grinned and jutted a tongue at her. "Sexy Lexi's single again."

She rolled her eyes. "Whatever *that* means."

"It means what I said."

"Like when you said, 'full but not full'? Your communication skills are, like, awesome."

He ignored this, because his communication skills actually were awesome. This he knew because seven years ago he'd attended a "High Impact CEO Communications" boot camp in Rutherford where he'd learned absolutely *nothing* because it was all as friggin *obvious* as the "open bag, eat nuts" instructions on a package of airline peanuts. At the end of it he'd received a dinky little medal, as meaningless as the one the Cowardly Lion got at the end of *The Wizard of Oz,* which he would've happily shown Lexi were it not encased in a frame on his office wall between a photograph of him with Derek Jeter and another one of him with Jeter's fellow Yankee Andy Pettitte. (Sara had not been the first to liken his office decorating scheme to a pizzeria's.) He said, "So, no more Pedro. Huh. *Now* who's gonna hook me up with some of that medical-grade shit?"

Glancing up from her phone, Alexis sighed and said, "Miguel, not Pedro. And did you even *hear* me just say he's not a dealer? You got ears or are those weird things just decorations?"

"So why don't *you* hook me up?"

"I'm *out,* okay? Which isn't cool 'cause of my you-know-what."

"The irritable butt?"

"You're the irritable butt."

Bah. Dave blew the air from his cheeks, motorboating his lips. Being deemed an irritable butt wasn't helping his present condition, which he suspected might be medical — a tapeworm? — and therefore qualified for some of that medical-grade weed to which it seemed, alas, he was no longer privy. He focused on *SportsCenter* for a while, but nothing that was said or news-crawled or headlined seemed to be sticking. His brain felt like a wide and leaky sieve, all these noodles of information slipping right on through. Nothing was plugging the holes. Was there such a thing as mental tapeworm? Tiger Woods came onscreen, shown in a practice swing, fanning the clubface in that killer takeaway of his. Dave wondered idly if Tiger had ever calculated how much he made with each swing, practice swings included. Had to be a lot. Also if Tiger ever felt this same way at 10:32 ... no, 10:35 on a Wednesday night, like a big glob of gorged dissatisfaction. A big glob of gorged dissatisfaction with ... weird ears. "What's wrong with my ears?" he asked.

"Nothing," she said, looking up at him. With an unexpected gentleness she assessed his head in profile and concluded, "They're decent ears, actually."

"Yeah?"

"Too bad they don't work."

"Huh." Dave nodded to himself. He'd never considered his ears before, and raising a hand to examine them decided they *felt* like decent ears, actually. Hairless and aerodynamic. This was something. This stuck. Take that, little tapeworm. Feeling brighter, he pressed Lexi again: "So what's the deal? With Pedro. Come clean."

"Miguel. Jesus."

"Yeah yeah, whatever. Him."

"Like, *nothing*, okay?" Down went her phone, and with a flat terseness, as if to close the subject, she said, "He was cute, that's all."

Dave smiled. The most important component of communication, they'd told him at that boot camp, is knowing what goes unsaid. (*Duh*, he'd unsaid.) "There you go again. *Was* cute. What happened, his face get caught in a deli slicer?"

"*Is* cute, okay?" Her shift to the present tense, he noted, demanded a measure of emotional exertion. "What's with the freaking interest, anyway? You want his number? Exploring your bi side?"

"Can't a stepdad be concerned?"

"A real one, maybe."

Crack: a line drive right back to the Irritable Butt Era. He chafed. "Hey, I'm just making conversation here," he barked. "It's my goddamn sofa. I'm allowed."

"Fine," she said, "I'm gone," but when she made to rise Dave lifted a hand and said, "Relax, okay?" He didn't want her to go. In fact, the thought of her leaving pumped a sudden spurt of despair through him, because then all he'd have was the empty sofa, and the *SportsCenter* guys, and the fancy Italian clock, and the plump wiggly tapeworm munching away somewhere inside him that might or might not be the source of this acute appetite he was feeling for something he couldn't describe or define except with the word *more*. Soothingly, he said, "He just seemed like a nice enough kid, is all."

Alexis peered downward, to where the closed and dingless phone was balanced on her thigh, and said, "It was just—I don't know, like a passing *thing*, you know? But whatever." She curled up her nose, absently running a fingertip along the glossy edge of her phone. "He was kind of a player."

"Uh *huh,*" Dave said. He'd caught something there, in that narrow little gap between the "you know" and the "but whatever": a flicker of candor, a passing glimpse of naked or at least semiclothed emotion, like her heart scooting by while clutching a bath towel. Years of phonework with debtors had sensitized him to these micro-moments, when through a verbal crack he'd catch something revealed, often something trivial but at other times an essential and game-changing truth. Rarely, he'd found, was it difficult to work that crack into a fissure. People went out into the world clad in armor, but what they really longed to do was shed that armor—it was why they got drunk in bars, why they went trolling the internet under the cloak of an alias, maybe why they fell in love. With a puckish smirk he said to her, "Well, he wasn't really your type anyway."

She stiffened, as he thought she might. "What's *that* mean?"

"Here we go again. It meant just what I said."

"Because he was Mexican? Is that it?"

"Maybe. Or maybe 'cause his dad's a fucking landscaper."

"So, what—you think I'm some sort of—gold digger?"

"I think you aim high, that's all."

"I'm not like my mom, if that's what you're saying."

"Whoa whoa *whoa,*" he said, with his hands splayed. This was an unforeseen swerve. "You calling your mom a gold digger?"

"I'm just saying," she said.

Raising his voice, he asked, "So what's that make *me?*"

She lifted one shoulder in an apprehensive half shrug, a touch of fear whitening her face.

Grinning, Dave said, "Makes me *gold,* that's what it makes me."

For a moment, Alexis was silent. Then her shoulders pitched and rolled as she fell into laughter, and for a full silken minute the two of them giggled, snorted, sighed, and giggled again, not looking at each other but instead at the television, as if the *SportsCenter* guys were cracking them up, and while Dave didn't fully comprehend why it was all so funny, he couldn't stop himself from laughing, not unlike when he'd gotten stoned at Thanksgiving and several times later. For the first time tonight, he realized, he felt almost happy, almost human, felt like he understood the velocity and spin and break of the pitch coming off the mound, felt as if the day was maybe finally shifting from dammit to donuts. Felt a little, well, *golden.* As he exhaled a laughter-concluding wheeze Alexis reached toward him and said, "Gimme the remote."

"Why?"

"'Cause this is *boring,*" she said, though not unhappily. She thumbed the channel back to the tiara-girl show, reconsidered, then dropped them into a rerun of *Jon & Kate Plus 8,* which struck Dave as less boring than excruciating. Then again, he decided, the mommy on the show was from a certain angle kind of hot. The rear angle, for sure. Also the three-quarter profile angle. Although all *she* did, too, was talk about her kids.

"What's all that shit there, on the coffee table?" he asked.

"College stuff. Course catalogs."

"Your mom says you got into Rutgers."

"I'm *so* not going to Rutgers."

As a Rutgers alum, he could've taken this as an insult, but chose not to. Alexis, he knew, had fatter dreams than that—getting out of Jersey, for starters, a desire he nostalgically if condescendingly understood from having over-absorbed Springsteen's *Darkness on the Edge of Town* album as a teenager. (This was before Bruce had gone all lefty, or maybe before Dave had noticed the trails of lefty crumbs in Bruce's songs.) Dave had never had the luxury of considering it, however. At eighteen, his in-state destiny had been dictated by his old man: *You going to college, and you going to this one.* Which is how it'd always been: *You playing football, not basketball, 'cause I can't stand all that fuckin squeakin. Fuck that job down the shore, you working for your Uncle Bobby at the Wawa this summer.* Alexis was angling for Richard Varick College in Manhattan, and, so far as Dave was aware, angling fairly well: respectable GPA, an application essay that she'd worked on for weeks before getting it honed by a not-inexpensive "essay coach," two retakes of the SAT and ACT tests. "Holding out for the city, huh?" he said.

With a slanted grin, she replied, "Aiming high, remember?"

"Yeah, I get it. Where's Miguel headed?"

"Oh, God. I dunno. Sussex County Community College, maybe? Working with his dad, probably."

"He was a player, huh?"

"Kinda?"

"Kinda, how?"

"Like, he was dating some junior. Supposedly they'd broken up. *Not* the actual case."

"Two-timing you, then."

"I guess." She peered down at her phone again, and then with an abruptly inflamed tone, as if the screen had relayed some red-hot reminder, she said, "He's just a *dick,* really. Just, like, *shrugged* when I found out about it. Was like, oh well, if *that's* how you're gonna be about it, catch you later."

"Adios."

"He didn't say adios."

"Thought it, I'll bet."

"You're such a jackass."

Dave raised his eyebrows, leaned in. "You need me to rough him up for you?"

"Right."

"I got ways."

She pursed her lips. "What ways?"

"My ways."

"You're all talk."

"Here," he said, feeling challenged, "gimme your phone."

In a swift protective gesture, she scooped the phone off her thigh and said, "What?"

"Just give me the fucking phone."

She was holding it over her head now, the way you keep a leaping dog from snagging a milkbone. "Why?"

"'Cause I'm calling this asshole."

She shifted the phone to an unseen point behind her neck, so that to access it he might conceivably need to remove her head. "Not from my phone!"

"Fine," he said, unholstering his own phone. "Just read me off the number."

"Why?"

"Just read me the number."

After a long hesitation, her eyes flipping from phone to Dave then back again, she did so, her face settling into a rubbernecker's expression of equal parts terror and curiosity. When Dave hit the speaker button, and peals of static-hemmed ringing filled the room, she removed a hand from her own phone and slapped the hand across her open mouth.

"Fuck, what's his last name?" he said. "Quick."

"Rios."

Miguel answered just as Dave was clearing his throat. "Miguel Rios, please," Dave said, as Alexis went skittering back into the couch pillows, coiling herself like a cornered rodent. Dave winked.

"Yeah, who's this?" came the kid's voice.

"Sergeant Dick Mancuso, Byram Township Police. What's your location, sir?"

At this point Alexis smothered her face with a pillow.

"Who's this again?"

"You heard me. Mancuso, with a, uh, M. Your location, please."

"I'm — I'm at home?"

"You're needed for questioning." Dave reached over and swatted the pillow pressed to Lexi's face, because her muffled squealing was making it sound like Dave was calling from a slaughterhouse. He'd made this call before, though not in decades; somewhere back in his brain was his original script, which he'd last used to get back at his dipshit cousin Victor for borrowing Dave's car to drive to a Giants game and parking in a handicapped spot. Two-hundred-dollar ticket. "We can send a cruiser over now, or we can schedule a meeting at the station at, let's see, eight tomorrow morning."

The anxious gulp they heard incited contrasting reactions: from Dave, a toothsome grin; from Alexis, a hard, cellphone-weighted slap administered to the pillow covering her face, followed by a pained moan. "Questioning for what?" they heard him ask.

"I'm not at, uh, liberty to say that at this point, okay?" Dave said. "Look, kid, don't make this hard on yourself. Don't be stupid, okay? We can do this with or without a warrant. Now or tomorrow?"

"You sure you got the right Miguel Rios?"

By this point Alexis was doubled over, face down in the pillow. Dave kicked her in the shin, to make sure she wasn't suffocating herself. "Student at Sussex High?" he said. "Yeah, you're the one, hotshot. Eight o'clock tomorrow. Sergeant—" He had to think for an extra moment here: Who the hell had he said he was? Oh, that's right—"Mancuso, with an M. Station's in Stanhope. You're gonna need to be accompanied by a parent or guardian, got that? I'm required to advise you that you have the right to be represented by legal counsel."

"Legal . . . ?" The kid's voice was cracking. "What's this all . . . ? I've got school in the—"

"That's not even close to your biggest problem right now, capeesh? How bout we'll write you a note?"

"But my dad has to—"

"Look. Clock hits 8:01 and a bench warrant gets issued. So be on time, is I guess what I'm sayin."

"Sir, can I ask—"

"Nope, you can't. Not till eight tomorrow. Catch you later."

And with that he hung up. Cackling, he wagged a middle finger at the phone before reholstering it. "'Catch you later,'" he quoted himself quoting Alexis quoting Miguel. "Did you get that part?"

Alexis lifted her face from the pillow, her cheeks imprinted with the pillow's weave pattern. "Ohmyfuckinggod you're awesome," she gasped.

"He's not getting a good sleep tonight," said Dave.

"You're insane."

"Mancuso, with an M," he said, continuing his own highlight reel.

"Ohmygod, that was so *wrong*."

"Told you I had ways."

She put a hand to her chest, clearing her lungs with a long *whoooo,* then looked up at Dave. For a short while her smile held—she had obviously enjoyed the submissive crackling in Miguel's voice, the vengeful little dart they'd thrown—but then something like a shadow passed across her face, darkening her expression. Her eyes narrowed and her lips came together as she stared at Dave in a weirdly searching manner, the way you look at some dimly remembered person whose name you can't quite recall, scanning for visual clues. Finally she said, "Why'd you do that, perv?"

"Whaddaya mean, why?" He grunted, pretending to be listening to the semi-hot MILF on the television screen who was rehashing a marital spat about the choice of a jungle gym. "'Cause you fell for this asshole, and the little asshole was two-timing you."

"Maybe I did," she said softly, so softly that Dave told her to repeat it. "Maybe I did," she said again. "I dunno." Together they listened or rather appeared to listen to the TV husband's side of the jungle gym dispute. "Why are guys such assholes? I mean, I gave him—I told him . . ."

When Dave looked over at her he could see just how far her expression had fallen. She was back to rubbing the edge of the phone again, as if it was some holy talisman, like the turquoise eye his Aunt Ida bought off some psychic in Ocean City to ward off fear that she used to rub the dickens outta whenever Dave's father cracked a beer at family get-togethers. Was that a tear in Lexi's eye? Oh shit, he thought. Now he'd done it. But done *what?* It occurred to him that maybe he shouldn't have merely prank-called that dumb little yardboy kid. Maybe what he should've said was: I hope that back-inventory tramp of yours is a swimsuit model, *pendejo,* because this girl right here is about as beautiful as they get. Or maybe, better yet, he shouldn't have said anything at all, to anyone. Maybe he should've just concentrated on the fucking *SportsCenter* guys until all the odd empty feeling had passed. Trying to skirt the issue, he said, "Which guys are assholes? This one on the TV?"

"No," she sniffed. *"Guys."*

"Not me," he said.

She snorted. "Naw, you're an asshole too."

He glanced at her, glanced away, and then staring at the television screen announced, "You wouldna talked to me back in high school, you know."

"Why not?"

"Because I wasn't gold then. Not even close to gold. Not even tinfoil."

"But you had the nice ears."

"Yeah," he said. "That's true." He was quiet for a while, as if pondering this—though he wasn't pondering it. He wasn't pondering at all. "Let's turn the fucking channel, okay?" he said, and she went sifting through the channels until she found one that drew an approving nod from him. An old Bruce Willis movie, midway through. She set the remote on the coffee table, followed by her phone, and then Dave said, "Put your head over here," which she did.

5

A MONUMENT WAS rising in his dreams. Sometime around the end of April, three months after Elwin's first meeting with the Waste Isolation Project Markers panel and two weeks after the second meeting, the mission was beginning a slow and peculiar creep into his subconscious.

This was unusual in multiple ways. Elwin didn't often dream, for one thing, owing to a case of weight-related sleep apnea that tended to constantly scramble his REM-state channel lineup. What the act of dreaming brought to mind were the ancient frustrations of watching TV with his younger brother David, who'd lie on his back in front of the Philco Cool-Chassis "Miss America Series" set with the channel knob lodged between his toes, rotating the knob every two minutes in fractured, commercial-free contentment while from the couch Elwin and Jane would hurl murderous threats and occasionally magazines or flatware. On those rare nights when Elwin did manage to sustain and remember a dream, however, the dreams were always oblique, immaterial, indecipherable except at the basest symbolic level: unsatisfying Dada dreams in which, for instance, Maura didn't return to him pleading for love and forgiveness, no, but rather a bucktoothed Dunkin' Donuts cashier with a vague if sufficient resemblance to Maura shorted him on his change. That was it: a dream yielding nothing in the way of enlightenment or even a sense of his mind processing its sorrows somewhere deep within its gyral folds—yielding nothing, really, save a healthful aversion to the Dunkin' Donuts in the Marasmus State student union. He missed the vivid, oversaturated dreams of his younger years, when whole civilizations would appear to him, as in a private sci-fi novel, his mind swarming with the delicious phonologies and morphologies of lost or never-were languages, leaving him flushed and eager when he awoke, caffeinated from the inside.

These newest dreams, to his great and bewildered surprise, were very much like those. The first one arrived the night after the panel's second meeting, at the Attero Laboratories Waste Isolation Plant near Carlsbad, New Mexico. There he'd been outfitted with a headlamp-equipped hardhat, goggles, and emergency oxygen pack, and dropped two thousand feet down in a wire-cage elevator for a firsthand look at where eight hundred thousand steel drums of radioactive waste would eventually be stored. With him in the elevator were a blue-suited safety officer; Byron Torrance, the Pollyanna-ish genome biologist; and the artist on the panel, Sharon Keim, a Nevada sculptor whose most notable work was a thirty-ton granite polyhedron on the outskirts of El Paso that several Hollywood actresses had commissioned as a monument to battered women. Elwin liked Sharon; she was thorny, subversive, eager to lance the more swollen egos on the panel, as in:

"I feel I should admit something," Torrance announced in the elevator, about a thousand feet down. This he said floridly, with that same grandiloquence he applied to everything he said—one sensed the cameras were always rolling in his mind—but since Elwin had yet to become accustomed to this he awaited the admission with suspense. Torrance sighed. "I'm somewhat—claustrophobic."

The others must have been similarly disappointed, because no one responded—not even the safety officer, whose job it was to respond. Obligingly, Elwin broke the silence by soothing, "Everything's going to be all right."

Sharon leaned into Elwin. "You're stealing his lines."

Elwin didn't notice any reaction from Torrance, or any sign that Torrance had even overheard; he was too distracted by the playful pinch Sharon gave his arm as they went sinking downward. The pinch felt lingering—if only by second fragments—and he chose not to acknowledge it lest he give her cause to stop or, worse, curdle the moment with some embarrassing overacknowledgment. Only after she'd released her soft pincers did it occur to him that his lack of notice could've suggested he hadn't actually *felt* it—that his insulating layers of arm-fat were thick enough to buffer tactile sensation. And only after that did it occur to him that he was thinking like a seventh-grade girl. He cleared his throat, trying to be a linguist again, an expert in soberminded descent.

They'd emerged into a floodlit gray salt corridor, thirty feet wide and fifteen feet tall, that branched into a series of smaller subcorridors appearing to stretch infinitely outward. The walls, chilly to the touch and stippled with violet crystals, had been carved with angles that struck Elwin as impossibly sharp, the corners crisp and level as if steel girders were positioned behind giant sawn slabs of salt, or as if ten thousand men with ten thousand chisels had been chinking away since antiquity. Elwin saw his seatmate Carrollton, the materials scientist, ogling them with openmouthed admiration; Carrollton even rubbed the walls and tasted his fingers, to verify their saltiness. Forklifts went clattering by, trailed by squawks of static from the walkie talkies hitched to the drivers' belts. Down one subcorridor workers on scaffolding were fireproofing a ventilation shaft. The workers were all wearing identical blue suits, and were as indistinguishable, at first glance, as the ants in an ant farm: a sub rosa colony of subterranean laborers. In the main corridor one shouted, *"Watch to your right!"* as he floored some sort of deep-earth golf cart past the doddering clutch of panelists. This one was wearing sunglasses, Elwin noticed, and with a doubletake he confirmed the set of Mardi Gras beads strung around the driver's neck: subterranean homesick blues.

In a cathedral-hushed voice, Sharon said, "It's like a—giant underground Costco."

"Or a Bond villain's cave," Elwin said.

Together they looked back at Torrance, to include him in their dumbstruck analogizing. Torrance glanced up from studying the instructions on his oxygen pack, his face drawn and greenish, and snapped, "What?" Elwin just smiled and shrugged while Torrance, grunting, resumed his studying. Maybe here (Elwin thought), in these bizarro catacombs, the secret self broke loose, in something like the way cicadas shed their exoskeletons after their thirteen-year slumber below ground: the phobic worrywart emerging from inside the famously blithe optimist, the unheartbroken pinchable linguist shedding his Snuggie of despair. Nice to imagine, anyway. The panelists bumbled about the tunnels in a meek herd. Men with clipboards gave presentations. Everything and everyone was sleek, orderly, deft, buttoned: Here was the sort of covert government competence Elwin had assumed extinct for decades, that virile federal prowess of Cold War–era movies and paranoiac spy thrillers.

Afterwards they'd ascended back to earth to tour the surface site where their markers would be built: "their canvas," as Sharon put it. Aside from the buildings and trailers and parking lots and various other human alterations, some of which would be dismantled when the encasement was completed in 2055 (leaving only a security post, which would remain for another seventy-five years), the landscape was 360 degrees of khaki flatness, a petrified alien nothingness that Elwin found himself unable to contextualize. This was not the mythic desert West of cowboys and cattle; this was not even like the baked powder of the Sahara. This was a scorched void, stasis translated into geology, the earth stripped of nearly all he considered earthly: a few scrubby gray plants here and there, looking like miserable tinder, and in the great hazy distance a serrated line of violet-gray mountains, but that was all. The panel members gathered in a semicircle, holding their caps tight to their heads to prevent the warm hard wind from hurling them after the few tumbleweeds skittering toward the horizon, while their guide from Attero Laboratories ran through the project's timeline. "After active control is abandoned, in 2110, this is what will remain," he said, pointing away from the compound to the flatness beyond. Everyone looked, nodding, seeing nothing. "So the only indicator of what's buried below," he said, "will be up to you."

Elwin frowned, feeling the mental itch of some distant associative memory, an evocation scratching at the door of his consciousness: that tip-of-the-tongue sensation he imagined his poor father had to contend with every few minutes or so. Some line, some fragment, some something, what was it—he'd grown to loathe these senile interregnums, however common, darkened as they were by his father's demise—but then wait (he thought), that was it, his dad, his dad and the phrase *lone and level sands* which appeared to him suddenly like an aerial banner over the landscape: it was the melancholy closing lines of Shelley's "Ozymandias," which his father used to read to him at bedtime: "Round the decay / Of that colossal wreck, boundless and bare / The lone and level sands stretch far away." Elwin looked at the desert anew, filtering the view through the veil of this allusion—

But only for a moment. As if on cue, his cellphone chanced to snare a signal from the wind and bleeped to denote accumulated voicemails: six from his father already, Elwin saw, and all of these before 9 A.M. Eastern time. Even here, even nowhere, he could not shed his life, not even temporarily. It was like all the excess flesh that swaddled him: inert, inescapable, Elwinized. His secret self was just his self.

On the bus ride back to the hotel, rowdy with excited expert chatter, everyone leaning over their seatbacks yattering with interdisciplinary abandon, Elwin called his father back. He had to stick a finger inside one ear to mute the noise.

"Oh El, thank God. I can't find your mother's number," said his father. "Does she have a new one?"

This clearly wasn't the time to remind him she was dead. Sometimes Elwin's father would respond "Oh, right," as if he'd forgotten an appointment; at other times, he'd go silent, choke up, demand the details of her death and, with clenched wrath, the reason no one had thought to tell him. "I don't—have it," Elwin said, which wasn't quite the lie it felt like, since, technically, he couldn't have what didn't exist. (Janie, on the other hand, had already graduated to unrepentant make-believe: "Mom's with me," she'd tell him, "but she's asleep.")

"Why not?" his father asked.

Across the aisle from him, Sharon was debating marker aesthetics with the panel's physicist, who was kneeling backwards in his seat with his arms folded atop the headrest. Elwin didn't much like the physicist, if only because Sharon seemed equally as drawn to him as she was to Elwin. Back in San Francisco, during the first meeting, he'd gotten himself inadvertently drunk at the hotel bar with Sharon and the physicist—Randolph was his name, from U of Washington—while trying to wait him out in order to secure Sharon's exclusive attention. He wasn't sure why: she wasn't particularly beautiful, if that mattered (lined leathery skin, prone to Mother Hubbard–type dresses, a cross between an aging hippie and a Dorothea Lange subject), and had something of the wistful, smudgy air of a retired party girl about her. The question wasn't about attraction so much as alignment; they seemed like pieces from different puzzles, he and she. So it was all irrational, the drinking and adolescent jockeying, and one of many things he'd cursed himself for the next morning though well down the cringe-list from his having given Sharon an abridged but unavoidably pathetic account of his marriage's collapse. Despite the finger plugging his ear, Elwin heard her ask, "But how do we ensure it won't be mistaken for art?"

"I'm traveling, Dad," he said. "New Mexico, remember?"

"Sure. The nuke dump."

He heard Sharon say, "Ugliness alone isn't enough. Think about Munch. *The Scream* is ugly. But *The Scream* is art."

"That's it," Elwin said to his father. Outside the window, he saw a guard waving the big bus through a fenced checkpoint. The bus turned onto a paved roadway, churning up a billow of colorless dust that left the windows coated with a bleak film: the lone and level sands smearing his view of the lone and level sands.

"Hey, odd question for you," he said to his father.

"Say again?"

"Odd question." He caught Sharon's eye; she looked annoyed, in need of support with whatever argument she was failing to advance. "Do you remember 'Ozymandias'?" he asked his father. "The poem?"

"Shelley. What about it?"

Elwin could hear a nurse in the background, probably come to dispense his father's pills. He said, "You used to read it to me as a kid."

"Yeah, of course," his father said. Then he said, "Wait a second," which Elwin gathered was to the nurse standing bedside, as a nurse did three times daily, with a paper cup of water and a palmful of pills. Elwin's father cleared his throat, and then recited, with deep verve and without a single pause for recollection, all fourteen of the poem's lines.

"That's the one," Elwin said quietly, listening to his father gulping the pills while the nurse said, "Okay, Mr. King of Kings, one more," and several thousand miles closer Sharon was saying something about the pitfalls of beauty and singularity to a physicist shaking his head *no.*

"What else you need?" his father said, with a bouncy new lilt to his voice that sounded, to Elwin, like pride. However inadvertently, Elwin realized, he'd just given his father a test, and the old man hadn't just passed it, he'd aced it. The flush of that achievement might cheer him for hours. This was good, Elwin thought. This made the sunlight softer, the bus seat less cramped and sticky. He said, "Nothing, Dad, I'll check in again later, okay?" and his father said okay and thanked him for calling.

For a few moments longer Elwin kept the phone to his ear, staring vacantly out the window at the vacant scenes beyond the glass while inside his mind a question was taking lumpy shape: Was memory a choice? In one ear, albeit muted, there'd been Sharon arguing that even accidental beauty could jeopardize the Markers project, since, cross-culturally, beauty is preserved while ugliness is discarded, and therefore any beauty—even the fearsomely ugly beauty of *The Scream*—could undermine the mission by drawing rather than deflecting attention, enabling rather than disabling memory, while in the other ear there'd been his father, denying the death of his wife of fifty-eight years yet still clinging to fourteen lines of Shelley that he couldn't have had cause to recite or recall in four decades. There were dire clinical implications for the latter, of course, yet still Elwin wondered: Could these clashing conversations have been like opposite shores of the same raw and unmapped landmass? Could memories be like works of art, the great ones hung beneath metal halide lighting on stark museum walls, for daily straightening and dusting, while the shoddy ones were abandoned to attics, yard sales, to that unheeded space above the headboards in off-ramp motel rooms?

He'd wrestled with this idea before, professionally at least, when he'd conducted linguistic fieldwork in Papua New Guinea back in the 1980s. In the remote village of Gapun, where about two hundred villagers still spoke a dying language isolate called Taiap, he'd interviewed a brother and sister in their sixties—twins, in fact: that perfect scientific model. Both had left Gapun in their late teens—migrating to the provincial capital of Wewak, the sister to marry a policeman and the brother to work in a hotel which he eventually came to own—and both had given up Taiap for Tok Pisin, the pidgin English that's Papua New Guinea's official language. Yet forty-odd years later the brother could still speak fluent Taiap while the sister had retained only a few dozen nouns. Rudimentary psychology offered one hypothesis—the brother, now a cosmopolitan hotelier, delighted in the rags-to-riches arc of his biography, flattering himself with the humbleness of his beginnings, while the sister, who blamed a wide and wicked conspiracy for her husband's lack of promotion over the years and the low economic gear this had stalled them in, went to great lengths to conceal her upbringing in Gapun. Yet this hypothesis, that motivation alone could induce first-language attrition, seemed too coarse to Elwin, and unsatisfying from a neurolinguistic point of view. Could the brain be so easily unwired, by mere emotion? Was there, indeed, an aesthetics of memory? Surely that's what Sharon was arguing—he looked at her now, and by her expression realized that he'd lowered the phone from his ear and must now appear to be stewing forlornly in his seat, like the neglected fat kid on the schoolbus that he'd never been—and maybe what Carrollton had been reaching for when he suggested burying the waste with no markers at all, the obverse of Nabokov's contention that by loving a memory you make it stronger and stranger. "Elwin," Sharon said, trying to draw him in from across the aisle, "do you not agree?" He stammered, clueless about what she meant and furthermore distracted because latching onto the syntax he realized she was a Southerner, long enough ago to lose the accent but not the syntactic imprint, and for some odd reason this seemed like an important detail for him to know—for him to remember—if he was going to fall in love with her, a possibility he hadn't considered until that moment.

"Yes," he answered, "absolutely I agree," earning himself a sneer from the physicist which in some small way felt like a reward in itself.

That was the night the dreams started. In the first one, he appeared as a kind of pharaoh, though not in pharaoh dress. (Just his same old 48x32 Dockers "Big and Tall" khakis and a Kenneth Cole shirt: a mallwear pharaoh.) Inside a giant sandstone cavern, a group of blue-suited slaves—how Elwin knew they were slaves wasn't clear, but they were—carted wooden boxes in on dollies while others pried open the boxes and still others stacked the boxes' contents in an exquisitely patterned way. In the shape of an arrow, it seemed; possibly a flower. For whatever dream-logic reason, Elwin didn't recognize the contents at first. But then he did. There was his old tackle box, here was his wedding suit, there was the wristwatch his father'd given him upon his high-school graduation, here was his medicine cabinet with gypsum-dusted screws jutting from its back as if yanked straight from the wall. These were *his* goods, he realized: his stockpile for the afterlife. He shouted for the slaves to stop, because surely he wasn't dying, not to mention that he *needed* this stuff—the medicine cabinet more than the tackle box, but still. The slaves ignored him. Panicking, he fled the cavern by clambering into a convenient elevator. For a long bizarro time the elevator rose and kept rising, despite Elwin jamming all the buttons. When its doors slid open, Elwin found himself stepping out into a

desolate sand-swept landscape littered with the broken ruins of a sculpture. Awe flooded through him, and with it a sense of tranquility. The
wind was warm against his face, like the nuzzling breath of a mother or
perhaps a lover. He saw two stone legs, tall as houses, sticking out of the
sand, and nearby a half-buried head. Something about the legs—cartoon-
ishly plump, with sneakers on the feet—struck him as familiar, but when
he walked to the head and brushed the sand from its face he toppled backwards in—

In what? That's when he woke up, his eyelids springing open despite
their heavy crust and his entire body feeling energized at once, as if by
electrical switch, a hot and instantaneous current he could discern in his
fingers, toes, penis, even his hair: a sudden and all-encompassing shock of
corporeal awareness. The sensation was so extraordinary, in fact, that his
first conscious thought, as he scanned the alien darkness of the hotel room,
was that he'd died. Like that, boom. Like the deer on Route 202, without
ever having seen it coming.

But then: No. Of course he hadn't died. These were not the stiff sheets
and scratchy bedspread of the afterlife. With scenes of the dream still swirling through his mind, he pulled himself up, noting the red digits of the hotel alarm clock spelling out 2:57 A.M. For several minutes his mind seemed
to operate on two separate frequencies, one mind replaying episodes from
the dream, even as they faded, while the other was engaged in mundane
physiological analysis of the dream's causes. Had he eaten anything unusual? Half a Cobb salad, he remembered, dismissing any gastrointesti-
nal basis. No one had salad dreams. Was it alcohol? No. He'd had just
two glasses of chardonnay at dinner, and hadn't even finished the second
glass because frankly the wine was awful. Some Australian mega-brand
that'd tasted like kangaroo pee. He tried recollecting the dream's ending,
the maybe-climax that had jolted him from sleep, but couldn't—that's
where the film had broken.

But then something else occurred to him. The silence. Not the exterior
silence: the air conditioning unit was thrumming beneath the window, the
whoosh of passing cars sounded with arrhythmic regularity, somewhere a
toilet was flushing. No, the interior silence: the yearlong conversations he'd
been having with Maura in his head had stopped. That aggrieved chatter
that spooled constantly, like background music, had disappeared, and in

his mind now was a strange and blessed sonic emptiness. He rolled out of the bed and went to the window, and drawing open the heavy Marriott curtains he stood there, breathing in the view: the hotel roof, the parking lot, an empty intersection. The feeling was one of loss, but, weirdly, without the ache of loss. Loss without *loss*. He watched a car slow for a red light, pause at the intersection, and then glide on through, and for some reason this brought to his face a faint smile of rapport. He felt as though he, too, were gliding through something, though just *what* he didn't know.

The dreams persisted throughout the trip. At first they seemed unrelated, save for their vividness and volume. Sharon made a cameo in one, wheeling by on a bicycle. Long-lost friends showed up, resurrected after decades of disregard. More than once his father appeared, one time swimming with Elwin in an antifreeze-colored river that cut through a decimated, abandoned cityscape, the two of them nevertheless splashing and laughing the way they'd done at the shore almost half a century ago. After the third dream Elwin took to hastily transcribing his wake-up memories on a bedside notepad, which was how he came to note the connective dream-tissue binding them together. In each of the dreams, he discovered, was a monument. Of a sort, anyway: his own pharaoh's tomb; a discordantly gleaming edifice in the midst of that blighted riverside cityscape; a skyscraper-tall stack of junked cars in one odd episode (made odder still by the stack's curator, the television actor Gabe Kaplan of *Welcome Back, Kotter* fame); a stone cairn that in another dream some children were building and pleading for his help to finish it. He mulled this thematic tie, but not too much. Dreams were just dreams, he figured, the byproducts of the brain's digestive tract, the off-gasses of cognitive fermentation. Still, the dreaming was pleasant, and, even back home in New Jersey, where the dreams dipped in frequency, he soon found himself looking forward to sleep, nestling himself in early for some REM-sleep entertainment.

He was in the midst of one such dream when a hard metallic banging roused him from sleep. Someone was knocking on the screen door. Bologna sounded a dim bark, less a warning against intrusion than a drowsy corrective for the disturbance. Elwin rolled out of bed and sat up. It was 3:31 A.M. Out of fresh habit, he immediately tried to seize the remnants of his dream, but this one went leaking out fast—all he could catch was the somewhat alarming image of infants swaddled in Saran Wrap. He sat listening, but there was only silence now. Minor house creaks, the patter of rain outside. Had the knocking been a dream too? A dream layered atop another dream?

But then the knocking resumed. Elwin struggled into some pants and went puffing down the stairs. His first theory, conceived halfway down, was that Maura had finally come back. It was the symmetry of it all that sold him on the idea: She'd dumped him at 3:30 A.M., and now here she was returning to him. This was her decisive hour. What would he say to her, he wondered, as though he hadn't rehearsed the scene a thousand times in his head. *Yes,* of course. He'd say yes. To whatever she asked. She was the sword he was fated to fall upon. Yet he felt an odd lack of excitement for this potential, evidenced by his slackening pace as he reached the bottom of the stairs. Here was his Christmas, and he wasn't sure he wanted his gifts. Stricken with apprehension, rather than joy, he cracked the door open for a peek.

It was Christopher. His hair was rain-soaked, and though Elwin couldn't be sure because of all the dripping, he looked to have been crying. He had a pillow under his arm.

"Doc! Jesus, been banging like crazy—saw the Jeep—figured you was back—just . . ."

"Is everything okay?" Elwin asked, adding the obvious: "It's kinda late."

Emptying his lungs through his nose, and lowering his gaze to his shuffling wet sneakers, Christopher said, "You mind if I crash for the night, Doc?"

"Yeah, sure, come'n in," said Elwin, glancing past Christopher's shoulder to make sure Maura wasn't lurking there, her reconciliation mission having been upstaged at the last minute. "What's up?"

"Fucking usual. Dad's being a prick."

"Couch or the guestroom—your pick. How so?"

"Couch'll do. Just won't stay off my fucking ass."

Elwin flipped on the living room light and assessed Christopher in its glow. The old saw about looking like a drowned rat, he decided, fit with an unfortunate precision: Christopher's sniffling runny nose evoking a rodent's twitchy snout, the rainwater dripping from his mustache as from whiskers, his eyes beady and raw. "I'll fetch you a towel," Elwin said. "Maybe some—dry clothes."

When he returned he found Christopher on the couch cupping his head in his hands. Elwin set a towel before him on the coffee table, and beside it a t-shirt and pair of sweatpants that wouldn't possibly fit him but oh well. Christopher didn't move. For an awkward minute Elwin stood there, rubbing his hands, until finally he asked, "You want to talk about anything?"

Christopher looked up. So he *had* been crying, Elwin confirmed: the red evidence of it was ringing his eyes. But he'd also been drinking. That yeasty beer smell. Owing to recent episodes in his own life, Elwin didn't need reminding that the two activities could sometimes conjoin. "Yeah," Christopher said, and then paused. "Y'know what I *wanna* talk about, Doc? *Fishing.* The Mets. This chick I met Friday at McGuinn's, gave me her number and all that."

Elwin blinked a few times. "That sounds pretty good," he said, while thinking: *but not at 3:30 A.M. when I've got an eight o'clock seminar to teach.* He picked the towel off the table and pressed it upon Christopher who gave his wet face a halfhearted swipe.

"But you know what I gotta talk about," said Christopher, *"instead?"*

Elwin shook his head.

Christopher screwed up his lips, as though preparing to spit, and rocking his head back and forth he began, "That motherfucking—that old fucking sonofa—"

Boomboomboom. Now came another knocking at the screen door, sharp and insistent. Christopher, knowing better than Elwin who was at his door, closed his eyes and went limp. "Hold that thought," Elwin said, thinking surely *this* time it was Maura, but when he swung open the door he saw:

Big Jerry. Red-faced but not red-eyed, dressed in a New York Giants nightshirt with a torn collar exposing a swath of wet pink shoulder in something like (but also very unlike) the old *Flashdance* style from the '80s. (Maura had torn her shirts like that back then, kicking her legs to Jane Fonda videos on the old TV, something Elwin had found unbearably sexy.) Big Jerry's hair was bed-crazy, gray spikes shooting everywhere, which only added to the air of toxic lunacy Elwin sensed. He realized at once that he'd dropped or been dragged into the bad middle of something.

"Sorry to bother you at this crazy hour, Doc," Big Jerry said, his hands forming and unforming fists, his big voice pinched and tense, "but I saw the light was on, and I'm looking for—"

At that moment he drew his gaze past Elwin's unexposed shoulder and there on the couch he spotted: "*Christopher!* You piece of *shit!* Get your ass out here!"

Elwin said, "Whoa, Jerry, let's calm down . . ."

Big Jerry wedged a foot inside the doorway while Elwin widened his defensive stance, their bellies lightly crashing. Big Jerry seemed oblivious to Elwin's presence, however, as if blocked by a fence or some other inert matter. "You can't hide from me, you little shit!" He was poking a meaty finger in the air toward Christopher, close enough to Elwin's ear to provoke evasive head action. "You gonna take it like a man!"

Recalling Christopher's middle-fingered response to his father on the night they'd cleaned the deer, and therefore wanting to be prepared for Big Jerry's inevitable blitz if Christopher did likewise tonight, Elwin glanced back at Christopher. But Christopher looked incapable of anything remotely like that. Perhaps the excess beer had emboldened him that far-gone night, or maybe the obstructed distance between Big Jerry in the bedroom and himself out on the driveway, or the safety net of his mother's hovering influence. But there was no safety net now, Elwin realized (save Elwin himself), and Christopher was cowering, his forearm raised to protect himself. With a despairing scowl, Elwin noted the forearm: the way Christopher was holding it appeared subconscious, almost instinctual, as if he wasn't even aware it was raised, a nurtured rather than natural response that signaled to Elwin all he needed to know about Big Jerry's parenting tactics. Christopher was twenty-two years old yet in that ugly and trembly moment he looked ten, or six, a teary-eyed boy afraid for his life. A quick fusillade of *ah-ha*s went rippling through Elwin's mind, as he recalled some of Christopher's darker quirks, like his hair-trigger temper and his tendency during tantrums to assault inanimate objects, or the bullying tone he developed after six or seven beers at McGuinn's and the related paranoia that somebody in the bar was keen to kick his ass. Dropped hints, mumbled clues, inscrutable little tics. It all made sense now—or if it didn't quite make sense, because nothing human ever did (Maura, for instance), it pointed in the general direction of sense. Big Jerry fathered with his fists.

Elwin felt a stiff turning in his gut, a revulsion spiked with outrage, and turning to Big Jerry and placing a palm against Big Jerry's chest he said with uncommon firmness, "We need to calm it down."

Big Jerry sneered down at Elwin's hand, through which Elwin could feel Jerry's chest throbbing, and leaning into the palm so that Elwin's forearm muscles went taut against the pressure, he hissed, "Move out the way, Doc."

"That's not a good idea," was all Elwin could think to say.

"This ain't your fucking business."

"But it is my — my fucking house."

Big Jerry leaned in harder, compressing the distance between him and Elwin so that their bellies were now in full contact, and bellowed over Elwin's shoulder, "You tell your new best friend here how you got fired from work? Didya?" Elwin could feel wet droplets of spittle cooling on his ear and cheek. "I didn't think so." To Elwin he said, "I set 'im up with that job, *me*. That was a legacy hire, right there. Fucking dipshit can't get to work on time. Made *me* look like a piece of shit."

"Maybe it's for the best," Elwin offered.

With a squealing lisp Big Jerry echoed him: *"Maybe it's for the best."* Now he leaned in harder, Elwin's leg muscles tightening as he fixed his stance. "Get the fuck out the way, Doc. This here is a family matter and you ain't got no right sticking your nose in it."

"Everyone needs to calm down," Elwin suggested, as much to himself as to Big Jerry, because the stiffening in his gut was now iron-hard and spreading, his shoulders tensing and the fingers of his free hand flexing. After glancing back at Christopher, still silent and crouched, he felt his weight shifting forward into his palm. It all felt like a slow-motion collision, their parts straining toward mechanical breakage.

Big Jerry felt it too. "Lemme ask you something," he said, his gaze pinned downward as though addressing the hand against his chest. "You been payin him for all that work on your car?" Tilting his head upward to lock eyes with Elwin, he snorted, a ribbon of irate drool unfurling from his bottom lip. "I didn't fucking think so."

"Don't be ridiculous."

"Just move your fat ass so I can bring that piece of shit back where he belongs."

"You need to go back home, Jerry," Elwin said.

"You need to *move,* fatass!" he shouted, emphasizing the word *move* with a two-handed shove to Elwin's chest. The shove was fully leaded; Elwin felt it all the way to his ribs, emitting an *oof* of startled pain. In his peripheral vision, as he listed backwards, he saw Christopher rise from the couch, and then, listing forward like the big weeble-wobble he was, as he regained his balance, he saw Big Jerry's enraged face as a giant maw of coffee-stained teeth and woolly gray mustache, a face that appeared to Elwin ten times its actual size, as if anger were inflating Big Jerry's head.

Elwin had never been in a physical fight in his life. The closest he'd ever come was in third grade, when he'd accidentally elbowed Danny Parsh in a recess game of touch football and Danny Parsh had jumped him to the ground, the boys forming a tight circle and chanting *fight fight* while the girls fled to alert the nuns. Back then he'd folded himself into a wimpy fetal ball, much the way a potato bug did when threatened with a stick, while Danny sat atop him trying to wrest him into submissive position, but before Danny could land a punch he was plucked off by a nun gripping his collar and then forced to shake hands with a quivering Elwin who was from that day forward never again a competitive touch-football player. So he had zero fighting experience, unless you counted being sat on as a nine-year-old. He was certainly without any adult precedent for what to do when physically challenged. He might've known, otherwise, how to defuse such a situation (when curling up like a giant potato bug wasn't a moral option). Or, barring a peaceable outcome, he might've known how much force to deploy or not deploy when responding to a shove like the one he'd just absorbed.

All he did know, at that moment, was that Christopher was closing in behind him, one horrible and conflicted step at a time, and that there wasn't any way he was going to allow Big Jerry a whack at his poor son under his roof, or, worse yet, watch Christopher leap in to defend him, watch this whole episode devolve into bruisy mayhem, and, somewhere else inside him, in a secondary but insistent voice, that Maura wasn't ever coming back, she'd dumped him and it was over, and even if she did come back his answer wasn't yes but *no,* because he was done with being sat on, he was done with being not-enough, he was done with being totaled, he was done with his own obsolescence, he was done he was done he was *done.*

So he shoved Big Jerry in the same precise way Big Jerry had shoved him, tit for tat because the only fighting tactic he knew was the one that'd just been used on him seconds ago. But despite resemblances this was not Big Jerry's shove: the *tit* far overwhelmed the *tat*. Into that shove Elwin funneled all his 334 pounds (according to his last weigh-in, six hours prior), exerting a sixth-ton of impact that sent Big Jerry floundering backwards and then, to Elwin's horrified astonishment, farther backwards, almost but not quite airborne, his wet slippers skidding across the porch, his thick lineman's arms pinwheeling, and then even farther backwards until his back slammed the porch post, and with a grunt of pain he went spinning leftward into the porch railing, and then slipping in a puddle on the porch, where a clogged gutter was spilling filthy sheets of rainwater, he went down in a jellied heap. And was still.

"Holy shit," he heard Christopher say behind him.

Elwin was staring at his hands as if they weren't his own. "I didn't mean to—oh God I'm sorry—Jerry?"

From the drenched pile that was Big Jerry came a moan. Rolling to his side, he reached up for the porch post, missed it, and then latching onto the railing he slowly and brokenly began pulling himself upward. Elwin stepped out onto the porch, shaking timidly, saying, "Jerry?" But Big Jerry raised a hand for him to stop, unloosing a watery-sounding cough as he unbent himself to stand upright, or rather almost upright, reaching around with his other hand to caress his lower back. Across the driveway Elwin could see Myrna behind the stormdoor, clutching her robe to her neck, squinting out at the black rain. Big Jerry rubbed his face hard, as if to squeegee the water from it, and then took two steps toward the porch stairs, his soaked slippers going *flop-squish-flop-squish*. With a forlorn sigh he took in the view: his twenty-three-foot Bay Ranger, his sons' matching Ford F-250 4x4s in the driveway, the fleet of quads in the backyard, the junked old BMX bikes leaning rusted and tangled against the fence, Myrna with a hand above her eyes peering anxiously out the stormdoor like a ship's watch. Slowly he pivoted back toward Elwin, who held up his hands and said, "I'm sorry—I didn't mean to do anything—even close to that—"

Big Jerry threw up a hand, waving away the words. "You can keep him," he croaked, shaking his head and grimacing. "I'm fucking through."

"Jerry, please—" Elwin started to say, but by now Big Jerry was hobbling down the steps, clutching at the stair rail. Elwin watched as he went limping across the driveway, pelted by the rain, his waterlogged nightshirt clinging to his back, and then, as Myrna opened the door, on into his house. Elwin saw Myrna's eyes widen, and before the stormdoor rattled shut heard her say, "What happened? Where's Christopher?" Then the entry light went dark, and outside there was only rain.

Back inside, Elwin didn't wait for Christopher to speak. "Go put those dry clothes on," he said, and obediently—maybe even fearfully—Christopher nodded. Elwin was still staring at his hands when he drifted into the kitchen, and with amazement watched them as they went through the routine maneuvers of fixing a pot of coffee. While the coffeemaker gurgled he sat down with his palms upon the tabletop, in his mind replaying scenes from what had just happened in much the same way he'd spent so many recent nights replaying scenes from his dreams. He found that he kept pausing, in his playback, at the moment Big Jerry had risen from the wet porch and fixed his wincing gaze across the driveway at his own house and arrayed accessories, his own accumulated monument: What had Jerry seen there, or not seen? What could've possibly gone through Jerry's mind as he'd surveyed all that—the sum product of his sweat and sacrifice, all of it rendered hollow by his terrified half-man son whom he'd then, out of spite or surrender, chucked to the curb? Maybe nothing, Elwin decided. Maybe he'd merely been catching his breath and gauging his injuries. Or maybe he'd been inventorying all he stood to lose if he uncapped the murderous rage he was no doubt feeling for his unneighborly neighbor. "The goal of life," Elwin's father used to say, quoting Jonas Salk, "is to be a good ancestor." The idea had always seemed clear, to Elwin—painfully clear, actually, when years ago the doctors concluded his immotile sperm were the cause for his and Maura's childlessness. But maybe it wasn't so clear, he thought now. Maybe Big Jerry harbored the same goal, and all that he'd seen in that moment—the rusted BMX bikes, the quads, the matching pickups; even the job he'd bequeathed to his son—was the concrete proof of his effort. In the midst of these thoughts Elwin found himself staring at his hands again, causing another thought to interrupt: How can I possibly understand another person if I can't even recognize my goddamn self?

"I think your dog's dead." This was Christopher, standing in the kitchen doorway. He looked ridiculous, awash in Elwin's XXL Marasmus State t-shirt and clasping the waist of his borrowed sweatpants to keep them from falling off. Ridiculous, and pathetic: a boy unprepared for manhood—or deprived of the means for it, same difference.

"No," Elwin said. "He's not dead. He just sleeps hard. You'll see."

Christopher nodded, and came shuffling toward the table. "What the . . . fuck, huh?"

"Yeah," Elwin said, knowing there was so much more to come, a whole lifetime of talking before sunrise. "You hungry?" he asked, and when Christopher nodded yes Elwin stood up and opened the refrigerator and pulled from it a package of thawed deer steaks. As the coffeemaker beeped its completion, and as Christopher started talking, fumblingly, as if in a new language he had just that night begun to learn, Elwin rinsed the steaks in the sink, watching the blood turn pink under the faucet and then dissolve altogether, flushed into the ancient pipes running invisibly beneath New Jersey, the buried iron channels undergirding the world, holding it up, and draining who knows where.

6

MATTY BOONE DID NOT, at first, show much promise as a scavenger. For one thing, he lacked the ability to carry in his head a mental inventory of needs, and therefore didn't know what to look for when canvassing the streets without Talmadge or Micah to guide him; he judged everything he found on its condition, rather than its utility, as in the newish-looking blowdryer he fetched out of a West Village trash bag and proudly delivered to Micah despite (a) her unblowable dreadlocks and (b) their lack of functioning electrical sockets, or the brass birdcage he found on Jane Street, or the size-XXL velvet Santa suit he pulled from a bag on West 15th Street just after Christmas. (He tried putting the Santa suit to use as pajamas, to blunt all the grief he was taking from Tal, but the floppy cuffs kept tripping him up, only sharpening the grief.) For another, he couldn't seem to grasp the ecological landscape of trash, the way some areas were ripe for the picking and others poor, no matter how much Talmadge tutored him ("Dorms and nursing homes and residence hotels are always good. Anywhere you find people moving in and moving out a lot"), nor could he get a handle on the fixed schedule of scavenging, the tidal regularity of when grocery stores cleared the old produce (typically Mondays and Thursdays) and when delis dumped their warmed-over buffet items (4 and 11 P.M.) and how the sanitation pickup schedule changed north of 28th Street. How pigeons managed to cram all this into their M&M-sized brains was one of those mysteries of nature that Matty used to enjoy seeing solved on the Discovery Channel after several bong hits and a Vicodin chaser. Now it just pissed him off.

For the most part, then, he spent his solo days skating a desultory, unproductive downtown route on his longboard, occasionally kicking curbside bags in much the same pointless way used-car buyers kick tires. What was in there? Garbage was in there. And as much as he dug what Tal and Micah were doing, how they'd engineered this whole presto-chango disappearing act from society, how they were giving a righteous middle finger to the whole capitalist grind, living pure and all that shit, still . . . garbage was garbage, man, it was tampons and diapers and smeary pink meat wrappers and chicken bones and cat litter and scratched CDs and dull razors and expired coupons and ballpoint pens that didn't work anymore. To hear Tal and Micah tell it, however, it was like some barely known wormhole into another dimension of society, the flip side, the ass end, where everything is genuine and raw because it's not meant to be seen — that garbage was the only *truthful* thing civilization produced, because that's where all the dirty secrets went, all the adulterous love letters and the murder weapons and the abandoned poems and the unflattering photos and the never-to-be-counted empty booze bottles and the wads of Kleenex dampened by a woman who can't understand why she rises from bed at 3 A.M. and goes creeping by her perfect sleeping husband and children to weep at the kitchen table about imperfections she can't quite name. It was all in there, Micah and Tal said, just waiting to be hacked: the secret files of mankind, dragged weekly to the curb.

"What do you see?" Talmadge asked him one morning, as they were peering into a dumpster behind a nursing home on Henry Street. Talmadge was deploying his guru voice, all wise and zenny-sounding: his dumpster Yoda routine. Matty squinted hard. "I just see paper," he finally said, with the peeved tone of someone who's failed a riddle, a flunking Jedi. Because, aside from the black and red bags, that's all Matty *did* see: a fat white mound of mail and document-looking stuff, as though a file cabinet had barfed.

"Look harder," Talmadge said, but without another glance Matty snapped, "Dude. *Paper.*"

Talmadge heaved himself upward, using his abdomen to balance himself seesaw-style on the edge, and then, kicking his legs back, lowered his upper body into a corner of the dumpster. "Come hold my feet," he instructed Matty, who did so, staring up at the grid of windows above him and wondering what all those old fucks must be making of the sight. If he rubbed his belly and pouted, he suspected, cookies might come raining down from the windows. "Okay," Talmadge grunted. "Got it."

When Matty pulled Talmadge back upright, he saw a ten-pound sack of rice in Talmadge's hands and a wide satisfied grin above it. Together they assessed the sack, looking for holes in the fabric indicating rat or insect damage, or any odd, disturbing stains. But it looked as clean as the day the Sysco truck delivered it. "Who the hell knows, man," Talmadge said, hefting the bag onto his shoulder. "Maybe someone over-ordered. Happens all the time. Excess, man. This'll feed us for, like, forever." Matty trailed him into a narrow alley that led out to Henry Street, on the way punting an empty bottle of Pepto-Bismol with the same force he'd once applied to penalty kicks. "Fucking paper, that's all I saw," he grumbled.

But Matty Boone was not without resourcefulness. His late grandfather had always insisted that the family's Boone-ness could be traced back to the original Boone, that being Daniel of coonskin cap fame, and though Matty, from an early age, smelled a ripe whiff of bullshit — Granddad Boone had also claimed to know the precise whereabouts of Jimmy Hoffa's body, about which he would say only, "It's not where you think" — he reserved just enough faith in the claim to put it to occasional use. His probably-not-but-possibly noble ancestry was like an emergency well he drew from in moments of lowered confidence: entering the Oregon State Penitentiary, for instance, or getting kicked off the Ole Miss soccer team, or, further back, when he was forced to meet Mark Coreno in the woods behind the Ramapo Ridge Middle School baseball field to settle the affections of Kaitlyn Stulik: *I got Daniel Boone's blood in me,* he'd tell himself. *There's no bear, panther, or Indian in the world I can't kill. Boone, baby, Boone.* True, this turbo-boost of confidence hadn't stopped Mark Coreno from beating the crap out of him, or his cellmate in Oregon, a short wiry Russian with a spiderweb tattooed across his face, from *actually* crapping on him one night while Matty slept ("So you know where you stand," the cellmate explained in the morning, shrugging, "nothing personal"). But like an itty-bitty reservoir of adrenaline secreted deep inside his brainpan, Matty's Daniel Boone gene, synthetic or not, kept him stiff-jawed and resolute through these events, allowing him to feel — even with a prison turd on his chest — unbroken and maybe unbreakable, down but not quite out, fated for better days. So he'd suffered a few setbacks; according to Wikipedia, so had Daniel Boone. And maybe, from another, wider, and, like, Buddhist angle, they hadn't really been setbacks at all: Last he'd heard, Mark Coreno drove a plow truck and had gotten banned for life from Dave & Buster's after sticking his boot through the screen of a NASCAR simulator game, Kaitlyn Stulik had one white baby and one black one and was stripping down in Passaic, and his cellmate Gleb, first impressions aside, turned out to be the best roomie he'd had since Tal. Gleb, in fact, had accorded Matty special status *because* of his lineage, since Gleb, too, claimed a famous ancestor. "My great-grandfather very famous inventor," Gleb said. "He invent pistol you shoot underwater." At the time Matty wanted to ask why anyone would need to shoot a pistol underwater, but because Gleb had shit on him forty-eight hours earlier he just said, "Wow."

So Matty figured it this way: Daniel Boone lived rough and wild, had to hunt for his supper, had probably also gotten pissed off at pigeons for knowing more than he did. Matty could endure it, then; at least for a while, anyway. Not that his present deal was really all that bad: He had a place to crash, even if it required a two-hour pitstop at Starbucks every morning in order to charge his cellphone, and he had Talmadge to buddy around with, even if Tal had turned kinda *priestly* since college. No rent, no bills, no pressure: just undiluted downtime, a big fat pause button he could press until he could plug in the next GPS coordinates in his life, could point himself *x*-ward. The scavenging sucked, true, but Micah had laid down the law, announcing a "family meeting" after he'd been there for a week—one of those awkward things, like an intervention—during which she said he'd have to "contribute" if he planned to stay. Matty'd thought he *had* been contributing, by letting Tal raid his weed stash whenever he wanted, but Micah meant food and shit like that. Afterwards Tal had taken him aside to apologize for Micah, saying she was "sorta hardcore" and wasn't actually harshing Matty despite, you know, the way it'd sounded. "Dude, it's cool," Matty said. "My last roommate took a dump on me."

But Matty'd known the score. If he wanted to prolong this ride, he needed to please Micah.

Wandering Union Square one grimy afternoon just after the New Year, a Kaopectate-colored sky pissing equal measures of snow and sleet onto his head, he noticed, in an open truck bay on 13th Street behind a giant gourmet grocery chain, a dude in a green apron tossing what appeared to be shrinkwrapped packages of meat into a space age–looking dumpster. This looked promising. Matty stepped inside.

The grocery dude was a fat white guy with a beard so orange and splotchy that from a distance it looked like a birthmark. From atop a loading dock, he was flinging the meat into the dumpster frisbee-style, fetching one package at a time from a waxed cardboard box at his feet and hurling it sideways so that the trays went whirling through the air before disappearing into the big steel bin. It looked like fun — frisbee golf with meat! — though the dude's puffy scowl argued otherwise. From his expression, you'd think dude aimed to *punish* the meat with those whirlybird slingings, somewhat like the way (according to Gleb) Russian gangsters chopped the arms and legs off their victims, then seared the wounds with blowtorches, before killing them. (This had struck Matty as a seriously inefficient use of time and energy, but, again, to Gleb he'd just said, "Wow.") Dude's scowl only deepened when he glanced up and saw Matty.

"Wassup," Matty offered warmly.

At least thirty degrees chillier in tone, the grocery dude replied, "Wassup."

"That stuff still good?"

Grocery dude rolled his eyes. "Don't even ask," he said, resuming his dumping chore though without his prior flair. The meat went *thwunk, thwunk* into the bin. Matty watched several red porterhouses go sliding from the dude's pudgy hands.

"Ask what?"

"This is private property."

"What is?"

"Everything you see."

Matty thought about this for a while, his eyes trailing a package of hamburger meat in freefall. "I was just asking if any of that stuff was, like, still good to eat."

"Yeah, I *know* what you're asking, man, and the answer's no. Store policy."

Matty nodded, stuffing his hands in his coat pockets. He stood there rocking on his heels while the dude finished emptying the box, wondering how long the meat would stay cool in the dumpster (the air inside the bay was fridge temperature, he guessed) but also why the grocery dude was being such a complete assbucket. When the grocery dude/assbucket was done, he stood there, six feet above Matty on the loading dock with the bloodstained box in one hand, and snorted, "What?"

"What about later?"

"Later, *what?*"

"After you close or something. When no one's looking."

"The dumpster's locked, man. And there's cameras. Don't even dream it."

Matty frowned, bewildered by this technical point. "Why do you lock up a dumpster?"

"Freaks like you," came the reply, and with that the grocery dude turned to go inside. But then he stopped, pulling his hand from the doorknob, and turned back toward Matty. Cautiously, and with what appeared to be frictional deliberation, he looked to his left and then to his right, leading Matty to suspect he'd softened and, having ensured no one was watching, was about to divulge classified instructions for when and how to raid the dumpster. Matty smiled up at him, awaiting benevolence.

"Here," the grocery dude said, and dropped the box down to the concrete. "Guess you can lick that if you want." An amused and self-satisfied sneer followed, but before Matty could respond, he was gone, his apron strings waving a caustic goodbye as the door squawked shut behind him.

"Fucker," Matty said, and hocked a loogie toward the loading dock. And *fucker,* he thought, for several hours afterwards, over and over again . . . that *fucker,* he thought, even when he *wasn't* thinking it, like when he'd get a song lyric auto-looping in his head (that McDonald's jingle, for instance, which for him was a recurrent mental rash: *Give me back that filet o' fish, give me that fish*) that'd play behind his thoughts or, worse, ooze right *into* his thoughts. That fatassed mother*fucker,* he thought, while trying to distract himself with a pile of skater mags at the Union Square Barnes & Noble, then while getting rid of the smoke *(fucker)* from a one-hitter by blowing it into the toilet in the bookstore's bathroom, then while roaming the aisles at Shoe Mania where he considered stealing a pair of hightops until a headsetted salesdude with telepathic powers pinged him with that *uh-uh* look, and finally, when the sky stopped dripping, while sitting on the park steps hoping an Asian tourist chick would ask him for directions or to help her shave her legs or something—*fucker!* What was dude's *problem?* Talmadge had warned him about the various trash-guarding assholes you encountered, like Mr. Unger the Stale Bagel Sentry, but he'd never suggested they'd be like . . . *that. Guess you can lick that if you want?* The High Emperor of Fuckers.

Prowling the streets in tightening circles around the store, he noticed steam roiling from beneath a manhole cover and felt like he was staring into a mirror. Identical puffs of steam, he felt sure, were jetting from his ears. What's worse, he was *hungry,* and not just normal hungry but day-twelve-of-being-stuck-on-a-lifeboat-in-the-Pacific hungry, the sight of those steaks having roused the inner carnivore he'd been sedating these past six weeks while growing sallow and limp from a diet of exhumed tofu and infinite variations on vegetable mush.

At nine, when the last shoppers trickled out of the grocery store toting reusable sacks filled with free-trade coffee beans and free-range *poussins* and organically farmed salmon and imported bottled spring water, and the saggy-shouldered store manager locked the automatic doors and penciled something onto his clipboard, Matty was watching from across 14th Street, leaning against a lightpole and swirling his tongue around the inside of his mouth like a snake prepping venom. He was getting those steaks. He was getting that hamburger meat. Matty Boone was going ninja on these motherfuckers.

Ten minutes later he was crouched behind the store, where one of the rollup doors had been left with a two-foot gap, peering underneath to survey the scene inside. Dude said there were cameras but Matty didn't see any. Who would train cameras on a dumpster, anyway? He rolled under the door, then scurried behind a giant rack of pallets the way he'd seen people scurry in action movies. Everything looked clear: beautiful. He bounded up the loading dock stairs to where the dumpster's hopper doors were spread open at its top. The bin was startlingly *deep,* maybe six or more feet downward, and must've recently been tipped out because there wasn't much inside it—a dozen or so bulging bags, a box of Eco-Planet Non-Dairy Cheddar Crackers with a squashed corner, a ripped bag of Organic Pizza Pie Puffs, several bunches of brown bananas . . . but there, seen as gleaming red bits peeking from beneath the other garbage, was the meat. Matty felt a sloshy agitation in his torso that could have been his stomach churning, his heartbeat accelerating, his Daniel Boone gene kicking in, or maybe all of these. He paused to listen for a moment, but heard nothing more menacing than his own breath. There were DANGER signs everywhere but there were always DANGER signs everywhere. He jumped.

Working swiftly and sharply, he uncovered the meat by digging out the bags and heaving them behind him, the way a dog digs, then swung his backpack forward and unzipped it. He wagged his head, grinning. The bounty was even better than he'd hoped: porterhouses, strip steaks, thick pink veal chops, two-pound packages of ground beef, a chuck roast, and also some sweetbreads which he passed on taking because he had an idea sweetbreads equaled testicles and some oxtail he likewise ignored because who wants to eat tails and what's an ox anyway? The sell-by dates were either today or yesterday — this shit was still fucking *good!* As he loaded up his backpack he did some rough calculating: $10.15 for the hamburger, $28.77 for two mega porterhouses, $17.54 for the veal, and so on . . . that was, like, fifty bucks' worth right there. And his backpack was barely full! *Now* he understood, at last, why Tal got so stoked about this — it was *free,* man, it was like wheeling your cart past the cashier and right out the fucking door, it was just like discovering back in college that every song you wanted was free for the downloading on BitTorrent networks. When he'd stuffed his backpack to the point of unzippability, he tried cramming the meat down harder, which didn't do the trick, then knelt there agonizing over what to leave behind — not the veal, that shit was pricey, and not the porterhouses either — maybe the ribeyes but man they were bone-in and thick and looked *good.* So he went at the meat again, grunting and panting as he squashed it down until finally he got the zipper around it all; when he was finished his backpack looked pressurized, as if a knock against a sharp edge might blow meat on anyone within a ten-foot radius. *Awesome,* he thought, and stood up, feeling as rich and giddy as he'd felt since his release, raising and lowering the backpack to guess at its weight: ten pounds, fifteen, or — ?

Sounds: the raspy squawk of the door swinging open, voices, footclomps on the loading platform. Matty went crumpling to the bottom of the dumpster and froze.

"They got no depth in the secondary," a voice was saying. "None."

"You don't even fucking *need* a secondary against Chicago, brah," said another, more familiar voice. "It's a total ground game." Matty recognized that voice: It belonged to Grocery Dude/Assbucket/Emperor Fucker.

Hunkered down on all fours, and holding every cell rigid lest he cause a bag to crinkle and thereby give himself away, Matty angled his head upward and stared at the ceiling, expecting, at any moment, to see Grocery Dude's round pale orange-fuzzed face appear above him. He could imagine the tickled sneer: like when Tom the cat would have Jerry the mouse trapped in a corner, with all that lip-licking and what-do-we-have-here theatrics. He scanned the dumpster but there was no decent escape. Getting out would require a slow graceless clamber up the side, directly to where the meatheads were standing, and even if he *could* somehow bust out of the bin without getting plucked in the process, the subsequent need to roll himself under the door would entail a fatal delay. For that matter, he wasn't sure his backpack would even *fit* under the door. No way around it: He was trapped.

A sudden shadow came into view above him, and he stiffened even further. But it wasn't a face. It was a bag, a big black bulgy bag that came sailing over the edge and landed squarely on Matty's back. It wasn't heavy, which was a relief, but something like a glass jar hit his spine, just south of his shoulder blades. With superhuman effort he suppressed the natural *ooooof.*

"They'll fucking run it on third and fifteen," he heard Dude saying. "'Cause there's no protection from the oh-line, zero."

"I don't know, man," the other voice said—sounding threateningly close to Matty, right above him in fact, but with the bag splayed atop his neck Matty's view was blocked. His spine was tingling with such disturbing force that for a moment he feared paralysis; he wiggled a toe for reassurance. He heard a clicking, followed by some kind of mysterious machine-like hum, but his attention was focused on much more appealing noises: the fading of Dude's voice ("the kicking game is what *should* be scaring you"), the raspy creak of the door in motion, and then, with a sound as beautiful to him as the three-whistle signal that concluded his old soccer games, the door slamming shut. Exhaling, Matty felt his muscles go rubbery. In the hummy almost-silence that followed he shook off the garbage bag and reached his hand around to rub what would clearly be a major bruise on his back, whimpering.

That's when the whole dumpster began to rumble. Matty's whimper segued straightaway into a yelp. What the fuck? Only when the bags at the front started tumbling toward him did he realize what was happening: The space age–looking dumpster was a trash compactor, and that click-and-hum had been the compactor firing up. "Oh shit," he said, two octaves above his normal voice, and grabbing a backpack strap he made a loose and gawky scramble toward the open end of the compactor, where a giant gray hydraulic ram had begun chugging toward him. Because of the positioning of the hopper doors, however, the only way out led over the ram itself. He hopped onto the pile of bags, thinking he might attempt a hail-mary leap, but the weight of the backpack pulled him backwards and screwed up his footing on the rolling heap. He got his hands on the ram, but that was all, and slipped face-first into the slowly cascading bags, flailing and flopping. When he got to his feet again, roughly a yard of light and air remained between the ram and the sealed portion of the compactor. He girded himself for another, even hail-mary-er leap, thinking he might just be able to scale the top of the ram before it shut him in completely, but the pause he took to compute his odds — if he got caught between the top of the ram and edge of the enclosure, he'd be cut in half in slow motion, or else extruded into the chute like a sheet of pasta — was too long. Already the trash bags were churning into his ankles as the ram plowed them forward with its nested steel blocks unfurling; he watched the last line of light disappear above him, and then: a fetid darkness, a low and unstoppable rumble, Matty feeling his way down to the empty far end of the chute where he now expected he might — Jesus fuck, might *die*. He banged the steel sides, screaming, the tight tinny echoes melding into one single reverberating howl. He'd give his left nutsack to see Grocery Dude sneering at him now.

The only previous time he'd faced death — certain death, anyway; he'd had an inkling of mortal danger when he found that turd on his chest — was at fourteen, when he and his mom watched a jackknifing tractor-trailer jump the divider on 287, hurtling into the opposite lane, right at them. But that sight had triggered a spooky calm — an out-of-body-type thing, as if he were in a video game and was about to forfeit a shitload of points, but nothing more serious. Only after his mother had accomplished a startling feat of Formula One–level driving, veering rightward onto the shoulder (one-handed, with her right arm fixed across Matty's chest) so that the tractor-trailer went barreling past her window, belting their car with huge, violent gobs of mud and grass, and they'd come to a stunned speechless stop—only then did Matty, blinking wildly, realize what had just happened, how close he'd just come to being a chunky red smear on an airbag. It had all happened too fast; there hadn't been time for awareness. This, however, was different: This was like sitting cross-legged on the highway while the tractor-trailer was bearing down on you at, say, ten mph, slowly enough for you to study the tire treads and to visualize their imminent effect on your face. This involved dread, reflection, calculations, the anticipation of a downtempo squishing. Given the choice, he would've much preferred the insta-smack of a jackknifing truck.

Yet from somewhere in his polluted subconscious came Daniel Boone, decked in a fringed coat and coonskin cap, calling for hereditary calm. Or at least that's how he'd later interpret it. How else to explain his sudden spurt of reasoning? If there was any chance of survival, he knew, he'd need to put something between himself and the rear wall, so, in frantic wailing blindness, he snatched as many bags as he could snatch and piled them behind him. Because he could only hear the ram, and not see it, he had no hint of how much time he might have left; when he thought he'd made a semi-sufficient cushion, he nestled himself sideways into the bags, with his back to the rear wall, holding his backpack close against his chest, and waited. The wait turned out to be excruciatingly long, though not long enough for him to decree any pledges or prayers, or to inventory his regrets, or to fathom the absurdity of his imminent smooshing, or to hatch even a single cogent thought. What sped through his mind, instead, was something like a TV news-crawl as hacked by an eighth-grader: a streaming sequence of profanities, *fuck shit piss fuck damn,* that went on and on until he felt the soft pressure of the ram pushing a buffer wall of bags into him, then a single bag rolling onto his head as another one flattened itself on his face, then an intensified pressure as the air in the bags swelled and then with deafening gassy bangs the bags blew, in quick succession like microwave popcorn, and he could feel the backpack growing harder and tighter against his ribcage and the sharp corner of something in a bag behind him being drilled into his ass cheek. Another bag popped, spurting some kind of gelatinous semi-liquid onto his face. He needed air, but his nostrils were goo-clogged. He sensed pressure on every inch of his body, especially his shoulders, and when the pressure turned to pain his mouth flopped open; an instinctual inhale brought a film of polypropylene into his mouth, and his lungs began thrashing.

And then the ram stopped. He heard another click, and the polypropylene sagged from his mouth as the ram commenced a backwards slog. From deep in his throbbing windpipe came a yawp of joy and relief, sounding like *ferfffff*, until he realized he couldn't move. Once again he feared paralysis, but no, he was merely squashed—the nougat center of a big squarish block of compressed garbage. He wriggled his legs, rocking the bags off one another, and then, with more effort, his arms, until the block crumbled into hunks of plastic so deflated they looked vacuum-sealed.

Matty rolled down to the steel floor just as light came flooding into the compactor from the ram's withdrawal and sat there, gasping, wiping the unidentifiable gloop off his face with his coatsleeve, as the hydraulic motor spun down and the compactor clicked off. His ears were ringing so profoundly, and the silence seemed so dulled, that he thought he might be deaf; he dispelled this newest fear by inserting an investigative finger into his ear, finding it caulked by that same fucking gloop. He spat. Still stripped of thoughts, a reasonless zombie operating on purely sensory consciousness, he stood up, fetched his backpack from the floor, fastened it onto his back, and climbed out of the compactor and onto the loading dock. As he descended the stairs, he heard the door sweeping open behind him, but he neither looked back or hurried his pace. "Hey!" shouted a voice whose ownership Matty didn't even try to determine: Grocery Dude, God, it didn't matter. He flung the loading door up, drowning the voice's second, harsher *hey!* with a thick steel clatter. "Come back here!" demanded the voice, but Matty was already on 13th Street, headed east on a sidewalk that felt ten feet below him, only barely aware of the passersby halting to stare at him openmouthed.

"Holy shit," said Talmadge, when Matty appeared in the doorway, rising so abruptly that his chair tumped backwards. From the recliner, where she was tuning her banjo, Micah glanced up and frowned. They had that lazy spent look on their faces, Matty noted, like they'd just finished one of the marathon fucking sessions they'd been having way too frequently and loudly for Matty's comfort. "What happened?"

Expressionlessly, and without a word, Matty unfastened the backpack and swung it down to the floor. "Dinner," he said, nodding flatly toward the backpack.

When it was clear Matty wasn't going to say or do anything further, Talmadge knelt down and unzipped the bag. He blew a low whistle through his teeth, then looked up at Matty with a mixture of bewilderment and apprehension. Matty's long woolly beard was encrusted with something greenish yellow, as if he'd been drooling wasabi mustard, though streaks of the same crud daubed his forehead and cap. His coat was splotched with some other, thicker, paler species of glop, yogurt maybe, while his boots gave the impression he'd waded home through an eight-inch flood of butternut squash soup. Several strands of spaghetti clung to his left shoulder, like a lowgrade epaulette. He stank, too—that dumpster-juice smell.

"What is it?" Micah said, her attention still half trained on the banjo neck. She plucked a middle string, warped the note with a tuning peg, plucked it again.

Talmadge fished the uppermost package out of the backpack and held it up to the candlelight: strip steaks.

"Awww, Matty," Micah said. "You know we don't eat meat."

Matty clamped his lips together and sighed through his nose, listening to Micah strum a punctuative banjo lick that sounded like a runty backwoods giggle: *ding dang ba dada ding dang:* like a musical putdown, to Matty's stuccoed ears. To quell the eruption he felt rising in his throat, some dangerously seething amalgam of physical and emotional bile bubbling just below his tonsils, he reached into the chest pocket of his coat for a cigarette. Realizing the condition of his gloves, however, he replaced the pack into the pocket, sighed again, slipped off his gloves, then repeated the fetching barehanded. A quizzical hush filled the room until Talmadge rose with a lighter and Matty sucked two monumental drags from the cigarette.

"If you fucking *knew*," he began, "what I just went through to get this shit . . ."

"It's organic," Talmadge noted.

Matty blinked down at Talmadge. They'd never once fought or even quarreled, not even after the night Matty swiped the keys to Tal's Land Cruiser and got it stuck up to the fenders in some remote Sardis Lake mudflat, but Matty was feeling the sudden sour urge to boot his old friend in the stomach. He resisted the urge. "If you," he began again, "fucking knew—"

"Have at it," said Micah, with the precise tone and meter commonly applied to the word *whatever*. She strummed the banjo, scowled, fiddled with another tuning peg while Matty aimed a long jet of smoke at her. Now he wanted to kick the banjo.

Talmadge asked, "What happened?"

"What *happened?*" Matty said, his gaze still locked upon Micah. "What *happened* is that I got crushed in a—in a motherfucking compactor. What *happened* is that I almost died getting this meat. What *happened* is that— is that I don't understand the whole reason why you guys can't get your fucking groceries through the front door."

Micah shot him a fast black glare, underscored by that dimple creasing beneath her left eye, then dipped her head back down to pick a short, forlorn-sounding arpeggio on the banjo.

"Where?" said Talmadge.

"Union Square, that big—I dunno." Matty's stare was drawn back down to Talmadge, who appeared to be suppressing something. His face was all quivery. "What?"

"Dude." Talmadge snorted, covering his mouth with a hand; his eyes were squeezed from what looked to be stifled laughter. "You look like a pterodactyl took a shit on you."

"That's funny. That's real fucking funny."

"Sorry, man." Trying to swallow his laughter, Talmadge emitted something like a baby's burp. "It's just—you stink."

Ignoring him, Matty said to Micah: "So you're not gonna eat any of this?"

Ding bada dingdang dingdang. "Me?" she said. "No, man. I'm a vegan. That means steak is way off the menu."

"I know what vegan means." Matty drew such a glowering drag from his cigarette that his whole face puckered. "But I thought this whole thing was about, like, waste. This shit was in the trash. It was gonna rot, and turn into worms or someshit."

"So fry you up a steak, man." She was watching her fingers spider banjo strings. "It's not like we're stopping you."

"What about the rest of it?"

Micah shrugged.

"What the fuck'm I supposed to do with the *rest* of it? There's, like, veal chops in there."

Talmadge dug the veal chops out of the meat piles he'd organized on the floor. He tried lifting them for display, but Matty batted them down. "Cut that shit out," Matty hissed.

Plainly annoyed, Micah propped the banjo against the side of the recliner and leaned forward, her eyes meeting Matty's for the first time since he'd staggered in. "Why'd you take so much?" she asked.

He grunted. "Whaddaya mean, 'so much'?"

"So much meat. We couldn't eat all that even if Tal and I ate meat."

"'Cause this shit's *good!* Check out those porterhouses! They're big as a—I dunno what. They're huge."

"Bigger'n a Texan's ego," said Talmadge, courtesy of Uncle Lenord.

Micah pursed her lips and looked away, signaling to Matty just how unsatisfactory his answer was. Why *had* he taken so much? Because he *could,* that's why. Because twenty-five pounds of it had been lying in the bed of the compactor, and, Jesus—he'd thought that was the whole point, "reclaiming excess" or whatever Micah'd preached. Because, look: Here was a cow. The cow had been killed—with that rad tool the serial killer used in the movie *No Country for Old Men*—then chopped up into pieces. Some of those pieces had been sold to the kinds of New Yorkers Matty had watched exiting the store: thirtysomething dudes in chunky square glasses and peacoats, coldfaced career mommies toting it back to their Park Slope apartments. The unsold pieces, on the other hand, had been flung into a compactor where Matty Boone had almost died—almost fucking *died,* people—rescuing them. Micah wasn't vegan for health reasons; she'd told him that. She was vegan because she despised the whole blood-money system: the cow killing, the cow parceling, the smug omnivores peeling the plastic wrap off their bloodless meat in their ethically lit kitchens before cooking up some kind of virtuous multiculti stew. Fair enough. But this meat—this was outside the system, it was *extra,* this was like the twenty-five percent overage that Matty had learned to tack onto floor tiling estimates the summer he worked with his uncle down in Paterson. If you really gave a shit about cows, it seemed to him, you'd eat it; to sit there picking on your banjo saying *awww, no,* he thought, was to, like, *disrespect* the stupid cow whose brain had been popped with a stainless-steel bolt. And, worse, to disrespect the crudded-up hero who'd gotten himself crushed inside a garbage square just to please you. "So an apple in the trash is, like, tragic," he said, snorting. "But a porterhouse, that doesn't matter."

He saw Talmadge wince, as he replaced the meat into the backpack.

"Not even close, man." Micah wagged her head. "You don't get this at all."

"So fucking *teach* me, okay?"

"Meat is the absence of a life." She'd switched to that crisp lecture voice that'd lately been driving Matty insane; he sometimes felt the presence of a teleprompter behind his head. "So to consume it is to support that absence — to endorse it."

"Yeah, but what I'm sayin is that the absence was already — absent. So the whole fucking deal gets turned. If this shit rots, then the absence is wasted. See?"

"I think what Matty's saying," Talmadge broke in, "is that once it's been dumped, there's, like, no ethical downside to—"

Micah cut him off. "I know what he's saying."

"All I'm saying," said Matty, "is that I've been hearing you guys talking this shit for weeks, and, okay, you don't eat meat, fine, whatever, but now you're telling me to take however many pounds of this and dump it back into the trash, and, I dunno, it seems like someone's principles might be seriously outta whack . . ."

"I'm sorry, you wanna talk principles?" She was riled now, her accent gone ornery: *you wan talk prince-pulls.*

"I got mashed in a fucking compactor, okay? And not for *my* fucking principles!"

"Then *eat* it, man!" Micah was up on her feet now, taut as a slingshot. "It don't have to be a party, okay? You wanna eat it, eat it. *Jesus.*"

"Fuck it," Matty said, "I will," as he gathered five packages into his arms and went stomping to the kitchen where he slapped them onto the counter and with a purposeful clamor shoved aside a stack of plates crusted with the remnants of Tal and Micah's fruit-mush breakfast and bean-mush lunch.

He tore the plastic off a package of two strip steaks, sniffed them, shrugged, and then tried to figure out, vainly, how the hell to light those stupid god-damn Boy Scout stoves. "Son of a bitch," he muttered, fiddling with the cap on the methanol can while entertaining baleful mental images of his beard ablaze in the aftermath of an explosion. As frightening as the potential pain was the potential irony: SQUATTER DIES IN COOKING EXPLOSION HOURS AFTER SURVIVING COMPACTOR CRUSHING. "Tal!" he shouted.

Talmadge came slinking into the doorway sideways.

"Light these fuckers for me."

"Don't be pissed, dude."

"Light both of 'em. I want 'em hot."

"I got it, got it. Here. Just be cool, okay?"

Talmadge retreated back to the doorway, as though he needed to re-main within Micah's view range, and there he lingered, half in and half out, while Matty banged two sauté pans onto the burners and unwrapped another package of meat—the veal chops. He plopped the strip steaks onto one of the pans, which wasn't yet hot enough to produce a sizzle. The steaks just lay there, looking very very dead. Matty poked one, arousing a feeble curl of steam.

"Might want some oil," Talmadge offered.

"I can handle this," Matty replied, dropping the veal chops into the other pan with an equal lack of sizzle. For several minutes he stood there, monitoring the meat with unblinking concentration, and thereby ignor-ing Talmadge, until, as commonly happened when he stood still for too long, he was jogged by the desire for a joint—he had one or two pre-rolled packed with his cigarettes, and he knew the drifting odor would curl Mi-cah's lip that much further. Extending his arm, he gestured for Tal's lighter by flicking his thumb against his fist; but Talmadge had vanished, which was probably for the best but made something sink inside him anyhow. Lipping the joint, Matty lowered his face to the burner and, with one hand shielding his beard, lit it with the hissy blue flame. Then, glancing around the corner to be extra sure of Tal's absence, he grabbed the bottle of olive oil and doused both pans. The oil, however, pooled uselessly to the imbal-anced sides. He poked the still dead-looking steaks again, inadvertently peppering one with fallen ash. "Shit," he whispered, brushing it into the meat. Then he heard Micah's banjo kicking back up. "Shit," he whispered again. From a pocket he dug his cellphone and a set of earbuds and with a few finger flicks drowned out the *ding a dang*s with ASG's "Yes We Are Aware": a fast filthy avalanche of guitar crunch and cymbal assault, the sonic antidote to that folk-fuck banjo noise and Micah's voice atop it, all that cooing about rivers and wildflowers and sweet Jesus and fair-n-tender ladies and better times a-comin. He tried flipping the steaks, but they were cemented to the pan; some violent scraping was required. Hankering for something even harder, he cut short ASG and switched to a song by the Scrambled Defuncts, a Moscow atmo-black metal band that Gleb had turned him onto. Yeah, this was better—like a jackhammer in each ear, engaged in a deathmatch race to crack his skull.

When he figured the meat was done or maybe-done, Matty stacked it all—two steaks, three chops—onto one overloaded plate and hauled it to the table. The room was dark, cave-dark, but Matty didn't care. He also didn't care that the meat was overcooked to the point of petrification; whatever else the compactor had done, it'd squeezed the hunger right out of him. When sawing the meat proved impossible, he just ate it with his hands. Only once did he glance toward the living room, where Micah was deep into singing—her mouth open and head uptilted, looking like one of those caroling kids from the Charlie Brown Christmas special—and where Talmadge was staring at him with the saddest punished-puppy expression he could ever remember seeing on Tal's face, maybe even worse than when Tal's dad had called him to say he was ditching his mom and afterwards Tal had sat there stunned with a cold bong on his lap for like two hours. For a fleeting moment, barely the duration of a single manic guitar riff, their eyes locked—until, pricked by guilt, Matty dropped his gaze to his plate. The shame was narrow and precise: He felt guilty for how disgusted he was with Tal. He knew Tal was prone to being pussywhipped— he'd gone to a friggin *John Mayer* concert once, with what's-her-name, that Memphis chick, who was hot but not *that* hot—but this, man, this was outer-limits whipped, this was like hibernating your nuts in a vat of liquid nitrogen, Matty just didn't *get* this. He didn't know what'd happened to his friend but he didn't like it. When he'd chewed the steaks down, he went at the veal chops though he could feel his gut resisting—maybe because it was full, maybe because the spongy gray meat tasted vaguely acidic and had probably been dumped for good cause, despite what Micah said about the sham of "sell by" dates and all that shit. Still, he had a point to make. Not a point he could've put into words, but a point just the same. He chewed, he chewed, while the Russian jackhammers blasted out his inner ear, until all that remained on the plate were T-shaped veal bones and blubbery strips of gristle and one of Micah's handmade napkins sopping up the scant juice. He glanced toward the living room, to be sure his victory had been witnessed and his whatever-it-was point had been made, but was disappointed to find it abandoned. He shut off the music, lit a cigarette, and decided he'd had enough.

Before eight the next morning he was already up and gone, and by nine he was inside the dumpster of that Henry Street nursing home, where Talmadge had fished out the sack of rice. But Matty wasn't looking for food. "Paper," he remembered saying. "All I see is fucking paper." For an hour he combed the dumpster, tearing open giant clear bags that were filled with smaller clear bags and sifting through the paper he found, ripping open envelopes, scanning page after page, all the while stuffing his backpack. He would've stayed longer had not a huge black orderly come upon him saying *The hell you doin,* forcing him out of the dumpster and saying *Gwine outta here* in response to Matty's ardent-sounding condemnation of "food waste."

Out on the street he dialed the number he had for Gleb's girlfriend in Seattle, which Gleb had told him was the best way to contact him. He didn't know the girlfriend's name—if Gleb had ever spoken it, he'd forgotten—but he did know, courtesy of photographs that Gleb kept under his mattress and didn't mind sharing, that one of her asscheeks was adorned with a snake tattoo and she smoked cigarettes while giving head. She was so warm and chipper on the phone that Matty almost felt guilty for knowing this. She told him Gleb had scored an iPhone in prison, sounding inordinately proud, like a wife noting her husband's promotion down at the plant. (He'd bought it from a guard, she said, which made Matty smile, knowing precisely which guard.) Matty texted Gleb: *cellie, wats ^? yr k9 nEdz hlp. bac east, got idea. cll l8r?* Half an hour later, Matty's phone rang. After explaining his idea, he listened for a long and serious while, nodding, frowning, saying *rad, okay, thanks,* and scrawling several numbers on his dirty palm with a perfectly good ballpoint pen someone had abandoned in the trash.

7

THE FIRST ITEM Alexis thought to add to her red plastic basket was shampoo, because everyone's hair gets dirty, meaning everyone needs shampoo, and therefore no one could draw any conclusions or for that matter think anything at all about a bottle of shampoo. Not her regular brand, however (she was fond of Tea Tree Special from Paul Mitchell, it had this weird-cool Altoid-y tingle to it and it wasn't tested on animals). She needed some other brand, one that couldn't be tied to her, didn't represent her. As she stood midway in the aisle at the CVS, adhered to the carpet by indecision, her ears picked up two competing frequencies: a piped-in Taylor Swift song, which sounded to her the way Bubble Yum tastes after it's been chewed for half an hour, and the magnetic buzz of the fluorescent lights above her, which was more than merely sonic. She could *feel* the buzz as well, as if she was caught in some force field or X-ray machine; she felt radioactive, and possibly a little nauseated, as she stood scanning the six stories of shelves for a brand of shampoo that meant nothing, said nothing, that was alien to her but unremarkable to anyone else. The shampoo, like the rest of the drugstore miscellany she was here to gather, was not the primary object of her shopping, but rather a buffer: a means of obscuring or at least diluting the truth of her mission.

She reached out a hand, then retracted it. Not Herbal Essences, no — that's the one Leighton Meester from *Gossip Girl* was modeling for, and Alexis *hated* that show, it was totally stupid. And not Kiss My Face shampoo, because she didn't want anyone to *look* at her face much less consider kissing it, and not Suave because that was sort of Walmart-ish, and definitely *definitely* not Pantene Pro-V because that's what her mom used. After a while her eyes came to rest upon a lonesome-looking bottle of Pert on the second shelf from the bottom, and her gaze lingered there, inscrutably, until with a prick of memory she made the connection: That'd been her dad's brand. She remembered that stout green bottle from her early childhood, perched high up in the shower caddy where her dad's razors and shaving gel used to live before he'd died and Aunt Liz had come in and scrubbed the house clean of his memory, just Lysol'd away every trace of him. Wanting to prolong and intensify the sentimental association she was feeling, she picked the bottle off the shelf and held it in one hand, lightly rubbing the label with her thumb. Her dad had always smelled so good, half-waking her up to plant a goodbye kiss on her cheek before heading off to catch the train to the city in the early early morning, the sudden blast of his cologne like a warm and welcome ray of sunlight alighting upon her face, his freshly-shaven-yet-still-scratchy cheek nuzzling hers, and God that'd always felt so . . . so *good,* him whispering *Bye bye sweetness* and her smiling drowsily without opening her eyes, savoring the kiss and her awareness that she had another hour and a half to burrow beneath her Powerpuff Girls comforter until her mom would come in barking, "Schooltime, Alexis, up and at 'em . . ." or some other dumb wake-up shit.

She startled. From around the corner a blue-shirted stockboy had emerged, pushing a flat cart loaded with cardboard boxes. He had bumpy pink skin and a high bony forehead but was mildly cute anyway, in an indie Brooklyn kind of way. He glanced at her, then immediately dropped his eyes as he rolled the cart toward her — forcing her, by not merely his presence but also his age and gender and semi-cuteness, to make her shampoo choice. The Pert, fine, whatever: She dropped the bottle into her basket with an affected nonchalance, even drawing a finger to her lips to suggest a half-remembered mental shopping list, then evacuated the aisle before the stockboy could put two and two together to figure out the monumentally fucked-up reason she was loading up a basket at a CVS store to which she'd driven 12.9 miles and 24 minutes, passing three other drugstores on the way. Rounding the corner, toward — where? the moisturizer aisle, okay — she felt certain that his eyes were trained on her back, that she'd roused suspicion, and her nausea doubled.

A bottle of Neutrogena. That'd do. She roamed the store, drawn to unpeopled aisles. In the makeup aisle she added Great Lash mascara (Blackest Black, straight-brush) even though she'd switched to Voluminous a year ago because Great Lash smeared. Then cottonballs. Sea Breeze astringent. Maybe a magazine? No, the checkout people sometimes paused with those, or made some comment about the celeb on the cover: *Is Kate still dating A-Rod? I don't know why people say Jessica Simpson's so fat. I saw that new Twilight movie, did you, ohmygod it sucked.* Stiffening herself, she drifted toward the healthcare aisles on the other side of the store, furtively noting the circular green signs (Wound Care, Warts & Lice) while making sure her eyes didn't catch those of the Indian-lady pharmacist surveying the store from a counter in the rear. Pain & Sleep, Eye Care. Allergy & Asthma. Laxatives, across from — there it was, oh God, Family Planning.

But she couldn't go there yet. Jesus. She added a jar of Tylenol to her basket, thinking she might actually *need* that. She felt the fluorescent buzz heightening, as if the light-tubes were straining under some gaseous pressure and would soon explode, one after the other, showering hot yellow sparks onto the floor and maybe easing this whole situation by killing her. Just . . . killing her. So that her mom could erase *her* memory, too, and so everyone could go on with their lives without stupid fucking *stupid* Alexis dragging them down. She heard a telephone ring, watched the pharmacist lady take the call then disappear behind some shelves stocked with fat white pill bottles. With a deep and resolute inhalation, Alexis made her move.

For the very briefest of moments, she skimmed the throng of products on the shelves, feeling assaulted by the profusion, all those brand names (First Response; Answer; Clearblue; E.P.T.) leaping at her, shouting *Pick me* in voices so blaringly strident she felt sure the whole store could hear. She couldn't do it. Panicking, she spun around, and found herself staring squarely at a shelf of enemas which immediately brought to mind her sorta-kinda best friend Gus, and which, under any other circumstances, would've caused her to laugh aloud. ("Sorta-kinda" best friend because ever since eighth grade they'd maintained a cycle of falling out with each other then reuniting then falling out again.) As a sophomore, Gus had pioneered the use of vodka enemas which he claimed got you drunk immediately and couldn't be detected by a Breathalyzer or by his mom's regular demands to smell his breath when he'd roll in on the weekends. Gus was big on shocking people—he sometimes wore flowery vintage dresses to school, played bass in an otherwise all-girl Lo-Fi Goth band called the Date Rapes, faked epileptic seizures when he was bored in class—but broadcasting his use of alcohol enemas had been, as even he admitted, an error: his fame had gotten so out-of-control that even incoming freshmen knew him for his enemas, and he couldn't go to the bathroom at a party without someone breaking in with a cellphone camera, hoping to catch him in the act, even though he'd abandoned the practice after about half a dozen woozy times. That fame was yet another reason Gus couldn't wait to get to New York City, where he'd been accepted to the Fashion Institute of Technology and was planning a triple career as a musician, reality-TV star, and designer of punk-inspired clothing he intended to market world-wide under the "Gussy" label. He was as dead set on her going to Richard Varick College as she was, to study finance like her dad had done. Gus said she could manage all the numbers for Gussy, be his chief operating officer ("I'll be your boo, you'll be my coo"), which despite her smiling assent was not in her planbook. She saw Goldman Sachs on the menu. *Had,* anyway. Now this. Now the maybe-this. God, she wished Gus was here right now, ordering her to chill, promising her it'd all be okay. But this—this was too fucked-up, even for Gus.

Noting the pharmacist's return, she plucked a box of laxatives from the shelf above the enemas—Dulcolax, her regular brand—and stood there awhile, reading the text on the package. *Active ingredient: Bisacodyl USP.* How could this be happening to her? *Also contains: Hydrogenated vegetable oil.* Who could she possibly tell about this? *Do not use when abdominal pain, nausea, or vomiting are present unless directed by a physician.* No one, that's who. No one and never. The pharmacist stood up again, toting a clipboard back behind the pill shelves, and Alexis swung around.

Why were there so many brands, and could it possibly matter? *Early result. New! One step. Digital. Color sure tip. Over 99% accurate.* Deluged by the choices, she went with an established tack inherited from her mother: She picked the most expensive one, burying it beneath the shampoo and cottonballs and mascara and moisturizer and Sea Breeze as she strode from the aisle. If she was expecting any relief from having *done it,* from having grabbed the test without anyone seeing her or confronting her or asking her if there was anything she needed to talk about, none came. Instead, she felt *truly* radioactive now, as if her basket was glowing, pulsing, smoldering, leaving a trail of glo-green drips behind her. En route to the front of the store she added a jumbo bag of Doritos, jamming it into the basket as if to smother the radiation. She felt tears forming just below her eyeballs, felt her cheeks scalding, and was struck with the new fear that she might faint.

At the registers things only got worse. The schlubby, mustachioed cashier she'd spotted upon entering had been replaced by a blonde girl just a few years older than Alexis. The girl had stringy yellow hair and puffy eyes and was apparently new at the job because she was having trouble scanning a sack of Cat Chow that an elderly woman was trying to buy. Alexis focused on the cover of the *Cosmopolitan* perched beside the register: *Wicked Things Other Women Do in Bed (Our Naughtiest Sex Poll!)*, read one coverline. *Are you a Bitch?* The old woman was digging through her purse for her CVS card while the cashier chewed gum. *The One Time to Tell Him "I Love You."* Alexis noticed she was shaking—uncontrollably, visibly—and pinched her forearm, as hard as she could, to distract her physical self—so hard she could feel herself bruising.

And then the cashier said, "Next." Afraid to look down at her basket, and determined to avoid eye contact, Alexis focused on the cigarettes arrayed behind the counter and counted to ten and then back down again while the cashier emptied the basket. She heard the crinkle of the Doritos, the swish of the cottonballs being scanned, flinching at every beep of the scanner. Would the beep be different, like the double-beep that sounded when you bought beer or cigarettes? "No," she mumbled, when the cashier asked if she had a CVS card. As she was signing her name with the digital marker, for a credit purchase, she caught sight of the cashier loading the test into a white plastic bag, causing her signing hand to collapse and her last name to go dribbling below the signature line.

"Have a nice day," the cashier said, and though Alexis tried avoiding her eyes, she failed. The cashier *knew.* Of course she knew. Alexis saw it in those puffy gray eyes, the downturned mouth, the way she'd stopped chewing her gum to stare at her, and with a sudden spasm of horror Alexis realized why: She was crying. She'd broken. Exposed, she looked straight at the cashier as if to plead for mercy or guidance or understanding or maybe shock or horror or disgust, aware of how wet her cheeks had gotten and what a sorry, mangled sight she must be, but the cashier just resumed her gum-chewing and said, "Next."

Alexis grabbed the two bags and fled: through the twin sets of automatic doors, and out onto the white-bright sidewalk beside a red-topped trash can. A sob came up, wrenching her body the way vomiting does, and she grasped the trash can to steady herself. *This is not happening to me,* she said to herself. Gleams of sunlight bounced off the cars in the parking lot. *This is not happening to me,* she told herself again. And then, as if to prove it, she pushed one of the bags into the trash can, and feeling a strange and welcome release, pushed the other one in too. Yet again she said to herself, *This is not happening to me,* and took two steps backwards, wiping her cheeks with her forearm, feeling her balance returning as she put several yards of concrete between the trash can and herself, as if she'd somehow purged herself of this toxin, and was free, *free.* More coolly this time, she repeated it to herself, *This is not happening to me,* and with one last glance at the trash can turned toward her car.

PART THREE

I

THE NURSES WERE always telling Dr. Elwin Cross Sr. that he should lie down. That all this shuffling and reshuffling of papers he did, all this frantic hopping from one book to another and constant realigning of pencils and pens and notebooks and notecards, did nothing but frustrate him—"stress" him, they said—to the brink of combustion. "Why don't you take a break?" they'd say, in that artificially chipper tone endemic to kindergarten teachers and restaurant hostesses, sometimes adding, "Nothing like a good long nap on a (rainy, sunny, winter, summer) afternoon . . ." When he'd resist this suggestion, as he always did, they'd point to his scarred and allegedly frail heart, sighing and frowning in what seemed to Dr. Cross the way a friend might note the wife and children of a man embarking upon an affair or some other reckless action—as though his sole duty in these swift and narrowing years was to coddle this one organ, to pledge above all else his custodial fealty to his over-monitored reptilian core.

This was, of course, a bunch of baloney. Dr. Cross didn't like lying down, never had. Sleep just left your thoughts unsupervised, a terrible danger. He did, however, like bologna, which reminded him—well, it reminded him of something, but something that couldn't possibly matter at the moment, because here he was, at his desk that was really a table in his room that was really a cell in this "assisted living facility" that was really a hospital in this hospital that was really a hospice, on page 235 of the book he was writing, the book he was too modest to call his "masterwork" aloud to anyone but his eldest son and maybe his wife (though she'd stopped listening to his shoptalk years ago, nowadays given to murmuring *uh-hmmmm, uh-hmmmm* from behind the veil of her *Time* magazine). He was midway through a chapter on the destruction of Melos by the Athenians during the Peloponnesian War, more precisely about whether or not the terrible massacre as described by Thucydides was in fact an instance of genocide as Chalk and Jonassohn had semi-convincingly argued five or was it twenty years ago, and, at present, he was sifting through the books on his desk in search of a note he remembered scratching in a margin. It was a penciled note — this detail he remembered — and would, if he could find it, lead him sideways to a quotation whose source and subject he couldn't quite recall at this moment. Yet he could, with photographic clarity, remember the note itself, scrawled three-quarters of the way down a densely printed page with tight acid-brown margins, a curlicue of graphite scrawl that read . . . *baloney.* Except: no. He scowled. Not *baloney.* Where had that come from? He would never have written *baloney* in the margins of anything. *Dubious,* maybe. *Questionable. Arguable. Unlikely.* At worst, *pshaw!* And in any case — now he was really frowning, scratching at the side of his nose — there'd be no point in searching for a quotation he'd deemed *baloney* since baloney wasn't quotable except in instances of scholarly aggression, something he'd outgrown decades ago.

He set the book down and craned his head forward to meet his hands, rubbing his temples and thereby dislodging his reading glasses so that one side fell dangling to his lips like collapsed scaffolding. Catching a reflected glimpse of himself in the window glass, a Jerry Lewis skit gone awry, he cursed, feeling faint twinges in his chest that if revealed would be cause for stethoscopes, diodes, flurries of *tsk-tsk*ing from the nurses, a compulsory prescription for horizontal torpor. Readjusting his glasses, he straightened his back into his chair and emitted the same classroom-volume *ahem* with which he'd shamed generations of whispery undergraduates. The *ahem* rang hollow, however: a bum tuning note, a failed engine crank. It occurred to him that he'd lost the ability to shame even himself. Suppressing another attempt, he thought: I can't go on like this. He needed to focus, he thought — pay heed, "show a little ginger" as his father used to say. He had too much work left to do.

In the same brand of leather-bound legal notebooks he'd used to write his four previous books (notebooks he continued to order by mail from a legal-supply wholesaler in Newark, Mr. Teague was the wholesaler's name,

Dr. Cross could rattle off the address—115 Norfolk Street—like an old song lyric), page 235 of the new book lay open before him. The page was blank aside from the handwritten "235" in the bottom right corner and at the top left corner three words: "prosperity or ruin." With a muddled squint he examined the words, struggling but failing to place them in context, then with a lick of his index finger he peeled back page 235 to see from page 234 what could have led to this grave-sounding polarity of prosperity or ruin. "Ah," he said aloud, with a mixture of relief and self-abasement, as when a search for misplaced keys ends in their most obvious resting place. The words were part of a quotation from Thucydides' Melian dialogue, when the Athenians were threatening the unsubmissive Melians with complete annihilation: "You have not more than one country, and upon this one deliberation depends its"—depends its what?, he wondered, turning back to page 235—oh: "prosperity or ruin." He picked up a pencil and hovered it over the page until gravity, rather than inspiration or just plain yeoman will, drew its point to the page. The pencil stayed motionless as he returned his eyes to the window, his attention drawn beyond his sour reflection to the sidewalk one story down where a woman in a short pleated skirt with a phone pressed to her ear drifted past, her right arm swinging in fierce gesticulation, her head bobbing as she paused beside a mailbox to drive home some essential and boilsome point—telling a tale of amazement he would never chance to hear. It wasn't this last realization, however, that provoked the sudden suck of melancholy he felt: a quick and desolate sense of a stopper being pulled so that his daily supply of lightness and energy—already meager—went circling a drain. It was the skirt, and the yellow light reflected on the sheen of her bare legs. He hadn't known, until that moment, that it was summer. No one had told him. All they ever told him was to lie down.

Summer! That meant Alice was in the backyard garden in Montclair. There was long-distance comfort in this image, a mental railing for him to grasp. He wondered how high the tomatoes were, and if the hornworms had assaulted them yet, and if so whether David had dropped one down Jane's shirt and whether Alice had punished him for it, which she rarely if ever did because David, as she was so incautiously prone to stating publicly, was her favorite child. Dr. Cross had never been fond of Alice's garden—he'd never understood her desire for all that grimy fuss, for the pruning and staking and kneeling and mulch-schlepping, or the way Alice would return from an afternoon's digging and weeding with the sated pink-chested glow of a woman fresh from a tryst with her Mediterranean lover—but now, in the ammonia-scented dimness of his room, he was overcome with the uncharacteristic desire to deliver her a glass of lemonade, to see her rise smiling and startled from the soil to accept it, smearing her forehead as she wiped the sweat from it with her arm, him leaning on the opposite side of the picket garden fence, the two of them talking of— of what? Of the children, of neighborhood or campus gossip, or of beautiful sunlit nothingness—the nothingness that comes after two people have co-existed for so long that nothing new can ever be spoken, nothing save goodbye.

The desire gripped him on an almost cellular level—he could feel his leg muscles twitch in preparation for movement, his weight shifting on the chair, his body poised to rise—before the realization swamped him: Alice was dead. Of course. His cells went slack, his bones folding back into the seat. Alice was dead. At least, that's what everyone told him. He didn't *remember* Alice dying, not the how of it nor the funeral nor the eulogy he was accused of having delivered, which was suspicious; sometimes he wondered if his children had concocted the story to protect him from some greater sadness, such as Alice having deserted him for some actual Mediterranean lover. Yet that scenario struck him as even more improbable and absurd than him forgetting her death. For one thing, Elwin Jr. was as shoddy a liar as his father, and as for Alice, well—Alice had always been faithful. So had he, though not without struggles he'd prefer to forget. Alice made fidelity look easy, like walking or drinking lemonade or the way your unmonitored heart beats on and on in your youth and middle years: like an instinctual response to love.

Had made it look easy, that is. It was so hard to keep the tenses right without any evidence.

He drew his gaze back down to page 235 and its prosperity or ruin. The words appeared to need a question mark, so he penciled one. Then he pondered it for a while as though he'd written himself an essay question. He looked up, down, around, surveying the room before deciding in a bout of Spenglerian gloom: *Ruin*. Ruin's what we get, ruin's all we get. Prosperity is just a phase, like childhood, and like childhood it lasts longer for some than for others—for people and civilizations, the same. If he'd concluded anything from sixty-some years of reading history, it was the absence of any unifying theory save transience: We come and we go, as we came and went. Greatness, however broadly or narrowly you defined it, was no defense or insulator against ruin; its bones and scraps were indistinguishable from those of mediocrity or worse. He lowered his pencil to transcribe this last thought before half remembering the front end of the quotation back on page 234. Damn it all, he thought. I'm wandering again. He slammed down the pencil just as a faint mewing sounded behind him.

The cat's name was Jack, or maybe John—possibly Joe. Not that it mattered. He was a small tabby Manx, with a rumpy riser for a tail, whose swirled black-on-gray fur patterns called to mind an oil slick or the sort of unctuous curbside puddles Dr. Cross recalled from his childhood in Brooklyn, gruesome-looking puddles he was never tempted to go splashing in. The cat was sitting in the doorway, studying him in a vaguely predatory manner. "Go away, cat," Dr. Cross said. The cat glanced around, yawny and unaffected, then returned its stare to Dr. Cross. "Shoo," he said.

The cat was death. That was the rumor around the Roth Residence, anyway. When the cat chose you, death followed quickly—someone clever had calculated six months, tops. Mrs. Odenkirk down the hall, for instance, had awakened to the sight of the cat lying at the foot of her bed; for three weeks the cat returned nightly, purring by her feet, until Mrs. Odenkirk passed in her sleep and the cat went on its way. After her it chose Fred Something-or-Other on the third floor; same outcome, a stroke felling him five weeks after the cat's first visit. Once word got around that "pet therapy" was in fact a death warrant, a few of the more despondent patients tried luring the cat into their rooms by leaving smuggled bits of fish from Friday dinner under their beds. Those of an opposite bent barricaded themselves in their rooms at the first sight of the cat roaming their floor. One fellow managed to score a water-pistol from his grandson, taking desperate potshots at the cat whenever it passed his doorway, while a woman three rooms down, halved by a stroke seventeen years before and unable to speak or feed herself, was somehow able to procure catnip from her daughter and went about sprinkling it on her comforter every night. Dr. Cross did not believe in any of this voodoo, of course, but he was nonetheless a cautious sort who'd never been keen to tempt fate, as in his boyhood when he'd avoided those poisonous-looking puddles all the other boys dared one another to leap during the walk to school. "Shoo," he said again, with a backhanded whisk of his arm. The cat either blinked or winked; Dr. Cross felt certain he'd seen the latter but had doubts cats could wink.

Grunting, he turned in his chair to face the cat, and was staring it down *High Noon*–style when appeared behind it two enormous blue legs. These belonged to Boolah, the nurse, who was carrying a small pink plastic tray and had a thin sheaf of envelopes tucked beneath his armpit. Dr. Cross looked away, embarrassed to have been caught in a staring match with a cat that might or might not have been equipped with the ability to wink and/or incite a tranquil death. With a toneless expression, Boolah glanced down at the cat between his feet, up at Dr. Cross, then down at the cat again. He pursed his lips. Somberly, he said, "Yo. Kitty."

"Get that cat out of here," said Dr. Cross.

"You don't like cats?"

"I don't like *that* cat."

"That's all b.s., you know." Boolah sighed. "Miss Snyder been sleeping with that cat for three years now. Ain't nothing wrong with her and Lord help me ain't nothing *going* wrong with her."

Dr. Cross said, "I just don't like him."

Boolah returned his gaze to the cat, which was more than small enough for him to step over or around or even, for that matter, on. Instead, though, he spoke to it: "Go on now. You heard the man. Pussy, *move*."

The cat gave no indication it had even noticed Boolah behind it, an impossibility given Boolah's seismic presence. With his crepe-soled shoe Boolah gave it a gentle giddy-up, kitty-up nudge, eventually — gingerly — lifting its rear end with his toe and rotating it on the glossy tiled floor so that the cat was facing the hallway. The cat stood up, twitched its little bump of a tail, and plopped itself down in the doorway so that Dr. Cross was once again in its whiskered crosshairs. "Uh-oh," Boolah said.

"Cut that out."

Cringing, Boolah stepped over the cat and set his tray on a bedside cart along with the envelopes. "Truth is," he said, counting pills into his hand, "I don't like that kitty much either."

"I don't know why they allow it here. It's a health hazard. Cats are dirty."

"He ain't dirty."

"He's for rats, isn't he? I'll bet he's for rats."

"Naw, supposed to make it feel like home here."

"Well," said Dr. Cross, and guffawed. "It doesn't." The word *home* went ricocheting through him. *Home:* of course. That was it, the answer to a question he hadn't quite formulated. He needed to go home. Yet another question, this one fully formed, came thumping along behind: Where *was* home? Was it Brooklyn? He saw the puddles: yes, Brooklyn, the pavement glistening in the aftermath of a springtime rain, the sight of his two-tone school shoes navigating the sidewalk cracks, the storefront windows filled with faded Ex-Lax placards, Fatima signs, rubber baby-pants, antique displays of antipasto and halvah and chocolates, down Carroll Street the steam gusts of a tailor shop exhaled onto the sidewalk like the breath of some great polar beast. But then, wait—

"I'm just reading from the script, my man," said Boolah. "You understand?"

Foggily, Dr. Cross said, "Well, it doesn't matter. I'm going home tomorrow."

Boolah ignored this. "I got your 'roids here, and grabbed your mail for you, too, 'cause I'm so nice."

"My what?"

"Your steroids. Your vitamins."

"My vitamins?"

"Your *pills,* man. I got all your pills."

Dr. Cross grunted. "I don't need those pills."

Boolah ignored this too, standing beside Dr. Cross's shoulder with a multicolored assortment of medicines on his wide expanse of palm, a glass of water in his other hand. He said, "Shoot 'em down for me."

"Blech," said Dr. Cross afterwards. "That big orange one—it's like swallowing a golfball."

"That one make you *strong,* man." Boolah curled his fist and leaned forward, flexing his bicep. "Put that ol' tiger in your tank."

"Huh. I don't need any tiger."

"Everybody need some tiger."

The sight of the cat sprawled in the doorway distracted Dr. Cross. Was this the tiger Boolah was talking about? "I don't like that tiger," he whispered.

"Say again?"

"That—tiger," said Dr. Cross, pointing to the cat.

"That ain't no tiger."

"But it . . ."

"What?"

"You said . . ."

"You want your mail?"

"Oh yes," said Dr. Cross, with a sudden swerve of brightness.

Boolah laid the envelopes on the desk. "All yours, tiger," he said, and gathering up the tray headed toward the door. He paused at the cat, and offered it a respectful nod before stepping over it with calculated stealth.

"And could you make that cat go away?" Dr. Cross shouted after him.

From down the hallway he heard Boolah shout back, "Pussy do what pussy want," which brought forth a yawp of old-lady objection from a neighboring room.

After turning his chair, with an exaggerated harrumph, so that his back was to the cat, Dr. Cross went sifting through the envelopes in his standard way, as always looking first for a personal letter—anything hand-addressed. There was, of course, nothing of the kind, and excepting the annual trickle of Christmas cards there hadn't been for years. This was partly due to email—Dr. Cross had once tried to use the computer in the common area, at Elwin's urging, but found the machine entirely un-likable—but more to do with all the crossed-out entries in his address book. Put plainly, almost everyone was dead. They'd all gone extinct. The only friend who still wrote him was Ted Blundell, but Ted wasn't really a friend—rather an ex-friend whose letters were all depressingly apologetic, a paragraph of wan news floating atop a ten-ton anchor of regrets. Back in the '80s, when Ted had been a rising star in the Montclair State history department, he'd borrowed $15,000 from Dr. Cross for a down payment on a Brookdale Park Tudor. Six months later, however, he'd ditched his wife, three-year-old twins, tenure track, and the handshaken loan agreement with his department chair to go gallumphing after the bass player in an all-female Hoboken New Wave band. (Until he resurfaced eighteen years later, the last Ted sighting, reported by a grad student, had been of him working the door at a Newark lesbian bar, collecting the $2 cover charge in an upturned Montclair State baseball cap with an expression of squirmy indigestion, as though this fat slice of life he'd bitten off had yielded him a case of existential dysentery.) Bathetic letters of remorse had started flowing from Ted in the late '90s — one of them ran to eleven damp pages — but for all their pleas for forgiveness they were notably devoid of checks. Still, Dr. Cross wouldn't have minded seeing one of those letters now — anything from a familiar voice, even a piteous one.

Yet there was nothing of the kind. He tore open the topmost envelope — something from the Veterans Administration. For sixty years he'd used an ivory-handled letter opener but letter openers weren't allowed in the Roth Residence and his had been confiscated by who-knows-who to who-knows-where for who-knows-what-reason. Perhaps to prevent him from eviscerating that cat whose sniper eyes he could presently feel between his shoulderblades. In those same sixty years he'd grown more than accustomed to VA mailings and the like, yet even now the familiar microshiver ran through him, a quick shudder of unsolicited memory: Here was his war, come back to him in a four-by-nine-inch plastic-windowed envelope. True, he'd made a life's work out of studying war, but for whatever obscure psychological reason these tangible reminders of his own relationship with it tended to unsteady him, as if they exposed the blood ties between the observer and the observed, between the historian and history, or revealed the first-person subjectivity hiding beneath the cool third-person veneer, casting doubt on the affirmed — or were they over-affirmed? — facts. But then, no, that wasn't quite it — or even it at all. That was just the story he told himself. The truth was that a gulf of difference lay between war and *his* war. One he understood, or had tried to understand; the other was incomprehensible, as even his quaking limbs knew.

This present shiver, however — he paused, gauging it — this shiver was different, this wasn't the standard-issue shiver he'd learned to extinguish with a fast wag of the head. This one ran deep and then deeper, the memory swooping with a violence he hadn't felt from it in years, screeching like an incoming hawk or artillery shell. He froze, his throat clogged with trapped air. The next of his old remedies — closing his eyes — also failed him. In fact this only intensified the memory by removing the counterbalance provided by the sight of his desk and room, training his mind's eye upon the memory the way the dimming of theatre lights trains your eyes upon the stage. Then he heard himself gasping the same gasp he'd sucked into his lungs in May of 1945, and though he tried to lift his eyelids, he couldn't; they shuddered but remain locked.

The memory comprised two separate scenes. They weren't quite segregated in his mind's eye, like a split screen, but neither were they superimposed upon each other; it was more like the way comic books were sometimes misprinted in the old days, with the colors bleeding outside the black lines meant to contain them.

The first scene was of the road to Gunskirchen Lager, the Austrian concentration camp that Pfc. Elwin Cross, as an eighteen-year-old "Doughboy" of the U.S. Army's 71st Infantry Division—a replacement just sixteen days into his overseas service—had helped liberate just before V-E Day. Alerted to the Allied advance, the SS had abandoned the camp days earlier, and hundreds of the camp's inmates—Hungarian Jews, for the most part: sickly, starving, skeletal—had swarmed through the open gates to the road where they greeted the approach of Pfc. Cross's unit with moany cheers and cracked-lip pleas for water and food. One man stormed the slow-moving Jeep in which Pfc. Cross was riding, gripping the top of the door and trying to run alongside it, but without the strength to lift his feet he was half the time dragged. "Cigarettes," he begged. Pfc. Cross handed him a half pack of Lucky Strikes and the man let go of the Jeep. When Pfc. Cross looked behind he saw the man stuffing the cigarettes into his mouth, chewing wildly. Nearer the gates lay a string of corpses on both sides: inmates who'd perished just yards into their freedom, as though felled by the shock of it, their rabid thirst sated by drowning. Then Pfc. Cross gasped: the same precise gasp he was gasping sixty-plus years later. There by the gates was a boy—twelve or thirteen years old, he reckoned, though starvation skewed any guesses—with his head in the split guts of a shellfired horse that'd been dead two days at least. The boy—or was it a girl?—glanced up as the Jeep passed, his or her face smeared purple and the eyes blank and dismal, and then without expression he or she turned back to the horse's belly and resumed gnawing. "Jesus," someone said, and the Jeep crunched to a stop. Skeletons surrounded the Jeep, pressing in and blocking Pfc. Cross's view of the child and horse. "*Víz,*" they pleaded, "*Wasser,*" and Pfc. Cross watched his canteen disappear into a desperate vortex of blue-nailed fingers.

This was the first scene, which he saw in his mind as fragments, as a broken montage, the images as jostled and disordered as the inmates who'd swarmed the Jeep. The second scene was from hours later. C Company had corralled a dozen German civilians from a nearby village to collect and bury the hundreds of bodies littering the camp and surrounding woods. Assigned a guard detail, Pfc. Cross was stationed atop a berm overlooking an earthen pit where the corpses were being piled. The pit was massive, at least sixty feet long, and reminded him of photos of meteor craters he'd seen in his science textbooks. For six hours he watched the Germans haul the bodies to the pit's edge—the corpses were so light that the Germans carrying them on their shoulders walked unperturbed and unhunched— where another contingent of German civilians slid them down and stacked them into long neat rows, like stacks of creosote ties down at the Brooklyn railyard. Pfc. Cross held a rag to his face to ward off the stench, an odor so thick and sticky you felt you could take it in your hands and mold it like putty. The Germans, by order of the lieutenant, were not allowed any such buffers. "Let 'em smell it," said Pfc. Cross's sergeant.

At first Pfc. Cross had tried to be hard, gristly, Sarge-like, fixing his stare upon the live Germans rather than the dead Hungarian Jews, whose blank open eyes and papery skin were too much for him to bear; more than any-thing else, at first, he feared his own tears. With a wave of his rifle barrel he'd shout "Shuddup!" whenever the Germans spoke to one another, even whispered or grunted or coughed from the odor. For most of the afternoon they obeyed him without acknowledgment, which Pfc. Cross preferred. These were old men, primarily, and Pfc. Cross was aware of how choked and boyish his commands must have sounded. Nothing had prepared him for this. On the long passage to Europe, standing at the ship's bow tossing cigarette butt after cigarette butt into the moon-colored wake, his great worry had been the standard-issue one: whether he'd be brave enough for combat, steady in the face of peril. Here there was no peril—just an open pit, unarmed old men, all those bodies—yet he could feel himself warping all the same, crushed by the unfathomability of it all.

Then one of the old Germans looked at him. The man—short and wiry, with a felt flat cap the same gray shade as his beard scruff—stood straight up from his digging and leveled a blank stare at Pfc. Cross. The look wasn't in response to anything Pfc. Cross had said or done, nor as far as he could tell was it a prelude to something. The old man just paused to look at Pfc. Cross without any expression whatsoever. Pfc. Cross returned the same glazed stare to the man, their eyes locking, the old man chewing his flattened lips while the young man held the rag tight beneath his watery eyes, until Pfc. Cross realized that, no, the rag was gone, he'd dropped it, and glancing down for it he realized too that he'd raised his rifle so that the barrel was aimed directly at the old man's chest. He didn't know what was happening. His body seemed to be acting independently of his mind, and while that should have reasonably sparked panic within him, it didn't; instead he felt a warm and almost pleasant absolution, the relief of surrender. He could feel his finger locked on the trigger, not moving so much as *growing:* thickening, as though his body—perhaps his soul—was redirecting all the blood in his body into that one outer point in order to force the trigger through arterial pressure alone, to swell it into action.

Astonished, he glanced down at the finger, feeling powerless to stop its distention even had he wanted to—and he didn't want to. He didn't want to fire the gun—not all his reason had been eclipsed, not yet—but he did want the gun to fire. Into his mind came a sudden but fully formed fantasy, then, in which he not only shot the German now staring at him with narrowed eyes—he saw the holes opening in the old man's shirt, his arms windmilling backwards as he fell—but *all of them,* the old Germans lurching downward as the bullets perforated them, the dying plunging atop the dead, the smell of fresh blood braided into the odor of rotted flesh, justice come at last.

This was not his body or soul mutinying against his mind now, this was his mind itself, the irrational overriding the rational, and the desire that flooded him felt as true and pure as any desire he'd ever had. It coursed through him like a sexual tremble, and he could see the rifle barrel shaking, could feel his finger twitching against the trigger. He had never wanted anything so badly in his life than to massacre these Kraut sonsofbitches, to not merely kill them but *hurt* them, to shoot them in the crotch, in the eyes, to rip them apart in jagged red pieces, to shoot them with such might that the bullets would pass through them to their children and through their children to their grandchildren, the bullets stained and then re-stained, unstoppable in their righteousness. The rifle was swaying in his hands now, every last ounce of his own blood pooled in his tumid fingertip, as he awaited the signal from the old man—the signal to open fire.

For years and years thereafter Pfc. Cross—later Staff Sergeant Cross and later still Dr. Cross—would wonder what would have happened had the old German given the signal: had he smirked at the quivering rifle, spoken a single guttural word, made a single tiny gesture: done anything at all, moved even an inch. Long after he'd returned from overseas, married Alice, fathered children, taken up golf, learned to semi-enjoy the taste of scotch, this question would shake him out of sleep, and often out of bed, sometimes screaming but more often gaping his mouth to scream but producing no sound, his long rangy arms flailing, Alice lying beside him on the shag carpet stroking his cheek and hair, lifting her head to shoo their roused and frightened children from the room, whispering *Hush now* into his ear, *whatever it is it's over.* It haunted his daylit hours as well, at first shadowing his historical studies—casting new and darker shades to his interpretation of ancient events—and then overtaking them. He'd pioneered the nascent field of genocide studies not because he'd witnessed genocide, as some of his closer colleagues presumed, but instead because he'd come inch-fragments away from *enacting* it—because in the course of a single April day he'd absorbed not only its horrors but its temptations, had not only witnessed the monster but for a short time become it.

Or rather *almost* become it: because the old man didn't smirk, didn't speak, didn't make any gesture at all. He just stared inscrutably at Pfc. Cross's trembling rifle and then lowered his gaze earthward and with the same vacant expression on his face resumed his digging without any sign whatsoever that he sensed how close he'd just come to joining the corpses stacked beside him. From atop the berm Pfc. Cross heard the *scritch scritch* of the shovels as he collapsed to his knees and vomited down the side of the pit before losing consciousness altogether.

"You all right?"

Whose voice was that? It was Sarge. Sarge had been there when he'd come to in the medic truck; they'd driven it a half mile from the camp to escape the smell. When he opened his eyes the white light was blinding. "Yessir," he whispered, and shut his eyes again.

"Yo, Dr. Cross." The voice was nearer now, and it didn't belong to Sarge. "What's wrong?"

"Nothing, sir," he said, opening his eyes again, a bed taking blurred shape in his vision, a file cabinet, books, then a hulking, frowning Negro medic—

"You're crying," Boolah said, plucking a tissue from a box atop the dresser.

"I'm not," said Dr. Cross, waving away the tissue.

"Why don't we try a nap, man?"

"Get away," Dr. Cross said.

"Now look—"

"Get the hell away from me."

Boolah raised his hands, walked backwards. "We're good, man."

"Just get out of my house," Dr. Cross said.

"I'm going, don't need to tell me twice, I was just passing by and saw you—"

A shrill cry went up. Boolah had stepped backwards onto the cat. With a low curse Boolah lifted his foot and the cat scurried sideways to a spot beneath the steel chair in Dr. Cross's room. Boolah looked at the cat, which was licking its mashed paw beneath the safe shade of the chair, and then at Dr. Cross, who was trying to fish something that wasn't there out of his right eye. Boolah spread wide his arms to denote his position between rock and hard place.

"Just go," Dr. Cross told him, and with one last sidelong glance at the cat Boolah obeyed.

The VA envelope and its contents had spilled to the floor, where Dr. Cross's memories of the war had followed them. He surveyed the room, incrementally remembering that it was his, though as usual not *why* it was his. He was more acutely confused, however, by the residual despair gripping him—perhaps Boolah had been right about the crying, he thought, rubbing the glossy evidence of his own tears between his thumb and index finger. Something had just happened to him, he knew, though he couldn't say what, but since heartache was what he was feeling he drew his hand to his chest. He found his heart racing violently. So that was it. He groaned. His goddamn feeble heart. And here Boolah had almost caught it in the act of timorous thrashing, flopping like a banked fish. That sure could've torpedoed his workday. Yet beneath his palm he could feel his heart beginning to calm, resuming its old elegant cha-cha rhythm, and fetching his eyeglasses from atop the pile of envelopes on his lap he said to his heart and to himself, for the dozenth time that day, *enough*. Because there on the bedside table was his work, his masterwork, possibly his life's final stitch. "The only thing that we can really make is our work," he remembered Edmund Wilson writing in a letter, because he'd quoted this to his colleague Peter Humes when Humes was stalled on his Benjamin Harrison biography, "and deliberate work of the mind, imagination, and hand, done, as Nietzsche said, 'notwithstanding,' in the long run remakes the world."

Yes, he thought. That was it. He had a world to remake. But first this mail, lingering on his lap. Even Edmund Wilson had to open his mail. Nietzsche, too, notwithstanding.

He opened the topmost envelope and glowered at what it contained: his credit card statement, with a total balance of—could that be?—$3,918.24. This was preposterous. He drew the statement to his face for a closer look, but no, there it was: larger and clearer, but bearing the same absurd amount. He'd avoided credit balances all his life, going so far as to channel the meager advance funds for his second book toward prepayment on their mortgage, rather than using it for a vacation (Alice's idea) or a pony (Jane's). But then wait, he thought—Jane. Why was he recalling or imagining some connection between Jane and his credit card account? Perhaps he'd allowed her to use his card? She *was* still in college, wasn't she? He re-adjusted his glasses, then ran a fingertip down the table of charges. $85.16 at someplace called Shoe Mania: well, surely *that'd* been Jane, a shoe maniac since toddlerhood. $50 to the Metropolitan Transit Authority/MetroCard: Jane zooming beneath the city, no doubt. $312.86 at the Longboard Loft Skate Shop in New York City: a total mystery, that one. $23.43 at Pipolo's Pizza, $16.39 at Famous Ray's Pizza, and many more like these: could've been a hungry Jane, he supposed, by now growing furious at her because clearly she'd embarked on what appeared to be a carbohydrate-fueled spending spree. (No doubt abetted by her mother, who'd be hearing about this in just a moment. Together those damn women tossed money like confetti.)

But then—look here, he thought, his fingertip gliding downward: a $275.00 charge from Yankee Stadium, followed by a $7.75 Yankee Stadium charge, and then another $7.75. He grunted blackly. Not Jane, no. Jane hated baseball. All his children hated sports, in fact, unless you counted David's long-distance-running habit which'd always struck his father as more neurotic than sporting, or Elwin's hunting, same diagnosis. Certainly there weren't any baseball fans in the family. In the Cross household, the sports section went into the trash in the same pristine folded condition in which it'd landed on the doorstep.

No, Dr. Cross knew, with a deepening sense of alarm, the statement trembling in his hand. Those charges were his own.

Not that he was a baseball fan either. Had he been, moreover, he would've never rooted for the Yankees. The Dodgers' abandonment of Brooklyn in '57 hadn't wounded him personally—not the way it'd crushed his older brother Tom, who'd traded in his prized '56 Dodge Coronet hardtop for a Chevrolet to avoid the partial if still painful evocation of seeing "Dodge" tattooed on his dashboard—but it had implanted a borough-loyal disdain for the Yankees that overrode his indifference to the game. But then these charges weren't about baseball, as he knew. They were about Katherine Bluestein.

Katherine was the Yankees fan. God, was she ever. And no casual fan at that: She knew Tony Kubek threw right and batted left, that by the 1960 season Yogi Berra was *bupkes* as a catcher but still valuable as a clutch hitter, that Elston Howard could loosen the cover from a baseball just by squeezing it, that Whitey Ford was prone to throwing "lollipops," that the Pittsburgh Pirates had a difficult time winning outside their home turf. (General Robert E. Lee, he'd told her, had a similar problem.)

Katherine worked as a part-time research librarian at Montclair State. Aside from aiding him with his infinite research requests (Dr. Cross was thirty-three that year, already a father of three, and at work on his first book), all he ever saw her do, however, was ogle the sports pages. He mentioned this to her once. "I've got to keep up with my boys," she protested, confounded when Dr. Cross asked who those boys might be. "You don't follow baseball?" she asked him, mouth agape when he admitted the game was "an utter mystery" to him. Katherine was a striking woman—in her late twenties (though she never divulged her precise age), with olive skin and an abundance of hair (lustrously unplucked black eyebrows, downy forearms, a gossamer fringe of vellus hair spilling down toward her jaw) hinting at an interior fecundity or wildness, a lavishness within—and when she replied, with a wink, "Well, I've got a lot to teach you then, don't I?" he felt something powerful go surging through his entire body, something fizzy and inebriating and dangerous and swashbuckling and altogether new. "Yes," he replied, "I think I'd like that," entranced by the serious way she looked up at him then, as though a pact had been brokered, a treaty settled, a journey commenced. For the remainder of the day he walked taller and straighter, slapped colleagues' backs, wrestled with his surprised young sons in the front yard. The next morning Alice noted that he might've overdone it with the cologne.

And thus began his single season of baseball fandom. He'd pick Katherine up at the library and drive on to Yankee Stadium where they'd plant themselves in the grandstand for what felt like endless summertime picnics, feeling as though they were (or at least he was) stealing all those languorous innings from life itself, as if he'd found strange passage into a more vibrant and slower-rhythmed alternate universe, a sun-drenched otherworld that was sticky-footed with Coke residue and scattered with peanut hulls. With a cigarette braced between her fingers, Katherine would pore over her fifteen-cent scorecard, faithfully marking in the boxes but sometimes ignoring the game to bite her lip and stare at Dr. Cross (whom she'd dubbed "Young Perfessor," riffing on manager Casey Stengel's nickname of "Old Perfessor") even in the midst of, say, a taut, two-out, bases-loaded situation. He'd blush and point to the field, as though he were the Perfessor of baseball and she the dewy student, rather than the opposite. But the score, he came to learn, was not her sole intrigue. Driving back from their third game together she confessed that what she loved most about baseball was not so much the game itself but, indeed, her boys: Roger Maris ("those magic blue eyes") and Moose Skowron and Bobby Richardson ("even though he's a fuddy-duddy who can't hit worth a damn") and Billy Shantz whose name sounded Jewish but wasn't and Eli Grba whose name seemed like a typewriter accident but wasn't. The way they moved in their uniforms, "like Greek statues that walked straight out of the museum," or the way they spat, scratched, punched their gloves, loitered at base with their legs spread wide. "I suppose it's rather carnal," she concluded, which wasn't a word he remembered hearing a woman speak aloud before, certainly not like that: so nonchalantly, unashamedly—so carnally.

He vaguely understood, but did not say, that his own interest in baseball was carnal, too. During their sixth game together, the first in a doubleheader against the Red Sox, she came leaping into his arms in the giddy standing-ovation aftermath of a Mickey Mantle homer, and when their arms came down he discovered her hand clasping his. Their hands remained like that, twined atop the concrete bleachers and mostly unacknowledged save for the occasional shy glance and bitten lip, for almost all of the next game, which neither of them seemed to follow very closely. And though he hated himself for thinking it, he could not remember being so savagely happy in all his life.

He cut it off after that—for a while, at least. He'd always been a terrible liar, and his ungainly attempt to explain away his mild sunburn to Alice— "maybe from mowing the lawn?" he'd asked, as if to draw out a better explanation from her—felt loathsome and excruciating. His wrestling with the boys vanished as swiftly as it'd come; instead he found himself barking orders at them, oppressed by their cap guns and bickering, incensed by all their toys underfoot which seemed like plastic symbols of all that was hindering him from . . . from what? He couldn't say. He was not in love with Katherine Bluestein, if he defined love in the traditional way—that is, he did not long to marry her, father her children (the very idea brought a shudder), grow old in her company. But neither did he want to merely lay her down, like some sailor on shore leave. He didn't think he wanted a new life, necessarily . . . just his same life, squared. But he knew this was impossible—absurdly so. There were laws of physics that applied to emotions. At night he'd lie awake listening to Alice snore and try cursing himself to sleep. To avoid Katherine, he even stopped working on his book for a couple of weeks, blackening his mood that much further.

But 1960 was a pennant year for the Bombers, and everywhere he went, it seemed, they were all anyone talked about. Had it always been like this, and he'd never been aware of it? Or were his antennae so overtuned that every eavesdropped mention of Hector Lopez, Joe DeMaestri, Duke Maas, *et al.,* or the Indians, Tigers, Bucs, or Orioles, no matter how distant or slight, whether in the butcher shop or the bookstore, on the sidewalk walking past the barber, or from the beat cops outside the bakery blowing the steam off the tops of their coffees, came flooding into his mind, swamping and drowning everything else? Without ever intending to, he realized, he'd carved a whole separate chunk out of his life, had created an alternate persona that both was and wasn't him—and from everywhere, from the radio and the television and the newspaper and the kids bopping down Main

Street in their navy-blue Yankees caps, it was calling him back. Against his own knotted desires and late-night curses he felt wrecked and powerless.

He and Katherine were chaste through their eighth game, and for most of their ninth. They even bickered once, when she made fun of him for not taking off his hat in the greasy July heat. But during the seventh inning of that ninth and final game, Dr. Cross emerged from the bathroom to find Katherine waiting for him there, her purse in hand. He somehow knew what was coming—he could see it in the severe, almost deranged frown on her face; in the slight wet parting of her unbitten lips; in the serpentine way her shoulders rolled as she came toward him at the wall—but was startled nonetheless when her face met his and with its violent entry her tongue shocked his mouth. How long the kiss lasted wasn't clear; he was only dimly aware of the sound of a bat cracking followed by the giant roar of the crowd, of her fingernails piercing his shoulders and his own arms hanging limp and heavy at his sides, of the rich, malty, tobacco-y taste of her mouth, of the muttered jostling men gave him as they came streaming in and out of the bathroom, of the wondrous and terrible gust of life battering its way through him. When finally he opened his eyes, as breathless as if to the crowd's wild delight he'd run the bases himself, he saw her eyes fixed upon his, seeming to penetrate them in much the same way her tongue had just penetrated his mouth. He stood motionless, eyes wide and blinking. She cocked her head, seeming to sense his reluctance which wasn't quite reluctance but something far more explosive than that: desire and fear, combusting. "There's more," she whispered, biting her bottom lip on which his own pilfered saliva gleamed.

More: He knew of course what more meant. And yet he didn't. Because even then, in the sweltering sauna heat of that stadium corridor, with her hands gently ironing out the creases her nails had left on his suit sleeves, and with what felt like a miracle of animal pleasure occurring in his elasticized limbs, he understood that with more came less. That there was an equilibrium to life, and that with everything you gained you lost something as well, in the same measure, so that whatever further bliss was available to him would have to be paid with equal degrees of pain. He had just one life, not two, meaning *more* was an illusion, a traitorous chimera. He slipped his hat off, rolling it in his hands in the thin space between them so that she was forced to let go of him and drop back a step, and he read and reread the label inside the crown as Katherine stood waiting, as if there inside that hat were the instructions he required, the biblical verse that could supply him fortitude. Then he nodded, and wiped his mouth, and feeling every cell in his body roiling in furious mutiny he shook his head no and turned glumly toward the exit, Katherine following along as a long train of sighs.

They never spoke of baseball again, or of anything beyond the humdrum administering of his research needs. A rejected chill came into her eyes when she'd lift them from the sports pages to field his requests, and he'd lower his own when she'd stand up to retrieve his books or documents. When the Yankees lost the World Series that year, in the seventh game to the Pirates, Dr. Cross was on his way home from teaching, oblivious to all the crestfallen boys in their Yankees caps kicking pebbles down the sidewalk, to the cops and the barbers wagging their heads while loudly second-guessing the Old Perfessor's decision to start Bob Turley on the mound rather than Whitey Ford, to the viral pallor of defeat on the faces of the men he passed. Alice made pork chops for dinner, and without exaggeration he told her they were the best pork chops he'd ever eaten, grateful for scraps his fussy children abandoned to their plates.

But now Katherine was back. Katherine Bluestein and the Yankees. How had it happened? He shook the credit card statement in his hand, as if to throttle it for more information, his insides blistering with anger. Why couldn't he ever *remember*? *Why*? How had she found him, after all these years—or, God forbid, had *he* somehow found her? Surely not the latter: Goddamn just look at me, he thought, with an acidly mournful snort. A decrepit and colorless sleeve of bones all but strapped to a hospital bed, with a heart so frail it couldn't take an ounce more burden or the slightest boost in tempo—nothing *more*. Of course he'd occasionally thought about Katherine over the years, because after everything had cooled and his life had resumed being livable, when it'd matured into being a statement rather than a question, he'd come to believe that it was in just these unknown and private moments that our true characters were made or revealed. This belief had depressed him, at first, because it seemed to undermine his work as a historian, seemed to undermine the practice of history itself: How could he hope to comprehend and chronicle

past lives—transmitted to him via the minuscule dripline of letters, autobiographies, recorded interviews, recollections of others, diaries which
were rarely as candid as they seemed—when he knew his own mild history, written by another or even by himself, could never include what he
deemed his most noble and ignoble moments—the primary but secret
truths of his life?

History records strong deeds; but the *truth* of history, he came to believe, was in the wavering. What if he *had* followed Katherine Bluestein
into that *More?* Maybe nothing, or close to nothing. Several years later
the sexual revolution would come charging in, as sudden and beguiling as
Katherine's tongue invading his mouth, and he would hear his colleagues
and students dismissing such dalliances as "just sex," which perhaps was
what they were. Maybe that was all Katherine Bluestein could've been, and
possibly wanted to be: a hobby of his, practiced in dim little Updikean motel rooms near the stadium, her cigarettes burning on the nightstand like
incense, his conscience parked outside by the door. Maybe he was both
over-romantic and priggish to think otherwise. But he did. And because
he hadn't followed Katherine Bluestein into that *More,* he'd dedicated himself—applying all that super-heated radioactive energy she'd brought forth
in him—to the idyll of who he was, or wanted most of all to be: an honest
and decent man, that creature civilization had spent four thousand–plus
years creating and honing, still and forever tilting against the windmills
of brute nature. The wavering had forged him, just as his wavering at the
edge of the burial pit at Gunskirchen Lager had forged him, when in that
terrible hinge of a moment he'd learned how easy it would be—how *natural*—to surrender to his urges, to submit to his wants. Yet neither of these
crucible instances would ever be known. They would be buried with him,
as maybe all true moments are. What we leave behind, he'd come to believe, is mere simulacra, the invented residue of our public selves.

But now. But now. Who *was* he, after all? His memory said one thing;
his lack of memory, another. He tried ripping the credit card statement
but its two pages were too durable for his weak hands to tear apart. This
felt like further indignity, and again his eyes dampened with frustration
and sorrow. But he was able to rip one of the pages, singly, first into halves
and then into quarters, and the remaining page after that, and then all the

quarters into smaller pieces and then, his curled arthritic hands twitching with pain, into even smaller pieces, until the bedspread was littered with unruly white shards, the shredded evidence of the man he was or wasn't or could've been.

That's when the cat jumped onto the bed. Dr. Cross yelped and threw his hands up and back, as if accosted by a mugger, as the cat closed in on him with predatory grace. It lifted one paw, stepped lightly forward. "Shoo, cat," Dr. Cross moaned. His arms remained fixed to the headboard as the cat arched its back and began kneading the bedspread, digging its claws into the cheap cotton layer atop Dr. Cross's belly and purring, the tiny scraps of paper bobbing on the bedspread like floating debris in an eddypool. "Shoo," Dr. Cross said again, but with such weakness that the cat dunked its head and seemed almost to smile, purring all the louder.

They stayed that way for a long while, until Dr. Cross felt the warm music of the purring loosening his shoulders and with them his fears. As the terror subsided he found himself lowering his arms and even offering a hand which the cat nuzzled and with its wet snout smeared. He felt his body slackening, but not unpleasantly—the way morphine must feel, he thought. Maybe the nurses were right after all: perhaps some rest was in order, the restorative anesthesia of a brief nap. Yes, that was it. A nap. Through the window, outside on Henry Street, he could see the sunlight slanting, bowing to nightfall's approach, and from the doorway he could hear the squeaks of the nurses steering their carts down the hallway, the eager babble from televisions in other rooms, the forlorn echoes of a distant unanswered phone going ring, ring, ring, ring, ring. The cat continued its kneading and purring, staring directly into Dr. Cross's eyes, and Dr. Cross, wincing as the occasional claw pierced the bedspread and went digging into his sheer and withered skin, lulled by the soft staticky purring and yet strangely and powerfully lucid, returned the stare harder, wanting to know what the cat saw, wanting to know what it knew. He wanted to know what was coming for him.

2

"**DUDE, SERIOUSLY,**" **MATTY** was saying. "I told you this was all on me. Will you stop scrounging the trash cans already?"

"Force of habit, man," Talmadge muttered, swerving away from the blue trash barrel. A tiny knot of annoyance gnarled the back of his neck: annoyance at Matty, for the way he was always belittling scavenging, but at himself, too, for the blinders he'd developed, for the way he'd come to view the world — Exhibit A, just then — as some kind of matrix for diving ops, a connect-the-dots trail of trash bags and dumpsters and recycling bins, as a treasure map without . . . he opted not to finish the thought, focusing instead on following Matty through the dense, round-shouldered, blue-jerseyed stadium crowd. It was just like he'd learned to navigate the human briars of places like Times Square: you got yourself behind some fast-walking native, your machete, or your ice cutter, and let that person carve you an open route right through those wadded-up tourists. You could draft whole blocks that way, as dreamy and unperturbed as when cruising an interstate. Anyway, it's not like he could've grabbed anything from the trash barrels in the first place: His hands were full, with a jumbo light beer in one and nachos in the other. Closely monitoring the beer, which kept sloshing over the cup's rim as he walked, he failed to notice Matty stopping, and in the collision splashed Miller Lite onto Matty's lower back, basically down his shorts.

"Thanks, dude," said Matty. "That felt *delicious*. We gotta turn in here. (Coming through, bro.) Our seats are down this way. (Seriously, man, you gonna let me pass? Jesus.) I think we've missed, like, the whole first inning. Here we go, down here. Damn, you see that asswipe? Just standing there. I was like, dude, coming through, *hello*."

"I'm just following you," said Talmadge, as they emerged from a gray concrete corridor into the massive sunlit bowl of Yankee Stadium—and the bottom of the bowl, at that, to a section along the first-base line that was almost level with the field. "Holy shit, what'd you *pay* for these seats, man?" Talmadge called out. Then a sudden grin quirked his face. "Or are we squatting?"

"Screw squatting." Matty quartered back as if to say something further but shook his head instead, swallowing whatever he'd been fixing to say, and then descended down the concrete steps. "They're *our* seats, okay? This row here."

"Oh, *man*," Talmadge said, more impressed than he wanted to be. Until this moment he'd thought his dad's box seats at the Superdome were the shit. But Dick Bertrand had nothing on these. Third row from the field, just to the right of the Yankees dugout. He was almost shocked to see the field up close as actual grass with actual blades; the anomaly of seeing genuine earth in this unearthly city never failed to stagger him. He was near enough to see the thick, sunlight-glossed forearm hair of the Yankees' first baseman, the rawhide curls on his glove, the weave of his socks. This was high-definition seating. He sat down in amazement.

To Talmadge's right sat a fortyish brunette whose enormous silicone breasts he couldn't help noticing first, though with nonbiological interest, and certainly no amazement. They were positioned unnaturally high, aimed skyward like anti-aircraft guns, and set just barely inside a blue satin dress that must've been custom tailored to restrict them within the confines of indecent exposure laws. To her right sat a distracted, sweaty man at least a decade older, cursing at something on his cellphone screen, who Talmadge presumed to be her husband. He had one of those lumpy misshapen bodies on which shirts never fit properly, shirts bunching and puffing as his was bunched and puffed now, but this didn't matter because at a certain tax bracket dishevelment was mistaken for charm. Dick Bertrand had a body like that, but without the bank balance to render it charming. With great agitation the man flashed the screen for the woman to see. She shrugged in the most noncommittal manner Talmadge had ever seen a person shrug, a scant lift of shoulder that could've signaled *There's nothing you can do right now about the price of crude* as easily as it could've signaled *I have no idea why you're showing me that battery-operated contraption.* Settling himself into his seat, with his beer between his legs and the nachos transferred to Matty's knee, Talmadge greeted the woman with a Southern hello. She pretended not to hear, staring expressionlessly up toward the Jumbotron or the blue sky beyond it, conceivably scanning for enemy aircraft. Talmadge tried not to mind. Even the snottiest matrons of the Gulfport Yacht Club—he was thinking now of Mrs. Dubuisson, to whom his father had devoted years of courting for insidious society reasons—would've made *some* gesture in response. (In Mrs. Dubuisson's case, a lavishly condescending return greeting that only later would you register as devastating.) He thought of what Micah would do, in similar straits. Probably plant herself on the woman's lap until either acknowledgment came or those boobs opened fire. But then Micah would never be found lounging in a field box at Yankee Stadium. The point was way beyond moot.

Just then the inning ended and the Cleveland Indians came jogging out onto the field. Their first baseman—copper-skinned, with Popeye-grade arms and an ornate black goatee—had a thick sinister shape to him, a streetfighter's physique crammed into the temperate uniform of a ballplayer. From the rows above and behind him Talmadge heard people yelling something to the first baseman. Something scraggly and bitter-sounding, the word hurled like a shotput. It sounded like *herpes.*

"Does he have herpes?" Talmadge asked Matty.

"No, man. That's his name."

"His name's Herpes?"

"His name's Hermes, dude. Hermes Ortiz."

At this point Matty joined in, cupping his mouth and shouting, "Hey, Herpes! *Herpes!*" Matty seemed pleased with himself, devouring a nacho as reward, but at this near distance, so close to the field and thereby to Herpes/Hermes, something felt off to Talmadge, as though at this point-blank range the partisan became personal. Evidently he wasn't alone. With a sharp crank of her head the woman beside Talmadge shot them a glare, withering upon impact, and her husband leaned forward in his seat and pointing a rolled-up program at them said, "Come on, boys." Even Hermes himself took notice, flashing them a quick but meaningful scowl. From what Talmadge could gather an unwritten code had been violated, and he found himself slinking down into his seat even as the fans in the higher seats, emboldened by Matty's breach, broke into a caustic mob-chant of *Herpes Herpes Herpes*. Talmadge was reminded of the way he'd felt when his Uncle Lenord, regrettably introduced to the open bar at his cousin's son's wedding reception, commandeered the microphone and concluded his toast by saying of the bride, "I'd slide buck-nekkid down a rusty razor blade into a pool of rubbing alcohol just to hear her fart over a walkie talkie." The bride's father chased Lenord out into the parking lot but ultimately it didn't matter because the marriage failed to survive a year; the investment had been bad from the start.

Not wanting to see Matty chased into the parking lot, Talmadge diverted him by asking, "Are the Yankees any good this year?"

Matty snorted. "You really don't follow, do you?"

"What do you mean?"

"Baseball. You don't follow baseball."

"I guess not."

"Well, they're in first. The Sox are three games back."

"What about Cleveland?"

"In third. Four and a half back."

"Okay."

"But Cleveland's on a big fucking streak right now. They've won seven road games."

"Gotcha."

"And the Yankees, man — injuries out the ass. It's tight."

"Okay."

After a moment Matty said, "So it matters."

"The game, you mean?"

"Yeah. The game."

With a perfect-sounding *crack* a Yankee batter hit a pitch high out to left field and Matty rose from his seat to watch it, lips parted in expectation. When it dropped into the outfielder's glove Matty dropped himself back down, lips resealed. "Thought he had the goods on that one," he muttered.

"I guess we're more like football people," said Talmadge. "In the South, I mean."

Matty's face clouded. "Yo, space dude, you forgetting who I am?"

"I'm just sayin."

What he was saying, he thought afterwards, as the teams switched fields and shouts of *Bye Herpes* chased Ortiz across the diamond, was that this — the game itself, the field box seats, his extravagantly rude and siliconized seatmate — was all foreign and exotic and vaguely incomprehensible to him, and not just because Micah (who at one time and maybe still was foreign and exotic and incomprehensible to him) had rewired his thinking so that every component of his life needed to jibe with their all-encompassing moral vision, all these square pegs needing to be rammed into impossible round holes. But then no, scratch that. He took a long swig of beer to flush out the confusion. Truth was, he *didn't* know what he was saying because he didn't even know what he was thinking — not lately, anyway. All his thoughts were clipped short, like the grass on the field. Maybe it was that he shouldn't have come here in the first place, maybe just that — that something was wrong about this, though precisely what he couldn't say. Where he should've been, he knew, was home with Micah — especially now. *Because of.* Except that — he cut the thought short with a sigh, revisiting his beer. But the thought unspooled anyway: Except that he couldn't *stand* to be home with Micah right now. *Because of:* again.

"Gentlemen?" Someone was calling to them from Talmadge's right. Looking over he saw a stadium guard leaning across the sweaty husband who seemed oddly okay with having his view of the field blocked. "Can I see your tickets, gentlemen?"

"Fuck," Matty whispered. "Be cool."

"What's going on? We *are* squatting, aren't we? It's no big deal."

"Just be cool," Matty hissed, passing the ticket stubs to Talmadge who had to awkwardly angle his arm in order to pass them to the guard without brushing his seatmate's inflations.

The guard checked the tickets and returning them said, "Enjoy the game."

"What was *that?*" Talmadge asked Matty.

"What was what?"

"Why'd you freak?"

"I didn't freak. Shut up, man. Jeter's up."

"You freaked, dude."

"Just shut up. I'll tell you later."

So something *was* wrong about all this: Talmadge's Spidey-sense stood confirmed. How much *had* these tickets cost, anyway? In his chivalrous effort to avoid boob contact he'd missed an opportunity to note the price when conveying the tickets back and forth. He rewound his memory to an argument with Micah that he'd had about a month ago: Matty had come home one evening with roughly thirty boxes of Ho Hos which he'd claimed to have found in a trash bag outside the Gristedes on Mercer Street. Alone with Talmadge later she'd called bullshit. "No one throws Ho Hos out," she fumed. "That shit's got the shelf life of chainsaw oil." Talmadge's response was along the lines of *so what*. "We're not running a hostel, man," she said. "If Matty wants to join forces, or even just show some goddamn respect for what we believe in, then it's cool, but otherwise . . ."

"Join *forces?*" Talmadge interrupted. "Since when are we at war?"

With a sadness that seemed to him terribly and even mysteriously over-wrought, considering they were fighting about Ho Hos, she put a hand to his chest and said, "You just don't get it, man," and by walking away left him smoldering and confused. He *didn't* get it. She was right.

But then he also didn't get where Matty had scored the cash to buy thirty boxes of Ho Hos unless he contemplated the obvious answer which Talmadge didn't want to do. So as the fresh Ho Hos continued to pile up in the cabinets and a new longboard appeared in the outside hallway and Matty's creased-up old Doc Martens were replaced with crisp new waffle-soled Vans, Talmadge willfully ignored it all, allowing Matty his charade ("Yeah, there must be, like, a recall on Ho Hos or someshit") while avoiding the topic with Micah with the same twisty exertion he'd just applied to dodging his seatmate's breasts. But now, as the theme from *Rocky* came raining from the loudspeakers above them: What the *hell*, man? Five hundred bucks for these seats? Maybe more? He took an anxious sip of beer as the Yankees orchestrated a double play to retire the inning and Matty rose up cheering.

"Something's up," Talmadge finally said to him. "You're back to dealing again, aren't you?"

Scrunching his face, Matty blew out a fat derisive *pshaw* sound. "I'm not *dealing*, okay? Will you just enjoy the fucking game? Did you even *see* that play?"

"I don't like it. It feels weird, dude. Like I'm sitting in a stolen seat."

Noting a beer vendor, Matty waved him over and signaled for two. He peeled off a twenty for Talmadge to pass down. As Talmadge stood to retrieve the beers he heard Matty say, "Watch out for those tits," and was this time relieved at the woman's deafness act. He did, however, sneak a glance down the engineered crevice of her cleavage which was gleaming with sweat droplets, a water slide to paradise or if not paradise then a reasonable imitation. He'd never fiddled with anything like them, he realized. Becky Annandale's, back in college, were reputed to be fake, but at the time he'd touched them he hadn't had enough experience to tell the difference; but then Becky's certainly weren't like these, mere pints to these gallon-plus jugs. When Hermes Ortiz took the field Matty waved to him like someone trying to catch a date's attention in a crowded restaurant. "Yoo hoo, Herpes," he called, and Talmadge noted a sharp hissing from his right, from the husband. Then in a low conspiratorial voice Matty said to Talmadge, "So what if you are?"

"Are, what?"

"Sitting in a stolen seat."

"Am I?"

"Keep your voice down."

Talmadge's voice twanged in anger, "What the fuck, dude?"

Matty shifted his attention to the field. A strike. Two balls. A softly popped foul that went arcing into the stands behind them, which Matty didn't crane his neck or even raise his head to watch pass. It was like he was watching the game without watching it. Another strike, followed by another. The batter punished the dirt with a sharp kick before heaving the bat to the batboy. One out.

"This stays between us, right? No exemption for the chick."

"Right," Talmadge agreed.

Matty paused to watch the next batter, some inner conflict torquing his face; he looked indigestive, licking his lips, his Adam's apple throbbing from his frequent swallowing. "Now batting for the Yankees," came the announcement, "Johnny Damon." Matty clapped, so Talmadge did too. One strike, then another, then a *crack* that sent the ball skittering past the second baseman out into center field, a ground-ball single that landed Damon on first base. "Way to play it, Johnny!" Matty shouted, as the loudspeakers blared some godawful techno song that Talmadge associated with amusement parks and other manufactured fun, like his other seatmate perhaps. Adjusting his helmet as he headed back to the base, Damon turned to give Matty a wink.

"You see that?" Matty bubbled.

He was stalling.

"Come on, dude," Talmadge urged.

"Okay." Rolling his shoulders like an on-deck batter, Matty cleared his throat and said, "I'm kinda doing this, like, entrepreneur thing."

"What're you talking about?"

He leaned in. "You know that dumpster, at the nursing home?"

"The one on Henry Street?"

"Yeah, that one. There was some valuable shit in there. And I'm not talking rice."

"What kind of shit?"

"Keep your voice down, man."

"What kind of shit?"

"Credit card statements. Bank statements. Social security papers. Motherfucking treasure trove."

"Dude," Talmadge said, with a burn in his chest. "Tell me you're lying."

"It's so freaking *easy*, man." Matty lifted his head at the sound of bat striking ball—but it was just a foul, shanked into the netting. "This guy I did time with, my cellie back in Oregon?" he continued. "He hooked me up with his, like, cousin or something, I dunno, this dude out in Brighton Beach. He can fucking do *anything* with that info, man. He's got this machine, right? In his basement. That basement's so fucked up, dude, it's like Satan's playroom. Anyway, there's this rad machine down there, and you just plug in the numbers and it spits out a credit card. With the little name and everything."

"Holy shit," Talmadge said, not sure what was impressing him, if anything. Probably the machine.

"I mean, it's not *that* easy. He don't pay me that much. It's mostly methheads bringing him shit so he just pays 'em with some tweak. But I'm going light on that shit, dude. Monya, he kinda respects that. We're on, like, cash and credit terms."

"Who's Monya?"

"That's the dude in Brighton Beach. Fucking Russian mafia, man. Face tats and all that. Honestly? He kinda scares the shit outta me." Matty unloosed an intensely uncomfortable laugh, like that of someone tickled to the point of pain. "But it's cool. It's cool, Tal. It ain't nothing to freak out over. It's petty, dude. It's just another angle."

Talmadge's face reddened, and shifting away from Matty he said, "Man, Micah would . . ."

"Micah's not gonna do *anything*, dude." There was menace at the bottom of Matty's voice: an unfamiliar substrate, to Talmadge's ears, despite all their years of friendship. "Okay? You follow?"

They sat in silence, only lightly clapping, while the Yankees chalked up another hit: a line drive by Matsui that bounced off the center-field wall and put Damon on third. Talmadge sipped his Miller Lite, which had a sour tinge to it—possibly the effect of its newly revealed status as contraband. None of this was really surprising, he concluded, just as it hadn't been a surprise two years ago when Matty called to say he'd been busted in a Portland sting operation, or two years before that, when Matty informed him he'd been booted off the Ole Miss soccer team for failing a drug test even though he'd chugged seventeen cups of goldenseal tea to cleanse the urine sample. If anything, Matty was the consistent one in their friendship, the steady control—his desires never deviating, their outcomes measured and predictable. Talmadge was the wildcard, the one with all the surprises.

"So who are we today?" he asked Matty.

"What do you mean?"

"Like, who comped our tickets?"

"Oh, yeah. Him. That'd be Dr. Elwin Cross Sr."

With equal doses sarcasm and earnestness Talmadge mumbled, "Sorry, Elwin."

"Dude, fuck Elwin." Matty's eyes flared, but after a quick survey of the field they came back softer. "Elwin's fine, okay? The banks eat up all this shit anyway. Bank of America, that's who's treating us today. People see the weird charges, they call the bank, the bank freezes the card and wipes the charges clean. It's, like, an operating expense. Monya explained it all to me. They don't even investigate it."

Talmadge mulled this for a while, as Matsui stole second and the stadium quaked with the sudden stomp of forty thousand people springing to their feet (Talmadge excepted), the slippery chords of Metallica's "Enter Sandman" overpowering the speakers and blowing sonic fuzz throughout the stands, Matty hoisting his beer to the sky and whooping and even Talmadge's other seatmate up on her heels now, rocking her knees up and down as though gathering the kinetic force necessary to launch herself skyward. Or was she dancing? Talmadge caught himself staring at her ass, which was respectable so far as asses went though he'd never been an ass man so he didn't really understand why his eyes felt suddenly locked to the thin blue satin clinging so faithfully to her buttocks. He had to remind himself that from all available evidence (the brusqueness, the store-bought tits, the tanning-booth patina, the sugar-daddy husband) she was flatly despicable—the tri-state equivalent of Sherilyn, his stepmom in technicality only, who'd transformed his father into a puddle of what he supposed was lust (though the idea skeeved him out) and in doing so sliced his family down the middle. He was both disappointed and relieved when the woman sat back down.

"Funny thing about Elwin, though," Matty said thoughtfully.

"What's that?"

"This card's been hot for, like, two months now. Normally you get a few days, max. I'm not even supposed to be using it like this. Mail-order only, that's Monya's rule. But fuck. The thing's hot. Elwin must have some serious bank."

Talmadge felt his face go hot. "Dude, are you insane? What're you, missing prison or something?"

"It's cool, man. I told you."

"Naw, it's bullshit." Matty always had to *push* it. That was the thing with him: Whatever it was, he pushed it till it broke. "I'm not digging this."

"Fuck you, dude. It's from the same trash you're scrounging through." He was misinterpreting Talmadge's objection as being on ethical grounds, though Talmadge hadn't even broached that yet, to Matty or himself. "I'm just, like, recycling the information. It's all the same."

"Whatever. It's a felony, man."

"Would you keep it down?"

"This explains the Ho Hos, too."

"The what?"

"All the Ho Hos you've been dragging in. You don't never see Ho Hos in the trash. They've got the shelf life of, like, chainsaw oil."

"Chainsaw oil?"

"Whatever. A ten-thousand-year shelf life."

"Awright, fine. Busted. Maybe I was trying to make your chick happy."

"She doesn't eat Ho Hos."

"So what if I was trying to make *me* happy, okay?" Cheering went rippling through the stands, which they both ignored. "They're fucking *Ho Hos*. I'm supposed to tell her, what, some old dude in a nursing home bought 'em for us? I can't believe you're busting my balls over Ho Hos. I tried bringing steaks back once and you saw how that turned out. What a fucking party that was. Micah, man." Talmadge caught a note of personal grievance in Matty's voice. "She's so, like—*hardcore*, man. Chick doesn't bend. I'm sorry, dude, but I don't know how you put up with her shit sometimes—"

"She's pregnant, you know."

The paralyzed expression on Matty's face mirrored Talmadge's own. He hadn't intended to tell Matty—not yet, at least. And God knows not like this. It was like he hadn't spoken it so much as allowed it to escape, had left the gate unlocked on this news that'd been fermenting inside him for three weeks now, this bubbling acid burning holes in his gut. He felt a panic beginning to swirl within him, second only to the panic he'd felt when Micah told him because now he'd just loosed it, brought it to life outside the narrow confines of their relationship, and in doing so had made it *real*. The weirdest thing was: He'd *felt* her getting pregnant, he'd actually felt the moment of conception as they'd exploded that night into some paranormal whoosh of synchronized climax, intertwined orgasms squared to the nth degree, as though right there, at the porthole tip of his dick, he'd sensed the sperm meeting the egg and doing whatever it was they did to begin construction on a microscopic head and heart, and when he'd rolled off her—Micah still quivering and spaced out, because her orgasms often resembled epileptic seizures, thrashy and prolonged—he'd felt strangely heavy, almost despondent really, despite having just experienced perhaps the deepest and most spectacular sex of his life. She'd fallen straight to sleep—which was also odd, because usually sex threw Micah into a talkative whir—and after a long dark while Talmadge found himself climbing to the roof and staring at the skyline as if somewhere in all those constellations of trembling yellow windows was the answer to a hard and essential question, if only he knew what it was, or how to ask it.

"No," Matty said finally, with a grim edge to his voice. "I didn't know. How would I know?"

"Because I just told you."

The bases were loaded now, the Indians' pitcher having walked Cabrera. On one of the digital signs over center field the word THUNDER appeared to wriggle and squirm. The stadium filled with the noise of banging and clapping, transfigured into a four-acre drum. Cellphone cameras rose from the crowds, held high and higher to record whatever might be coming from ten thousand vantage points at least, in an immense surge of preservation. Inside that volatile rowdy bowl it felt as though only two people remained seated.

Matty had to shout, "So where you guys gonna move?"

It was so brazenly self-serving, the question caused Talmadge to flinch. But the flinch was not without other origins. "That's the thing," Talmadge shouted back. "She's saying we're *not* moving."

"What the fuck, dude? You gonna raise a baby in a squat?"

"That's kinda what I said."

"And she's not open to, like, going to a clinic—"

Talmadge cut him off, knowing just where he'd been headed. He'd visited the same clinic in his own mind. "No chance, man. She wants this baby."

"Go out diving for baby food?" Matty said, veering back. "Dude, I seen enough to tell you you'd have better luck finding Ho Hos."

Giambi was up to bat, and after two balls and a strike, the crowd settled into an eager hush, holding its breath for him.

"I hear you, man, I do," Talmadge said. "You know how she is. You said it yourself."

Matty grunted, looking almost satisfied to no longer be on the defensive. "And you think I'm the fucked-up one."

"And the worst part, man," Talmadge went on, with a squeak to his drawl, "is that I can't fucking talk to her about it. She's always going on about the way her dad did things. The way he raised her. But her dad, man—he's batshit crazy! Everyone but Micah thinks he killed her mother! He got hauled into court when she was a kid for, like, child neglect or something."

"Like I said," Matty muttered.

"Yeah, well." Matty was over-hammering the point. "You're fucked up too."

Matty disliked Micah. This was clear and maybe always had been, as much as Talmadge longed to deny it. That wink he'd given Talmadge, that very first Thanksgiving night: It'd signaled he would play along for however long Talmadge needed, that he'd be there when this fever broke. But what did Matty know? He'd never been in love, as he freely admitted. He'd never even had much in the way of a girlfriend, so far as Talmadge knew. All his feelings were aimed inward. But then who else did Talmadge have? He'd whittled his allegiances down to two, and just one if you discounted Micah: the wild kid from Mahwah who'd cradled Talmadge's head above a Deaton Hall toilet one long-ago night, after Talmadge had mixed two hits of blotter with a couple ecstasy pills on top of bourbon, sponging the vomit from his lips and assuring him over and over again, as Talmadge bawled in hallucinatory terror, that he wasn't going to die, to stop talking like that, that everything would be okay, that he wasn't going to let him die no matter what. The memory sent a tremor of affection through Talmadge's chest, and swishing the last warm remnants of beer in his cup he said, "I'm empty. Can ol' Elwin buy me another beer?"

"Ol' Elwin'll buy you anything you want, man."

Giambi struck out, retiring the inning and with his last whiff at bat sucking all the oxygen from the stadium, causing everyone to gasp and sink back into their seats as if felled by the toxic fumes of dashed hopes. A low mutinous grumble overtook the stands as Matty disappeared to fetch more beer. In the solitary interim Talmadge tried to unknot what he was feeling but found himself distracted by the legs of his seatmate which, now that she'd perched her feet on the armrest in front of her, thereby jackknifing her legs in Talmadge's direction, were both obnoxiously and breathtakingly close. They were Ole Miss legs, he realized, though of an older and slightly distressed vintage: of that variety of shatteringly perfect limbs he'd come to know and ogle from his first day at the university, as seen on the girls navigating Sorority Row in their hiked-up Umbro shorts, the negligible variations in shape and skin tone melding into a burnished uniform gleam as they'd go power-walking up or down the hill in clutches of three or four, those legs like sharpened scissors cutting straight into the monkey recesses of his stupefied brain. In the languid sunlight the woman's legs appeared not just shaved (they were) but sanded down to their lustrous core and then oiled to bring out the barely perceptible grain, like the mahogany gunstock of his grandfather's .30-30. He wanted to touch the leg nearest him — mere inches from his hand, he could almost detect the 98.6-degree heat it was exuding, could almost feel the microclimate of her skin — as he'd been allowed to touch his grandfather's rifle as a boy: with a sacred reverence and an awareness of danger that prickled the skin on the nape of his neck. He pulled his hand away, however, cursing himself and looking the woman up and down with a sneer that seemed callous but necessary. Micah had amazing legs, too, of course. She did. He loved the downy chestnut hair on them, the way the hair submitted to his tongue when he'd run his mouth down her lower legs leaving a slickly flattened row —

Who am I? The question burst into his consciousness with such jarring suddenness that he glanced around to see if maybe someone else had just stabbed it into his brain. Maybe the announcer? But no, the announcer had another script before him as he broadcast the start of a between-innings race featuring a trio of people dressed as bottles of ketchup, mustard, and relish. He chanced a quick peek at the woman's lower thigh, as though it could supply him the answer. He wasn't convinced it couldn't. Maybe this was the question he'd meant to ask the skyline that night. Or maybe the skyline was no wiser and no more forthcoming than Dick Bertrand's prized bug zapper. As usual he didn't know.

When Matty returned it was clear that he'd been pondering Talmadge's situation; he wore a gently worried expression, and when he asked Talmadge how he was feeling it was with therapeutic warmth. "It's just, like, this is for keeps now, you know?" Talmadge blurted, three weeks of desperation finding sudden vent. "I mean, look, I admire Micah's principles more than I can even —" He stopped at that edge, because he *did* admire Micah's fundamentalism, and he didn't want to insult it with hyperbolic bullshit. "Go to hell, mustard!" they heard someone bellow, and both he and Matty glanced to the field where ketchup was leading mustard on a dash around the bases with relish far behind, the foam costumes bouncing atop stocking legs. "I mean, she's right," he said. "She's totally *right,* dude. Her way of living—our way I mean. It's the only moral way to even *exist* in the world right now."

Matty shook his head and looked away toward the field, where ketchup was now claiming an oversized check for charity and the Yankees were jogging out to claim their positions. "I don't get how that matters."

Talmadge ignored this. "But you bring a kid into it," he went on, "no fucking *way,* man. Right? Battle's over. It's one thing to take on these sacrifices, and, like, put your money where your mouth is—"

"More like your anti-money."

"Fine, whatever. But you get what I'm saying, dude—removing yourself from the system, living below it or above it or whatever we're doing. The whole anti-civ bit. You can do that when it's just *you,* or just us— when you're making your own choices about how to flip off the world. I mean, I *believe* in what Micah's saying. She's right. She's a hundred percent right. You'd have to be a blind prick to look at the world and not agree with every damn thing she says."

Matty raised a protesting finger, which Talmadge also ignored. "But you bring a kid—a *baby*—into it? Uh-uh. You can't hand those sacrifices down, you know? Maybe you can—write letters. March. Give money to, like, groups or someshit. Start groups, I dunno." He hesitated, disliking the path he'd just gone down, before gathering the force for the conclusion he'd been flailing toward: "But you gotta ease that kid into the world as it is."

Matty went quiet for a while, squinting into the sun dipping slowly into the upper deck above third base. "You tell her that?"

"Yeah," Talmadge said. "Of course. That was the epic throw-down we had Saturday night."

"I knew something was up. That's why I broke loose."

"What the fuck am I supposed to *do?*" In his voice was a choked urgency, a deep blue wretchedness that until this very moment he hadn't fully unleashed. "She won't bend. And that's my kid."

The Indians were already down two outs. Matty leaned back in his seat, propping his legs over the open seat in front of him. Talmadge felt his chest heaving, and the sweat on his face was cold and still. When he brought his beer to his lips the cup was shaking; the harder he gripped it, the harder it shook. "Fuck," he said, by which he meant everything, and Matty turned and gave him a hangdog look that felt as consoling as Matty taking his hand in his would've felt. "You're gonna need some cash, you know. Doctors' bills. Diapers. That sorta shit."

"I been thinking about it."

"I'm guessing you guys won't be disposable diaper people."

"Fuck off, dude," Talmadge said gently, with the faintest curve of a smile.

"It's not hard to get, you know. Same trash bags. Same dumpsters."

Talmadge wagged his head no, though his insides surrendered immediately to the idea. "It's like I told her," he said. "We can live pure and change the fucking world, or we can have this baby. But not both."

"I think you've nailed it, dude," Matty affirmed.

"Yeah?" Talmadge said, watching Matty purse his lips and nod contemplatively. They took synchronized sips of their beers, their heads turning in further tandem as a Cleveland batter knocked a pop fly out to left field, where Matsui nabbed it effortlessly from the sky, closing the inning. The woman beside Talmadge slipped off her heels and angling her leg toward him she flexed her toes in what remained of the sunlight. It was such an obvious violation of his space that she murmured an apology, which Talmadge accepted with a nod and then added, clumsily, "Go on and let those dogs loose." On her face there was zero reaction, but the golden legs crept forward, releasing their ache into the oily heat of the stadium. The call of a roving hot dog vendor came drifting down from the stands above, as measured and ancient-sounding as a church bell tolling on a Mississippi Sunday morning: *hawt dawgs, hawt dawgs, get yeh hawt dawgs heah.* Rotating to search the stands, Matty asked, "You wanna vegan hot dog?"

With a crooked smile Talmadge said, "Fuck off."

Matty stood, raising two fingers high in the air, as the Indians took their places on the field. "How you feeling, Herpes?" he shouted while waiting. Ortiz threw his head back, rippling his neck muscles in mutely indignant response, as Matty's call sparked an erratic chorus to detonate in the higher seats: *"Herpes! Herpes! Herpes!"* Matty climbed up onto his seat, exhorting the crowd by raising his outspread arms high and then higher, an orchestral conductor urging mayhem with a wide cocky smile emerging from the top of that lavish black slab of a beard, looking "nuttier than a squirrel turd," as Uncle Lenord would've put it, and as the crowd roared in beery, full-throated obedience, the chant spreading from section to section, Talmadge saw Matty glance down at him, to prod Talmadge into joining his choir. But he didn't need to. Talmadge was already shouting.

3

SARA WAS AT LUNCH with her sister Liz when she said it. The restaurant, set inside the three-story Soho: Kitchen & Home department store on lower Broadway, was called 'Vore, though it didn't bill itself a restaurant: A SUSTAINABLE CURATION, rather, at least according to the menu which was printed on FSC-certified post-consumer paper and stapled to squares of cardboard recycled from the store's delivery boxes that (also according to the menu) would be composted at day's end along with all the placemats, sugar-cane fiber napkins, and leftovers. Sara had ordered a "massaged" raw kale salad with Meyer lemon, black walnuts, and mint, joking to Liz that at least some part of her would be massaged that day, while Liz sent back her kasha and orzo with veal meatballs for being "kind of gummy," confiding to Sara afterwards that she hated "to be a bitch but they're composting it anyway." Her backup choice, housemade falafel with garam masala and Long Island apricot, was also gummy, and though the waiter offered to compost that too, Liz reluctantly said she'd stick with it, and went about nibbling the edges like a martyr. She was fresh from hot yoga, her skin still weeping sweat despite the restaurant's glacial air conditioning, and before Sara had even thought to reach for her water Liz had drained three glasses along with a watermelon-ginger-lemongrass "cooler" out of a Mason jar that, again according to the menu, had been reclaimed from a defunct Amish jammery in Middlefield, Ohio, not fifteen minutes from where Liz and Sara had been raised. They noted this in passing, thinking the coincidence might hold significance, but finding none settled languidly into inventorying their standard laments: Jeremy's on-again depression

(Liz blamed his job at the Rainforest Protection Network, noting that at the end of their recent ten-day vacation to Costa Rica, during which she'd barred him from both laptop and phone, he'd said, "Of course it was a great time. Only 1,370 species went extinct while I was gone"); the apparent futility of behavioral therapy for Aidan's autism ("thirty grand a year to get the same kid coming out as the one going in"); and, on Sara's end, the twined hardships of living with an increasingly frustrated husband and an increasingly reclusive teen daughter. "I swear," Sara said, ribbons of kale speared on the fork hovering just below her mouth, "sometimes I think Alexis loves Dave more than I do."

This wasn't what she'd meant to say. From across the table she saw her sister's face warping with a mixture of confusion and concern. What she'd meant to say instead was, "Sometimes I think Alexis loves Dave more than me," though even that sounded ambiguous as she realized upon correcting herself. "What I *mean*," she re-amended, "is that it feels like she loves Dave more than she loves me. Sometimes. Oh hell."

Liz swallowed dryly and rearranged the napkin on her knees. She'd never been good at hiding her distaste for Dave, although Sara (who characterized herself as a "staunch independent" to mask her lack of interest) had always chalked the divide up to politics, to the Sunni-Shi'a split of the contemporary American electorate: Dave's rigidity clanging against Liz's. Cautiously, Liz said, "Maybe that's because Dave isn't the disciplinarian."

"Oh God he isn't," Sara agreed. "He's like—her enabler."

"So it makes sense in a way. Of *course* Alexis seems drawn to him. Whenever you're saying no, he's throwing her a big life-ring of yes."

"That's probably it," Sara said, lifting the kale into her mouth and chewing it without registering any flavor. She knew this theory was insufficient—Alexis wasn't *really* a discipline problem; Dave didn't *really* have authority in parenting matters to begin with—but she liked its cleanliness. The muddier truth—that her husband and daughter seemed at times enjoined against her, a two-person cabal trading inside jokes and sneaky remarks and furtive glances—had a paranoiac smudge to it, and risked the impression that Sara was swamped with self-esteem issues: *No one likes me,* et cetera. Which she wasn't; no more than the average American woman, she figured. "Teenagers," she groaned, wanting suddenly to close this subject she'd so awkwardly opened. "Just you wait."

"It's one day at a time, with Aidy," Liz said, poking through her falafel for specks of apricot. "The challenge for us, I think, is going to be separating out what's neurotypical—you know, hormonal—and what's the disease. What's normal and what's not. Jeremy and I have been taking this online course, through UMass, on behavioral intervention in autism." She posed this last bit as a question, as though the prestige of the program might be known to Sara; it wasn't. "Well, *I'm* taking it at least. Jeremy's just going through the paces." With a frown, she dug a finger into her mouth to pluck something from her back teeth. "I really should've sent this back too. What's the deal? All the reviews made this place sound like nirvana."

"Mine's good," Sara offered.

"Speaking of that," Liz said, not clearly at all, "how's the whole, you know, sex issue?" The leer on her face was the exclusive product of her Midwestern inability to broach the topic of sex without sniggering; neither her issue nor Sara's was particularly leer-worthy.

"Ugh, the same," Sara said. "The pressure's so intense that even when we *do* have it it's not enough for him. It almost makes things worse, because then he thinks the next night's in play. Let's not even go there. You?"

Liz shrugged. "He still claims it's because of the antidepressants. Though he won't ask his doctor for, you know, the other pills. For . . ."

"Right."

"So nothing's changed on my end, either." She sighed, staring at her falafel as though it represented her gummy, send-backable sex life. "Still *nada.*"

"If only we could trade husbands," Sara said clumsily, regretting it even before Liz's face warped again, this time from undisguised revulsion. She could see Liz picturing the scene the way Sara had once uncharitably described it to her—Dave entering the bedroom nude and hairy-bellied with his penis already stout and erect, having prepped it in the bathroom to signal his desirous expectation the way beach flags signaled surf conditions—and felt a stab of defensiveness, her imagination retorting by throwing up images of Jeremy asking meekly and creepily to rub her feet, maybe, if that was okay, just a little bit. Sara was about to claw back the remark when the waiter appeared tableside, wanting to know if everything was all right.

"Don't ask," Liz said blackly, and when the waiter probed further to see if the falafel was to blame, Liz and Sara broke into a familial concert of blushing laughter, forcing his baffled retreat from the table. This had always been their way: laughter ricocheting between them, no matter the strains it covered, bound and sustained by their sisterly ties. As teenagers they'd sometimes interrupted screaming matches with cackling and joyful-sounding time-outs, before resuming the quarrel to the confoundment of their parents. After an inherited baritone snort Liz blurted, "Oh shit I'm turning into Mom," refueling their laughter so that neighboring diners must've thought them the happiest sober women in New York City.

It didn't occur to Sara until halfway through her train ride home that this—the Main Line train out of Secaucus Junction—was the very place she'd met Dave. Possibly this very car, in fact, except no—it'd been one of the newer cars, if she was remembering right. She'd been shopping in the city that afternoon—and could list everything she'd bought that day if pressed: the Christian Louboutin suede platform pumps and ivory Loro Piana metallic evening shawl from Bergdorf Goodman; the double-pocket calfskin Prada hobo purse from Neiman Marcus; and the Badgley Mischka sequined bodice gown from Saks that she hated not being able to wear anymore owing to her augmented bust—and had to squeeze herself onto a rush-hour train, needing but failing to receive wide berth for all the shopping bags she was carrying. At least a dozen men refused eye contact with her, studying imaginary text messages or pretending to look out the window at the black tunnel walls while she'd stood there, crooked beneath the weight of all those bags, before Dave, whom she hadn't noticed at all, rose up behind her. With merely a tap on her shoulder, not so much as a single word, he'd directed her into the seat he'd just vacated for her—out of *instinct,* or so it'd seemed to her then, and while later he'd profess to have done so out of admiration for her rear, she didn't quite buy that claim. That brash and boorish side of him struck her as overcompensation for what she still considered (if less confidently) his decent and vulnerable heart, all that jock posturing a means of obscuring a fundamental goodness that (she suspected) his father had tried hardening off. She'd always found that combination irresistible in a man—the Alpha exterior masking the Beta interior, the hard candy shell around the nougaty center—and it flattered her to think this revealed something complex about her, something that harked back to the high-school incongruity of her quarterback-craving cheerleader self dating the clove-smoking drama boys on the side: the very breadth of her attractions suggesting an essential and untypecastable wholeness.

None of that was yet apparent that evening on the train, however, when the man beside her got off at Kingsland and Dave slipped into his seat. What attracted her then, strangely, was his rage. Somehow he'd fished her history from her: the stunted acting career, marriage and motherhood, and then 9/11 though not its tangled aftermath. The way he'd responded was, in retrospect, almost absurdly overwrought. With tears in his eyes he'd hailed the bravery of the cops and firefighters who'd died that morning, and also what he'd personally do to Osama bin Laden when "they catch that motherfucker," pounding the seat in front of him so hard that its occupant turned around to protest but reconsidered after seeing this burly six-foot-three man with wet feral eyes. Nothing about his behavior would have been unusual in the weeks or months after 9/11, but by this time the wound was three years old; even Brian's dad could discuss it dispassionately. Yet something about that rage, however unearned and jingoistic it might have been, instead of repelling Sara drew her in. She'd dealt with Brian's death so coldly, she realized — her flash-frozen grief having been reconstituted as hatred for Jane L. Becker, Brian's mistress — that she'd failed to absorb the wider tragedy, all the anguish that wasn't exclusively hers. Dave's unhinged wrath felt cathartic, and spoke to a fury that she hadn't even known occupied a place within her. In that moment it'd felt as if they shared a mutually murderous heat. She gave him her number. She married him.

Had it been a mistake? Possibly. But then she had to be candid about her motives. Part of the reason she'd married Dave — a significant proportion, for sure, though she refused to quantify it as the majority part — was financial. No one was ever supposed to admit this, though she legitimized it to herself by noting this motive was the unacknowledged bedrock of most Victorian marriages — even the fictional ones she'd swooned over in college, like Jane and Rochester's in *Jane Eyre* or that of Jane Bennet and Charles Bingley in *Pride and Prejudice*. Not that poverty was a risk for her. Not *real* poverty, anyway — the fear of tomorrow versus the fear of next year. Between Brian's life insurance and the payout from the Victim Compensation Fund, Sara had been able to clear the mortgage on their former house and still hand over to an investment advisor what had seemed then like a tremendous sum—until the stock market went chipping away at it, and, if she was honest with herself, until she'd done some chipping of her own. The finiteness of the number, as it appeared in her monthly Smith-Barney statements, disturbed her—this was it, for life? With anxious dread she'd imagined herself at eighty, opening those envelopes and gaping at a much-dwindled figure. And then came Dave, gaping (he claimed) at her backside on that packed NJ Transit train, and somehow wooing her by venting all that patriotic steam from his ears. After their fourth date she'd searched online for the market cap of his Acquisitions and Asset Recovery Corp., which she was unable to find because the company was privately held. The futile inquiry left her feeling seamy and pathetic but she stood by its chilled necessity. She'd married for love the first time, and look how that had turned out. Idealism was something you outgrew, like miniskirts and over-the-knee boots.

At the Ridgewood stop a man boarded the train and claimed the seat beside her. He was handsome, in a starchy, lean-limbed, gray-templed, se-nior-bank-vice-president way, and she found herself consciously averting her gaze from him, as though mere eye contact might somehow endanger her. On this train line, after all, it had been known to happen. Peering out the window, as the train went curving through a gritty narrow trough, she saw trash scattered along the sloped trackside: shopping carts and bent chairs and rusted bicycles and even a sofa and then, as the train crossed the access road to an abandoned-looking industrial park, a tragic-looking teddy bear, of the oversized Day-Glo variety they awarded at carnival games, with poofs of white stuffing oozing from its neck—a throat-slashing victim for sure. She thought it would make a fine subject for an arty photographer, a William Eggleston type whose photo would raise the ominous question: Who would cut the throat of a teddy bear, and why? But then how had it ended up here, she wondered, broadening the question to include all the garbage she saw streaming by. It looked as though it had been hurled from the train, but of course that wasn't the case. She didn't see any houses up at the top of the slopes, to account for transient renters plowing all their unwanteds down the hill to get their deposits back. Perhaps a flood had left it in its mucky wake, though she couldn't recall one occurring here—down in Passaic, maybe, but not up this way. She was jogged from this investigative reverie, however, by the man beside her clearing his throat, and soon she found her eyes drawn down to his hands—long slender concert-pianist hands, like those of Timmy Westrick back in high school, whose hand she'd placed directly on her crotch one night during a make-out session because she knew he was too afraid to place it there himself. (Knew wrongly, as she learned years later: He'd actually been too *gay* to put his hand down there.) As she studied the man's hands, with their elegant topography of bluish veins and tanned creases and glossy, perhaps too preciously maintained nails, while almost but not quite connecting the mental dots between them and Timmy Westrick's and therefore her crotch, the thought occurred to her: What if it was that easy? If she spoke, if he spoke, if something he said found unexpected traction within her. What if you could change your life as easily as changing trains?

Well you *could*, she supposed—wasn't that the gist of *Eat Pray Love*, which everyone but Sara seemed to be reading that spring? Unless you had kids, that is. With a drawn-out sigh she shifted her gaze back out the window where a river had replaced the garbage-strewn slopesides: a clear and perfect-looking stream that beneath a sumptuous canopy of bending tree limbs went gurgling over smooth round stones, like a scene from the cover of an ambient music CD. It looked almost fake, in fact: the work of a civic-minded volunteer group that'd painted it onto a curtain to conceal the debris behind it. Here was something else she couldn't ever admit publicly, not seriously anyway: She'd never wanted children. A family—that had been Brian's idea, and when you got down to it his imperial command. Perhaps she should've known what to expect, marrying into an Irish family: the ancestral desire for strength in numbers. As one of six kids Brian couldn't imagine life outside an unruly freckled mob. As for the Tetwicks, Liz had apparently sopped up all the maternal genes in utero, before Sara'd ever had the chance to claim some. Liz excelled at mothering—Sara sometimes agreed with Dave that Aidan's autism was less a medical condition than an excuse for Liz to exercise her mommy muscles, to escalate the marathon of motherhood into some sort of an ultradistance Ironman race—whereas for Sara it'd never come naturally. Breastfeeding appalled her, and though she'd given it a valiant effort, because you were considered some sort of monster if you didn't, that harsh grabby clamping on her nipples, the leaky alien sensation of her body being drained—it'd just made her nauseated, and she'd abandoned it as swiftly as social censure allowed. The same with potting Alexis in front of the television, which she understood to be detrimental to child brain development and all that other highminded highmoraled Liz stuff, but what else was she supposed to do? Alexis just dribbled and banged. Sara had never learned to speak baby, not the way Brian did—with his perfect fluency he'd been able to withstand goo-goo time almost indefinitely, seeming to actually *enjoy* his second or third hour of lying on a blanket poking Alexis's belly to make her kick. Though Alexis had come squirming out of Sara's body she'd been Brian's from the start.

If not motherhood, then, what had she been meant for? In her formative years she'd dreamt of fame—as less of an actuality, she supposed, than a loosely defined concept. Sara Tetwick: star. That was it. Probably every girl fantasized about tossled romances with the movie-star idols smoldering down at her from posters tacked to bedroom walls: in Sara's case Rob Lowe and Tom Cruise and Don Johnson and Corey Haim and Patrick Swayze and River Phoenix. (Liz's bedroom, in contrast, had been lined with posters of endangered whales.) But not every girl, she thought, had constructed a lifeplan built around achieving them; from the age of thirteen she'd started lobbying her parents for acting classes, and by the end of high school she'd been voted Most Likely to Make it Big in Hollywood. Had that been the crest of her idealism? Maybe. Back then she'd been almost hypersexual, if you could call it that—oversexed (in her estimation) to the point of dismaying self-concern, to the frequent degree of self-loathing. On the night of her junior prom she'd masturbated while showering for the dance, had unfulfilling sex with Mark Rinehart in the back of his dad's Suburban, and then, at 3 A.M., in the dim yellow nightlight glow of her bedroom beneath the unblinking audience of all those wallpapered movie stars, masturbated one more time, immediately dissolving into muffled sobs afterwards because something had to be wrong with her, this much wanting couldn't be normal. It was like what Liz had just said about Aidan at lunch, about mapping that divide between what was hormones and what was disease. An undiagnosed disease was what it'd felt like, then: a cancer of desire. The polymorphous liberties of college had straightened her out, of course, as had New York City, where her acting classes often felt like sexually teeming petri dishes, everyone rubbing their future stardoms against one another, grinding into iridescent powder the pixie dust that seemed to coat them as young talents in the city. She'd made peace with herself by making another kind of peace with others, and then with Brian who for all his public loutishness (he was always the one chanting *chug chug chug* in a barroom, the one whose buddies christened him a verb, i.e., to "brian" was to ogle a woman with such shameless vigor that your body rotated 360 degrees) had been an endlessly giving and tender lover — but *no,* she stopped herself cold. Let's not go there, as she'd said to Liz. Let's never ever go there again.

The kill or the cure: That's what Jane L. Becker had been. In those tormented days after Brian's death and Sara's discovery of his affair she'd felt something go dead inside her, felt something shrivel and dry as a grape becomes a raisin. Or maybe that wasn't right — it was more accurate to say she felt something disappear, as though Jane L. Becker had reached inside her and snatched it away. Precisely what *it* was she couldn't quite say: her dignity, she sometimes thought; her faith in the idea of love, which as a child of the sixties was the only faith she'd ever had; not her future (the terrorists stole that) but her past; her trust in appearances, so that even the sight of a river from a train window was suspect; but her sexuality, too, snarled amidst all those other things and robbed from her just the same. That raunchy, delirious desire whose strength she'd once mistaken for malignancy.

She'd faked it with Dave. Not the orgasms, which were genuine but hollow, the Muzak version of a song she'd once adored, but her interest, her willingness, the shivers she issued at his touch. As an actress she'd thought she could sustain it, akin to the way she'd played Anya night after night in *The Cherry Orchard* (and would've kept playing her forever, with jubilance, had the investors not pulled out of the show): "Why is it that I no longer love the cherry orchard as I did?" she used to say, the resonance of her voice almost otherworldly inside that dingy little third-floor theatre on West 46th Street, feeling the smattering of an audience clinging hard to her pauses. "I used to love it so tenderly. I thought there was no better place on earth than our garden." Yet there were limits, she'd learned, to playing another kind of character — one you didn't understand or didn't want to play. In bed with Dave she was the Coast shampoo girl all over again, cooing, "Oooooh, that scent!": a single note, strained and artificial.

Sustaining that note had proven as difficult as sustaining any note, the reason opera singers earned ovations for their *tenuto* holds—eventually you give out. And she had. About a year ago, give or take a few isolated and wine-driven exceptions, which had left Dave discontented and tetchy, a black cloud of frustration trailing him from room to room. She'd misgauged the narrowness of his affections, she guessed; maybe, as he'd joked (or not-joked, she had to assume), the shape of her butt had been enough for him that evening on the train. He'd spoken to her as to the broker for her body, negotiating the terms. Would it be different with someone else? She looked at the man beside her again—ogled him, really, if ogling meant imagining what sex would be like (Brian always claimed otherwise, noting that he ogled sportscars too but didn't, in his words, "want to stick my dick in one"). No, she decided, as the train slowed toward her stop. It was her. It was all her. All the posters from her teenaged bedroom coming to life wouldn't make a difference.

She found Dave at the kitchen table when she got home. He was gnawing a crust of pizza and glowering at some paperwork that was so thoroughly disarranged across the table it appeared he'd shoveled it there. She fetched a bottle of chenin blanc from the refrigerator, but only after she'd banged its base onto the table did he half acknowledge her, without glancing up. "How was lunch?" he muttered, a spitball curve on the last word.

She twirled a corkscrew into the bottle, sneaking a glimpse at the paperwork which looked legal: those telltale fourteen-inch sheets. "What's up?"

"This shit?" he said, with a shoo-fly wave at the messy tabletop. "Nothing. We're being sued again."

She paused, the cork halfway out. "We?"

"The company. Fair Debt Collection Practices Act, Section 15, yadda yadda bing-bang."

"Oh." With a wet pop the cork sprang loose. "You're always being sued for that."

"Yeah, but this time the freakin lawyers are all wetting their pants. It's the social networking shit."

She stepped back from the table as though clearing space for a bow. "Who said that was shady? Especially that girl thing . . ."

Sara had said it: that was who. This had come during dinner with Tim,

Dave's VP and general manager, and his wife Susan, several months before. The men were gloating about their latest "innovation," explaining how they'd been successfully exploiting debtors' social network accounts— Facebook, Myspace, Twitter, the like—in their collection pursuits. The "innovation" was code-named Mandy, and she was a recent ARC hire, fresh from Marasmus State's business school, whose real name went unmentioned. Tim pulled up a photo of her on his phone: She was a seductive-faced bleached blonde who Sara agreed was attractive, albeit (she didn't say this) in the style of the women on Turnpike billboards advertising gentlemen's clubs. They'd established a fake Facebook identity for her—Dave and Tim called it their "favorite-ever day" at work, the two (or three) of them holed up in Tim's office inventing the most irresistible "hot girl" imaginable, charting her likes, her fictional history (Tim: "We had her go to Florida State, because those girls are eee-zeeee"), and even convincing "Mandy" to provide bikini snapshots as well as a photo of her dog—and then set her loose shotgunning friend requests to as many male debtors as she could find online. The acceptance rate, they said, was staggering—more than seventy-five percent of the men befriended her back. ("What a surprise," Susan mumbled, rolling her eyes in Sara's direction.) With access to the debtors' lists of family members and friends as well as to their personal data (cellphone numbers were something of a holy grail in the collections business), Mandy had been able to ambush them into a "sensational" number of settlements. ("Some guy posted pictures from his vacation in Vegas," Dave explained, Tim beside him panting *Yeah yeah this is great.* "Mandy leaves a comment like, 'Looks like a fantastic trip! I'd love to go there myself. Can you give me an idea of the cost? Was it more than $1,348?'—or whatever the amount he owed us was. Guy was on a payment plan within the hour. And you know what? He didn't unfriend her!") The experiment was working so well, in fact, that they'd already expanded the payroll to include Kaitlyn, Gaby, Kristal, Megan, Holly, Blaire, Dani, Kristy, Gina, Nicole, and Tina. (As Tim explained, "We're posting help-wanted ads at sorority houses.") Pressed by Sara, they admitted female debtors had proven tougher nuts to crack. An equivalent experiment, with a young male employee Dave and Tim deemed "GQ-ish" (Tim pulled up his photo as well, to crinkle-nosed reactions from the women), had fizzled, though Tim noted that women were "way more" vulnerable than men to their family members being contacted. "I don't know," said Sara. "The whole thing seems shady to me." The men emitted loud unchastened grunts. "It's not shady," Dave argued. "It's brilliant." According to the documents Sara was presently skimming over Dave's shoulder, a Florida judge was the one who'd be parsing that distinction.

"Are you worried?" she asked him.

"Naw, not really. I'll just be pissed if they shut us down."

"Shut the company down?" Sara felt something go fluttering down inside of her, like a bird shot from the sky. The sip of chenin blanc she'd intended expanded into a sudden mouthful.

"Not the company, babe. The social-network ops. Fred's thinking the judge might grant them an injunction. I'm trying to sort the shit out, okay?"

"Oh." Drifting to the far end of the table where a cardboard pizza box lay open, two slices congealing inside, Sara asked, "Where's Alexis?"

"I dunno." Dave lowered his face closer to the paperwork, either his weakening eyesight or what he was reading painting a scowl onto his face. "She grabbed half the pizza and ran off to her room."

"I told you to go easy on the pizza," she said, shaking her head as she tallied the number of slices this meant. "You know she needs to watch her weight."

Alexis flat-out refused to discuss all the weight she'd gained—which was dismaying Sara, both Alexis's reticence and the sight of her once lithe and athletic daughter going flabby and schlumpy—though Sara knew just how much it bothered her. (She was eighteen, and about to start college: of *course* it bothered her.) Two weeks ago Sara had taken Alexis to the doctor to get her immunizations certified, something Richard Varick College required of incoming freshmen. They'd gone to the same pediatric clinic where she'd been taking Alexis for years, though, as Sara learned that day, Alexis's longtime pediatrician had decamped for a clinic in Princeton. A nurse led Alexis onto the scale, balanced the weights, and announced, "One hundred and twenty-nine pounds." From behind, Sara noticed Alexis's shoulders begin to shake, and she stepped forward at the same time as the nurse put a hand to Alexis's arm and asked, "Are you okay?" Alexis was crying, or rather, they saw, struggling not to cry: squeezing her eyes shut to stifle the tears, her front teeth clamped hard upon her lower lip, her quivering shoulders racked by the effort. Together the women stroked Alexis's hair and told her not to worry, the nurse peeling back the chart and saying, "It's just a gain of . . ." but electing not to finish the sentence. Sara promised, "We'll put you on a good diet. That 'Half Way to Healthy' one, the one everyone's always talking about?" With a deep and approving nod the nurse said, "My sister's lost twenty pounds on that," before shepherding Alexis and Sara to the examination room. An unfamiliar male doctor — to Sara, he looked barely older than Alexis — dashed in and went about quickly scribbling down Alexis's absence of health complaints, aside from the Irritable Bowel Syndrome which she said she was managing with medication; that she said she was presently and normally menstruating; that he'd palpated no abnormalities; and that he'd given her a shot of the chickenpox vaccine Varivax to comply with the college's immunization requirements. Noting the stunned look on Alexis's face as she rose from the exam table, Sara whispered to her, "Yeah, I'm thinking the same thing. Dr. Michaels never rushed us through like that." Then Sara showed her the purchase confirmation from Amazon for the copy of *The Half Way to Healthy* she'd just ordered on her phone. "Okay?" Sara said cheerily, and Alexis nodded, that dazed, spooked expression still lingering on her face.

"She *asked* for pizza, okay?" Dave said, and with a burst of irritation lifted his head from the legal papers. "What'm I supposed to say? No? Your mom says you're too fat?"

"Don't you bite my head off," Sara snapped back. "I'm not the one suing you for your 'ass-quisitors' or whatever you call those girls."

"Tim called them that. *Once.* At dinner after way too much wine. Goddamn." Haphazardly gathering the documents, as though to heave them into the garbage, he mumbled, "This is always how you act when you come home from seeing Lizbo."

Another sip of wine ballooned into a mouthful; it tasted bitter, and hot on Sara's throat. "When are you going to finally come off that? The whole lesbian joke wasn't funny the first time and it's even less funny the millionth time."

"I never thought it was funny," Dave said quickly. "I thought it was true."

Just then Alexis swerved around the corner into the kitchen. She was wearing baggy gray sweatpants and was braless in an oversized navy V-neck t-shirt that, unless Sara was mistaken, belonged to Dave. Her hair hung down in lifeless brown strings, and her movements were sluggardly, dumpy, depressed. The impression was of someone who'd just been drained by a vampire. "Hey, honey," Sara said.

Alexis pulled open the refrigerator and stared into it vacantly, as if to air condition her frontside. "What are you guys fighting about?"

"Whether your aunt is a lesbian," said Dave.

"Oh, totally," she said.

Dave leveled a vindictive smile at Sara. "See?"

"No," said Sara coolly, "Dave's just upset because he's being sued for pretending to be hot girls on the internet."

With a drowsy frown Alexis turned from the refrigerator. "You can get sued for that?"

"Of course not," sniffed Dave. "The entire internet is people pretending to be hot girls."

"You would know," said Alexis, and shutting the refrigerator she moved to the open pizza box on the table and gave it the same empty stare she'd given the interior of the refrigerator. She picked up a slice and drew it toward her mouth.

"Alexis, honey," Sara intervened. "Haven't you already had some pizza?"

Alexis went rigid, the slice drooping limply from her hand. "I'm still hungry, okay? Am I not allowed to be hungry anymore?"

"Calm down—Jesus," Sara said. "What is it with you guys today?"

"Maybe we're on the rag," Dave said, and a twitch quirked Alexis's face as she shifted her gaze down and away.

Softening her voice and curling her lips into a compassionate pout, Sara said, "Honey, I'm just thinking about that day at the doctor's office, and—"

"Can I please be in charge of the size of my own ass?" She took an oversized and resentful chomp of pizza. "Can I?"

"It's just that the weight is so much easier to gain than to lose . . ."

Alexis threw up her hands, her cheeks bulked and round. "This is like, so—pleasant." Her voice was gulpy and doughy. "You're *really* making my dinner."

"Mine too," Dave sneaked in.

Flushing, Sara pressed her palms onto the tabletop to steady herself.

This was what she'd tried but failed to describe to Liz: Alexis and Dave's magnetic alignment, the way the dividing line always seemed to be drawn between them and her. It was more than unfair; it was unendurable. Over-compensating from the effort to hold back a scream, Sara spoke coldly and sharply: "Well please excuse me for not wanting my daughter to start college in two months looking like—" She fumbled for an analogy, and with a numb glance at Alexis found it instantly—"like she's about to give birth."

Immediately the kitchen went silent and motionless, like paused video, or as if the sounds of an intruder had just registered and everyone was fro-zen in that pre-panic moment of stiffening comprehension. But Sara her-self was that intruder, she realized, as Dave let out a low, grave-sounding whistle and with bunched-up fury Alexis hurled Sara a look unlike any she'd ever seen on her daughter's face, or on anyone's face for that matter. "Fuck," Alexis spat, "you."

Lobbing the half-eaten slice back into the pizza box, Alexis flounced out of the kitchen. "Oh, shit," Sara moaned, and tracking the echoes of the stomps she followed her daughter into the hallway and through the living room then up the stairs where she heard the slamming of Alexis's bedroom door punctuated by the icy click of the lock. Gently, Sara rapped on the door. "Honey?" she said to it. "I'm sorry, honey." No response. She knocked again, adjusting her voice. "Honey?" Crisp, sweet: the voice of a mother bearing oven-warm cookies. When that yielded nothing she ad-justed it again. "Honey." Deeper this time, more somber: as if needing to inform her about the passing of a distant relation. Then Sara cracked— "Alexis!"—and grabbing the doorknob with her left hand yanked it and shook it, the door shuddering against its hinges and Sara flooding with a sadness and rage that felt alien and unwarranted to her, less like something churned from within her than like something injected into her, a poison someone had slipped into her overheating bloodstream. When the rattling proved ineffectual she surrendered herself against the door and from be-hind it heard Alexis sobbing, long hoarse wails she must've been smoth-ering with a pillow. "Honey," she said again, with honest pleading in her voice, aware that it was futile. She felt no longer like a mother, nor even an actress playing the role of one. She was just an intruder, and a failed one at that.

Retreating to the kitchen, she went straight for her wine. Dave was still sitting in the exact position as when she'd left, staring off into the ether beyond the bay window where in the gold-green twilight two deer were grazing on the fescue. "What just happened?" she said to him.

Maintaining his gaze out the window he answered, "You opened your mouth and a cruise missile shot out." Then he turned to her, with a soft and unfamiliar cast of melancholy to his face, and said, "That's what."

Sara shouted, "I'm trying to *help* her!" She brought a fingertip to her mouth to dab the wine that'd just leaked out. "I mean, Christ, she's pre-loaded her freshman fifteen. Her freshman *thirty.* And that—that *attitude.* What in God's name is up with her?"

Dave said flatly, "Beats me."

"No." She braced herself with another dose of wine, then refilled her glass. This was how bad actors drank in plays and movies; an acting teacher had once cued up a clip from *Casablanca,* that scene where Humphrey Bogart downs vehement shots of something-or-other after Ingrid Bergman re-enters his life, as an example of how even great and subtle actors can overdo it. "No one drinks like that in real life," he'd said. But here she was, in her own real life, slugging wine like a cut-rate Bogart. "No," she said again, wagging her head and swinging around the table to station herself directly across from Dave, jamming his view out the window. "No, that's not true. It doesn't 'beat' you. What is *up* with her?"

He lifted an eyebrow, studying her. "I'm not catching your drift."

"I feel like I don't know my own daughter, okay?" Her grip felt wobbly on the stem of the glass and she could feel herself swaying, though not from the wine. "And maybe I'm not sure—I've ever known her."

"That's not—"

"You're the one who knows her," she interrupted, "you're the one she talks to." She added bitterly, "You're the one she loves."

"That's not true." His jaw was firm, his tone anchored and businesslike. Their positioning at the table and the official-looking paperwork between them sent a fleeting shadow through her mind: a foreshadowing, perhaps, or maybe just a bleb of repugnance at the way Dave appeared to her, like a negotiator tabulating risk and profit. "That's not true at all. I'm just the one who pays *attention* to her."

Gasping, Sara swiveled around to the bay window to collect herself.

Noting her sharp movement, the deer outside flicked their white tails and gawked at her dumbly, chewing their pilfered share of her lawn. Then spinning back, uncollected, she yelled, "I don't pay *attention* to her? How dare you say that to me?"

His own sudden movement — striking the tabletop with the heels of his hands as he threw himself back into his chair, red-faced and erect — startled her, and her left hand flipped upward in instinctual fright, like the tails of the deer. "You don't pay attention to *either of us!*" he thundered.

From the recoiling expression on his face she could tell that he'd startled himself as much as her. He glanced down at his hands and flexed them. In his wheezy shock she sensed a vulnerability, some underlayment of resentment he hadn't meant to expose, and drawing a cold and livid conclusion she said, "Oh, right. I get it. We're back to your blowjob deficit."

His shoulders went limp. "I didn't say anything about blowjobs."

"But you were thinking it."

"Right, fucking guilty." His own sarcasm came close to drawing a vinegary laugh from him. "Because my chances right now, they're about as good as ever, aren't they?"

"So we're here again. The same old fight? How should we play it this time, Dave?"

"Actually, no. You're the one who steered us here. I think the word I said was — *attention.*"

"Is that your code word for it?"

"Lexi," he said calmly, pushing down the air in front of him. This was clearly a gesture rehearsed over the course of a thousand business meetings: *Guys, let's stick to the issues here.* "If you remember, we were talking about Lexi."

She spluttered, "Who —"

Spluttering over her he said, "Who excuse me for saying so could use a little more attention to things besides her — besides her grades, and her future earning capacity, and the size of her fucking ass."

"Oh no. That is *my* daughter and —"

"Did you even know she had a boyfriend?"

Sara's rage stalled. In her mind she went rifling through a cache of half-remembered glimpses of Alexis's Facebook page, looking for missed clues. "What boyfriend?" she finally said.

"Name's Miguel. Or Pedro. No, Miguel. He's Pedro's kid."

"Who's Pedro?"

"The Mexi?" Dave said, indicting her with a raised eyebrow. "Does our landscaping?"

The landscaper's son? Their—landscaper? (The landscapers always worked in teams of three or four, indistinguishable in their quick and wordless efficiency: unloading their machines from the trailer, launching a rapidfire assault on the lawn and plantings, disappearing in a puff of single-stroke engine smoke.) None of this made any sense to Sara, and her expression must've reflected that; bewilderment often brought a sneer to her face, incomprehension disguising itself as contempt.

Dave nodded at her, his lips pursed in disappointment. "Yeah," he said. "That's probably why she never told you."

She ignored this, concentrating instead on the sudden gush of relief she was experiencing. The weight gain, the schlumpiness, the woe-is-me demeanor, the unfathomable yin to the yang of her graduation and preparations for college: It was all just puppy love, off-the-rack teen heartbreak. Finally it made sense. "So is that what all the crying is about up there?" she said, too lightly. "They broke up?"

"What crying?"

"She's up in her room sobbing her guts out."

"No." He knotted his face. "They broke up—I don't know, four or five months ago."

An extreme case of puppy love, then. It happened: the cancer of desire, or in this case the flu. She'd deal with it. In the meantime she glared at Dave and scolded, "You could've made things a helluva lot better around here if you'd just *told* me."

"Told you?"

"Told me. You know, talking? About other things besides your blue balls and your creepy work innovations?"

Something snapped inside him as he rose toward her and with looming and vaguely sexual menace roared, "You could've fucking *paid attention!*"

She leapt back from the table, fearing he might come swimming across it in order to—to what? For the first time in her marriage—maybe in her life—she felt physically threatened; not acutely enough to cower, but enough for his offense to revolt her, and for that revulsion to transform itself into a cold bionic alloy inside her. With that steel girding her voice she said, "Yeah, right. I don't think we're talking about Alexis anymore."

He was panting now, upright out of his chair, and with a wince he reached his right hand to his left shoulder, as if in the early throes of a heart attack. Sara felt a bubble of cruelty rise within her as it occurred to her that she might not attempt a rescue if he was—she might, but hard deliberation would preface any action or inaction. He didn't look threatening now, but pathetic instead, like one of those cable-news blowhards he was so fond of watching whose argument has just been decimated, whose slimy lobbyist's motives have just been exposed. That rage she'd once found so compelling: It *had* been absurd, and in its later manifestations even more absurd, a bratty, petulant response to life refusing to pay him the exorbitant amount he demanded. In a crumpled gesture he waved a hand toward all the paperwork between them and said, "I'm getting sued."

Perhaps this was his oblique way of apologizing or explaining, she didn't know. Or even care, she realized. She watched him in skeptical, predatory silence.

"Fred says they might try to smash us with fines, make an example out of us," he said.

"Serves you right," she hissed, and with the satisfaction of a withering last word she turned from the table and walked out of the kitchen, the clicks of her heels on the polished terrazzo floor throwing spiteful echoes against the walls. In the living room she slipped off those shoes and flung them to the carpet. She stood there for a while, thinking how she wanted a cigarette right now even though she'd never smoked, except briefly onstage for a role, and how preposterous that would be, to smoke one now, to blow dragon plumes of smoke into her goddamn living room which the decorator had said would evoke 1920s Manhattan but with its eighty-two-inch flat-screen and Dave-inspired Italianate kitsch instead just evoked twenty-first-century New Jersey. She dropped onto the couch, abruptly exhausted and longing for her wine but not nearly enough to go fetch it with Dave in the kitchen. So Alexis had a boyfriend, and Sara's ignorance of this fact was grounds for—what? Dave had delivered that revelation as a power ploy, had brandished it against her like a club. Because everything was power to him. As in the collections racket ("the *acquisitions* business," she could hear him protest), information was the ultimate weapon; you lorded it over

people, you battered them with it, you twisted their own facts and histories against them, their families too if it would help your extraction, and if
lying was further ammunition (Mandy), you did that too. Because everything was power to him, she repeated to herself. Sex included: the extraction of her body, the settlement of his pig-grunt finish. After a while Dave
passed through the living room muttering goodnight; Sara turned her
head. She listened to his footsteps up the stairs, disgusted that he would or
could sleep right now, then differently disgusted when she heard the chim-
ing startup of the computer in his upstairs office. She knew what he did in
there some nights. Unless he had a chronic sinus condition triggered only
by his office's atmosphere, the wadded Kleenex in the trash bin confided all
she needed to know.

Only after she'd turned on the TV did her tidal surge of anger begin to
recede, exposing scoured stretches of sadness. Drifting through the cable
channels, she was stung by the sense that something had ended tonight, or
rather had begun to end — not her marriage, though that seemed possible,
and also not her shaky grasp on motherhood, though for a moment, before
she'd figured out (months too late, because of Dave's strategic informa-
tion-hoarding) that Alexis's problem was run-of-the-mill heartbreak, she
had thought that imperiled. No, it was something blurrier, more shape-
less, and now, she supposed, less fixed: her sense of self. Who she was,
and who she'd thought she was supposed to be — or play. The role of Sara
Tetwick Tooney Masoli: question mark. Even the television seemed to af-
firm this uncertainty as she went scrolling through the channels, yearning
for anything that might speak to her, distract her, entertain her, fulfill her
for even half an hour, from channel 100 through channel 1195 and then
back through again, through wedding disasters and shark attacks and old
movies (there went *Casablanca*) and political partisans wagging fingers at
the screen and faith healers setting hands and bombs strewing body parts
across Middle East markets and other kinds of markets tracking up or
tracking down and batters hitting baseballs and the arctic ice shelf melting
violently into the sea and on and on and on. How obscene and astonishing
it was, she thought, that amidst all this digital plenty, there could still be
nothing.

4

THE FIRST SATURDAY after schools let out for the summer, in New Jersey, is yard sale day. This designation is unofficial but adhered to just the same. The hand-lettered posters start sprouting on tree trunks and signposts at least a week before, and by that Friday they're clogging every corner, thick as campaign signs. Then, on Saturday morning, the earlybirds having already cased the block in their low poky sedans, out onto driveways, lawns, and curbs comes the stuff: the unjacketed books and the high-density polyethylene yard-toys and the outmoded VCRs and boomboxes and printers and floppy disks and the crib mattresses and the souvenir shotglasses and the rued leather pants and the puckered deflated basketballs along with the power tools, waterbed components, Bundt pans, stationary bikes, encyclopedias, telescopes, toaster ovens, silk flowers, fishing reels, vacuums, puzzles, folding chairs, Ping-Pong tables, and often out back the mildew-speckled trampoline, free for the taking, buddy, if you've got a way to haul it.

Elwin's intention was to obey this tradition, in order to rid himself of what he'd come to see as his glut of postmarital excess, but he quite literally couldn't get his shit together. Formal blame went to a late-May meeting of the Waste Isolation Project Markers panel, where he'd been appointed co-author (with Sharon) of the Warning Message text, as well as to the increasing demands of his father's decreasing condition, but these were wan excuses and he knew it: the pablum of procrastination. On more than one night — more than a dozen, actually — he'd stared down all the boxes and bric-a-brac marked for disposal, with their demand to be sorted, assessed, adjudicated, and priced, and shook his head *no* or rather shook his head *later,* which he understood to be the same sentiment dolled up with lipstick. Yet he had to do it; this much was clear to him. The surplus alone wasn't the problem, although Christopher's remark that Elwin didn't qualify as a bona fide hoarder because "you can still walk through the house" suggested, at the very least, an underlying issue. No, the problem, as Elwin diagnosed it, was that he was living in another man's house: the man he'd been before Maura had marked *him* for disposal. If he truly was *done,* as he'd concluded that awful morning when he'd slammed Big Jerry against his porch post and inadvertently adopted one of Jerry's sons, then he felt he had no choice but to reboot — to remake himself in a new and frankly alien image. The first step, he figured, was ecological: remaking his own environment by purging from it all these mementoes of failure and indulgence and failed indulgence. The upright piano he'd bought Maura for her fortieth birthday, for instance, after she'd been citing her lack of hobbies as a source of malaise in conjunction with a remembered decree from a piano teacher, from when she was twelve, that hers was an "extraordinary talent": This wasn't merely a five-hundred-pound oddment, sucking space from the living room. It was an emotional bloodstain, a big red reminder of who he'd been or had failed to be. For him to become someone else, it had to go.

And so, forgoing the traditional yard-sale option, onto Craigslist he went, with a barrage of digital advertisements.

First he checked in with Maura about some of the stuff — the shared-custody debris, like the piano, that'd once been theirs but now seemed to be his. He felt he needed Maura's blessing, which she gave — but reluctantly, and only after she'd asked him to itemize the inventory for her. This reluctance both pleased and displeased Elwin: pleased, because her wavering (about a shabby-chic vanity table, circa 1995, she'd said nostalgically, "Oh God, do you remember buying that?" — which he did, but differently than Maura did; what she remembered was the black teenaged warehouse worker who after cracking the vanity mirror while loading their car begged them, with genuine tears in his eyes, not to tell the store manager, while what Elwin remembered was the surprise sex they'd had later that afternoon, after hauling the damaged table into their bedroom, the way Maura had tugged him down onto the bed by his belt, as if high on the opium fumes of commerce and minor-league charity) seemed to show some remnant of emotional attachment to their former life, and thereby him; but displeased, too, for the very same reason, because if that attachment remained — even partly, barely — then why had it come to all this? What the hell had he done — the old self-pitying question, on a permanent orbit 'round his mind — to deserve all *this?*

All *this,* indeed: Elwin clicking off the phone and setting down his clipboard and then setting down himself in a room piled high with his own spurned history, his brain struggling to uncouple the familiar comfort of Maura's voice from the still-novel sting of it. He sat there, oblivious to the NPR newscast drifting from the kitchen radio, to all the complicated traumas and vital global dramas floating across the airwaves, and then the traffic report, the buildup at the Bayonne Bridge, the three-car accident on the Goethals Bridge, the car fire on the Garden State, the disabled linguist at the Morristown house. How much easier it would be, he thought, if people were merely good or bad, as in comic books and television dramas, instead of suspended in the hoary in-between, goodbad creatures swerving from acts of valiant decency to craven negligence in the very same day/hour/minute. How much easier it would be, that is, for him to *hate* Maura. To regret their years together as a bitter miscalculation, a foul wrong turn. To chuck all the physical residue of their marriage into a rented dumpster upon which he could climb late one night in order to piss on everything, her ghost-memory included, his dick in one hand and a half-drained bottle of something macho in the other. To be able to deem her a "bitch," as Christopher did. Yet that wasn't Elwin. And that wasn't Maura, despite everything she'd done or hadn't done. "Free to good home," he began many of his advertisements, because a good home was what all this stuff had been meant for — himself, perhaps, included.

By this time Christopher had been living with him for almost two months. Their agreement, such as it was, was for Christopher to stay until he'd landed a new job and with it the funds for deposits on an apartment, etc. The job search, however, was conspicuously lagging. Though Elwin had noticed a blank AutoZone application on the kitchen table, its fate remained unknown. Not that it was easy for Christopher to look for jobs from inside Elwin's garage, where he spent most of his time making further upgrades to the Jeep that by now were stretching way beyond the functional. Way *way* beyond: A recent afternoon found Elwin banging his horn while stuck in downtown Newark traffic. What came trumpeting from beneath the hood—to his immediate, Diet Coke–spitting horror—was the riff from the song "Tequila" at a hundred-plus decibels. "Oh Christ," Elwin croaked. When it looked to be going on forever—other drivers were craning their necks out their windows to see who'd just blasted that, pedestrians halting mid-stride—Elwin hit the horn button again, hoping that might squelch it, but instead he started the riff all over again: *duh DUH duh duh da da DUH DUH.* A man peddling roses from the median paused to do the cabbage-patch dance. Kids hooted from a school bus. A tanktopped guy in the car beside Elwin awarded him a vigorous fist-pump and shouted "Tequila!" as Elwin pressed his forehead to the Diet Coke–sticky steering wheel, cursing his Charlie Brown life.

But Christopher—whose response to that incident was to exclaim, "Is that the coolest fucking horn ever or what?"—wouldn't be stopped, even after Elwin threatened to close down the AutoZone account, even after Elwin pleaded with him to "soup up" his own truck instead. It somehow wasn't enough for Christopher to merely resuscitate the dubiously totaled Jeep, to return it to its shaggy former state as Elwin's mobile depository for paperwork and junk mail and empty Diet Coke cans and Altoids tins, his comfortably anonymous ride. No, Christopher was determined to make the Jeep perform tricks it had never been designed to perform: to strut, intimidate, peacock, crack jokes, dance. This meant a double-tube chrome front bumper and Bushwacker fender flares. A shift-light tachometer gauge above the dashboard, first alarming and then annoying Elwin every time that red bulb flashed. A cold-air intake that made the Jeep sound like a vacuum cleaner when Elwin gassed it, along with an American Thunder performance exhaust system that set off nearby car alarms in the A&P parking lot. "A chrome gas cap?" Elwin asked one typical evening. "You're going to tell me that was necessary, too?"

"Oh yeah, it matches the new bumper. Hey, you see the radiator scoops? Stick your head under the hood. Fuckin pain in the ass to install. Had to drill the shroud to be able—"

"What the hell are those?" Elwin pointed to a jumbo pair of wheels stacked beside the Jeep, their tires corduroyed with deep wavy treads, like a moon buggy might have.

WANT NOT313

"Those?"

"Yeah. Those."

"Sand paddles, duh. For driving on the shore."

Elwin let out an exasperated, end-of-his-rope chuckle. "Wow." Here he was, attempting to de-hoard his life, and there was Christopher, sneaking crap back in—and not just crap, but moon-buggy crap. Sand paddles? "It's never even *occurred* to me to drive on a beach," he said. "I wouldn't even think it was legal."

"That's because until now you *couldn't.*"

"No, you're not getting it. The actual *desire* has never occurred to me."

"Yeah, right. Because you can't desire what's freakin *impossible.*"

"Of course you can. That's all I ever do. That's all anyone does."

"You just wait, Doc." Christopher paused to glug down what looked to be an entire can of Keystone Light. "This thing's gonna be the *shit,* man. When I'm done with it, this Jeep's gonna get you *laid.*"

"Howzabout it just gets me to work instead . . . ?"

"Laid," came the reply, as Christopher tossed the beer can to the garage floor and dug an arm down into the engine to carburet Elwin's future sex life.

Moments like this one were frequent enough to tempt him to offer Christopher on Craigslist, too. "Free to good home," went the imaginary ad. "21-Year-old central N.J. refugee. Leaves towels on bathroom floor, flushes toilet approximately 10% of time, skilled in the use of all machinery except for 'too fucking complicated' laundry machines. Will force you to watch allegedly hilarious YouTube videos in which young men light farts or animals hump inanimate objects. Excellent way of ensuring beerless fridge & ridiculously tricked-out car. No phone inquiries, please." But this grumpiness tended to pass as quickly as it came; Christopher always seemed to be able to grin his way back into Elwin's sympathies. And truth be told, Elwin half- or three-quarters-enjoyed Christopher's company in the evenings, even if he didn't quite get why footage of a turtle mounting a plastic sandal was funny enough to demand repeat viewings. At the hard bottom of loneliness, he'd found, there is just a single letter, one bereft of curves and ornament, a short straight line that's capped on both ends as though to stifle growth or blossoming: *I*. Merely shifting that to *We*—two letters, one reaching upward and the other sliding sideways—felt sometimes like enough: just the regular presence of another human, not to cure the pain but to blunt it, the way an Excedrin dulls a migraine down to tolerable levels without vanquishing it completely. An analgesic for the menacing stillness. He also couldn't deny the self-satisfaction he derived from helping the kid out—the dim halo of benevolence he felt hovering above his scalp. Christopher was a callow wreck, yes; but if he could leave Elwin's care even a smidgen less wrecked—a few degrees wiser, more sure-footed and self-aware—then Elwin might have accomplished something. Twenty-four years of lecture-hall enervation, he realized, had not entirely driven the pedagogical impulse out of him.

Only once had he encountered Big Jerry, partly because Elwin surveyed the shared driveway before leaving for work in the mornings, to confirm a Jerry-free route to the garage, and also because he'd also shifted his outdoor time to the other side of the house, by the fire escape, where a small gravel patio sat beneath the shade of a maple tree. Yet there was Big Jerry, one pink-sky evening, unloading his pickup in the driveway when Elwin returned home from Newark. Elwin stared straight ahead as he piloted the Jeep into the garage, for the first and likely last time grateful for the pimped-out tinting with which Christopher had darkened the Jeep's windows. For an awkward while he sat inside the Jeep, monitoring Big Jerry via the rearview mirror, but soon enough it occurred to Elwin that what he was doing was hiding, curling himself up like a potato bug, and that Big Jerry would arrive at the same realization soon enough too, if he hadn't already. So Elwin pulled himself from the Jeep and exhaled a big what-the-hell gust of breath and went trudging out of the garage down the driveway toward the porch steps. Along the way he gave Jerry a single glance and a solemn cowboy nod, but Jerry, who'd paused to watch Elwin pass, offered no expression in return, as though Elwin were precisely as invisible as he longed to be.

Halfway up the steps, however, he heard Jerry call from behind him: "He doon alright?"

Elwin stopped, then turned around slowly. Before answering, he searched Jerry's face and replayed the question in his mind for any clues as to how Jerry had meant it (earnestly, angrily, regretfully, sarcastically). But there was nothing. The question just hung there—unshaded, textureless, impenetrable. When Elwin finally spoke — "Yeah," he said, with a whole palette of shadings — Jerry had already turned his attention back to the truck bed, as if the asking were all, the answer gratuitous. Saying no, Elwin realized, might've yielded the same non-response; as on Craigslist, a firm no-returns policy seemed to be in effect. Elwin added gratuitously, "He's doing fine." Once inside, however, he found Christopher asleep in his boxers, still in bed at 6 P.M., a video-game joystick propped loosely in his inert hand. In the kitchen, scouring the back reaches of the refrigerator for a nonexistent beer, Elwin found himself mulling the semantic ambiguity of the word *fine*.

Incorporating Christopher into his Craigslist campaign, then, struck him as a sound and possibly even fine idea. This would supply Christopher something else with which to occupy himself — besides hot-rodding Elwin's poor, dignity-stripped Jeep — while granting Elwin some scant mental remove from the dispersal of Maura's abandoned estate. Since money was never an object, he offered Christopher a fifty percent commission on everything he helped sell. This arrangement seemed promising, at first. Elwin wrote the ad copy while Christopher took the digital photos and posted the online ads. The inquiries went to Elwin's email address, and he forwarded them to Christopher for response. As he explained it to Christopher, "You're the salesman, and I'm the sales manager." With more than fifty items for sale, the inquiries numbered more than a hundred — Elwin was startled by the hunger for secondhand stuff out there, especially the way people leapt on the freebies — which gave him faith that they'd be done with this unsavory business in a week's time tops. But night after night he'd come home to find the greater bulk of the stuff still *there,* stacked in the unused and now unusable dining room, while the inquiries continued to swarm in: *Is the item still available? Will you take $10 for the shoe rack?*

Christopher claimed most of those inquiries were from spammers, trolling Craigslist for valid email addresses they could then flood with ads for cut-rate Viagra and antidepressants and such. But after Elwin noticed that all the buyers arriving at the front door in the evenings were youngish women, and conspicuously attractive ones at that, Christopher came clean: He'd been plugging the names from the email inquiries into Facebook, and only responding to the "hot ones." Not a single male had warranted a reply. "Jesus," Elwin said. "You turned my—you turned this into—some kind of screwy dating scheme?"

"Sorry, Doc," Christopher said. "Was kinda thinking of the chicks as my, uh, dividend."

"Your what?"

"My dividend."

Elwin sighed. Maybe the kid was hopeless after all: *finito, kaput-ski.* He felt compelled to scratch a lesser itch, however: "You're not using the word correctly. It's from the Latin, *dividendum.* Thing to be divided."

"Yeah, no," Christopher said. "I'm using it right. 'Cause they all got little round ends I'd like to divide."

At which point Elwin, as sales manager, fired his salesman.

For about a week Elwin's one-man digital yard sale felt oppressive, and not just emotionally. Even just the emailed haggling and appointment-making felt like a full-time job—which also happened to be what the Waste Isolation Markers project felt like, sitting atop his primary full-time job as director of the Trueblood Center, which come to think of it was stacked one layer above his ostensibly full-time job studying language death, squashed into a wafer at the bottom.

Christopher, as it turned out, had been right about the scammers. After Elwin wrote, "Yes! Still available!" in reply to several inquiries (in retrospect, suspiciously vague), his inbox went haywire with emails like this one: *Calibrate love success life! Howbeit you not make lamentable passion damage with your substantific distress poker? She meantime hearken for downright hornifier for assuage unlarded quiver. Discontent her love bean nevermore with free shipping!* (A whole new species of language death, Elwin thought, or perhaps the opposite: the nascent pidgin of contented love beans.)

Stashed among all those scammy inquiries, however, were genuine ones, from genuine people in genuine places—Milburn and Tewksbury and Hopatcong and the Oranges and Linden and Branchburg and Camden and even White Plains, New York, and Allentown, Pennsylvania— wanting to claim Elwin's excess, the junked pieces of his heart. Soon his appointment calendar was as haywire as his inbox: On Tuesday at seven was a lady for the vanity table, followed by a fellow at nine ("I work in the city so I can't be there until late") for a free half bag of mortar mix left over from repairs to the patio's stone wall, then on Wednesday at six a man scheduled to buy Maura's old bread machine ("possible to try it before paying the ten bucks cash?") followed by a woman at six-thirty (when presumably the test-bread would be rising) for a box full of Maura's unwanted shoes, plus another woman at eight for Maura's cookbooks for which Maura seemed to have no further use now that her unlarded quivers were being assuaged by the chef. Thursday, much the same. Friday too. And the weekend, in Christopher's words: "Fucking mayhem."

Sometimes the buyers or claimants brushed in, grabbed their goods, and left without a single warm word: straight business. More often, however, they stayed to chat, and after a while Elwin realized he'd stumbled upon a strange variant of a social life. He was the maître d' of his divested stuff, a party host of dispossession, welcoming in guests to dismantle his ex-life. One man—the city commuter, picking up the free half bag of mortar mix—stayed for a garrulous half hour, taking as an extra Maura's makeup mirror, for his teenaged daughters, and leaving Elwin, as a reciprocal extra, a bottle of his "famous" homemade hot sauce, a vicious-looking crimson liquid in a recycled sixteen-ounce plastic Pepsi bottle on which he'd written, with a thick black marker, "NJ SuperFun Sauce." (Aware that he'd never be hungry or brave enough to sample a stranger's homebrewed hot sauce from a Pepsi bottle, Elwin ditched the bottle in the trash, but afterwards felt so guilty about it—how proud the guy was, detailing the exotic pepper varietals he grew in his garden—that he fished it from the trash, rinsed the outside of the bottle, and tucked it into the pantry.) From others he received tips on the best Mexican food in Newark; two requests to be Facebook friends; a homeopathic arthritis remedy for Bologna; an invitation to attend services at a Pentecostal church in Dover; and four compliments on the Jeep, which one excitable guy in a Budweiser do-rag deemed "smokin'."

Many of these visitors also asked to go combing through the sale/giveaway pile, for further treasure, which Elwin let them do. More rarely, they'd point to random items in the house and ask if they could have those too. The parents of a six-year-old girl, for instance, went about hushing her, and shooting Elwin embarrassed smiles, when she asked for his television. They'd come for Maura's old Pottery Barn desk, because the mother— twenty-one at most—was starting community college in the fall, for a nursing degree, and needed a desk for studying, this because she was "so over" waiting tables at the Hackensack Hooters though not nearly as over it, she said, as her furiously tattooed husband/boyfriend was ("She don't need that scene," he mumbled). Elwin had listed the desk for fifty dollars but within minutes discounted it to five. "Oh man," the woman said, elated at the forty-five unexpected bucks headed back into her purse. "You have no idea." That's when the little girl asked for the flat-screen. "I'm sorry," the father said to Elwin, reaching his hands around the girl's belly and gently pulling her into him, saying to her, "It's not a *store,* sweetness," then to Elwin, "We're saving to get ours fixed. It kind've got in the way of a soccer ball." Elwin looked at the TV and then the little girl, who had doubtless been in league with that soccer ball, and then back to the TV. Why not? He rarely watched it, and when he did it was usually to give his eyes something to do while his mouth dispatched half portions of junk food. And hadn't Maura picked it out? It qualified, then. "Take it," he told the couple, who glanced at one another in wary astonishment, the father's hands tightening against the girl's round belly. "Seriously?" the girl asked. "Seriously," said Santa Elwin. The father shook his hand so hard and for so long that for the remainder of the evening Elwin worried his wrist was sprained. "You *really* have no idea," the woman kept saying, and when the family pulled out of the driveway in their mufflerless Camry, Elwin heard the parents ordering the girl to wave, which she did, as big white bursts of reflected sunset went bouncing off the TV propped sideways in the backseat beside her. Elwin lingered on the porch until the sputtering of their car dissolved into the usual traffic thrum, feeling strangely lighter and more vibrant, as when emerging from a dream, the tangerine sky above Morristown streaked with red-velvet clouds, a postcard scene from a place no one ever sent postcards. Then Christopher came in from the garage, and after discovering what'd become of the TV, threw a seething fit during which he threatened to move out—to where he didn't know, just *the fuck OUT.*

Inside Elwin, however, something had clicked. An odd squirt of dopamine, maybe, or perhaps something deeper: a mild eureka of the heart. With every sale or gift he could feel his broken life dematerializing, its old scarred edifice crumbling, the invited looters fleeing with its junked remnants, and with that feeling came astonishing relief. These were not insignificant objects, however trivial they sometimes appeared as they were carted off and slipped into backseats and car trunks. They were totems, idols, talismans, artifacts, witnesses, volatile with memory and meaning, each one a marker on a trail that'd once seemed so promising but had petered into a dead end.

He thought of all the self-help and diet books he'd devoured in the last year, with their consistent hectoring that for positive change to occur, it had to originate *inside.* Yet here was the obverse: the outside changing, and the inside following giddily along. Was this how Maura had felt, after abandoning the 340 pounds of dead weight in her own life (him)? The parallels were too coarse, he decided, but still. If such minor episodes of divestment felt this good, he thought — then how much better would *more* feel? The example of the little girl and the TV said *very.*

The next person to arrive at his front door — a middle-aged woman wearing denim shorts and a Pipefitters Local 274 t-shirt, come to pick up a hallway mirror — put her hand to her chest when Elwin told her to take almost anything she wanted. He watched her go wandering the house dumbstruck, then overheard her in the living room saying into her phone, "Honey? Can you borrow Bill's truck and meet me in Morristown? Right away, yeah." This time, when Christopher came in from the garage, he surveyed the denuded living room, which earlier that day had housed a couch and two leather chairs, and announced he was off to McGuinn's, because at the bar, he said, unlike here, there were places to sit down. "Great idea," said Elwin, deaf to the acid curdling Christopher's tone. "Just give me a minute to change my shirt."

It was that night at the bar that Elwin heard from Sharon, while checking email on his BlackBerry during one of Christopher's bathroom breaks. *Hey Big,* she wrote. *Turns out I *will* be in NYC next week (meeting with the Wall St. suits about that commission, which I should pretend to be ambivalent about but won't). Would it be a gruesome imposition for me to venture out to NJ to see some Elwin? Intentions are work and pleasure. We need to chop the legalese outta that statement text. And I sho could stand to see a friendly face in this mean ol blues song of a world. xo Sharon.* He read it twice, the first time smiling and the second time grunting and finally frowning, and laid the BlackBerry on the bar when Christopher swung back onto the barstool beside him, trailing a muskratty odor freshly purchased from the coin-op cologne dispenser in the bathroom.

Sharon's email was not entirely unexpected—she'd broached the idea of a visit the month before, when she and Elwin were together at the panel meeting, though in that loosey-goosey, noncommittal way people tended to plan things nowadays, leading Elwin to think it wouldn't happen. (A dismaying number of Elwin's friendships had degraded down to staggered email chains in which a friend suggested dinner and then, when Elwin asked when, disappeared for months, as though the friend were victim to repeat kidnappings—or as though the asking was all, the answer gratuitous.)

Nor was Sharon's *xo* tone any surprise: Over the course of all the meetings they'd developed a chumminess—that was the safe and vaguely rotund word Elwin would use—that was one part political alliance (the Markers panel had broken into two factions, which could be crudely called the Torrancians and the anti-Torrancians, or the optimists and the pessimists) and three parts something else. Whatever the component parts of chumminess were, he supposed. These latter parts had involved at least four late-night talking sessions—at grimly overlit hotel bars, drinks sweating onto Formica boothtops—during which Sharon had unfurled her own broken-life story: the artist husband who'd ditched her for a younger woman ("a student of his," she'd explained, adding, "why does it hurt so much more when it's a cliché?"), the daughter she'd raised alone who was now at USC on a film scholarship, the way you woke up in the middle of the night and found yourself sitting on the edge of the bed wondering if it would've all been different had you played by the rules and then wondering if maybe you actually *had* played by the rules, whatever the rules even were, but there you were regardless, adrift and unwanted, perched on the edge of the mattress at 3 A.M. with your cast-off misfit love. She was one of those divorcées—Elwin supposed he'd be counting himself as one, too—whose life had been knocked off its axis midway through, and who couldn't help viewing their lives through the binary of *before* and *after*. Nevermind that she'd achieved renown as a sculptor, and carved for herself what sounded like a rustically idyllic existence on the fringes of Taos (straw-bale house, one hundred percent solar-power generation, chickens and goats, bookish desert solitude), and raised a daughter whom she couldn't talk about without breaking into what she called her "dumb proud hayseed grin," no. She still compressed the story of her *after* life into three words: "I've muddled through."

Here was the danger or downside of romantic idealism, she and Elwin finally decided, two drinks later. "You shoot for the moon," he said, "but when you don't make it . . ."

"You can't bear to look at the moon ever again, right?" she said, but not quite to him — to the ice cubes melting at the bottom of her glass, or maybe whomever she saw reflected there.

No, the surprise, for Elwin, was how *he* felt at receiving the email: terrified. But of what? He sat there chewing his own melted ice while Christopher quizzed the bartendress on whether women could really squirt the way they did on the internet. Terrified of what, he asked himself again, sifting his thoughts: of the chumminess ripening into something warmer, sure. But also of it not. Terrified because the former carried the power to validate Maura's leaving by proving that, yes, these feelings of ours are all transferable, and that maybe the moon was never the right destination to begin with, because maybe we were all just atoms bouncing into one another in the black swirl of space, bound and released by the ebb and flow of something like static electricity, or like items in the marketplace, bought and used and disposed of and then if we're lucky, salvaged and reused. But terrified, too, that the latter — fixed chumminess — might also validate Maura's leaving, by exposing and maybe confirming once and for all his big fat undesirability. His essential not-enoughness, as Maura had so ungently put it. In the McGuinn's bathroom he splashed his face with cold water and assessed himself in the smudgy mirror, his face framed by angry-looking stickers for punk bands and skateboards. Wet like that, and cast in the snotty green glow of the fluorescent bathroom light, he looked like a bullfrog. The bullfrog said to him: *Just tell her you're sorry, but that you're out of town that week.* When a guy came barging into the bathroom he found Elwin nodding so deeply to the mirror that he immediately backed out with apologies.

The spooked bullfrog, however, was no match for Christopher and the bartender, whose name was Kelly, and who had a semi-agreeable habit of pouring shots of Jameson whether they'd been ordered or not. In a chemically induced semi-agreeable moment, Elwin showed the email to Christopher who passed it to Kelly who Googled up a photo of Sharon from her website and proclaimed her "smokin," just as the Budweiser pirate had deemed the Jeep. "So tell me what's the issue here?" she asked.

"Doc ain't sure," said Christopher, which was surprisingly incisive, because Elwin didn't recall admitting he was unsure.

Kelly scowled as she passed Elwin back his phone. "Ain't sure of what?"

"Anything," said Doc, not nearly as comically as he'd intended.

"Miss 'XO' here, on the email—is that it?" she said. Was it the Irish whiskey, or had everyone in his vicinity developed incisive superpowers? Was he the only one stumped by the riddle of his life? "'Cause the answer's yes, Mr. Big."

So that's what he wrote her, *yes,* tapping it out on the BlackBerry while Christopher steered the conversation back to other aspects of womanhood he'd learned from the internet, Kelly vigorously rolling her eyes as she went about debunking them one by one. *The state of New Jersey welcomes you for as long as you'd care to stay.* Elwin hitting *send* was celebratory cause for another round of Jameson shots, which this time he refused, passing the shot glass down to Christopher. "So you're obviously okay with sleeping on the couch for a night or two?" Elwin asked him. Christopher winced, wiping the whiskey residue off his lips with the back of his hand. "Doc," he said, "that chick ain't flying ten thousand miles from New Mexico to park herself in a guest room."

So his incisiveness had been a one-off. Elwin said, "Here's another lesson about women for you," prompting Kelly, who'd been leading this 101-level class, to take three steps backwards while shaking a cocktail, and lean in for a listen. "You don't ever make assumptions."

"Truth," Kelly said.

Cornered, Christopher held up his hands. "Awright. Fine. But here's the thing, Doc." A grin hijacked his face. "You gave away the fucking *couch* today."

"Oh shit," Elwin said.

So he shifted Sharon's visit down the Shore, to a short-term three-bedroom rental he found on Brigantine Beach, near Atlantic City. For one thing, Christopher had nowhere else to go during her stay—the idea of him sleeping out in a backyard tent went belly-up when Elwin remembered he'd sold his tents—and, for another, the house was in an accelerating and conceivably disturbing state of undress, as the Craigslisters went ransacking it daily. Hence the Shore. Per Elwin's invitation, Christopher would be coming along: With sobriety returned the murky terror, and

Elwin saw Christopher as a sort of buffer, a kind of funhouse version of a chaperone, or a preemptive excuse if things went awry. The kid was ecstatic: The only times he'd been down the Shore were as a boy, when Big Jerry forced his twins to guard the baitpail while he went wading into the crowded surf at Sandy Hook with a hangover and a Beefstick surfcasting rod, and once as a high schooler, when he'd gotten into a boardwalk brawl at Wildwood with "some Bergen County assholes" who'd knocked his ice cream cone to the ground. He was so ecstatic, in fact, that he disappeared into the garage for two straight days and nights, with instructions for Elwin to (a) borrow his truck to get back and forth to Marasmus State, and (b) not peek through the garage windows for any reason. Though sacked with another kind of terror, imagining or rather failing to imagine (because he'd already bumped the limits of his automotive nightmare-vision) what fresh hell his Jeep was being subjected to, Elwin obeyed — almost thankful for the comparative subtlety of Christopher's pickup with its raft of plastic skulls strung from the rearview mirror and its rear-window decal of a boy peeing on the Ford logo.

The morning of their departure, after Elwin had carted all his luggage and medicines and coolers to the porch, Christopher led him out to the garage for the unveiling. "You ready?" Christopher asked, and like a defendant girding himself for his jury sentence Elwin pursed his lips and nodded. Christopher rolled up the garage door, with its metallic racket for a drumroll, and there she was: Elwin's formerly deer-mangled Jeep Cherokee, looking like no Jeep Cherokee he'd ever seen or wanted to see. The polished-everywhere chrome shone like a wintry sun: the 22-inch chrome wheels, the chrome tube bumper, foglights, that damn chrome gas cap. Underbody LED lights threw a blue disco glow upward, to where Christopher had festooned the body with flame decals, long orange and yellow licks extending all the way to the rear. The way the Jeep was waxed and buffed and impossibly gleaming called to mind a bodybuilder flexing onstage — even the interior, which Christopher opened the door for him to see, bore an immaculate shine. "I don't know what to say," said Elwin. The backseat, he noted, was draped in a beige hammock; Christopher had been waiting for his puzzled expression. "That's for Bologna," he said. "Some kind of microfiber shit. To keep his hair off the seats. 'Sposed to be comfortable for him, too." At which point Elwin felt something sloshing inside him: revulsion mixing with affection. It was laughably appalling, and somehow the kindest gesture anyone had extended him in years.

"I'm speechless," he announced.

"I fucking told you, didn't I? I *told* you it'd be beautiful. Wait'll the old man sees this thing, right? I *told* you, Doc."

"You told me," Elwin whispered.

Whether Big Jerry ever saw the Jeep that morning as Elwin drove it slowly down the driveway—perhaps through the kitchen window, alerted by its adolescent rumble as he sat glowering into his coffee—went unknown. But Myrna saw it, and waved to them meekly through the screendoor. Christopher scooted his butt onto the windowframe and from over the top of the Jeep shouted, "Hey, *Ma!* Check it out, huh?" Whatever she said back, however, was drowned by the engine. "We're taking it down the Shore!" Someone else's reaction, however, was dominating Elwin's mind, and as he merged the Jeep onto the Garden State, headed toward the Bay Head train station where they'd planned to pick Sharon up for the two-hour drive south to Brigantine, with other drivers pulling alongside to take cameraphone snapshots or to confer admiring thumbs-ups, he tried warding off the self-conscious dread. He recalled the way his mother was always berating his father for the condition of their '65 Plymouth Belvedere, which even in Elwin's earliest memories was a rustbucket shambles, her asking, "Just what do you think that car *says* about us?" and Elwin Sr. answering, "I didn't know it was supposed to *say* anything." *Elwin,* he could hear her saying now, with a light sprinkling of Sharon's accent stirred in. *You're a fifty-four-year-old man driving a . . . clown car.* If he hadn't been the amalgamated middle child, perhaps, he might be bold enough to respond: *So what?* Somewhere near Perth Amboy, in the midst of these thoughts, two boys in a Chevy Tahoe drew alongside, the driver revving the engine as invitation to race. "Doc, we can totally smoke 'em," Christopher urged, but Elwin, as grand master of his own perverse parade, just smiled and waved. The driver gunned his engine, cutting them off hard while the passenger raised a middle finger out the window.

"Well that was rude," Elwin said.

"Shoulda fucking *smoked* 'em," Christopher shouted, punishing the innocent glove compartment with a hard whap.

Emerging from the Bay Head train station, with Elwin sheepishly toting her bags behind her, Sharon pressed a hand to her chest in much the same way the woman who'd first raided Elwin's house had done. She stopped and stared openmouthed at the curbside Jeep against which Christopher was leaning, as if posing for an official portrait, a cigarette balanced not-quite-dashingly upon his lip. Even at idle the Jeep sounded like a thunderstorm.

"This is—yours?"

In a graceless attempt to divert her attention Elwin pointed to Bologna's jowly face hanging out the rear window, with its curlicue of silver slobber dangling from his mouth, and said, "That's Bologna, that old guy there . . ."

"Oh my stars," she said. Her eyes went walking up and down Elwin in what looked like bafflement or possibly remorse. "I wouldn't have pegged you for . . ."

He sighed. "Me neither."

"But *this,*" she said, approaching the Jeep in what looked like awe but was probably, Elwin figured, more like distasteful caution—the way people came sidling up to touch a python draped across a handler's shoulders at some zoo show. She was wearing a crochet-trimmed tanktop above an ankle-length patchwork skirt. Her skin was tanned to the color of paper shopping bags, the muscles of her narrow freckled shoulders defined and redefined with every movement of her arms. She adjusted her cat's-eye glasses, squinted, and then turning to Elwin with a grin she said, "This is a work of art."

Elwin muttered, "Oh please."

"Just nailed her down last night," Christopher broke in, blowing a thick stream of Marlboro smog from his nostrils. "Doc helped me with some of the work early on, but I'd guess you'd call me, like, the mastermind or something . . ."

"This is Christopher?" Sharon said to Elwin. After his affirming nod she turned to Christopher and said, "Well, from one artist to another, Christopher, let me tell you—this is spectacular work."

The way Christopher stiffened and straightened—he came off the Jeep as though it'd just delivered him a mild electrical shock, his flattered smile causing his cigarette to droop from his mouth's sunken middle, his darting gaze pitched toward the sidewalk in ecstatic embarrassment—said to Elwin that no one, himself included, had ever told Christopher that anything he'd done was spectacular. And maybe it *was* spectacular, in its own skewed, heavy-metal, Matchbox car way: what the French called *belle laide,* or ugly-beautiful. There wasn't time to develop this thought further, however. Sharon was already in the Jeep, tying her blonde-gray hair back in a ponytail while hollering for some highway.

They took Highway 9, which at times threaded them in and out of the Garden State Parkway but for most of the way offered them a narrow pike through the soggy green coastal lowlands, '70s rock-radio blaring from the beefy aftermarket speakers (Elwin turning it down, Sharon cranking it back up) as they went roaring past low-rise motels and ice cream stands with bleached-out signs and car-repair shops where mechanics slapped one another on the arm and pointed to the Jeep, past Johnny Muffler and the Jersey Hooker, past the Sprinkle Shack and the Shark Fin Inn, Christopher playing air guitar in the backseat and/or complaining about Bologna's hot Purina breath, Elwin gunning the Jeep southward with his sun-pinked left arm propped out the window, Sharon waving to the legions of Jeep-gawkers and proclaiming, "I swear, it's like I got off the train and walked into a goddamn Springsteen song."

"Okay," Christopher said, when they'd made it to Brigantine island, "turn in here." They were stopped at the sand's edge, having made a trivial wrong turn on the way to the rental house. Behind them, the sun hung as low as it could hang in the sky while remaining whole, the calm purple water of Reeds Bay lapping at its bottom. Elwin, who had the Jeep in reverse to turn around, asked, "Turn in where?"

Christopher pointed ahead, to where a sand-track road went curving off between some grass-stubbled dunes. "There."

"Do you see the sign?" Now it was Elwin's turn to point, at a wooden sign that read NO DRIVING ON BEACH WITHOUT PERMIT.

"Oh, fuck that," Christopher said. "It's Jersey. Everything requires a permit but no one ever checks 'em."

"Oh come on," said Elwin.

"I vote yes," Sharon said.

"What about the sand paddles?"

"What about 'em?" said Christopher.

"Isn't this what you packed them for?" The damn things were taking up two-thirds of the rear compartment, or the "way back" as Sharon called it, and had forced Elwin to leave among other things his cooler back home on the porch. They were also the reason Sharon's floral fabric suitcase was now coated in dandruffy dog fur, as the only open space for it had been next to Bologna in the backseat.

"Aw, we'll be okay. Just stick it into four."

"Whaddaya mean, we'll be okay? What'd we buy them for, then?"

"In case we're *not* okay. Just go."

"So they're what — sand insurance?"

"Voting yes over here," Sharon said. "Does women's suffrage count for anything in this hot rod?"

This last point was hard to contest. With a grumpy exhale Elwin clunked the Jeep into four-wheel-drive, mashed it into first gear, and then grannied it onto the sand. "Give it more juice," Christopher said. "You need momentum to keep from getting stuck." Elwin gassed it, the wheels spinning and then with a fierce lurch catching, and Sharon let out an exhilarated squeak as she was thrown back in her seat. "Doc's on the loose now!" Christopher bellowed, whapping Elwin's headrest. The trail cut through low dunes to where the beach opened up, where a few lonesome surfcasters stood knee-deep in the shallow surf and where the last straggling sunbathers were bookmarking pages and closing umbrellas and folding up chairs. Elwin skirted left, away from the people to where the beach appeared deserted and more rugged, throwing a breaker of sand off the right side of the Jeep. "Hot damn," Sharon said, and as if by contagion Elwin mouthed the very same curse, *hot damn,* as the Jeep hurtled forward. Horrified by the prospect of getting stuck, Elwin gunned the Jeep hard and then harder, his morning's coffee cup shaking so violently as the Jeep went skittering across the sand that the cup came jiggling up and out of the cupholder, splashing cold black coffee onto the floorboards and his feet. He veered rightward, toward the waterline, and Sharon shrieked as the front right tire threw cold salt spray up into the open window. Drifting farther to the right, for the same effect only more, he felt the tires go slumping into the silt and pulled it roughly to the left, toppling Christopher onto Bologna who huffed out an offended baritone woof. He honked the tequila horn, fishing a squeal of appalled glee from Sharon. Elwin couldn't help himself: A whinnying *yee-haw* of a laugh came pouring out of him, an ebullient and peculiar sort of laugh that surely he'd sounded before in his life—but when? He couldn't recall. The sun had lowered itself into Reeds Bay by now, the prismatic smear of its passage spread across the entirety of the sky, and Elwin banked the Jeep in a satiny ribbon of surf's edge sand near the northern tip of the island, still laughing, almost gasping now—though at what he couldn't say.

Christopher was out first, stripping down to his boxers and launching himself into the waves. Bologna came out next, and then Elwin, evicted from the Jeep by Sharon who said she'd be changing into her swimsuit and wouldn't "stand for any winderpeepin." Elwin stood outside with his back to the Jeep watching Bologna plod his way to the water's edge where for a hesitant moment the old dog stood, the waves lapping his paws, as if trying to hoist this familiar sensation from a deep well of memories. As a pup he'd adored nothing more than rushing the sea beside the Santa Monica pier, Elwin tossing tennis ball after tennis ball into the Pacific and against all natural odds Bologna retrieving them, at times returning with draggled hanks of seaweed on his head or tail, barking at Elwin to throw the ball again and then barking at the waves for his own private canid reasons, a big wet mutty sea monster in love with the surf. Elwin watched now as Bologna hazarded a step farther, a splash from a wave dousing his head, the dog recoiling but then licking at the salt on his droopy gray snout and standing firm as another wave rolled into him, perhaps wondering if at last he was back home. Then Sharon came out of the Jeep, in a skirted one-piece that would've taken Elwin's breath away had he dared give it more than the timid passing glimpse he allowed himself, and like Christopher she went plunging into the water, hooting as she came up for breath. "Get in here," she hollered, and from deeper waters Christopher howled the same.

He hadn't counted on this, quite dumbly in retrospect: the swimming, and the near-nudity it required of him. In the preceding decade the only people who'd seen him shirtless were Maura and his physicians, and not one of them had left positive reviews. "Naw," he shouted back, with a wave of his arm meant to suggest this was all for them, that he was fine, like the way his father used to lurk at the edges of the tree on Christmas morning, ungifted but seemingly content. He saw the two of them out in the water—diving and surfacing, Sharon's legs scissoring the violet sky as she descended headfirst—as collections of perfect limbs, as fantastical creatures of no apparent relation to his schlubby self, a merman and mermaid he'd just released into the wild. He heard the ocean roar, "Get your ass in here," aping Christopher's voice, and watched Sharon urging him in by pulling both of her thin muscled arms toward her, like the signalmen on runways guiding jumbo jets to their gates. "Come *on*," she called.

They weren't going to let up, he realized. It was literally sink or swim. And so he emptied his pockets and kicked off his flipflops and, just as Bologna had done, he trudged to the edge of the world and let its cool alabaster frothiness come raging softly toward his feet, while from beyond the breaking surf they continued to shout at him, these two people who just a year ago had been unknown or barely known to him, but who weren't fantastical creatures at all, he understood—just bycatch like him, cast adrift with their misfit love.

As he waded in deeper, the water now slopping at his shirttails, he was struck by a sudden memory of the shore as it had been in his boyhood, back when the surf was porcupined with floating syringes from all the medical waste dumped at sea and the waterline was sometimes fringed with rainbowed slicks of oil. Him standing above a desiccated fish or the sickly stringiness of a beached condom or a washed-up tire with crabs skittering about its black hollows, with his mother or more often Jane screaming *Don't touch it El whatever it is don't touch it.*

A rush of water rising between his legs brought a yelp from his throat, and he spun around to block any further sea-nipping of what Christopher would call his "junk," backing himself out to sea. From this vantage he saw the Jeep in its new coat of armor gleaming at the twilit shoreline, its flanks adorned with those ridiculous flames. He'd give it to Christopher when they got back to Morristown, of course. Maybe he'd known that all along. The water was rising or he was sinking—he wasn't quite aware of who was driving now, himself or the Atlantic. But he wasn't terrified anymore, that much he knew. "Out here," he heard them call, as he came up for air, treading water while spitting it from his mouth in a long childish stream, the seawater briny and almost sweet-tasting. Everything is salvageable, he told himself, as he sank beneath the waves into the cool bruisy darkness and then, turning, began paddling toward their calls. Even you.

5

ON THE SAME late September day when Matty disappeared, Micah felt the baby inside her die. She witnessed its death inside a dream, her still and silent baby being scooped from her open belly by men in khaki uniforms, but when she came jolting awake from the dream, with a single frantic gasp, she knew that the baby was gone—that the dream had been real. This was not unforeseen. The cramping had begun two days earlier, and with it the spotting—light at first then progressively heavier until by the time she'd gone to bed the night before a steady rust-colored stream was draining out of her, like when you pulled the plug on the oilpan of a pickup engine, and every last towel and washcloth and rag in the apartment was soaked and stained from their shifts inside her underwear. After the dream she peeled the bedsheet off her clammy body and made her way to the bathroom where her pee struck the toilet water in gloppy bursts. She shone a flashlight down between her legs into the bowl. Floating in the water, dyed orange from the mixture of blood and urine, were clotted bits of her insides, of her voided womb, of her—child. She turned the flashlight off and let it fall to the floor. She had felt its conception, as Talmadge claimed he had, but now, eleven weeks later, she alone had felt its death, and sitting on the toilet in the humid black bathroom she dropped her head to her knees and began weeping and then—strangely, almost uncontrollably—praying. "For you formed my inward parts, you knitted me in my mother's womb," she whispered, her father's infinite cabin recitations of the Book of Psalms floating back to her on a southerly gust of memory. "My frame was not hidden from You, when I was made in secret and

331

wrought in the lowest parts of the earth. Your eyes saw my substance, being yet unformed, and in Your book they all were written, the days fashioned for me, when as yet there were none." She banged her forehead against her kneecaps as an ungovernable trickle fell out of her into the bowl, and a great sob engulfed her. "Search me, O God, and know my heart," she said, in a fevered mutter, "try me and know my pain; and lead me please oh fucking please in the way everlasting."

Several hours later, as dawn was creeping through the streets outside, Micah sat propped against her pillow in their bed, a towel wedged damply between her legs, and stroked Talmadge's long beautiful hair as he slept. He twitched, but lightly, like a porch-dog dreaming. He'd secretly hoped for this, she knew. Had maybe even willed it, if you believed such things possible. Into her mind drifted a memory of that day she'd found him swimming in the white gypsum dust of the Playa, and how Lola had instructed her, as they'd loaded his elasticized body into the van, to give him "the security of a womb." That a womb could be insecure, hers especially, had never occurred to her. Outside, the hydraulic brakes of a sanitation truck hissed the prelude to the glassy music of empty gin bottles being collected from the cocktailery down the block. A narrow sliver of sunlight broke through the edge of the plywood covering the window, and Micah tracked its path across the room to where the far wall had captured it, to where a sword of silver-white light lay embedded in the graffitied plaster. Adjusting the pillow behind her, she felt her breasts slosh against her t-shirt, their gorged and futile soreness drawing fresh tears from her eyes. She continued to stroke Talmadge's hair as the tears dribbled down onto her lips. All wasn't lost, she tried telling herself, even as the noise of Matty rising from the living room floor mangled the quiet. She listened to him rummaging through the kitchen, heard the crinkly tearing of a Ho Ho wrapper, noted the difference in the clomps of his footsteps once his shoes were on, and savored a rinse of relief when she heard the door close behind him and his footsteps descend the stairs. Her Eden restored, or at least what was left of it.

It was unusual for Matty to wake first. The typical morning scene, which Micah had come to detest, involved her and Talmadge navigating their way around Matty's sprawled snoresome body on the floor. Half a day might pass that way. Micah had found her banjo to be an effective alarm, prodding Matty to lift himself onto his elbows and with a groggy scowl mutter, "Fuck," or, "Jesus fucking Christmas," or some variation thereof. She'd begged Talmadge to evict him, over and over again she'd pleaded, nagged, threatened—but he was so timid with Matty, as though fearing him (though she couldn't see why) or bound to him by some confidential and unpayable debt. Talmadge acted different around Matty, too: harder, caustic, with a shriveled sense of purpose or self. On prickly occasions she was reminded of the Lusk boys, flopped on the couch in their trailer, stretching out a single dirty joke for hours, pulling it like taffy, while empty beer cans gathered at their feet and cigarette smoke left a yellow film on their faces. As recently as Monday Talmadge had been promising Matty would be gone by week's end. They'd been talking about it, he'd said, and while Matty didn't know the reason for it, the urgency was clear. But here it was Saturday, with no signs of packing or of the celebratory send-off she knew Talmadge would arrange. She didn't think she could face Matty today, imagining her grief smashing onto the rocks of his glib cluelessness, the violence of an overdue reckoning.

But that reckoning would never come. Only from the police, a day and a half later, would she learn the skeletal facts about why Matty had risen so early that morning, and where he'd gone.

His first stop had been a Starbucks down on Broadway, just across Bleecker Street from his ultimate destination: the Best Buy store down the block. Matty wanted to be there when it opened; he'd concocted a muddled rationale for this, thinking the store managers would be preoccupied with opening checklists and the cashiers still too foggyheaded and undercaffeinated to pay much attention to IDs and such, but his truer motivation was simpleminded excitement. Matty was going shopping, and he couldn't wait. For more than an hour he charged his cellphone while disagreeably nursing the double espresso he'd bought to earn him access to the electrical outlet and, more important, to the bathroom. He despised the bathroom in the squat, with its Superfund-level cockroach colony stationed beneath the iron tub, and couldn't bear to take a shit in there except on those regular occasions when Micah's dumpster cuisine sparked medical emergencies in his combustible bowels. Of course, he also hated the espresso at Starbucks, having been schooled and spoiled by the coffeeshops of Portland, but in exchange for a roach-free potty he would've suckled a gasoline pump. At 10 A.M., when the Best Buy opened, Matty was already positioned outside the store, on the sidewalk beneath the six-story cast-iron-fronted building that housed it, smoking a cigarette while watching a street vendor array kebabs atop a dirty-looking brazier. Then he went in.

He got sidetracked almost immediately. On his shopping list was a single item: a laptop computer, which he'd been wanting for months. With a laptop, he thought, life would be different. He could watch movies instead of captively listening to Micah wank that goddamn banjo or, worse, in the evenings, listening to her and Tal read aloud from a trove of ancient letters they'd scrounged from that nursing-home dumpster. His insides would go flopping when he'd see one of them tweezing a letter from that foot-long wooden box on the sidetable. Half of them were written on gray Red Cross stationery that was so thin you could almost see through it. Tal liked to stress that they were from World War II — "combat letters," he'd say — as if the minor balls of that fact outweighed the extraordinary pussy-ness of the letters' content. To Matty it was awful beyond compare: "'Does she comprehend the mad depth of my devotion?'" Talmadge would read, in character, as the Leo to Micah's Doris. "'Does she think of me as I think of my Doris, restlessly, hungrily, so constantly that even sleep and combat are no'—I can't . . . is it, repair? No, reprieve—'are no reprieve? When she thinks of the future does she see only me, as I see only her? Not only me versus other men, no no no, but me versus *everything.* Me *only,* the way the moon covers the sun in an eclipse.'" And then would come Micah, fifty times worse: "'In my eyes there is only Leo Vakolyuk.'" ("Leer Vac-you-luck," in her hillbilly pronunciation.) "'I breathe you, I hear you, I am more closely attached to you than I am to God (you will object to this but I can only speak heart's truth). You say I am brave. I am not! It's just that my fears are all concentrated. Facing a day without a letter from you, facing the thought of losing you—this and only this is what produces genuine terror.'" Because Micah objected to Matty sticking his finger down his throat to pantomime retching, he'd taken to plugging in his earbuds to drown the readings with scads of Russian death-metal. But you could only endure so much of chainsmoking while watching human beings—one of them, for fuck's sake, your old ace boon coon, your best friend—melting themselves down to pathetic candlelit puddles via their self-enacted dumpster soap opera. With his new laptop, Matty figured, he'd be able to download a gazillion movies from filesharing sites. (He'd scored the wifi password from the bar down the street, whose signal was intermittently hijackable in one corner of the living room.) And it'd be good to have porn back in his life—by now he'd exhausted his mental fantasy reel of Asian chicks polishing his knob.

But a display stack of new cellphones by the entrance brought him to a sudden standstill. He dug his own phone from his pocket for comparison. It was stupidly outdated; was the same phone, in fact, they'd returned to him after his nine-month vacation at the Oregon State Penitentiary, and the phone had been obsolete even before his arrest. (You could play Tetris on it, but that was it for games.) He browsed the new phones, which were tethered to the display by a plastic-coated metal wire, but after a while a look of befuddlement darkened his face; he needed a prepayable phone, with no calling plan, and he couldn't tell which models qualified. The last thing he wanted was employee attention—his goal was to get in and out quick, because until now he'd stuck to petty shit, shoes and skateboard gear and Yankees tickets, and he suspected he was promoting himself to felony level today; plus he was *really* flouting Monya's rules now, though, the way he saw it, Monya didn't understand the situation he had on his hands, didn't know Matty had lucked into a Supercard that wanted to give and give and give—but without knowing which phones were available with the prepay option he was screwed. He submitted to a salesman's offer of assistance.

With his spectacularly round shape and blue shirt and matching blue pants, the salesman resembled a globe on which the continents had been erased, or, as Micah would probably put it, a globe representing the apocalyptic future when warmed risen seas would swamp the earth. His cheeks were the size and color of pink grapefruits. He steered Matty toward a Nokia phone he called an "excellent convergence device," confusing Matty with an appended chuckle. Matty felt compelled to ask, "Is that a real thing—a convergence device?" The salesman chuckled again and said, "You know what movie *that's* from." Matty didn't, because nine months in prison followed by nine months in an unelectrified squat had left him culturally bankrupt, but he pretended to anyway. Real or not, he liked the sound of a convergence device, and the phone's price was a mid-range $149. "Sold," he told the salesman, who wiggled his hands in the air and exclaimed "all *riiiight!*" in what Matty understood to be another movie quotation. Dude was kind of funny; Matty liked him.

He admitted he'd come for a new laptop when the salesman asked if there was anything else. "Walk this way," the salesman said, and with a goofily hunched back led Matty deeper into the store. Matty was pleased, this time, to get the reference: that was from *Young Frankenstein,* an oldie his Grandma Boone used to shove into the VCR when she'd babysit him. Matty's plan was to keep the purchase under a grand, which was the line he'd drawn in his head between grand and petit larceny, based on a guess. Just a bare-bones laptop; nothing ostentatious. But as the salesman pointed out, the $799 model Matty was eyeing didn't have anywhere near the hard-drive capacity for storing movies, and when Matty said battery life was an issue the salesman snorted and claimed the battery would die long before he'd get to "see any bad guys killed." Plus, he added, could you really *enjoy* a movie on a fourteen-inch "peephole" screen? One by one they dismissed their way through the laptops until they came to an HP model called the "Dragon," with a twenty-inch high-def display and four gigabytes of RAM plus this bad-assed adjustable screen-hinge with which you could move the screen closer or farther from you, depending on—on something, Matty wasn't sure what, but it was cool. He kept moving it back and forth, test-driving the hinge, while the salesman disclosed bonus details about a new filesharing site with hyperspeed servers where he claimed you could find *every movie ever made,* probably even *White on Rice III* or *The Girls of the Whore-ient Express,* Matty thought to himself, reserving this tip for future investigation. But the price was crazy: *batshit* crazy. He couldn't even bear to look at it. The salesman had a point, however, even if he wasn't aware it was his point: Why take the risk Matty was taking on a machine that wasn't worth it? He played with the hinge some more, watching his own reflection in the glossy black screen receding and returning as he wormed his way into the idea. This would be the last time, he promised himself. He'd chop that life-giving Supercard into little plastic shards the moment he got home.

The total with phone and taxes came to $4,654.30. Matty gulped, declining the service protection program. This was so much more—obscenely more—than he'd intended to spend, and for a frenzied blood-pounding moment he heard a voice which might well have been Daniel

Boone's saying: *Get the fuck outta here, dude. Do a facepalm, say you forgot your wallet, and walk right out the door.* But like a big blue stray puppy the salesman had followed Matty all the way up to the register, where the female cashier turned out to be (fuck!) a first-day trainee, and because the salesman wouldn't shut up about how cool *Spider-Man 3* was going to look on that dual-lamp screen (Matty didn't even like Spider-Man), his pinched and quotation-larded voice adding a scrambled top layer to the fierce argument Matty was conducting inside his head, wise old Daniel Boone squaring off against the desire for that techno-wicked hinge thing, Matty wasn't fully aware as he handed his credit card and fake ID to the cashier. Not until scrunching her face and rotating the card swipe machine sideways she asked: "What does this mean?" When the salesman leaned in with a squint, Matty noticed his nametag, in particular the words ASSISTANT MANAGER: whoops. "Oh that," the salesman-turned-manager said. "That just means call for authorization." This was Matty's whistle to make a fast but smooth beeline for the doors, a whistle he obeyed. The giant black security guard nodded as Matty passed, smiling, "Have a nice day."

Which he might've had, if not for the fake ID he'd left on the counter. The one Monya had supplied him, courtesy of a mole inside the Brighton Beach DMV office, with Elwin Cross's name printed beside his own unmistakably fat-bearded face which even the most rudimentary face-recognition software (he'd seen this shit on TV) would link instantly back to his Oregon State Penitentiary file photos, or that any downtown beat cop (oh why the fuck hadn't he gone uptown?) could put to quick spotting use. With his hands gripping the bar of the door Matty froze. He needed that back. After a quick and energizing inhalation, he spun around and dashed back to the counter, snatching his ID just as the manager threw some kind of signal to the guard. His two-handed, index-fingers-pointed-inward motion was weird, and probably a physical movie quote, but regardless of its origins it still transmitted the same message to Matty: He was *fucked*. The guard was on him like a three-hundred-pound land octopus. "I'm clean, dude, check me," Matty protested, "my girlfriend just texted me—she got hit—by a bus," but the guard wasn't listening. Matty heard the manager tell the cashier to dial the police. He also heard her ask how.

Snared within the hulk arms of the security guard, Matty gauged the distance to the glass doors—eight or nine yards, max. A five-second sprint. He thrashed, trying to twist himself out of the guard's tentacled grip. When that didn't work he threw a loose and panicked haymaker punch that caught the guard smackdab in the jaw. It was like hitting a cinder block. "You try that again," the guard seethed, "and I'll shit down yo throat." Matty looked again to the doors. By now passersby had stopped to watch, their faces cupped to the glass: bad, meet worse. If he didn't try it again, however, he knew someone else would be shitting down his throat, and not just metaphorically: whatever comrades of Monya's were stocked inside Rikers Island. He swung at the guard again, who grabbed his arm in mid-swing and with sumo grace wrenched it behind Matty's back. Matty watched the polished floor rise up to meet him as he was dumped face down, and felt it cold and grainy against his cheek as the guard bound his wrists with zip-ties and announced, "It's shit time."

The 9th Precinct station was on Avenue C at East 8th Street, really just sneaker distance from the squat. Matty had walked or skated by that gray fortress a thousand times—did his laundry at the coin-op across the street from it, in fact, and had spent a multitude of nights with Tal picking through the trash of the Associated Supermarket cater-cornered from it across Avenue C. He and Tal had even bullshitted with some cops who'd been smoking outside the precinct one night, watching them scavenge. "You find any donuts?" one of the cops joked, and when Talmadge replied, "Naw, but we'll keep an eye out next time," the other cop noted the accent and asked where they were from. When Tal answered Mississippi they laughed as if he'd made it up, like he'd said Narnia or something. "But me, I'm from Mahwah," Matty added, without quite knowing why, because he couldn't possibly care what random cops thought—except maybe he didn't like being laughed at, or wanted to insert some distance between Talmadge's current Oscar the Grouch incarnation and himself. But the cops hadn't cared, they'd just gone on laughing about Mississippi.

No cops were laughing now. This was just the slightest indicator that, as of this morning, everything was different, everything had changed. He'd fucked it up. Rocking back and forth on the bench in his holding cell, Matty was overcome with a strange nostalgia for those early days, him and Tal sneaking off to the roof to get high, or reminiscing about college while poking through trash bags, all those free afternoons he'd filled with solo longboard circuits through the city, even for the dangerous semi-satisfactions of Micah's dumpster cooking—for those few months before he'd developed an angle. Tracking back through his memory he was able to pinpoint the very moment it went sour: that night after he'd escaped death in the compactor, when Micah snubbed his miraculous delivery of scavenged ribeyes. With that realization a scorching anger burned out the nostalgia. He thought: If that vegan bitch had just said thank you. If she'd said, thanks for almost dying for our fucked-up little eco-movement. If she'd said, thanks for abiding by one of the fifty commandments of our sick-ass, made-up, Amish-y religion. If she'd said, hey, thanks for letting me pussywhip your best friend into an unrecognizable garbage fairy.

A homeless guy with bughouse eyes and scabs all over his face took a seat beside Matty and asked, nonsensically, if he knew where they kept the insulin around here. Matty ignored him, mouth-breathing to avoid the guy's poisonous odor cloud. He pressed his back to the wall and closed his eyes, listening to the holding cell's six other inhabitants moaning amongst themselves; turned out everyone had been arrested on the same all-purpose charge, that being "some bullshit." This was Micah's fault, he decided. All of it; everything. Him sitting here right now even, inhaling ass. Maybe not *all* her fault, because leaving his ID on the counter was his fucktard move—but a lot of it. Most of it. In his imagination he stabbed her like a voodoo doll.

A middle-aged detective named Meyer oversaw Matty's transfer to an interview room. The detective skimmed the report, and then, with what sounded like a mystified grunt, dropped it onto the table and said, "What the hell happened at Best Buy, Mr. Cross?"

Matty dunked his forehead toward the table. I'm not a Cross, he wanted to say. I'm a Boone. *As in Daniel Motherfucking Boone, the King of the Wild-Thing Frontier, Slayer of Panther, Bear, and Injun, Capper of Coonskin, the MVP of American History, His Royal Fringe-Coated Badness:* that's who. What he said instead—nimbly, but in a quaking voice—was: "I don't wanna go back to prison, okay? I got some shit for a deal. Shit you'll like." The detective's eyebrow curved upward as he leaned back in his chair, preparing himself to be curious. Six hours later, after an assistant district attorney had passed through, followed by an assistant U.S. attorney (peeved to have been called in on a Saturday, barking at the detective, "You told me he was *Russian*"), plus a lackey from the Public Defender's Office whose sole apparent duty was to conduct a pattern analysis of his necktie, the detective came storming back in, and, as before, dropped the now-thickened report onto the table. This time, however, Meyer was pissed. "If you're gonna lie to us, this is a waste of time for everyone involved," he said. The attorneys glanced up in mild alarm. Matty was expressionless. "I just got off the phone with your folks in Mahwah," the detective said. "The ones you said you been living with? Your mom wants to know when you got back from Oregon." Matty felt his nostrils flaring, watching the assistant U.S. attorney, his face long and steeled like a garden spade, begin to stack his notepad and file folders. I tried, Matty consoled himself. Tal, dude, I tried. But you'll be better off this way, man. I swear to fucking God you will. Spreading his fingers on the tabletop, Matty stared up at the detective whose anger wasn't really anger, he saw, just as the salesman's helpful cheer hadn't really been cheer; everyone was just doing his job. So Matty did what he thought was his. He gave up the squat.

The police didn't make their way there until late the next afternoon. For Talmadge and Micah, Matty's disappearance had not been cause for distress. The opposite, really: In their unfamiliar twosomeness they stretched and yawned like purring cats, grateful for the unexplained reprieve though not precisely reveling in it. For most of Saturday Micah was desultory and subdued as she struggled with telling Talmadge she'd lost the baby. Fearing the arid delicateness of his reaction, the sudden telltale glow in his eyes exposing his secret relief, she opted to wait; until when, however, she wasn't sure. They'd nestled themselves into a night so soft and languorous as to verge on the narcotic, taking their letters of Leo and Doris early to bed where Talmadge's voice wilted away in the midst of a drowsy reading. When Micah raised her head to urge him onward she found him asleep, Leo's letter beside his head on the pillow like a nerveless lover's farewell. For her, the day and night felt like old age, or what she thought old age might feel like: the mindlessly fixed routine (scavenge, nap, scavenge again, eat dinner, bathe, Leo and Doris, sleep), the sedate and measured pacing, the long and tender silences that passed between them, but also, perhaps most essentially, a bittersweet impermanence shading every moment with its bluesy pall, a sense of sadness on its way. It might've just been Leo and Doris's letters inspiring these elderly connections, Micah didn't know. The letters were so brittle in her hand that by merely blowing a stream of air at one she thought she could blast a tear in the paper. Yet the passion they contained was so impregnable, or seemed to be. (They had only made it halfway through the correspondence.) When she finally fell asleep, hours after Talmadge had, she felt more like the paper than what was written upon it: tenuous, fragile, splotched with whorls of dried tears.

Then Sunday. Indian summer in the city: every window ajar to beckon inside those last warm gusts, the retreating summer breezes which the previous night's chill suggested had already been vanquished. People fled onto the sidewalks in a confusion of garments, some decked in sweaters and others wearing shorts, and the trees reflected this confusion, some having yellowed their leaves for the approach of autumn, others squeezing a final and vivid spurt of green down their branches, loath to surrender. The sky had a music to it, as if in longing to stay current it had expanded into multimedia. Mere color insufficient, it had to sing. And it was singing, or at least it seemed that way to Talmadge and Micah: a song of New York City you can hear only once, and only as young lovers, an evanescent, intoxicating music—parts Gershwin, Charlie Parker, the Ramones, and coffeehouse Dylan, and overlaid with a symphonic veneer of streetsounds: jackhammers and carhorns and keening sirens and the subway's dragon-grumble and the polyglot chaos of a hundred different languages dispersed into eight million conversations plus the lonesome elegant sawing of that wizened Chinese violinist down below the Times Square station—that causes some people to spend the rest of their lives there, cemented to the city for the chance of hearing it again. It played all through that Sunday morning, as Talmadge and Micah made their regular rounds, roaming the streets the way foragers roam woods. Discovering a sack of bruised apples and half a dozen containers of just-expired Greek yogurt outside the Gourmet Garage on Seventh Avenue, they hauled their find to the river and sat beside the water's edge, Talmadge slicing the apples with his pocketknife for Micah to dip into the yogurt. They tossed the bruised wedges into the Hudson, wondering if fish would rise to them, and what those fish might look like. The apples lay motionless on the surface, as if thrown into wet concrete, and noting this Micah raised her eyes to survey the whole river, which showed no signs of movement at all, looking as stilled and molten in its passage as Micah felt she was. For this one morning they seemed exempt, the river and her, from the obligations of flow, from the gravitational laws of life. She smiled at Talmadge, and fed him a yogurt-smeared apple.

On their way back home, on a side street near the river, they passed the open door of a restaurant or bar in the early stages of a gutting. Permit notices were splashed across the windows. Micah swiveled back, her intrusive gaze having latched onto a face—in a photograph or painting hanging on a far wall—whose resemblance didn't fully strike her until she'd already taken several steps past the door into the crosswalk. It was her father. "What are you doing?" Talmadge asked, as she went right inside the restaurant, her footsteps crinkling on the brown paper taped to the floor. The room was barren save for a massive and ornately carved mahogany bar to her left where in the blotched mirror behind it she caught sight of herself passing, momentarily startled. An open bottle was on the bar beside a paper-stuffed clipboard. When Talmadge caught up to her Micah was standing beneath the picture—a lithograph portrait she could tell was ancient, from the subject's high unfurling collar and wide waistcoat lapels, but whose likeness to her father stopped her breath just the same. "What is it?" Talmadge asked.

Before she could answer him, another question rang out: "Can we, uh, help you?" They looked to the kitchen door, where a thirtyish couple was standing. They were both exquisitely tattooed, the woman's arms inksleeved like Micah's left arm, purplish foliage overflowing from beneath the man's shirt. His beard was braided, and his head was capped by a porkpie hat. "We're not quite open," the woman said, tittering at the obviousness of this.

Talmadge apologized, and tried pulling Micah by the arm. She asked, "Who is this?"

"Him?" The woman stepped forward, joining Micah beneath the portrait. "We don't know!" she said, tittering again. "He came with the place. Do you know who he is? He looks so—so mean or something, we thought it'd be bad luck to take him down. At least for now . . ."

Without looking from the portrait Micah said, "I thought I might know him." Mean wasn't the word she would've used, though she groped through her mind for a replacement. Possessed, maybe. "He looks like—my daddy."

"Wow," the woman said, with a black note of sympathy.

"You guys from the neighborhood?" the man asked Talmadge, who with slight exaggeration said yes. "Then welcome to day one. Or I guess it's day two—right, baby? You'd think I could keep track. We just got the permits Friday. You guys ever come here when it was the Austrian place? No? I guess they just couldn't keep it together. Not really the right neighborhood for it."

"We're hoping to do a little better," the woman said, establishing her titter as a constant tic.

Micah remained beneath the portrait as Talmadge and the couple talked their way over to the bar. She half listened as the couple ("I'm Joe, this is my wife Donna") explained their concept—*haute* Jewish cuisine ("like Mario Batali cooking a Seder dinner")—and recounted all the toils of acquiring the place. "I mean, *you* know what a bitch this neighborhood can be," Joe said to Talmadge. "We're still fighting the liquor permit process. Twenty-seven seats with just beer and wine is a tough road. We thought about knocking back into the kitchen, for more front-of-the-house space, but the kitchen's tiny already. I've been in walk-ins bigger than that kitchen."

"Plus *he'd* have to come down," Donna said, pointing to the portrait.

"And the curse would befall us," Joe added, mock-ominously. Jutting his chin toward the bottle on the bar, he asked, "You want some champagne? We just opened it. A neighborly taste of what's to come."

"Sure thing," said Talmadge. Joe fetched two plastic cups from behind the bar, wiggling one toward Micah who with a faint smile declined.

"She's pregnant," Talmadge said, and the couple, already in celebratory mode, let out congratulatory whoops.

The whooping forced Micah to join them at the bar, though blankly and off to the side, where with a sulky fingertip she drew squiggles on the bar. The couple had a two-year-old girl, who was back home in Brooklyn with Donna's mother, and Micah nodded gamely as Donna pelted her with breezy childbirthing advice ("Don't resist the epidural, seriously"). The men discussed the restaurant business, Talmadge bubbling out a story about a restaurant—"a James Beard Award place," he noted, piquing the couple's attention—where he'd briefly worked during college, about the temperamental chef who'd fired him after Talmadge had mistakenly topped a crème brûlée with salt instead of sugar. "No matter how long I torched that thing, it wouldn't caramelize," he said. "But you didn't send it out?" Joe asked. "I sent it out!" Talmadge exclaimed, and everyone screeched in high laughter save for Micah, who wanted to ask what a crème brûlée was. Joe's confession that he'd once been a temperamental chef drew a smiling rebuke from Donna, who said she'd missed the memo that he'd gone into rehab. (Titter.) Talmadge hooted, tipping his plastic cup toward Joe to accept the offer of a refill.

A thousand mental miles down the bar, Micah flashed back to a family dinner she and Leah attended in India, and the way she'd felt when the hosts kept dipping into Hindi: the smile she'd manufactured in response to the incomprehensible words swirling 'round the table, the discomfort of her exclusion. She felt the same discomfort now, positioned outside this warm and spontaneous circle. Talmadge's salt story was new to her—he'd mentioned the restaurant once, but only to cite the unconscionable food waste he'd witnessed—and watching him now, as he leaned knowingly into Joe's stories about working the line at a restaurant whose name seemed familiar and impressive to him, she found herself marveling at Talmadge's fluidity, the way he could slip in and out of the World with such smooth and mellow dexterity. She'd seen this before, of course, though not with such starkness; it had always struck her as more of a skill than a trait. But then how could it not be? He was an auto dealer's son, with a genetic knack for small talk, armed from birth with social faculties Micah couldn't imagine herself possessing. Her eyes were drawn back to the portrait on the wall, to the glowering gray face of the restaurant-to-be's patron saint or demon. Her own inheritance had been a vision. A mutated certitude. An *idyll*.

When the champagne bottle was empty they waved goodbye to their new friends, who invited them to come back when the restaurant opened for a "Manischewitz cocktail," the bird-chirps of Donna's laughter trailing them down the block. Talmadge's hand found Micah's, but she struggled to keep up with his rhythm and pace, which were lighter and faster than usual, big moonwalk steps that left her straggling behind. When she stopped to investigate some trash bags outside a Sixth Avenue deli, he tugged her forward, saying, "Not now." She obliged, and let him lead her. On his face was the softest imprint of a smile, and she kept glancing at it as they walked in clasped silence, simultaneously troubled and reassured, as though the contentment she saw had once belonged to her, and her loving satisfaction at seeing him smile was offset by the emotional and physical hollow scoured from her insides. The sense of motionlessness returned, despite the city blocks clicking by, the preppy cobblestones of the far West Village giving way to the grittier mishmash of the East—a treadmill sensation, with the mileage of their walk as distorted and elongated as their own two-headed shadow in front of them was. She clasped his hand tighter, and he replied with a lingering squeeze. The moment was like that dessert Talmadge had described botching: creamy and sugary but crusted with charred salt. A sweetness contaminated.

They saw it together, from all the way down the block: their steel cellar doors splayed open to the street, with a police cruiser parked beside. The champagne fizz vanished instantly from Talmadge's eyes. "Oh God," he said, breaking into a rash and wild sprint. Micah stuck to the corner, watching. Arriving at the doors he peered down inside, and then looking back at Micah he threw up his hands in panicky indecision. The best course of action, she knew, was to stay put. Lola, who'd been through squat raids in Oakland and Vancouver, would've called their situation ideal: Wait out the cops, she'd advise, then gather your shit and vamoose. The best police contact is no police contact. But Talmadge was already going in. At the top of the door she saw him waving a desperate hand for her to follow. Micah found him at the bottom of the basement steps, buckling with fear. "What do we *do?*" he begged. She felt a small kernel of disgust pop inside her: That same debilitating timidity that'd kept Matty glued to them for all these months was now smeared across Talmadge's face. She shook her head as she passed by him into the basement, hearing his high-pitched cursing as he fumbled for his penlight.

Two uniformed patrol officers were in the apartment. One was a pink-faced guy with a linebacker's neck and tiny but predatory eyes; the other, who emerged from the kitchen just as Micah stepped through the apartment's open doorway, was a short black woman with a dense, squat figure whose bewildered, congested expression was either a permanent facial condition or her reaction to the squat and its residents. "What's going on here?" Micah asked her.

She didn't answer, deferring to her partner. "That's a good question," he said, sly and challenging. "You the ones live here?"

Talmadge was in the apartment now, flush-faced, and mouth agape. "Yessir," he said.

"You and who else?"

"We've had a friend, uh, staying with us—"

"Matthew Boone."

"Yessir," Talmadge said, his eyes ticking from the cop's face to Micah's.

"What's he done?" Micah asked, the unspoken word *now* dangling at the question's end.

"Done?" The cop was enjoying this, amusing himself further by imitating Micah's drawl. "Who said he *done* anything?"

Talmadge asked, "Is he okay?"

"Manner of speaking. He's in custody." The cop was staring hard at Talmadge now, sizing him up. "He took a swing or two at a security guard down at the Best Buy on Broadway. Was doing some shopping on a fraudulent credit card." His tiny eyes narrowed into blackened slits. "That sound about right to you?"

Talmadge shook his head, anxiety seeping into his face.

"Anyone else living here?"

"Nossir."

"Just you and Boone and the lady."

"Yessir."

"Let's pull out some IDs."

The cops were divvying them up: Talmadge to the male cop, Micah to the female. Micah's followed her into the bedroom so that Micah could fetch her passport. Noting it was expired, she asked if Micah had any other ID. When Micah said no the cop sighed and after an allergic survey of the bedroom wagged her head and sighed again, Micah stiffening against the scorn.

Back in the living room they found the male cop holding Talmadge's satchel in his hands. "Whose bag is this?"

"Why?" Talmadge asked.

"That's not an answer. Is it the lady's? This your purse, miss?"

"My name is Micah," she said.

"Okay, Myyyy-kah." He repeated her name like that, with even more relish. "This your purse?"

"It's mine," Talmadge said.

"It's your purse?"

"Yessir."

"Mind if I look inside?"

Talmadge shook his head no, his eyes beginning to puff. The cop gave it a brief and theatrical look-see; he had clearly ransacked it earlier.

"That's not a good bag to be claiming, is it?" he said.

"Nossir."

"Why?" Micah broke in.

"Whose bank statements are those? Whose credit card statements?"

Talmadge shrugged, looking pulverized.

"But they're not yours, right?"

"Nossir."

"But that's your weed in there, is that right?"

Talmadge shut his eyes, as if reeling from intestinal pain. "Yessir," he whispered.

"Where'd the bank statements come from?"

"They're just trash," he answered, his voice quivering.

"Say again?"

"They're just trash."

"Trash. Right." The cop straightened his back and nodded to himself, the button of his chin pulsing in and out of that thick neck. "You been working with Mr. Boone?"

"I'm not employed, sir," Talmadge said, and the cop let out a harsh booming laugh, its peals bringing stuttered flinches to Talmadge's face.

"Yeah, we can see that." The cop did a fresh study of the living room, reading or rereading the line from Matthew 8:20 painted on the wall. *Foxes have holes and birds have nests but the Son of Man has no place to lay his head.* "You paint that?"

Talmadge said no.

"Who did?"

"Someone before us."

"Someone before you." The cop chewed on this for a moment. "How long you been squatting here?"

"Almost a year and half," Micah said confidently. She glanced at Talmadge, who stood hunched in defeat. Matty on a shopping spree with a stolen credit card, financial garbage stuffed in Talmadge's satchel: these revelations had yet to congeal in her head.

"A year and a half?" The cop scanned the room again, re-coloring it with this fact. "Damn." He threw a look of repulsed disbelief to his partner. "Kept it pretty quiet, didn't you?"

No one said anything.

"Could've burned the whole block down. All these candles. That heater."

"We're real careful," Micah said.

"Bet you are," the cop snorted, and to demonstrate the hazards pushed an unlit candle from the sidetable onto the floor. Then he pushed another one, this time spitefully. "You're aware this is an illegal tenancy."

"The building's abandoned," Micah said.

"That makes it yours?"

"It makes it nobody's."

"Which makes it *yours?*" A tickled expression brightened his face; he was going to enjoy recounting her logic later at the precinct house. "The world doesn't work that way, hon. This little real-estate joyride—it ends today."

Micah bristled; she didn't know what was happening with Talmadge, though the pieces were beginning to bump together in her mind, but on this aspect she felt solid. "I know how the world works," she said, with an assertive twang. "And I know that after thirty days of adverse possession y'all need a court-ordered eviction."

"Adverse possession, y'all," the cop aped. "Yeah, not so much." He grunted. "All I need to do is make a quick call to the FD to get this place barricaded as a fire hazard."

Micah felt herself falling back in retreat. She didn't know if he was lying or not; Lola's playbook hadn't addressed this particular threat. "Is that what you're doing?" she asked coolly.

"We're doing a couple things here. That's one of them, yeah." He tossed his partner a heads-up. "The other is that we're arresting you for unlawful possession of marijuana."

"Oh come *on,*" Talmadge wailed, his eyes roving toward the female cop. "It's not even an ounce."

"We've got other things to talk about," his cop said, directing Talmadge to place his hands against the wall. "Things like trash."

"Ma'am?" Micah's cop said to her.

Micah blinked at her obliviously.

"Need you to do the same," she instructed.

Vacantly, Micah said, "You're arresting *me?*"

"The weed's mine, I told you," Talmadge protested. "She's straight edge." He gasped as the handcuffs clamped his wrists. "She's—she's fucking pregnant."

The cop's hands went soft on Micah, in mid-frisk. "Is that true, ma'am?"

"No," Micah said, and shot Talmadge an unfocused stare. "The baby's dead. I miscarried."

The room seemed to tilt with this statement, so that everyone—maybe even the cops, she wasn't watching—rebalanced their feet on the floor, like when the subway takes off.

"What?" Talmadge moaned, but Micah could see the confused relief dribbling through him. Even handcuffed, a weight came off his shoulders, and on his face was a wreck of collided emotions only partially masked by a willed expression of dismay. Whatever sentence he'd been fearing had just been reduced, and just as she'd expected she felt a cold brute anger spasming her. "When?" she heard him ask. The chilled pinch of the handcuffs on her wrists dilated the anger, as by now the clues were gelling together, a blob of indictment taking unruly shape in her mind: Matty and Talmadge had been scrounging data from the trash. Just how it all worked she didn't know, but Lola used to bitch about the guys (they were always guys) who did that in San Francisco. "Paper divers," she called them, citing them as the reason she and Micah found so many dumpsters padlocked; they were ruining it for everyone, Lola complained. Garbage was the only pure crop that civilization produced, she and Lola used to say, because no one owned it, no one wanted it, no one fought over it, no one had ever launched a war to claim it. Land, air, water, people, animals: all these had been commodified, sacked with pricetags, and enslaved on that vast plantation known as

civilization. Only garbage was free, in every sense of the word. Except—
that wasn't true, she understood now. Even that had been corrupted. And
there was its corruptor, staring at her with stunned, sad-dog eyes, his lies
scattered between them on the floor. This had all been an adventure for
him; nothing more. His were borrowed principles, returnable at will.
"This off-the-grid thing, it's an action, not a life," he'd argued, as if these
were distinct, as if your actions were spendable, but your life was an invio-
lable fund. When the stakes were revealed, he'd bailed.

"Micah," he whispered, but his voice bounced off her. She recognized
the iciness overtaking her; she'd felt it with Leah, when Leah dropped the
rupee note into the boy's hand and somehow with it Micah's devotion. The
sudden immunity to love. Its swift and unsalvageable disposal. "Micah,
look at me," he begged.

"I'm taking Trashman here to the house," the male cop told his partner, rotating Talmadge into the doorway. "You want to stay with her,
Shenice—see if she needs medical, okay? Meyer's on his way over."

The apartment was darkening now, the fading afternoon light dissolving into the plaster and plywood. "Can I sit down?" Micah asked, and the
cop said sure, her voice different now that her partner was gone: blunted,
less intrusive, recognizably female. There's a specific trick, Micah discovered, to sitting down while handcuffed, and when she swayed and stumbled the cop gripped her shoulders and lowered Micah into one of the
metal chairs. She felt an almost violent desire for tears, to map the extent
of her losses with sobs: the baby, Talmadge, the squat, the future she'd just
seen smashed. Yet nothing came. Her chest felt constricted, cuffed. Even
her mouth was dry.

"That your boyfriend?" the cop asked.

"Yeah," she said, and not knowing how to amend or append resorted to
adding, "Kinda."

The cop looked as though she wanted to ask something else, something
unofficial, woman-to-woman, but stopped herself. She shifted on her feet
so that all her weapons and gear shuddered and clinked. "You need a hospital, ma'am?"

Micah shook her head no.

The cop studied her. Her radio squawked, but she ignored it. "Look,"
she finally said, kneeling so that she could meet Micah's eyes. "There's a

sergeant on his way to take you to the precinct. Is there anything you need from here? Because I don't think getting back in here is gonna be an option for a while. Maybe ever."

Micah nodded, sensing uncommon charity. "There's a bag, in the bedroom. The striped one by the bed. It's got my money in it."

The money was what was left of a cash-stuffed envelope Leah had given Micah upon her arrival in San Francisco: "walking-around money," she called it. Micah had never counted it, and rarely plundered it in the years since. At least half of it remained, a stack of hundreds as thick as her ring finger. Or at least she hoped it remained. She hadn't checked it in forever, and what she'd just learned about Matty caused an ember of fear to redden in her mind. When the cop returned with the bag Micah asked, "Will you look inside it, please? There should be an envelope."

The envelope was there, and the cop peeked inside it. "Where'd the cash come from?" she asked, laxly suspicious.

"It's mine," Micah assured her. "I been saving it—for years now."

Peering up from the bag, the cop regarded the room with soft bewilderment, then narrowed her gaze back to Micah. "Can I ask you a question, then?" she said. "If you got money—why you living this way?"

Micah had the answer, of course. Her life was the answer. Just as the World outside, and the cop standing before her like one of the deputies who'd taken her from her home when she was ten years old, was the answer. The cop's eyes were receptive, even beseeching, but in the desert of Micah's mouth there were no words, just the ashes of a thousand sermons. "There's one more thing, in the bedroom," she was able to say.

"What's that?"

"My banjo, up against the wall."

"A banjo?" The cop stiffened. "I ain't getting no banjo."

"Please," Micah implored. "It was my mama's. It's all I got of her."

"Shit," the cop said, rising.

When Micah walked out of the 9th Precinct with the banjo strapped to her back, five hours later, it was like she'd been spat from the belly of a whale. The detective, Meyer, had spent three hours harrying her with questions like: Who was Monya? Had Monya ever visited their building? Had she ever been to Brighton Beach? What about Coney Island, then? What was the last thing she'd purchased? What was the last gift her boyfriend had given her? What *was* the source of their income? Were they anarchists? Was she sleeping with Matty too? And then, near the end: Did she consider herself dumb, or was there another way she could explain her ignorance of her boyfriend and her roommate selling dumpstered financial data to the Russian mafia? He was clearly frustrated with her; when another plain-clothes cop pulled him from the interview room, she heard him mutter "fucking oblivious" before the door clanged shut.

Only once did she see Talmadge, as she was led past the holding cell where he was standing in a back corner, staring down at his shoes. Another prisoner let out a lecherous grunt as Micah passed, and Talmadge raised his head, from alarm or intrigue it didn't matter. Their eyes met, just glancingly, yet in that brief optical connection there was an unjoining, a release, an elastic moment in which Talmadge was flung toward his clouded future and Micah toward hers, even cloudier. When Meyer finally released her, Talmadge had been transferred from the cell; she scanned all the faces behind the bars, but none was his. At the front desk a sergeant returned her bag and the banjo and laughed openly as he watched her strap it onto her back.

It was after midnight, and Avenue C was crowded. The groups of twos and threes that slid by and around her had a boozy lilt to them, and from down the avenue she heard trebly music seeping from open doorways, and the cackles of smokers gaggled outside. For a long and vacant time she just stood there, looking north then south and then north again, thinking and feeling almost nothing at all. Here was the antithesis of the motionlessness she'd felt earlier that day, an eon ago: Everything seemed accelerated, the taxis glistering by in fire-colored flashes, the traffic signals flickering greenyellowred greenyellowred as far down as she could see, the passersby hurtling forward with loose but furious purpose, all of it gathered into a neon hive of motion. She teetered in the hive's center, awash in what the detective had deemed, perhaps correctly, her oblivion. When sensation finally came, it was base, unthinking, mechanical: hunger. The last thing she'd eaten was the apples and yogurt for lunch. She glanced north again, then south, and started walking.

6

THE SAME NIGHT, 10:49 according to the cellphone in Alexis's hand, she was in toilet stall #1 on the third floor of Westervelt Hall at Richard Varick College, her favorite or rather her least-hated of the toilet stalls. They weren't actually numbered except in Alexis's mind, which was probably the only place they were rated too. The protracted bouts of toilet time generated by Irritable Bowel Syndrome tend to force these sorts of insights and judgments on a sufferer; solitary confinement is part of the sentence. Texting, Facebook, celebrity scandal news: These carried you only so far. Eventually, and inevitably, it came down to you and the bathroom you were shackled to. Her familiarity with stall #1 bordered on a kind of surface omniscience: She knew the precise number of tiny bronze-ish hexagonal floor tiles in the stall (482), the number of paint drips marring the cream-colored divider wall (3), the amount of paper the dispenser held (4 rolls), the number of bolts that had never been properly tightened into the door brackets or had worked themselves loose (2), and that if you craned your head forward and a bit to the side you could almost use the big chrome door latch as a mirror. She favored stall #1 for two reasons: It was in the corner up against the wall, offering a fractional degree more privacy than the other two stalls, and the toilet's automatic flush sensor was less prone to going off for no reason, drawing unwanted attention or, worse, transmitting a false message of hope to any girls waiting for an open stall. The last thing you wanted was social pressure when you were knotted in pain. And Alexis was, at this moment, in pain.

This was different, however, from the standard-grade IBS pain. That felt like someone was inflating your stomach with a bicycle pump, with a blunt bloated ache that rose into your ribcage. This pain was almost its opposite: as if her stomach had been so thoroughly vacuumed that its lining was sucked into a tightly compressed ball, a hard fist she could feel flexing and rotating beneath her breastbone. The cramps were coming in their typical waves, though from her back to her front this time, and she felt an angry heaviness in her lower gut, as though a lumpy jagged rock was being squeezed through her large intestine and was presently lodged in some hairpin turn, its rough stubbly corners abrading her bowels as her body tried to heave it through the bend. She didn't understand it; for dinner she'd eaten some cafeteria oatmeal and glugged down a bottle of Ensure, which experience told her should be passing without incident, certainly without trauma. But then also—with a wince of regret she remembered now. While watching a movie afterwards she'd raided her roommate Amanda's stash of Oreos and Mountain Dew, which were what Amanda lived on. Alexis knew better. Oreo filling went to concrete in her belly.

Amanda was gone as usual tonight, and established routine said she wouldn't be back until tomorrow afternoon, for her 2:45 chem class. She was up in Connecticut with the boyfriend she'd retained from high school, who played some preppy sport—tennis? lacrosse? Alexis never could remember—for UConn. Amanda spent every weekend with him, partly (Alexis suspected) because she couldn't stand Alexis, or rather couldn't stand Alexis's IBS, which had come to dominate her college experience. All those students roaming the campus buildings in their t-shirts and sweatshirts and butt-print shorts emblazoned with the college's initials, RVC— Alexis thought hers should be monogrammed with IBS, so inseparable had it become from her identity. She knew Amanda hated hearing about it, but Alexis couldn't help talking about it—whining, cursing, analyzing it—because it was consuming her: rendering her so listless and fatigued that she often skipped classes; leaving her withdrawn and antisocial, because hanging out was too fraught when you feared having to scramble to the bathroom, mid-conversation, for what could be an hour-long stay; and even degrading her appearance, because how much effort did you want to apply to your makeup just to stare at your warped funhouse reflection in the chrome latch of a stall door? Her mom blamed stress for the flare-ups—the stress of starting college, the stress of her weight gain, the stress of urban life. Amanda, who was an art major, had by now developed a boilerplate response: Alexis needed to get herself to campus health services. "I don't know why you're telling me all this," Amanda said once, exasperated. "I'm not a friggin doctor. I'm not even pre-med."

A sudden gush of pee surprised Alexis. This was weird. She'd just peed a short time ago, when she'd started her layover here in stall #1. Weirder, she wasn't so much squirting it, in the normal way of peeing, as allowing the urine to come bursting out; clenching her bladder had zero effect. And weirder still, the pee kept going forever, going and going and going some more, splashing into the toilet in less of a stream than a slosh, like water dashed from a bucket. Then it diminished to a steady leak, but still, it kept going, leaking and leaking and leaking out of her. (How much freaking Mountain Dew had she *drunk?*) Anyone overhearing this deluge, Alexis thought, would be hard pressed not to comment—the way the girls used to do, during the first few days of dorm acclimation, before word of Alexis's medical condition got around. As if by conjuring, someone entered the bathroom, and as if by plain bad luck another prolonged cramp went rippling through Alexis. She stifled a yelp as the someone appeared as feet beneath the metal door, feet positioned in front of the sinks that faced the stalls. Alexis frowned. Whoever this someone was was wearing new flip-flops, unfamiliar bright orange ones. Alexis knew all twelve girls on her floor by their flipflops, if not all of them by their names. The someone pivoted from the sink, and with a glimpse of the toenails Alexis identified her as Megan from down the hall. Megan painted her toenails in varying pastel colors, like eggs in an Easter basket. Megan disappeared, and then Alexis heard the squeak of the shower handle followed by the *ch-ch-ch-chwah* of the water stuttering out. The shower static filled the bathroom, and Alexis was relieved to be able to breathe again. When she did, however, a horrible dying-old-man groan came rumbling out of her, a sound that felt far beyond her control, as a breaker of nausea rolled through her at the head of a brutal, spasmy cramp, as though the rock had been dumped out of one bend but had just stalled hard in another. She hoped Megan would be showered, dried, and gone by the time the rock wound its way out of her; she sensed this was going to be explosively humiliating.

A new wave of cramps billowed through her, followed by another, and then, to her great alarm, another. They felt connected now, like someone flipping a jump rope inside her. She crunched herself down on the seat, noting the imprint of sweat her forehead deposited on her kneecaps. For an odd while, then, there was nothing, and she wondered if this crunched positioning was the key; she was panting, but the pain was absent, and a flicker of hope sparked inside her. But then another cramp engulfed her and she was thrown back upward, and as another one came fast behind it she bit so hard on her lips that she tasted the metallic tang of her own blood. She tried pushing out the rock with all her might, but it was stuck, the rock was jammed somewhere down in the tangled nest of her intestines. Another cramp struck, this one so vicious that it lifted her pelvis off the toilet seat; her hands went flailing behind her for something to grip. Nausea came, with shaking. She moaned, fear seeping into her now, especially as a new and separate kind of pain, unlike any other she'd ever experienced, gripped the front of her, down at her vee-jay. It was like the rock had made some unfathomably hideous wrong turn. She looked down, and would've gasped had a tortured yowl not overwhelmed her throat. Her labia were spreading around something black and gooey and round. With an ungovernable scream she tried tightening her muscles to suck it back in; the thing vanished, but only for a moment, until another cramp-wave shoved it back out. She reached down a hand to try to push it back inside.

She had to get out of here, she realized. She had to get out now. The shower was still going, Megan presumably soapy beneath it. Totteringly, Alexis rose from the toilet, the automatic flush drowning out her weepy grunts. She could feel it falling from her now, gravity greasing its exit, and her eyes brimmed tears of pain and confusion. She was able to get her sweatpants up but she couldn't close her legs or stand anywhere near upright; her posture was that of someone straddling an imaginary horse. She knew she couldn't scream, not with Megan in the shower, though that was all she wanted right now: to eject this terrible pain from her body in one sustained and lung-emptying shriek. She promised herself that scream just as soon as she was safe in her room, where she could destroy a pillow with it, but until then the scream had to be denied, she had to pretend the pain didn't exist. She could do that, she could. She clicked open the latch and hobbled sideways out of the stall, her legs akimbo, her back hunched, her face distorted with smothered torment. Enough of the girls had seen her go fleeing into the bathroom in a state of writhing pain; maybe seeing her come out that way would seem as natural.

The shower stopped. Hearing Megan blow out a refreshed exhalation, Alexis froze, thinking she should retreat back into the stall to wait her out. But she couldn't retreat: The pain was driving her forward, like kicks from an invisible torturer booting her from behind, along with an uncontrollable urge to just *push*. She wheeled toward the door, the blood from her bitten lip flooding the crevice beneath her bottom teeth, and was just through the wooden door as the contented *thwip-thwap* of Megan's flipflops came echoing from the showers.

Her room was directly across from the bathroom; she'd requested that positioning, owing to the IBS. From down the hall she heard a mixed ruckus of voices—everyone left their doors open at night, as an invitation for passersby to pop in to interrupt their studying—but the hall itself was empty, shimmery from a fluorescent light down the way that was trying, with buzzy struggle, to stay lit. She wambled across the hallway, with her legs spread wider now, her torso pitched lower, feeling the thing pulsing in and out of her as she went. When she got inside her room she collapsed straight to the floor, kicking the door shut behind her, and cupping her bloody lips against the carpet she vented a huge scream into its dirty fibers. She crawled forward, on her hands and knees, to the edge of her bed, but that was as far as she could go; when she tried rising again her body bucked in resistant agony. She tugged down her sweats and panties and kicked them by the door.

She both knew and didn't know what was happening to her. For the last eight months she'd been equipped with two separate and opposed brains, imparting two separate and opposed realities upon her. They'd demanded she choose between them, and, unconsciously, she had chosen, allying herself with the brain whose explanation for what was happening to her body, and her life, was less devastating. This didn't mean the other brain was entirely eclipsed. At the doctor's office with her mom, for instance, its voice had been loud and insistent, and inside that examining room she'd fully expected to have the choice made for her, the irreconcilable realities reconciled. But when the doctor said nothing, when he removed his hands from her abdomen and asked foggily about her IBS meds, the other reality came roaring back: *See?* it said, reassuringly. And then there was Gus's visit, when he'd come to see what Varick life was like, and said to her, "Who knocked *you* up?" She'd gone apeshit on him, goaded by that alternate reality, dismissing him as a "faggot" (which was what the jocks called him, but never ever Alexis, no matter how hard the two of them had fought), and with tears in her eyes she'd fled down the sidewalk from him, later blocking his texts after he wrote, *Srsly. Not a weight joke. WTF?*

Because it couldn't be otherwise. *Couldn't be.* Because, for one thing, she'd been on the pill, though not all that regularly. The pill played havoc with her goddamn IBS—something about hormone absorption and the lower intestine, she'd looked it up online after noting how her symptoms subsided when she was taking the one week of white pills versus the three of blue—so she'd tended to go off it during flare-ups, figuring she had enough residual hormones or whatever to coast through a few days or a week. But, for another—and here was where her mind always seized up, here was the chasm between the one brain and the other—she couldn't say who the father was. Miguel, probably, which was bad enough. But—God. Possibly Chico, his best friend and cousin, whom Alexis hooked up with two days after she discovered Miguel's cheating. It was just to get back at him, that was all. She'd never felt that way before: so *used,* so *disposed* of, so monumentally worthless. Like he'd taken his bite of her, and ditched the rest. The thing with Chico: It was just one half-drunk night, at a party Stacy Friedkin threw when her parents went to Bermuda. Poor Chico, he was such a loser, as awkward and ditzy as Miguel was smooth and connivingly smart. She'd attacked him like a vampire, up in Mr. and Mrs. Friedkin's bedroom—a vampire wanting Miguel's blood, to avenge the bite he'd taken from her with a bite of her own. In his stunned helplessness Chico lasted less than a minute, and putting his jeans back on he muttered something in Spanish that Alexis understood to be pleas for forgiveness from God or his cousin or both. She had expected to feel better afterwards— restored, atoned, *equal.* But instead she felt like death, her worthlessness compounded, and Miguel's cheating almost validated because who would want a girl like herself? Despite all her rehearsals she'd never even told Miguel. She'd just gone on the same way Chico had: like it had never happened.

The two brains were arguing now, waging a last-ditch battle for her consciousness. One ordered her to dial 911, while the other called that insane, an act of certain suicide. But she needed *someone,* she couldn't bear this alone, it was suicide either way. Gus, yes Gus—but not Gus, she'd hurled him from her life and anyway he was the least stable person she knew. In an act of compromise the brains threw up Dave. Dave would understand. Except, no: No one could *understand.* She didn't *understand.* But Dave was good at keeping secrets, Dave knew how to cover things. Plus he was in the city for a dinner meeting somewhere uptown; she knew this because earlier in the day she'd blown off his text about delivering her some jackets or warm clothes or somesuch shit her mom thought she needed. She positioned the phone in front of her as her hips rocked, her body determined to push but her mind objecting, the burning and the bulging bringing more tears to her eyes. *Sick,* she was able to type, sliding the phone up and away from the tears dripping onto the screen. *Need u plz.*

A minute later came his reply: *On my way home. Seriously?*

A contraction forced her head to the carpet and she clamped her eyes shut against it. She wanted to push so badly but she couldn't, wouldn't; she didn't want that thing out of her, it had to stay there until she figured this out. When her body slackened she punched out: *Hlp me.*

By the time the phone rang, with Dave's numerals flashing, she was weeping. She wouldn't have been able to answer it had she wanted to, which she didn't. A text pinged shortly after: *Turning around.* She dropped her head again, letting it hang loosely from her neck, swaying. Texting him was a mistake; he couldn't keep this secret, and therefore couldn't help her. Her *life* was at stake now, every future she'd ever dreamt, every desire she'd ever had was being obliterated by this blackness forcing its way out of her, and the only possible thing he could do was make it all fucking *worse.* Barely able to control her fingers, which were like end points for the pain, shot through with its electricity, she typed *nvrmind.* She knew him. The easy way out was always Dave's preference, and this would be enough for him. The phone rang, Dave again. He'd assume she was stuck in the bathroom, unable to talk. That one of her intestinal tornadoes had just blown its way through her. *Nvrmind:* that she'd finally crapped it out, keep driving.

But the arguing brains, she realized, didn't matter. They weren't in control anymore, and neither was she. She felt another scream gathering in her lungs and grinding her lips into the carpet she redirected it through her nose, a blast of air shooting through her nostrils as from a gas station tire pump. A ribbon of snot slapped her upper lip and she licked it off, mingling it with the blood on her tongue. Her vee-jay felt suddenly ablaze, with the flames spreading back toward her butthole, as though everything down there was melting into a single deformed orifice. Out of instinct she reached a hand beneath her, to try to ease the pain with some kind of adjusting, and she saw droplets of blood on the dorm-room carpet. Abandoning the adjustment, she yanked the duvet off her bed, raising one knee and then the other so that the fluffy, floral-printed duvet was bunched beneath her. Another contraction detonated, and she choked off her guttural scream with the carpet. Then she dragged a corner of the duvet up toward her face, to escape whatever foul graininess the carpet was gluing to her lips. The duvet smelled like the Febreze Amanda was always spraying through the room, and Alexis ground her face into its lavendered plushness as a massive *push* surged through her.

When she lifted her head she could tell something had changed. The fire was out, at least partially. She heard a foamy, sputtering noise, and reaching beneath her again she felt the terrible wholeness of a — oh Christ, a head. It was dangling out of her. "God no please," she moaned. Then the flames returned, even hotter than before, and unable to withstand it she reached underneath the head which swiveled in her palm and as she pushed she felt its knobby edges sliding inside her. Then came a giant fast *squish* as it slid out of her into the soft folds of the duvet.

For a half-moment she felt a torrent of relief — physical relief, as though three hundred pounds of pressure had just been sucked from her body, every one of her cells twitching in grateful astonishment. But then she looked between her knees and saw it there, a blue and gray thing coated with blood and creamy white stuff. For another half-moment she felt another kind of relief: If it was blue, it was dead, or almost dead, and if it was dead then . . . but no: She could see it pinkening, and making bubbly noises as it moved or fell onto its side and jerked its limbs outward. The fact of its life, undeniable and irreparable, ripped a hole of terror through her mind, and to flee it she took two crawl-steps forward. But a squiggly blue cord, swinging out of her like a snake, was linking her to it. She reached back to pull the snake from her but the pain was excruciating; it was caught on something inside her. With a fierce grunt she tried pushing it out, but to no avail; the cord just dangled there, rebuking her, shouting *Look this is yours.* She had to disconnect herself, unlink herself, she had to cut the cord—

Cut the cord. That's where the saying came from. She'd just heard her mom say it the month before, as Alexis packed for college: *cutting the cord.* The umbilical cord. She crawled forward another six inches, more of the cord slithering out of her, until she could reach the desk drawer where Amanda kept her art supplies. She groped inside the drawer, trying to feel for scissors. When that didn't work she wrenched the whole drawer from the desk, and a shower of supplies—paint-tubes and markers and brushes and colored pencils and glues—clattered to the floor. She fumbled through them until she found scissors.

Gingerly but determinedly, she turned herself to a sitting position. It was squalling now, along with the voices in her head, and to them as much as it she murmured *shutupshutupshutup.* To muffle its cries, and to avoid her having to see it, she draped the duvet cover over it, focusing on the cord. It was flaccid now, and whitish blue, a thin rope of slime tethering her to the bump in the duvet. She fixed the scissors on it and squeezed, but the scissors slipped sideways. The cord was too tough, it was like wet rubber, and she let out a mewl of defeat and pulverized sorrow. She lifted the cord between the blades and tried again, sawing at it now, and from it popped a small blister of blood. Then she squeezed with both hands, and with a red spurt the cord fell apart from the scissors. From its end of the cord came a faint trickling; from her end, as she rose to her knees, the swinging cord spattered droplets across the duvet cover's pansies. Her body was heaving again, the cramps re-activating, as she reached down to attempt again to pull the cord from inside her. But it was too slippery; it slid right through her hand. She threaded its bloody end around and between her fingers and pulled again, gently, and as if to aid her her body issued a minor but effective wave, and then another, and she felt something come slithering out of her and land with a viscid splash.

She'd pulled out another it, oh God, another baby: This was her first panicked thought. Then another thought blew in, only slightly less alarming: She'd pulled out her liver. Her fucking *liver!* How else to explain the limp, purplish organ in an oozy puddle on the duvet? She measured her breaths, fully expecting death to claim her at any moment, because she

knew you couldn't survive without a liver, and for a swift and weirdly ecstatic moment she welcomed this end, invited death to strike her, because
her dying meant that none of this mattered, because death would annihi-
late her future the same way life was doing, except without the pain. Then
she looked down, and saw the duvet moving, and heard the bottled-up
cries from inside it. Her heart was still beating; she could feel it, banging
beneath her breasts which had never felt so sore and anxious as now. She
didn't want to be but she was alive.

All that remained was it. If not for it, everything would be okay. If
not for it, all she'd be facing was—a laundry crisis. She leaned back and
surveyed the room, which looked like a murder scene. Stabilizing herself
with the corner of the desk, she rose to her feet, but lightheadedness overwhelmed her, and she dropped her hands to her knees to keep from faint-
ing. She had to get rid of it, she knew. It wasn't healthy, she told herself—
that blueness she'd seen, all that goop. It couldn't survive this—things
like it, they required hospitals, nurses, complicated machines, tubes, heat-
ers, antibiotics. She glanced down at herself, horrified to see the smears of
damp blood painted down her thighs, and the trail of red spatters on her
t-shirt. She slipped off the t-shirt, dumping it first in the laundry hamper
and then, reconsidering, stuffing it into the trash along with her sweats and
underwear. She found she was able to walk, if very unsteadily and against
a turbulent headwind of exhausted soreness, and with drips painting the
carpet with every step she took. Stealing a maxipad from Amanda's stash,
she pulled on fresh undies, fresh sweatpants, a t-shirt, her own flipflops,
tucked her phone into the waistband of her sweats: just like normal. A
wincing glance in the mirror, however, confirmed her fears of how horrid
she looked, the girl she'd once been reconstituted as a monster. With her
bathrobe, hanging from the door, she scrubbed the blood from her chin
and then her hands. Then she turned her attention to the duvet.

Bending down, she unfolded the duvet off of it. As if in response, it let
out a tremendous bawl, a shrill, pinched cry that caused Alexis to swoon,
and almost faint right on top of it. She had to get it off the duvet somehow.
The bathrobe, she thought, yanking it from the door hook. With the bathrobe spread beside it, she rolled it over, and from that one touch alone, or
so it seemed, it went suddenly and expectantly quiet, mewing in anticipation. "I'm sorry," she heard herself saying, in a voice that sounded distant

and not quite hers, echoing up from the dark bottom of that gulf dividing the two brains. She wrapped the other side of the bathrobe around it, noting as she did the strange slack hose jutting from its middle, which looked inhuman, an alien appendage. She tucked in the loose ends to make a kind of white terrycloth bundle which she lifted onto the bed.

The duvet was a sick mess, its pansies splotched with blood and other mysterious fluids. No way was it going into the trash can, a small bin already overflowing with her stained clothes. Amanda had some giant silvery trash bags, Alexis remembered, that she used for wrapping big canvases when walking them over to Sullivan Hall in the rain. She stuffed the duvet into one of the bags, and then fetched her clothes from the bin and added them to the bag too. She was breathing hard now, like she'd been running, and was startled to find her cheeks soaked; she hadn't known she was crying. She held the open bag while staring at the bed, wiping her face with the back of her hand. A thought flashed, then was immediately expunged. She dragged the bag to her closet and crammed it inside, and by pressing the weight of her back against the closet door she was able to snap it shut. She was almost okay, she told herself, as she hobbled toward the bed, and with a grimace gathered up the bundle. She was almost okay.

She didn't know the time. Midnight, one, maybe later. She took the emergency stairs, the elevator not even a consideration, easing herself down by sliding her left hand down the rail while her right hand secured the terrycloth bundle to her chest. It wasn't crying so much now, not like before. The students weren't supposed to know the security code for the back service door but everyone did; that's how they sneaked their hookups and/or boyfriends in and out. Though she'd never used the service door herself, Alexis had heard the code relayed in hushed conspiratorial tones, seen its four digits slyly enumerated in grin-backed sign language. She plugged in the code, and pushing through the door she emerged into the dark service alley.

Outside the night was warm, even balmy, and for the city it seemed unusually quiet. She fell back against the wall beside the door, beneath the dirty yellow glow of the security light which unlike the lights back home was unbombarded with insects, paid no attention by the world. She stayed like that for as long as she could, or until a tiny crinkled fist poked its way out of the bundle. She bent it back inside, and tucked the bundle tighter. A hospital, she thought. Or a church. Either one would accept it, right? But then who'd be at a church at this time of night, and at a hospital—surely they wouldn't just let her drop off a baby. Not without a blitz of questioning. She could say she found it, and run—except no, she couldn't run in her condition. She could barely walk. Maybe—maybe *near* a hospital, against the wall by the Emergency Room door, where surely someone would hear it, surely someone smoking outside would be drawn to it, peek inside . . . she pulled out her cellphone, thinking she could use it to find the nearest hospital, and it vibrated in her hand. She answered it out of instinct, or maybe confidence, imagining this would all be over soon.

"I'm just parking," Dave said. "Where are you?"

She couldn't think, couldn't speak: "I'm—I'm—"

"Lexi?"

"I'm okay," she said weakly. On the final syllable, the fist appeared again, and throwing off its terrycloth cloak the baby let out a full-throated cry of protest.

"What's that?"

"What?" Covering the baby again, squeezing it close to her to try to stifle its wailing, the phone squashed between her ear and shoulder, impossible to disconnect.

"That baby." The word itself was like a key, opening some kind of lockbox in Dave's mind where all the clues had been sequestered, the suspicions discarded, the incomprehensible what-ifs abandoned. She could almost hear the clack of his thoughts behind his dazed, heightened breathing. "Oh Christ. Oh Jesus of course. Lexi where are you? Lexi don't hang up just—"

She snatched the phone from her cheek and pressed END. Almost immediately it came alive again, glowing and shuddering, and she slipped it into her waistband and let it quiver madly against her hip. "Fuckfuckfuck," she said, because she'd been so *so* close, so fucking close to putting her future back together again, rebuilding it from all these shattered bloodstained pieces, but in a moment of fear and weakness she'd cried out for help, when she didn't *need* help, when if she'd just waited—she cursed herself again, and in mining her body for strength she latched onto a vision of her father, whose desire for success she'd inherited along with his eyes and crooked grin, whose spectacular ambition had put him at his desk at the

World Trade Center that horrible blue morning, which was the thing her
mother still hated him for, refused to forgive him for, was the reason she
refused to speak his name even all these years later. Nothing got in his way;
that's what everyone said about him. Uncle Robert most of all, he'd said it
a hundred times: "Your dad never let *nuthin* ever stand in his way."

The hospital plan wouldn't work now. She'd blown that by answering
the phone. Dave was somewhere close, possibly at the Westervelt Hall Residence stand, ordering an RA to bust open her room. She had to get rid of
it fast. She twirled her head, desperate for someone to just — to just hand
it off to, and flee. But there was no one in the dim yellow-black service alley. No one but her.

Her gaze fell against a row of dumpsters down the alleyway. There were
three of them, two green, one black, the black one's door propped open.
Then she startled at a noise, and thinking someone — thinking Dave —
was entering the alley she flung herself back against the wall in a lame attempt at hiding, hating that lifeless security light now, its empty bugless
glow. She slid sideways against the wall, in the direction of the dumpsters,
and then started walking, tender and hesitant steps that drew her closer
and closer to the open dumpster and farther and farther out of the light.
There was a kind of solace in the darkening, as though invisibility equaled
nonexistence and nonexistence equaled absolution. This was all she had to
do, she heard a voice telling her (a voice hers but not hers), and everything
could be okay again. She could talk Dave out of his panicked conclusions,
she wasn't sure how but somehow. Guys were easy, as Chico had affirmed.
Guys heard what they wanted to hear. This one small . . . act, which no
one besides her would ever know about. Especially not her father, who
she knew wasn't in heaven because the men who'd killed him thought they
were going to heaven, and that irreconcilable divide had for her negated
the idea of heaven. Almost to the dumpster she stopped, deaf to everything
beyond the drumming of her heart, which was thrashing against her ribs in
mutiny, as if wanting to escape her chest for another one, and for that she
didn't blame it. She understood it. Her heart didn't want her and neither
did this baby; maybe no one ever would. Her formerly opposed realities
had merged, in the incontrovertible fact inside the terrycloth bundle, but
now a new split cleaved her mind: between what was and what could be.
She was at the dumpster now, peering at its gnarled steel rim as though she

were staring off the edge of a cliff. What was unclear to her was whether leaping was suicide, or staying put was.

Now came another noise, just like before, but this one so close to her that she staggered backwards and against her will let out an ambushed yelp. From inside the dumpster a head popped up, and, pounded with terror, Alexis tried to run. But she couldn't run. Her pelvis felt smashed, and her abdominal muscles were still scorched and smoldering. She tripped down onto one knee, almost dropping the bundle, but the knee wouldn't hold, it buckled under her weight and she felt herself tipping forward. She yelped again, and rotating herself in the air was able to hit the ground on her back, the bundle bouncing securely against her chest, her arm tight around it. She rolled herself over, but couldn't stand with the bundle weighing her down, and so instead she crawled away, one hand on the ground, grinding her knees into the pebbly asphalt, glancing only once behind her to see what was coming for her: a monster from the dumpster's belly; an assailant, a rapist who'd been biding his time outside the dorm; Dave, hunting down her secret; her own writhing conscience; all of these, attacking her at once. She tried crawling more, but couldn't go on, paralyzed by a horror that was coming at her from the inside as well as the out.

"Sorry," said a voice, with a weird and exotic melody to it. The voice was climbing out of the dumpster now, and coming toward her. Alexis was too scared to raise her head. What she saw were the creature's feet, just like in the dorm, where she knew everyone by their feet. These feet were inside ratty Birkenstocks, hippie shoes, with rainbow-striped socks extending into the swirls of an ankle-length dress. She tilted her head up, blinking. She saw a woman towering over her, with dreadlocks, and a silver stud in her nose that was glinting in the distant glow of the security light. On the woman's face was a sad and bewildered expression, but a gentleness too, blunting Alexis's fright. The woman said, "I didn't mean to scare you."

Micah stared down at this strange and collapsed girl wearing what looked like pajamas, and trembling like she'd seen a haint. Her eyes were puffed and her face was smeary, like she'd been crying hard, and her lips were seeping blood from several cuts. She was gripping a bathrobe (Micah could tell it was a bathrobe from the terrycloth belt dangling down) like her whole life was inside it, her hand shaking against the fabric. She wondered if the girl had just been beaten, and dropping down to one knee she asked her, "Are you all right?"

You awl right? Alexis nodded, whispered yes. But the baby flailed again, throwing off its covering and bawling a long and infuriated scream, as though whatever patience it had was exhausted now. Alexis fumbled the robe back over it, and again tried to rise, to rise up and run, but the bundle wrecked her balance; she couldn't get up.

"That's a baby," Micah whispered, and stepped forward with an out-stretched hand. "That baby's—newborn. Is that your baby?"

"No," Alexis said, in a sharp threatened tone, but whatever power her voice carried immediately dissolved: "No," she quivered. "No, it's not mine, it's not."

"Here," Micah offered. She could tell the girl was traumatized, reeling, unfocused. "Hand it to me so I can help you up."

Alexis didn't hesitate, but her body did; her arms resisted the handover, and she had to will her hands off the robe. She watched as the woman unfolded the flaps of the robe and broke into a wide, awestruck, and (to Alexis) unseemly smile, an expression of joy being the least imaginable response at this moment, the most inapt emotion possible. In fact it made the woman appear insane: How could she smile right now? Scrunching a robe flap in her hand, the woman brushed the baby lightly, cleaning it, and the baby cried even harder now, giant howls of discontentment that drew a laugh from the woman, another insane reaction. She told the baby *shhhhh.* "She's a little girl," she said to Alexis, with a look of amazement that this time didn't strike Alexis as insane.

Because Alexis herself hadn't noted that essential detail, she realized. It had just been it. Not her: it. She'd seen without seeing, and something about this revelation crushed her with a pain worse than the pain of delivery had been, a deathblow of comprehension that drove her back toward the asphalt, all the feuding voices in her head going abruptly silent at the revealing of this one obvious and essential detail. Alexis thought she might vomit, but retched out only a sob.

"She's yours, isn't she?" Micah said, waiting for the answer. When the girl finally lifted her head it was clear in her eyes.

"No," the girl pleaded.

"What were you . . ." But Micah knew the answer to this, too. The baby was just minutes old, and with its drying crust of amniotic fluid Micah knew the baby hadn't been delivered by a doctor, or a midwife, or by anyone else but the girl herself. And the girl was at the dumpster, where Micah had been scrounging for a change of clothes. The college dumpsters were always good for those, and Micah had nothing but the clothes she was wearing. But she had to ask anyway; she needed to hear the answer. "What were you gonna do with her?"

Alexis felt the answer lodged inside her throat, choking her. It wasn't a complicated or even satisfactory answer: She didn't know. That was the answer. She'd been standing at a cliff, without knowing what the cliff meant. But she couldn't say anything now, not even the empty-sounding truth, and for sure not the darker truth lurking behind it, the truth that was too heavy and unwieldy for her mind to carry: the truth of the skewed desires that'd led her here, desires she recognized now as unsayable, flimsy, plastic, chintzy, knocked-off, dead. "Help me up," she begged, and the woman extended a hand. Alexis took it, uncrumpling herself skyward.

"She's yours," Micah said, but it wasn't a question now. It was a statement, a command.

"No," Alexis moaned, and backing away she wagged her head and repeated it, her cheeks streamed with tears. Frightened by the woman's tone, and by the prospect of the woman forcing the baby back into her arms, Alexis spun around and tripped feebly to the service door, where she glanced back once before tapping the keypad beside the door. It didn't work. Her sight blurry from the tears, she entered the code again, but again it failed. She flustered, then remembered: The outside code was different from the inside code. Amanda's boyfriend had attempted the same trick. She looked back one more time, to where the woman was gaping at the baby, the baby's fists flailing just beneath the woman's jaw, and then floundered down the alley, in a drained and feverish welter, to where an open chainlink gate led to the street.

On the other side of the chainlink she squinted at the freakish and dizzying spectacle: streetlights and taxis and motorcycles and shifting herds of people roaming the sidewalks as if nothing had ever happened, not to her or to them. It overwhelmed her, and she fell back against the chainlink, threading her fingers into the aluminum lattice to keep from collapsing, and with a vexed metal clatter the fence bowed and recoiled against her back. Like insects to a lightbulb, people came buzzing toward her, first a hand-holding couple, a decade or so her senior, and then a lone girl her own age, wearing strange and witchy-looking round eyeglasses, who stood off to the side, gawking. She heard one of them ask if she was okay, heard her ask if there was someone they could call. Alexis felt her cellphone vibrating; it had been vibrating the whole time, which she only realized when she lifted out the phone to give it to someone, and her hip ceased quavering. She heard coordinates being given; she heard herself described as "not so good."

The streetlights were bending down now, the taxis rising like airplanes off a runway, the people's heads inflating and deflating except for that of the girl in the evil round glasses, who just stared in pale fury, knowing everything. Then she felt herself in Dave's arms, though for a moment she didn't know they were Dave's. Slumping into the safety of his chest, she was seven years old again, and wrapped in her father's arms as he went loping and shuffling around the living room to the mangled beat of his own a cappella, Long Island Irish-brogue rendition of "Thunder Road," the greatest moment of her life intruding now on the worst. "It's all gonna be all right but you gotta come clean, okay?" she heard Dave saying, and didn't nod so much as throw her head back and forth, still dancing through a memory.

"You're pregnant, aren't you?" he said, and when she nodded again Dave felt the bottom drop out of something, and maybe everything.

"Did you—" It was unthinkable, but he'd heard the cry. "You had the baby?"

Another nod, more unfocused than the others. He was losing her now. "Where's the baby, Alexis?"

Her head wobbled, her lips fell open without sound.

Dave pushed her back against the chainlink, so hard that her body sank into the fence and charged back at him limply. The couple who'd spoken to him—the woman had—was still standing there, along with the other girl, and seeing this the guy intervened tentatively, saying, "Hey, whoa man, easy," and placing a hand on Dave's shoulder which Dave furiously shrugged off.

"Where's the baby, Alexis?" he asked again, his voice choppy and strangled, and he shook her by her shoulders to eject an answer. He felt something filling him, not adrenaline but something thicker and more complex, a molten surge of emotion and comprehending that he sensed might drown him. A volley of what-ifs went bubbling through him, and with them came an understanding that this was his sin, too, if not in commission than in something more vague and amorphous but no less damning. He'd never visualized or even considered human consequences before—something so obvious in abstraction but foreign to his daily life, where what mattered was him, what mattered was more, what mattered was what he said mattered—and now here were those consequences, in stark and condemnatory relief; and filed directly behind this sin, he knew, were hundreds or thousands of other sins, a witheringly long line of human debts long out of statute but due just the same. All this went flushing through his mind in scarcely a millisecond, in an electrical impulse of black awareness; only later, in a hospital waiting room, as the emergency-room technicians pored over Alexis and the cops jotted notes and Sara texted updates of her grim 3 A.M. progress across New Jersey on I-280, would he translate that shock of awareness into words, would he feel his myriad lusts curdling within him. Right now, however, he just needed the baby. "The baby," he growled at her, yearning to pry open her drooping, bulged eyelids so that she'd look him in the eyes. "Where's the baby?"

"A woman," was all she could say, flopping her thumb back in the direction of the alleyway. "Over by the dumpster. I gave it to her. I gave her to her."

Dave flung her aside to open the gate, and then took off running down the dim alleyway. He jogged to a stop at the dumpsters, sticking his head into the open one but seeing only big bags of trash overlaid with a banjo someone had thrown out; the other dumpsters were locked. He called out, "Hello?" The respondent silence made him feel stupid and powerless. He flung himself farther down the alleyway, to where it joined the sidewalk, and dashed right into the center of the street to search both sidewalks. A taxi came to a lurching overwrought stop in front of him, the driver throwing his arm out the window in the standard irritated manner. Dave ignored him, twirling on the pavement as he scanned the block, but this was a campus side street, anchored by the Richard Varick College bookstore which was dark and vacant, and the only people on the block were three lonesome-looking young men walking off their midnight cravings, their hands uniformly hidden in their pockets. He ran to the corner, the taxi driver issuing an appreciative note of "Fuck you, crazyguy" as he squealed the tires. Dave didn't even know what street he was on; the streets were crazy in this part of downtown, all squashed and nowhere-leading. He ran one way, not even knowing what precisely he was searching for: woman, baby. He realized he was looking for a woman pushing a stroller, and the desolate ridiculousness of this brought him to an impotent standstill. He went hurtling into a park—what park was this? where was he?—but the park was empty, just a bleak gray statue ringed by a copse of trees whose sagging black-leafed boughs gave the impression of the dark forests of gloomy fairy tales, the places children ventured to be cooked and eaten. He jogged through the park, almost afraid for his own safety now, but one side looked like the other, and he circled back around it. At one corner of the park a homeless old man was sprawled on the sidewalk beside a cardboard sign advertising his destitution. Out of breath, Dave asked, "A woman . . ." But before he could draw the air to finish his question the old man cackled and proclaimed, "We all got our wants, friend-sir, we all got our wants."

By this time, Micah was already at the twenty-four-hour Duane Reade drugstore near Times Square, just two blocks south of the Port Authority Bus Terminal, hushing the baby as she unpacked an overloaded blue basket onto the counter—bottles, nipples, formula, four blankets, disposable diapers, flushable wipes, diaper-rash cream, and pacifiers, along with two cheap school backpacks, identically decorated with SpongeBob SquarePants, for carrying it all—and then fetched the envelope out of her bag, plucking two hundred-dollar bills from it. The young speechless cashier—who would later say, under police questioning, that he had no memory of the woman on the surveillance video—ignored her completely, passing back her change while idly monitoring a pair of drunk tourists who for their own soused reasons were trying on sunglasses in the middle of the night.

At the Greyhound desk at the Port Authority she peeled off another hundred, for a one-way bus ticket to Johnson City, Tennessee; she was just in time for the 3:45 A.M. departure to Richmond, Virginia, where eight hours later she would transfer for Johnson City. As the bus rolled out of the city, swiftly through the Lincoln Tunnel and then out onto the New Jersey Turnpike, Micah ran a fingertip softly across the baby's cheek as the baby suckled a bottle, whispering, "So hungry, little one," and skimming the lightest paintbrush of a kiss onto her dark forehead. With the baby on her shoulder Micah congratulated her for a burp, then cradled her against her chest and draped her with two blankets, the baby drifting effortlessly off to sleep, soothed by the diesel thrum of the bus engine and the lullaby being sung to her by the giant, southward-spinning tires.

Micah peered out the window, New Jersey passing by in a Turnpike blur of tollbooths and scrolled iron bridges and all-night refinery flames burning sacredly in the low distance near smokestack ruins and the enormous, mantis-like gantries of the industrial ports, her reflection superimposed upon all this, her eyes sometimes watching her eyes as the hours slid by and New Jersey turned briefly into Delaware and then became Maryland, and dawn fuzzed the horizon. Soon they'd be home, Micah and the girl. She could almost smell it approaching, beckoning her onward: the caramel scent of freshly split pignut hickory, the wintry char-smell of woodsmoke haze, and out in the woods the springtime onion-odor of wild leeks giving way to summer's grape-soda perfume of mountain laurel along with the musty, vibrant, fern-rot funk of the stream bank, beside the water's distilled silver chill, where as a little girl she'd lured a trusting fawn within six feet of her, a record her father called unchallenged in the history of mankind. She watched her reflection dissipating in the blooming sunlight. What John Rye had done wrong, Micah would do right. And what John Rye had done right, she would do better. This was all the remaking of the world she could do, for now. The tiny sleeping girl in her arms, she thought, could dream the rest.

7

THE CALL CAME to Elwin after he'd just unburdened himself of the very last of his Craigslist offerings: the remaining venison in his deep-freeze. He'd posted the ad as a lark, a tongue-in-cheek farewell to his Craigslist odyssey, never for a moment expecting a response. "Ten-month-old roadkilled venison, frozen. About 20 lbs. left, predominantly roasts. Competently butchered (I hit it myself), packaged, and sealed. Have eaten plenty of it myself, with no ill effects, but it's not on the new diet and frankly I'm tired of it. Free to first taker. Serious inquiries only. (Ha!)" Within four hours he'd received a dozen inquiries, at least half of them serious or at least convincingly deadpan. The first claimants turned out to be a pair of unsmiling brothers from Morristown by way of Honduras, and they came to pick it up on a Monday evening, saying little as they mined the meat from the bottom of the deep-freeze and dumped the brown, frost-gilded parcels into recycled plastic ShopRite bags. Elwin shook his head in droll bewilderment as he watched them drive away, then immediately called Christopher.

Christopher had his own place now, an efficiency apartment in a complex over by the mall. The apartment was within theoretical walking distance of the AutoZone where after just three weeks Christopher had been promoted from customer-service rep to parts sales manager. The store manager liked Christopher parking the Jeep out front, instead of behind the store where the other employees parked, on the grounds that the Jeep was good advertising. A girlfriend was also said to be in the picture, though

Elwin hadn't met her. Kelly at the bar said she was "nice enough," dropping her voice a notch, however, when noting she didn't take her gum out when she drank beer. This struck Elwin as an entirely forgivable flaw, and from Kelly's wounded tone he surmised, improbably, that Kelly had something of a crush on Christopher. Stranger things had happened.

"You'll never believe this," Elwin said to him. "Someone took the deer meat."

"You really posted that? I thought you were shittin me."

"I did," Elwin said, and pricked by Christopher's incredulity he added, "I mean, there wasn't anything wrong with it . . ."

"Punk, Doc. Super punk." An interjecting series of beeps from Elwin's phone clipped off the rest: "That's—whole new—punk."

"Hold on, Chris, there's another call coming in. Okay?"

Happily, confidently, Christopher said, "I got nowhere to go."

On Elwin's other line was the director of the Roth Residence. Elwin's father was dead. "He went peacefully, during a nap," the director said. The voice was consoling but robotic, the inflections corroded by over-routine. "We think his heart just stopped."

Elwin said, "I'll be there in an hour."

"There's no rush . . ." the director said.

En route to the city he called his sister Jane, whose audible tears came as a surprise to him. He didn't think he'd heard her cry since the time she'd come in third, despite being heavily favored to win, in the five-hundred-yard freestyle at the Greater Essex Conference Championship; his impression, from having observed her through two divorces, financial semi-ruin, and the death of their mother, was that she'd given up competitive swimming and crying on the very same day. He certainly didn't expect this particular loss to break that streak, considering the peculiar grudge she'd been holding against their father for all these years, but there she was, honking exotic sobs into the phone, then briefly collecting herself before smithereening into sobs all over again. His call reached her in St. Lucia, where she was vacationing with husband number three, the anesthesiologist, and for some reason—perhaps the strange imbalance he felt on the line, with Jane reduced to tears by precisely the same loss dry-eyed Elwin was suffering—he apologized to her for ruining her vacation. "Oh El," she said warmly, "don't be such an ass." Jane volunteered to tell their brother

David, wondering aloud if the number she had for him in China would actually ring all the way over there. "Well, it's supposed to," Elwin said carefully, chalking up the ditziness to her unfamiliar emotional state. This led them into a reminiscence about the time as children they'd tried digging to China through the backyard, all three of them, unearthing a hole deep enough to swallow David whole, and how in discouraging their expedition their mother had cited the earth's volcanic core while their father had urged them ever downward. Elwin remembered it oppositely—their mother had been the lover of digging, their father the lover of fact—and this, coupled with the warbly timbre of Jane's voice, suggested to Elwin that it might be cocktail hour in St. Lucia. He reconsidered Jane's tears in light of this, though not uncharitably, his only conclusion being that Jane would always be a mystery to him, as perhaps he was to her.

Next he called Sharon, and reaching her voicemail instead he found himself stammering, because calling her in the first place was a bit odd, and to leave her a message about his father's death odder still. So instead he claimed to be calling about the Waste Markers project, which was a less-than-sturdy lie since their work on that was all but complete, their report on its way to a government printing office. Two months after the flirty languor of the shore trip, their chumminess—he was beginning to loathe this word but had yet to find a replacement candidate—had developed a pressurized edge, awaiting one or the other to address it. The poor but persistent analogy that came to Elwin's mind was a Saran Wrap–covered bowl of leftovers heating in a microwave, with the plastic ballooning dangerously from steam; if you didn't vent the Saran Wrap, you got a messy microwave. The closest they'd come to venting it, he supposed, was while drinking away the aftershocks of the Markers panel's most rancorous day, when Sharon grasped Elwin's hand across the table in a gesture of sympathy for the point he was making. The touch had stalled them both, because it felt so powerfully conjugal, almost fated, and they'd let out synchronized sighs while gaping dumbly at their enjoined hands. "We're such old goobers," Sharon finally said. "Let's just let what happens happen, right?"

This had come at the end of a rough three days, when the panel met in San Francisco to draft its final recommendations. Elwin had stayed to the side of the debates on what they called physical messaging—how to use architecture to scare future generations away from the sixteen-square-mile radioactive site. One doomed but popular idea was to construct a "land-scape of thorns": sixty-foot concrete spires jutting from the desert at ran-domly jagged angles, with sharply tapered branches, to evoke a 240-acre briar patch. Cost projections, however, killed that one, along with the odds-making of how a proposal like that would fare in Congress—even its fiercest proponents could envision the concrete thorns showing up in negative campaign ads, the perfect visual for wasteful government boon-doggles. The consensus idea was to propose massive earthen berms, like river levees, surrounding an assortment of twenty-five-foot granite mono-liths which the materials scientist Carrollton assured them wouldn't be as cryptically Stonehenge-ish as they sounded. Engraved upon those mono-liths would be a varying series of warning messages, which was where El-win—and the rancor—had come in.

Byron Torrance's side was lobbying for a strong language component, language being in their estimation the most unambiguous form of commu-nication. You could blame Elwin's thirty-plus years of studying language death for his resistance (as the Torrancians did), but Elwin found this po-sition almost criminally naive. Of the seven languages they proposed for engraving the warning message, one (Navajo) was already endangered, and the others—Arabic, English, Spanish, Chinese, Russian, and French, the six primary languages of the United Nations—were, by his projections, unlikely to survive another five hundred years in anything close to their current states. His counter-proposal: a warning message based upon pic-tograms, which he'd sketched out for the panel (cartoon figures fleeing the site in horror, corpses, mayhem, a version of Munch's *The Scream* that Sharon unhelpfully noted had a closer resemblance to the kid from the "Home Alone" movies). He'd gone so far as to fish out from the surviv-ing boxes in his basement his childhood cache of "Henry" comic books, and passing them out to the panelists he stressed how comprehensible and entertaining they were, despite their absence of words, or language of any kind. Einstein, Elwin reminded them, didn't think in words or numer-als—rather in images, which he then translated into words. And the oldest enduring communications, he noted, were Paleolithic-era cave paintings, which when you got down to it weren't so very different from "Henry."

"But knowing what a cave painting depicts isn't the same as under-standing the message it's conveying," Torrance shot back. "That's the real trick. Infinite clarity. Take a stick figure holding a spear, painted beside a bear. What's the message? Lots of bears here, good eating? Or instead: Watch out, hungry bears here, make sure you're armed? Or maybe no message." He nodded toward Sharon, as if to joggle her well-known alliance with Elwin. "Art for art's sake. The painter working out a dream he'd had about killing a bear. Understanding what it is doesn't mean we understand what it says. Especially when you factor in all the elements we can't decipher — the handprints at the Chauvet caves, good example."

"Interpretation of imagery can be ambiguous," Elwin granted. "But if conveyed in a dead script, there *isn't* any interpretation."

Torrance wagged his head, sliding away the issue of "Henry" unopened before him. "We can't base deep-time communication on a comic book."

"And we also can't send the equivalent of the Voynich Manuscript into deep time," Elwin blurted back. A low mumble circled the table, and Sharon leaned in with an inquisitively raised finger. "A fifteenth-century codex," Elwin explained. "Written in an unknown language that no one has ever been able to decipher. Not even World War II codebreakers. Definitely not linguists." Shooting a dark glance toward Torrance, he added, "A lot of scholars suspect it's a hoax. Which I'd call our worst-worst-case scenario."

Torrance twirled a pencil through his fingers, impatiently flexing his jaw. "So it comes down to your sense of futility versus ours," he said, but before Elwin could respond the panel's legal expert (surely a middle child) chimed, "I'd call that a good argument for redundancy." Torrance disagreed, however, and so did the others. There would be minimal images: primarily the trefoil radiation symbol, which struck Elwin as as useless an image as the biohazard symbol in his father's bathroom at the nursing home. It was like attempting to communicate with a newly discovered Amazonian tribe via naval signal flags. The panel also voted to add translations of the warning in several more Native American languages as a compensatory gesture for secreting a quarter-million barrels of toxic waste beneath sacred tribal grounds. Elwin might have just as well stayed home.

"You're really wadded up about all this, aren't you?" Sharon said later, at the bar of their Mason Street hotel.

"Am I?" Elwin said. "Maybe I am. I don't know. It's just the *arrogance* of it. This idea that there will always be more. That civilization won't ever stop growing, won't ever emerge from puberty. That the arc of human history has to swing upward—"

"It's a *preliminary* report on a *proposal*," Sharon cut in, flexing her jaw with impatience the same way Torrance had. "For a project that won't be implemented until 2030 at the earliest, and probably won't be implemented at all if the Republicans have their say in it."

"But—"

"For a waste dump, El. For a garbage dump."

Absorbing this like a slow poison, he said weakly, "For the only epitaph we're likely to leave on this goddamn planet."

She stared at him in a peculiar, head-tilted way, as if noting something new about him, an unplayed B-side. "This isn't *your* epitaph, El," she said, and that's when her hand came down onto his, with the weight of not merely affection but some heavier, warmer element, too. Fate, love, mercy: one of the dense nouns, the ones into which we stuff all the mysteries of existence. With a strange palpable swiftness Elwin felt the future narrowing, the deep-time horizon shrinking back so that all he could spy of the future was its foreground: the next hour, or maybe the next week or month or year, or perhaps, if he squinted out toward the furthest point, the one, two, three decades remaining in the life of Elwin Cross Jr. But nothing more. "Let's just let what happens happen, right?" he heard Sharon saying, and he latched onto a liberating tone in that otherwise empty-sounding notion, the dissonant bliss of surrender: *let it be,* like the song said. Because what was going to happen, *would* happen. Languages would die, despite Elwin's efforts at triage. His father would die. He himself would die. Civilization as we understood it would die. And had he gotten his way, in five or ten thousand years someone—human, cyborg, extraterrestrial—might have come upon his granite comic book of horror and wondered, perhaps, why anyone would've thought it mattered, why anyone might've cared. We came, we saw, we trashed. One futility versus another.

And now, Monday evening, the on-ramp to I-78 looming just past the next red light: Now it *was* happening. His father had died. The expectedness of this event—moving a parent into a nursing home is nothing if not an act of anticipation—somehow didn't blunt the sorrow of it. Loose tears didn't flow, as they had for Jane, but instead there came to him a tightening sense of gloom, of a finality that can't be felt in advance, no matter the

forecast, no matter the certitude. Out of bridge-and-tunnel instinct he dialed in the traffic report on the radio in his new car—he'd bought a brand-
new Ford hybrid, despite Christopher's bilingual objection that it lacked
"cojones"—but flicked it off just as fast, realizing that the traffic didn't really matter. His route was his route. Plus, as the director said, there wasn't
any rush. Slowness, in fact, felt like a virtue. This would be his last drive
down to Henry Street, and he almost wanted to savor it—not because it
was enjoyable but because the drive had become a component of his relationship with his father, an act of devotion that doubled as a means of as-
suaging his guilt for having interred his father in that human junkyard, in
that scrap heap of obsolete ancestors. He watched the familiar sights sliding by—the merkin of suburban leafiness giving way to the obscure and
dilapidated factories on the outskirts of Newark, the salt domes, the billboards he'd read a thousand times, the heat-wobbled air above the smoke-
stacks, Manhattan appearing as a serrated grayness on the horizon—as his
car was funneled into all that teeming metal hurtling eastward on I-78 and
then the Pulaski Skyway, the toxic green swirls of the Meadowlands roiling
far below him. When Sharon called him back he told her about his father,
and she told him to be strong. "I'm there with you, El," she said, and he
drew solace from the idea: that amidst all these thousands of people gliding
beside him, someone was with him, even invisibly, even merely as a sympa-
thetic cliché.

At the Roth Residence, Boolah led Elwin into his father's room. "I'm
real sorry," Boolah said, with a genuineness that had eluded his boss. "I'm
gonna miss your dad. He was a real pain in the ass. You just holler if you
need anything."

Elwin sat down on the edge of the bed, inhaling the same scents his father had awakened to every day: the wafting antiseptic sourness, the fake-
floral reek of prescription moisturizing creams, soiled undergarments fermenting in big blue plastic bins. He wanted to think of his father as he had
been before all this, out of filial loyalty, but it was impossible. Broken by
the Alzheimer's disease into the *before* and the *after,* they were like two different people, related but separate. The before-father he'd already lost, at
least partly; this loss, of the after-father, felt like a physical disappearance
trailing years behind the dwindling of his essence, as though the mind had
finally claimed the body too. Yearning for a moment of what Jane would

call closure, even forced closure, Elwin recalled his father's oft-stated ambition, cribbed from Jonas Salk: to be a good ancestor. "You were," he said aloud to the room. The room said nothing in return, certainly no indication that Elwin was a good descendant. The man who'd consecrated his life to the study of the past, Elwin thought, had bequeathed just one thing to the future: his children. Jane, Elwin, and David: These were his sole attempts at deep-time communication.

Elwin didn't know where to start. He'd brought bags with him, and there were cardboard boxes in the trunk if he needed them. He picked his father's eyeglasses off the nightstand and mindlessly wiped the oily smears from their lenses with his shirttail. The eyeglasses had been resting atop one of the leather-bound notebooks his father'd always favored—demanded, really—for his writing. One of his many stubborn quirks. He refused to write in anything else, and a year ago, when Elwin discovered the company that made them was fading into bankruptcy, Elwin had bought an entire case of them. The unopened case was still in his basement, and though he'd briefly considered posting it for sale on Craigslist, too, he'd held off. He'd never shaken the dumb hope, he supposed, that his father would find some secret back exit out of the diagnosis, would refute all the clinical forecasts, and fill every one of those notebooks with his hyperactive pen-scrawl—the hope Jane was always upbraiding him for. He brought the notebook to his lap, and opening it to the first page he began to read.

Hopes aside, on some pragmatic level he knew that Jane had always been right: that writing and dementia could not coexist. He girded himself for the comeuppance of gibberish. Yet he frowned, seeing something else. His father's penmanship, true, evinced terrible effort—Elwin could see the hesitations riddling the script, the spaces between the letters suggesting that words had been started but forgotten midway through, then pieced back together again—but the thoughts expressed were lucid, if sometimes repetitive. *Often* repetitive, he admitted to himself, flipping forward and then back, trying to make sense of what he was reading. Not that it was nonsensical; it wasn't. He skimmed a long and fluid analysis of the Peloponnesian War that any historian would claim with pride. What didn't make sense, to Elwin, was that his father had written it.

With the notebook in hand he moved to the chair, where he'd spent so many hours sitting by his father while the old man kvetched and bewailed.

He knew the book was intended to be a treatise on genocide—they'd talked about the book, he and his father, and the subject after all was his father's historiographic specialty—but Elwin wasn't prepared for his father's radically grim thesis, for his intimate tone, for the almost biblical pronouncements it contained. *Genocide, defined as the systematic and deliberate annihilation of specific groups or classes of people, is not incidental to the history of civilization,* he read. *It is in fact a <u>function</u> of civilization, in that civilization developed as a means of resource control, and the most effective control of resources lies in broadening resource availability while limiting resource consumption and therefore depletion.* Elwin reread those sentences, to ensure he was understanding them correctly. *Genocide was less an anomalous tool than a necessary component, sewn into the fabric of the earliest proto-agrarian societies. Its history demonstrates that it cannot be viewed as a reaction, aberrant or otherwise, to external factors, nor can it be seen as a unique and uniquely contemporaneous perversion of civilization. If we unlock genocide from its semantic restraints, as I will do in the pages that follow, we can clearly see that it has occurred, in one part of the globe or another, and in varying scope and intensity, on nearly every day of recorded history. It <u>is</u> civilization. If you are reading these words it is part of you, as it is, painfully, part of me.*

Elwin looked up in confusion. He'd never heard his father express or even allude to thoughts like these, nor had his father ever injected the personal into his writings. Even the acknowledgments in his previous books were written in the third person ("the author wishes to thank . . ."). Even the *birthday cards* he wrote were like that: "Your father wishes you a happy 12th birthday." As for his father's thesis, it seemed slightly deranged—demented, even—and for a moment Elwin wondered if his father hadn't struck back at his Alzheimer's-destroyed neurons by slapping civilization with a fatal diagnosis of its own. Except that, reading farther, Elwin found himself nodding at the arguments, his nodding bolstered by his thirty-plus years of watching the world's languages and thus its human heterogeneity vanish word by word, sometimes through systematic linguicide and other times through the gradual consumption of larger dominant cultures, or just lost in the flood. He flipped to the end of the notebook, hoping for a resolution, for a cogent and synthesized closing defense of his father's premise, but the writing—worse and worse as he followed it deeper into the notebook, compound sentences giving way to bare and repetitious declarations, declarations giving way to false starts and to thoughts that went dribbling down the page—stopped at page 248, with his father still mired in the massacres of antiquity, in the early building blocks of his case. Elwin closed the notebook, feeling his loss sharpened now, because after all these months of making small talk, he now had questions, questions for which there would never be answers: how and why his father had drawn these dour conclusions, what they meant to him, what . . . but Elwin had only this single half-filled notebook, this physical question mark, preserved in the amber. This inscrutable map of what the son had missed or ignored.

He tucked the notebook into one of the bags he'd brought, for safe-keeping. Precisely what he'd do with it, he didn't know. Such deliberations were for later. To the bag he added the eyeglasses for no other reason than that they'd touched his father's face, and the bare fact of that tactile connection seemed precious, and worth preserving. He decided to start with the walls, because they would be easy. There wasn't much on them—just three framed photographs of Jane's two kids, fashionable young professionals whose overscheduled lives had permitted them just two or three annual visits to their grandfather, a ten-minute cab ride away. They weren't bad kids; just typical. Had their grandfather been on Facebook he might've drawn their affections. These photos he put in another bag, for Jane if she wanted them. Books were everywhere, overrunning the windowsill and piled haphazardly by the bedside, and these Elwin mounded into two rickety stacks in a corner of the room, for later boxing. He investigated the file cabinet he'd delivered to his father last year, presuming it to be empty because despite months of his nagging his father had seemed oblivious to its presence, but no, he'd finally used it; the top drawer was crammed with notes and photocopies and what looked, at first glance, like a diary or journal. Sorting these was too much for Elwin to deal with now, so he turned to the dresser.

There at the top—who'd folded all the clothes so nicely? Boolah? His father?—was the shirt he had bought his father last Christmas. Its positioning there felt like either a wry rebuke or a heart-cracking affirmation. He'd purchased it at Walmart, thinking his father—something of a dandy in his prime—was too far gone to pay attention to his clothes, yet after unwrapping it he'd rubbed the sleeve between his thumb and forefinger and said cagily, "You got a pretty sweet deal on this shirt, didn't you?" He shut the dresser drawer, not wanting to deal with the clothes now, either, and with the frantic agitation of being trapped in a maze he went spinning back to the nightstand, home base. He could feel something building in him now, a grippiness in his lungs, a low throbbing murmur at his temples.

In the nightstand drawer he found his father's wallet, the same tattered, overworn black leather one he'd carried for as long as Elwin could remember, probably since before the advent of credit cards. Inside it was his father's expired New Jersey driver's license, with a photo Elwin had never seen — a photo he wished he could tease his father about, because the startled wide-eyed expression suggested someone had goosed him just as the camera snapped. There too in the drawer was a string-tied packet of the letters Elwin used to write him from California, buoyant and contentment-soaked letters (delusive, in retrospect) from the sunnier coast, with all their bragging about the weather and tenure and minor awards and too their unremitting assurances, in closing, that Maura sends her love. There were postcards, too, from Jane (why?), along with — Elwin gasped — whole chapters of David's novel (it was real!) stuffed into big manila envelopes bearing flamboyant and exotic Chinese postage. Digging deeper, he found a scrap of paper his father must've "laminated" by himself, with endless reels of Scotch tape, on which was written, below the name Alice, their old Montclair phone number — so he wouldn't forget how to call his dead wife. Elwin watched the taped-up paper tremble in his hand, and scanning the room he felt himself smothering under the ghost-weight of it all, of his father's everywhere presence, its jumble of the known and the unknown. He felt himself cracking beneath the weight, his eyesight smearing.

Boolah overheard Elwin as he passed down the hallway: a stifled, coughy weeping. Ducking his head into the room, he found Elwin crunched into the chair with the scrap of paper still shaking in his hand. "You doing all right?" he said gently.

Elwin looked up at him, his cheeks smeared, his eyes already reddened. "What do I do," he begged, "with all this *stuff?*"

8

EXCERPT FROM THE *Preliminary Report on Deterring Human Intrusion into the Waste Isolation Plant,* Attero Laboratories report ATT94–1783/UI-409, p. D-67. Co-authors: Drs. Elwin Cross Jr. (Trueblood Center for Applied Linguistics, Marasmus State College); Byron Torrance (Harvard University); Sharon Keim (independent artist); Richard Carrollton (Columbia University); Jose Nunes, Esq. (Georgetown University School of Law); Thomas B. Rankin (Duke University); Ronald Shapiro (University of California at Berkeley); Jacqueline Boesinger (Case Western Reserve University); James Dees (Western Research Group, Inc.); Randolph Yates (University of Washington); and B. R. Weems (Richard Varick College).

The entire site will be a message in itself, the framework for redundant and reinforcing levels of communication integrated into a holistic system of messaging. The message will be imparted both non-linguistically (via the unnatural syntax and negative entropy of the site design as well as through Level I communications) and linguistically, in the six primary languages of the United Nations (Arabic, English, Spanish, French, Russian, and Chinese) and in Navajo, as follows:

THIS IS NOT A PLACE OF HONOR. NO HIGHLY ESTEEMED DEED
IS COMMEMORATED HERE. NOTHING IS VALUED HERE.

THIS PLACE IS A MESSAGE. THE MESSAGE IS A WARNING
ABOUT DANGER. YOU MUST HEED IT.

WHAT IS HERE IS REPULSIVE AND DANGEROUS TO US.
THE DANGER IS STILL PRESENT, IN YOUR TIME AS IN OURS.

THE FORM OF THE DANGER IS AN EMANATION OF ENERGY,
AND IT CAN KILL. THE DANGER IS UNLEASHED ONLY
IF YOU DISTURB THIS PLACE.

THIS PLACE IS BEST SHUNNED.

SENDING THIS MESSAGE WAS IMPORTANT TO US.
WE CONSIDERED OURSELVES TO BE A POWERFUL CIVILIZATION.

Acknowledgments

The author wishes to acknowledge a debt to the physicist Gregory Benford, whose book *Deep Time: How Humanity Communicates Across Millennia* (Avon Books, 1999) was frequently & shamelessly raided during the writing of this novel. Credit also goes to the writer and activist Derrick Jensen, whose ideas—in sometimes mangled form—are strewn throughout this book. *Always In Our Hearts* (Record Books, 1999), by Doug Most, provided guidance for several scenes.

The excerpt from the Waste Isolation Plant warning message is derived, almost verbatim, from the warning proposed in *Expert Judgment on Markers to Deter Inadvertent Human Intrusion into the Waste Isolation Pilot Plant,* Sandia National Laboratories Report SAND92-1382/UC-721, p. F-49. That said, this is a work of imagination, and is in no way intended to accurately reflect the inner workings of the WIPP.

For their generous expertise, the author wishes to thank Dr. David B. Givens, Ph.D., from the Center for Nonverbal Studies; Christine Foy Stage, from the Orange County Attorney's Office in Goshen, New York; Tom Rankin; Mary & Hershel Ladner; Kate Dubost; Sarah McCusker; Skyler Gambrell; and Ben Weaver, for joining me on that buffet line of West 36th Street trash bags. Gratitude is also owed to Matthew Teague and Tyler Johnson, and to Bob Schluter and Rosemarie Curti as well. This book, and arguably its author, would not exist without the love & support of Catherine Miles, whose atypical lapse in judgment, when a small-town Mississippi landscaper-slash-"writer" twisted a paper bar napkin onto her finger and asked her to marry him, still seems, fourteen years later, nothing short of a miracle.